The Sin-Eater's Daughter

By: Michele L. Hinton

The Sin-Eater's Daughter

Cover Art by: Cody Scott

ISBN-10: 0988292602
ISBN-13: 978-0-9882926-0-4

The Seashell Books
An eBook Publishing Co. and eBookstore.

www.theseashellbooks.com
Email: seashellbooks@gmail.com

Dedicated

To

Kim Bussey

AKA Purrfect Tale

A wonderful author and friend.
Though we've never met face to face,
she followed this story with great interest and
became involved with the characters.
Thanks for your valuable comments.

A Very Special Thanks

To Michael Smith Hester
and Brian Durski for their
touching comments about this novel
as well as their contributions
in assisting me to polish it.

Chapter 1

Year 1847 – Black Water Swamp

The sounds of the night filled the cool air of Black Water Swamp. Bullfrogs croaked their love songs to any female that would listen. The hissing of a snake echoed in the breeze as it was about to acquire a meal. Leaves rustled on the trees, and dead branches fell to the ground. The chaos of the night sounds blended together as a soothing noise. Suddenly everything stopped. The quiet was deafening.

Paloma awoke from her sleep and drew a deep breath. She sat up and looked at her husband, Benjamin. He was sleeping peacefully. She slipped out of bed and headed for the kitchen. After taking a small pouch of herbs from the cupboard, she put a shawl around her shoulders and went outside. The moon was full and a dark, thin cloud, shaped like a crooked finger, stretched across its face and pointed downward.

Benjamin was aroused from his sleep by the smell of smoke and found his wife missing from his side. He adjusted the patch he wore over his dead right eye, got up and went to the door. He saw her sitting on a log bench looking into a fire. As he leaned against the doorframe and stared at her for a moment, he thanked heaven for her presence in his life. She was the only bright spot in his existence. Though he was a man kept at a distance by the town's people he served, he was also the envy of every man in it, for Paloma was the definition of beauty, whereas he was the beast - just as in the fabled story. He left the porch and sat down beside her.

"Something's bothering you." Benjamin brushed a strand of black hair behind her ear and put an arm around her. "I've seen this look on you before."

Paloma looked lovingly into his good right eye and caressed his scarred cheek with her hand. She turned back to the fire, took a pinch of herbs from the leather pouch and tossed them in. They sizzled and crackled in the flames, and a ringlet of smoke circled upward. "A child was born tonight." She looked up at the sky. "He was born under a bad moon. Life will be hard for this boy."

Benjamin watched the finger-like cloud dissipate. "I'm sure there were several children born this night. Does that mean all of them will have misfortune?"

Paloma took another pinch from the pouch and threw it into the fire. "No, I just see this one."

He didn't doubt what she said. They had been married for fifteen years, and her predictions were, for the most part, spot on. She was rarely wrong. Being of Gypsy descent, he figured she came by it naturally. Her family had come to America years ago and traveled most of her childhood. She had inherited her grandmother's gift of prognostication. Her father had been a physician of sorts, who had taught her all he knew about healing and medicinal herbs. They would go from town to town telling fortunes and selling her father's remedies. Most people called his elixirs and powders "snake oil," but Paloma had told him that her father's medicines had true curative abilities, unlike the other peddlers whose remedies were equivalent 90 proof gin.

"Will this child of misfortune have anything to do with us?" Benjamin asked.

Paloma threw another pinch of herbs into the flame. She closed her eyes momentarily and hesitated before answering. She gave him a sad smile "It's unclear."

Benjamin felt a chill in the air and shivered slightly. "What do you say we go back to bed and warm each other? I don't want you to catch your death out here." They both stood. "You go on in. I'll put out the fire."

Paloma did as her husband asked. She put away her pouch of herbs and leaned against the cupboard. A single tear rolled down her cheek. She couldn't bring herself to tell him that his death would signal the arrival of this boy.

New Orleans – Same Night

A child was born under the light of a full moon in the city of New Orleans. The mid-wife put the child in his mother's arms. Hattie was counting his little fingers and toes as her husband came into the room. He knelt down beside the bed.

"He's beautiful!" exclaimed the new father as he kissed his wife on the forehead.

Hattie kissed her son. "Have you decided on a name?"

John Lucas took his son in his arms. "I'll call him after my father – Jedidiah Lucas."

***

For the next five years, good fortune and happiness smiled on the Lucas family, until John came down with a fever. Upon his deathbed, John made his wife promise to remarry. Even though he'd secured enough money for his wife and son to live modestly for many years, he wanted her to give his son a father who would teach him how to be a good man.

Hattie was a comely woman with light, curly brown hair and green eyes. A year after John's death, she put away her black mourning dress. Though she would have been content to stay the widow of John Lucas, he was right. Jedidiah needed a good father figure to emulate.

Several men came to call on the Widow Lucas. One of her suitors was very persistent. Homer Bedlam, to her, seemed to be a good man. He lavished Hattie and Jedidiah with gifts and never uttered a harsh word to either of them. Her other callers seemed to be shy or standoffish where her son was concerned, so she consented to marry Mr. Bedlam when the boy turned seven.

Shortly after the wedding, Homer Bedlam showed his true nature. He was a harsh and jealous man. If another man ventured to say good-day to Hattie, Homer would accuse her of infidelity, and she'd receive a beating. Eventually, she wasn't allowed out of the house without him accompanying her. Jedidiah often tried to protect his mother from Mr. Bedlam's wrath, but would receive a smack from the back of his hand whenever he tried.

Jedidiah and his mother did their best to not upset Mr. Bedlam, but as time passed, he became angry with Hattie for not producing him a son of his own. Nothing she did pleased him. He'd started drinking more, and the small fortune that Hattie's deceased husband had amounted was practically gone. It had become evident to her that Mr. Bedlam only married her for her inheritance, but there was nothing she could do about it. To others, he presented himself as a loving, devout husband and stepfather, but such was not the case. He was a cruel and unforgiving man.

In June of 1861, Jedidiah turned fourteen. He was forced to quit school and went to work for Haskill & Son's Wheelwright. He figured it would take him about a year to save enough money to take his mother away. He saved a few cents from his pay and gave it to his mother to hide for safekeeping. The rest he was ordered to turn over to his stepfather. "You're old enough to pay your own way in my house," is what Mr. Bedlam had said.

The day after Jedidiah received his first week's wages his stepfather came to Mr. Haskill's shop and inquired about the amount of money he'd paid him. Mr. Bedlam told the man that he just wanted to make sure his stepson was being paid fairly, but Jedidiah had already foreseen that possibility and asked his employer to tell his stepfather the amount – less the few pennies he'd set aside for his mother. Mr. Haskill didn't like or trust Homer Bedlam and agreed to the boy's request.

Homer Bedlam kept a close eye on the boy. Jedidiah was becoming taller and stronger, and he predicted that one day, he would no longer have control over Hattie's son. When war broke out between the states, the heartless man saw his opportunity to be rid of him. Soldiers were in New Orleans enlisting the aid of men to join the Confederacy. Homer slipped a few dollars into the pocket of one of the officers, and Jedidiah was forced into the army.

Chapter 2

1865 - Four Years Later...

Jedidiah fought in the war for almost a year. After being shot in the leg during the battle at Mill Springs in Kentucky, he was captured by Union soldiers. He was thrown in a prison without much medical attention. A week later, a portion of his leg just below his knee had to be amputated when gangrene set in. He lived through the surgery, and when he had recovered, he was transferred to a prison camp in Louisville, Kentucky for three years.

Life was harsh for the young man. He was fed only enough to keep him alive. Many times he wished for death, but the one driving force in him, were thoughts of his mother. He had to keep living for her. Upon his eventual release, he planned to take her away from Mr. Bedlam, even if they had to steal away in the night and work in the cotton fields to earn their way.

When the war was over, Jedidiah and other prisoners were set free. They were being sent home by rail and loaded into boxcars like cattle. But when he returned, Jedidiah found his mother under the doctor's care. Her face had been severely burned, and she'd been unconscious for the past three days. His stepfather had told him that he was awakened by the sound of her scream, and he found her lying on the floor by the fireplace with a kettle of water over turned on the floor beside her. He suggested that perhaps some type of flash from the fireplace had caused her injury; however, Jedidiah had seen a skeptical look on the doctor's face when Mr. Bedlam gave his explanations. He had his doubts also, but no proof.

Jedidiah spent the next two days keeping vigil at his mother side, but the doctor said he doubted she would live long. She was wasting away, and infection had set in. The doctor said there was nothing more he could do for her. In the last few minutes of her life, his mother finally regained consciousness.

Hattie couldn't see her son, for her eyelids were swollen shut. But she could hear his voice and that eased her tortured mind about his wellbeing. Her husband had confiscated and burned his letters to her. Though she wasn't allowed to read them, just the knowledge that her son had written to her meant he still lived, and that gave her some measure of relief.

"My beautiful son," Hattie managed to say, for the slightest movement of her mouth gave her excruciating pain.

Tears came to Jedidiah's eyes when she mumbled the words. "Don't try and talk, Mother, just be still and rest so you can get well." He pressed her hand to his cheek.

"Did they treat you well, Son?" She tried to see his face with the touch of her hand. "Your face feels thinner."

"It wasn't bad," he lied. "I was treated tolerably." He didn't tell her about the stump he had for a leg. He didn't want to give her cause for any more grief than what she had already.

Hattie felt she didn't have much time left. A tear trickled from her eye and burned as it rolled down her scared face. The memory of what Mr. Bedlam had done to her weighed heavily on her mind. "I need to tell what happened."

"You need your rest, Hattie," said the doctor.

"There is no rest for me until Mr. Bedlam pays for what he did to me!" she gritted out through her pain. "I want others to hear what I'm about to say. Is there someone else in the room that can bear witness?"

The doctor called his nurse into the room, and Hattie told them what had happened. She was pouring Mr. Bedlam his morning coffee. Her hand trembled slightly, and she accidently poured the scalding liquid on his hand. Though she apologized whole-heartedly, it wasn't enough for him. Homer wanted to teach her a lesson. He smacked her and forced her to the floor. He'd straddled her, stuffed a handkerchief in her mouth to muffle her cries, and poured the pot of coffee over her face.

Hattie gripped her son's hand and concluded, "And then he asked me how it felt."

Jedidiah felt a lump in his throat. Tears rolled down his face. What Mr. Bedlam had done to his mother intensified one hundred fold. "I'll kill him!"

"No!" she gripped her son's hand to keep him by her side. "I can't go to my rest if your life is compromised. "Let the law deal with him. He'll be guilty of my death." She turned to the doctor and asked him to write down what she'd said. Afterward, she'd signed the paper.

"I'll see to it on your behalf," the doctor replied.

Hattie spoke again to her son. "Swear to me you won't seek revenge."

Jedidiah crossed his fingers behind his back. "I promise," he lied.

With her last breath, Hattie told Jedidiah she loved him. He wept and the doctor consoled him.

"Justice will be served, son," said the doctor, holding up Hattie's sworn statement. "This paper and our testimony will assure Homer Bedlam a long prison sentence – or a hanging!"

Jedidiah wiped the tears from his face. He picked up his crutch from the floor and stood. He looked back at the doctor before leaving the room and repeated coldly, "Justice will be served!"

"Now don't do anything rash, Jedidiah!" the doctor shouted, but it fell upon deaf ears.

Jedidiah saw his stepfather talking to a group of men across the street at an outdoor café. He wanted to beat Homer Bedlam with his own two hands and choke the life out of him, but he literally only had one leg to stand on. Where once his body was strong, prison had turned him into a thing that resembled a hobbling skeleton. He crossed the street to the general store.

"How's your mother, Jedidiah?" the elderly shopkeeper asked. "Is there any hope of recovery?"

Jedidiah smiled sadly. "Her life is in the Lord's hands."

The shopkeeper nodded in agreement. "So true, so true." He cleared his throat and changed the subject. "What can I do for you today?"

"I'd like to test one of your best pistols. I thought I might do a little hunting."

"A rifle would be more effective," the shopkeeper replied.

Jedidiah tapped his stump of a leg with his crutch. "A rifle would be a little hard for me to manipulate."

The shopkeeper stammered slightly and replied, "I – I see your point."

The older man handed him the most expensive weapon, some bullets, and said the target was in back. Jedidiah loaded the gun and walked to the front door.

"You can cut through the storage room," said the shopkeeper.

He gave the man a stone-faced look. "I have a target in mind."

Homer Bedlam was still talking and laughing with his friends. He couldn't take the chance that his stepfather wouldn't be convicted. He'd heard of guilty men getting off scot-free. It would be his mother's statement against his stepfather's declarations.

The time Jedidiah spent in the army, before his capture, had made him a crack shot. He had a clear line of sight on his stepfather. "HOMER! HOMER BEDLAM!" he shouted angrily.

His stepfather looked up, and the laughter spewing from his mouth instantly ceased. His friends scattered when they saw the boy raise a pistol. Homer was stunned momentarily, and then he grinned, self-assured that Hattie's son was a spineless weakling and wouldn't pull the trigger. He laughed. "You won't shoot, you piece of white trash. Your mother is a useless whore and…" but that was the last word from his mouth. Homer Bedlam fell instantly to the ground - a bullet went right between his eyes.

When the shopkeeper saw Jedidiah raise his weapon and heard the shouting, he nervously fumbled the bullets as he tried to load his own gun. But he was too late to stop the killing. He pointed his weapon at the young man. "Put it down, Jedidiah!"

"Justice is served," Jedidiah said, as a tear ran down his cheek. "My mother went to heaven. I just sent Homer Bedlam to hell!" He lowered his arm, handed the man the gun and sat down on the step. "I'll wait here for the law."

***

Jedidiah spent a week in jail before his trial. He felt at peace with what he suspected would happen to him. Even though he had a lawyer to speak on his behalf, he knew he was going to hang.

The streets of New Orleans were usually teaming with activity during that time of day; however, that day was different. Several shopkeepers had closed their doors temporarily, and only a few wagons rolled down the street. Everyone gathered in one place – the courthouse.

The room was crowded with people anxiously awaiting the jury to return with a verdict. Jedidiah looked around at the faces of the spectators who were vigorously fanning themselves. He heard the lady sitting behind him say to her husband, "I wish they'd hurry up and come back. I'm about to melt!"

The young man laughed inwardly and thought: *Why don't you just go outside then?* But he knew she wouldn't. Like everyone else, she didn't want to lose her seat to someone standing in the back of the room.

Jedidiah turned his gaze forward. He agreed with her. It was sweltering in the building, but to wish for the jury to come back any sooner would be like wishing his life away a little faster. While he waited, he closed his eyes and prayed for the soul of his mother. His lawyer had arranged for him to be released temporarily for her funeral. The owner of the general store had been a friend of his mother's since their school days, and he gave Jedidiah a new, black suit to wear for the service when he'd heard the true story of how Hattie had died. The truth had spread quickly, and the young man received several messages of condolence from people his mother knew and gifts of decent food while he was incarcerated.

Jedidiah's musings were interrupted when the door opened to the jury room. The twelve men entered the courtroom and took their places. The bailiff came out a few minutes later and announced, "All rise for the Honorable Judge James Harcourt." The people in the gallery stood until the judge was seated. He pounded his gavel twice - everyone quieted and took their seats.

"Court is again in session." The judge looked toward the jury. "Gentlemen of the jury, how say you?"

The foreman wiped the sweat from his brow and stood. "We find the defendant guilty of a – justifiable killing."

The people in the gallery mumbled among themselves. Jedidiah looked behind him and saw some heads nod favorably, and a few mumble their disappointment, shaking their heads in the negative.

The judge banged his gavel again, and order was once more restored. He paused for a moment to gather his thoughts. "Will the defendant rise and face the court," he said stoically.

Jedidiah swallowed hard and stood with his arms behind his back. His heart beat steadily in his chest. He knew what the sentence would be, for Judge Harcourt was renowned for his use of the rope. Now all he had to do was wait for him to announce the day of the hanging.

The judge looked at him with a stone-faced expression. "Jedidiah Lucas, the jury finds you guilty of murder. According to the dictates of New Orleans' law for murder, you are hereby sentenced to hang by the neck until dead."

With that announcement, several people from the gallery stood and shouted their objections. A few of Homer's friends applauded.

The judge banged his gavel several times. "Quiet!" he shouted, "Or I'll fine every man-jack in this room for contempt of court!" When everyone was reseated, Judge Harcourt continued. "The law dictates that sentence."

He looked at Jedidiah. "Though you are guilty of killing Homer Bedlam, this court is not without compassion and understands what brought you to violence. The way this court sees it, you saved the taxpayers of this city the expense of lodging Mr. Bedlam in jail, for it was only a matter of time before his dishonest dealings with people would have brought his sorry ass before this bench." Then his voice softened. "Your mother was a good woman. Hattie will be missed." His face became ridged. "I suspend the sentence under the condition that you leave New Orleans and seek life elsewhere." The judge banged his gavel again and dismissed the court.

Several people, including the doctor, patted Jedidiah on the back and wished him well. He sank in his chair. He was shaken by the sentence and expected to join his mother in death. Now he was alone in the world and knew barely anything of it. His life had been filled with violence and misery with his stepfather's maltreatment of him, the war, and prison.

Jedidiah left the courtroom. He headed for home to collect his meager belongings. Homer Bedlam had borrowed money against the house so the bank basically owned it. Everything else was to be auctioned off to pay for his mother's entombment, the lawyer and court costs. He was now practically a pauper.

He went to the fireplace, removed a loose stone and pulled out a small sack in the niche. It contained about twenty dollars in coins. It was the secret hiding place where his mother hid money.

***

The judge had given Jedidiah a week to settle his affairs and leave town. He visited Mr. Haskill, the wheelwright, before he left. The man had fashioned him a wooden leg. During the war, Jedidiah had seen several men wearing wooden pegs in place of a lost limb, but the one Mr. Haskill had fashioned actually looked like a leg and even had a shoe on it. It felt awkward and slightly painful to use, but he figured that in time he would get used to it. He thanked the man for his thoughtfulness.

Jedidiah hadn't a clue where he would go, so he went into the stage office to purchase a ticket to anywhere two dollars would take him. He needed to conserve as much of his limited funds as possible. The man in charge said there was a stage heading for Baton Rouge, and it would take him that far; however, the man had heard Jedidiah was an excellent shot and told him that if he'd act as shotgun and ride with the driver, he could have a free ride to the end of the line. Jedidiah graciously accepted.

The first few days went well. They stopped at several small townships to pick up and drop off mail and passengers, until they left the town of Laplace. The only passengers were a man and his wife. They also carried a sack of mail and a strong box with an undisclosed content. As they approached a bridge they needed to cross, the driver quickly reined in the horses. He and Jedidiah climbed down from the driver's box. The passengers looked out the window.

"What's the hold up?" the man asked.

"The bridge is out," the driver shouted back.

Jedidiah looked at the bits of mangled wood scattered about. "It looks like someone blew it up."

"I crossed this bridge last week," the driver said. He bent down and picked up a piece of wood and sniffed the burnt edges. "This was recently done."

Jedidiah cocked his rifle to make sure there was a round in the chamber and looked about.

The man got out of the coach. "What do we do now?"

"Take a detour. We can't cross here - the water's too deep. There's another bridge about ten miles downstream to the left…" he pointed, "…or a shallower crossing about three miles to the right, but it's a rough ride. It's an old road full of ruts and rocks."

"My wife and I are anxious to get to Baton Rouge. Take the shorter route," the passenger ordered.

"I don't know, Mister," said Jedidiah. "Whoever blew it up might expect us to take the shorter route."

"As I see it," the man replied, "It's a crap shoot either way. If you have an extra rifle, I'll take it just in case."

The driver went to the coach and pulled another rifle from the front boot and threw it to him. "Let's get out of here." The driver spat the juice from his chaw of tobacco. "I don't like it here. The hairs on the back of my neck are standin' on end." They headed back to the coach.

They left the well-traveled road and drove down a rough, rarely used path. The driver said that this was the old road to a township called Black Water and hadn't been used in years. The newer road was several miles back. They were about a mile down the old road when a band of ten raiders came galloping up behind them firing their guns. The driver snapped the reins and the horses took off in a gallop. The coach bounced and pitched along the rough path, but Jedidiah still managed to hit three of the riders.

He heard the man in the coach firing, but he was a poor shot.

"I'm hit!" the driver suddenly shouted. But as soon as he spoke the words, the man dropped the reins and slumped over in the driver's box – dead.

The horses ran uncontrollable, and before Jedidiah had a chance retrieve the reins, the coach hit a rut in the road and turned over. Jedidiah was thrown to the ground, and his head struck a rock, knocking him out.

***

The sun was setting when Jedidiah came to. He sat up and felt dizzy and a little disoriented. There was dried blood on his shirt, and he felt the gash on the side of his head. He made his way to the overturned stagecoach. The lock had been shot off the strong box and was empty. Letters from the mailbag had been opened and littered the area. He figured the raiders searched them for money. He looked inside the coach. The two passengers were dead. The woman's neck was broken, and the man had been shot in the head. He was surprised that the robbers hadn't shot him as well, but surmised they thought him dead also and didn't bother to waste a bullet. He checked his pockets. His money pouch was gone.

He looked at his surroundings. The area was wooded on both sides of the creek. The driver had told him that they were close to Black Water Swamp. Jedidiah decided he couldn't leave the bodies lying there for the buzzards or any other wild creature to feed on, so covered them with a tarp he found in the rear boot of the stagecoach and gathered stones from around the creek bed to cover the driver and two passengers. After gathering his things, he took a canteen, filled it in the creek and then washed the dirt and blood from his face. He wasn't sure how far the town of Black Water was, but that's where he decided to head. The authorities there would be able to send a wire to either New Orleans or Baton Rouge when he told them what happened, if they had a telegraph office.

Jedidiah walked as far as he could while there was still light in the sky, but when darkness fell upon him, he settled down by an inviting tree for the night. Thoughts of his mother filtered into his dreams and he woke. He leaned against the tree and closed his eyes. The realization that he was alone weighed heavy on his mind. Tears streamed down his face, and his loud cries reverberated in the night. A short time later, a noise came from deep within the woods. It was as if someone had answered his cries. The words, "I'll be here for you," came to his ears in a whisper. He knew it was just the wind blowing through a hollow log or something, but it also gave him some measure of comfort, and he was finally able to lay his head down to sleep.

Chapter 3

BLACK WATER TOWNSHIP

It was almost dark when Dr. Jackson was summoned to the Welch residence. He listened to the heartbeat of Alvin Welch and then held a circle of glass up to his mouth and nose. He turned to Erma Welch, and the friends who'd gathered at the old man's bedside. "I'm afraid he won't be with us long."

Erma held a handkerchief to her eye and cried. "Is there nothing else you can do?"

"It's in the hands of the Maker now. I can only do so much," said the doctor as he put away his instruments.

A slightly plump woman put a comforting arm around her friend. "His will be done," said Sally Gooch. "Your husband led a good life."

Dr. Jackson had his doubts about how good Alvin actually was. He'd been a secretive man during his life, and it was a mystery as to how his wealth had mounted so quickly. But he was the Mayor of Black Water and the town's leading citizen who was also instrumental in its growth and prosperity. The elderly doctor looked by the door and saw Henry, Alvin's only son. He thought the young man looked like Alvin when he was a man of twenty-seven. Henry was tall and thin. He had light brown hair and sported the same style of thin mustache as his father.

The doctor approached Henry and whispered to him softly, "I suggest you have someone ring for the Sin-Eater. His services may be required shortly."

"How long?" Henry looked toward the bed of his dying father.

"Who can say?" Dr. Jackson replied. "A day - an hour. His breathing is shallow and his heartbeat is faint. The venom from the snakebite was too overpowering. I'm surprised he's lasted this long."

Henry smiled sadly. "It doesn't surprise me. He's a stubborn old bird." He folded his arms and leaned against the doorframe. "I told him he needed to stay out of that damn swamp - that he wasn't a spring chicken anymore. But he never listens to me."

"Besides Benjamin Day, why would anyone want to go there?" Dr. Jackson shivered.

Henry shook his head. "I don't know. He would never tell me. All I know is he'd be gone for a day or two ever-so-often and return happy as a meadow lark."

Henry Welch had no great love for his father, but neither did he disrespect him. He was a busy man with the affairs of the town and had little time for him while he was growing up. But he doted on his mother, and Henry wanted for nothing. Only when he was older did his father pay any sort of attention to him. Alvin had started grooming his son to take his place as leader of the town after him. They weren't like father and son. Henry felt it was more like businessman to apprentice.

Henry turned to the household servant. "Fetch the Sin-Eater."

BLACK WATER SWAMP

Paloma stood on the porch of her small cottage that was in a clearing of the swamp and looked out into the night. Her beloved Benjamin had now been dead for a week. She missed him terribly. She was now sixty-two, and though she was fairly healthy, she hadn't the strength to take care of her husband's remains. She secretly went into town and sought out Alvin Welch, Benjamin's only friend. He'd helped her carry her husband's body from the house to the funeral pyre she'd prepared. Burying him would have been pointless, since anything buried in the swamp wouldn't stay buried for long. She also doubted the town's people would allow his body in their cemetery. Alvin Welch had just visited her again the other day and brought her a supply of coffee, tea, sugar and flour from the general store. He'd told her that he would come back every-so-often to see how she was getting along, but when he'd given her a friendly hug good-bye, she had a sense of foreboding. She'd warned him to be careful, but she had an uneasy feeling that she would not be seeing him again.

Paloma sat in her rocking chair and thought about Benjamin and Alvin Welch. She laughed slightly. The two friends had a still set up in another part of the swamp and would spend a couple of days out of every month getting drunk together. She remembered Alvin telling them that in his younger days, he secretly made and sold bootlegged whisky and had amassed a tidy sum of money. His bootlegging career ended when he entered the Calvary. She'd thought it funny that the town of Black Water was dry as far liquor was concerned. He only drank when he visited them. Alvin thought it wouldn't do for the citizens of Black Water to know that their Mayor indulged, especially since he was largely responsible for the ordinance that kept liquor, saloons and houses of ill repute out of the town.

Suddenly, Paloma heard two sounds that were carried on the wind. The first was a familiar sound she'd heard many times over many years. Someone was ringing the bell at the edge of the swamp. They were summoning the Sin-Eater for someone who was either dead or about to die. But this time the bell would go unanswered. Benjamin Day, the town's Sin-Eater, was also dead. Neither she nor her husband believed in the practice of sin-eating, for they were brought up differently. However, the people in the town did, and it provided them with an income of sorts for things that the swamp couldn't provide for them. Paloma figured she would leave a note at the bell in the morning. The people feared her, and she rarely entered town. Except for the occasional boy who entered on a dare to look for the cabin of the swamp witch, Alvin Welch was the only person to pay them visits.

The second sound she heard was an eerie cry. It too was familiar, but from a past dream she'd had seventeen years ago. Paloma stood and walked to the edge of the clearing toward the cry. "I'll be here for you," she shouted into the night.

***

Jedidiah wondered if he'd made a mistake going to Black Water Township. The road had disappeared after several hours of walking. It had been over taken by the woods and was swampy in areas. He stopped several time on his journey to rest, for he wasn't used to walking on the new wooden leg.

Day had turned into night, and that meant another night in the woods. He was cold and hungry. Water barely satisfied his empty stomach. He'd seen a few bushes with berries but feared to eat them, for even though animals may be able to, that didn't mean it was safe for people. During the war, he'd seen a hungry man eat from an unfamiliar plant, and he'd watched him die in agony. Jedidiah didn't fear dying. It was the agony part and dying alone in the woods, with the possibility of some animal devouring him while he was still half alive, that didn't set well with him. He shivered at the thought.

The next morning, Jedidiah woke and started on his way again. His stomach thought his throat had been cut. He didn't know how much further he could go without food. But then he came upon a wall of stone that blocked his way. It was stacked just about eye level, but it was still too high to view over. He put his hands on top of the wall, balanced himself on his wooden leg and found a foothold in a crevice to push his self upward. He looked across a vast field of young soybean plants, and in the distance, he saw a town. "Finally!" he said. "This must be Black Water." He looked down the expanse of the wall. It stretched for as far as he could see in both directions. He figured it was built to keep the woods and whatever creatures lurked in them at bay. After gathering his things, he climbed over to the other side and looked down at the soybean plants. He sighed, wishing those precious beans could be eaten straight from the plants, but unfortunately they were poisonous until processed.

The soybean field ended at the edge of town. Jedidiah thought it a good-sized town and was impressed by it. It seemed quiet and orderly as opposed to the hustle and bustle of New Orleans. He passed shops of various types, a nice looking hotel and a couple of restaurants which made his stomach rumbled. But the first order of business he figured was to notify the law about what happened to the stagecoach.

As he hobbled down the main street, he saw people staring. But that didn't surprise him. He probably looked like something the cat dragged in, not to mention he was a stranger. It didn't take him long to find the Sheriff's Office. He looked through the window before entering and saw a middle-aged man wearing a star on his three-piece suit, sitting at a desk reading the newspaper. He went to the door and opened it.

***

Sheriff Hiram Wright sat back in his chair reading the paper he'd just received from New Orleans. It was a week old, but that was normal for the news that came from outside Black Water. He read the headline:

HANG'EM HIGH HARCOURT SHOWS LENIENCY

In an unprecedented decision today, Judge James Harcourt resends his own sentence. Accused of murdering his stepfather....

His reading was interrupted when the door opened. He put down his paper and looked up to see a haggard young man enter. "Can I help you, boy?"

"I want to report the holdup of a stagecoach bound for Baton Rouge," Jedidiah replied.

"Where?"

"About a mile or so from the bridge on the old Black Water road. Raiders blew that up too."

Jedidiah introduced himself and told the story of what had happened to the sheriff. Afterward, he asked the man if there was any place around town where he could work for a decent meal and a place to sleep for the night. Suddenly, he saw a strange look come over the sheriff's face. He jumped up from his chair and called to his deputy.

"Sam! Get out here!"

A young man came out from the back room and leaned his broom against the wall. "Yeah, Sheriff?"

"Sit down and make out a report," the sheriff ordered. He turned back to Jedidiah. "Stay right here, sonny!" He grabbed his hat off the hook by the door. "Repeat everything you said to the deputy, in detail, so he can write it down. I'll be back shortly."

He didn't quite understand why he had to repeat it all again, but the man was the sheriff. The young deputy pulled some paper from one drawer and an apple from another. Jedidiah watched him take a bite and felt his stomach rumble. "Have you got another one of those?"

"Sorry, only one I got. You know the saying, *Apple a day keeps the doctor away.*" He took another bite, dipped his pen in the inkwell and posed it over the paper to write. "Okay fella', shoot!"

Deep in the recesses of his mind, Jedidiah thought, *If you don't hurry up and finish that apple, I will shoot you and take it!*

Chapter 4

THE GOOCH RESIDENCE

Henry Welch paced the floor of the home of his father's friend, Judge Victor Gooch.

"Settle down, my boy," said the older man.

"How can I!" Henry exclaimed. "My father has been dead for these past two days. Mother refuses to have him interred until a Sin-Eater can be found."

The judge sat back in his chair and sighed. "Benjamin's death was unfortunate. He provided a necessary service to this community."

Henry stopped pacing and leaned on the desk before him. "The point is – what are we going to do? Isn't there a vagrant or someone we can get to take his place?"

Victor scratched his head. "Unfortunately, Sheriff Wright does his job well. And before you ask, the jail cells are empty. I've checked."

There was a quick knock at the door and Sally Gooch, the judge's wife, entered before being asked. She was quite distraught. "I'm sorry for the interruption, Mr. Gooch," Sally said wringing her hands. "Mrs. Dubois just left quite beside herself. Her mother is sick, and she fears she may not get better. The news of Benjamin Day's death has spread like a disease."

The judge stood, put an arm around his wife and patted her on the shoulder. "There, there now, Mrs. Gooch. Young Henry and I were just discussing the situation."

"The people are beginning to worry," she replied. "So am I. It's bad enough having a witch living in the swamp. I don't think I could live in a town full of unsettled ghosts also."

"Now, you know Paloma has never caused anyone harm, my dear," Victor scolded mildly. "In fact, wasn't it she who was instrumental in finding the Miller boy last year when he got lost in the swamp?"

"Yes," she admitted, then added a bit sarcastically. "But the ladies of my sewing circle believe it was she who enticed him to enter the swamp the first place."

Victor shook his head and walked her to the door. "Be that as it may, everything will be settled soon." He kissed her on the forehead. "Go on now, and don't worry."

She sighed in relief and looked at Henry. "I'm sorry, Henry. I know this situation concerns you more than any of us at the present. When you go home this evening, tell your good mother I'll be around to see her tomorrow."

Henry kissed her hand. "Certainly, Mrs. Gooch, you've been a great comfort to her."

The judge closed the door behind her. He walked back to his desk and looked out the window. "After all these years, the women of this town are still jealous of Paloma Day."

"I don't know," Henry replied agreeing with the judge's wife. "They may have a point. She scared me when I was a child."

Victor laughed. "Don't tell me – let me guess. Your mother told you stories of her flying around on her broomstick. That's what my wife told our daughter, Barbara, when she was younger."

Henry chuckled slightly and shoved his hands in his pockets. "No, my mother told me she catches naughty little boys who enter her swamp, boils them in her big, black caldron and eats them."

"You believed her?" Victor grinned.

"Not at first. I believed it was just a story she told to keep me out of the swamp, until Byron VanHorn and I went looking for her."

"And?" the judge prompted when Henry hesitated to laugh at the memory.

"After some considerable amount of looking, we found her shack and hid behind a large tree. She was stirring something in a big, black pot. Her back was to us. It surprised the hell out of us when we heard her shout out, 'Boy's, lunch is about ready. I just need to add a few more ingredients. Care to join me?' Then she turned and looked right at us. We took off running like a pair of scared rabbits."

Victor laughed. "You still afraid of her?"

"No," he replied tentatively. "But when you're nine-years-old, it makes one hell of an impression." Then he changed the subject. "Speaking of children, where's Emmaline? I haven't seen her in a few weeks?"

"She's gone to visit Barbara and her husband in Baton Rouge," Victor replied. "Why?"

"Oh, no reason, just curious," he said shyly.

Victor laughed inwardly. Emmaline had come to live with them after her parents died of influenza seven years ago. She was now nineteen. He knew young Henry had feelings for his wife's niece, but was hesitant about asking for his permission to court her.

A few moments later, the household butler knocked on the door and entered. "You have a visitor, sir. Sheriff Wright wishes an audience."

"Show him in," the judge replied.

The sheriff entered the room. "Good afternoon, gentlemen." He shook their hands.

"What can I do for you today, Hiram?" Victor asked.

"I have a young man in my office. He claims the stagecoach out of New Orleans was robbed a couple of days ago. He said he buried the bodies of the driver and passengers on the old road. I thought you might like to talk with him."

"Why? Do you doubt his story?" asked the judge.

"The young man is crippled, so I don't doubt his story." Hiram smiled deviously and looked toward Henry. "But he's also penniless, hungry, and looking for some type of work."

"Interesting." Victor folded his arms and pulled at the white hairs of his goatee. He turned toward Henry. "My boy, it maybe behoove you, in more ways than one, to come along and interview this poor, unfortunate soul."

Henry wasn't dim to what either of the two men suggested. This stranger could possibly kill two birds with one stone. If he was credited for finding a Sin-Eater, it could possibly cinch his election as the new mayor, and his father's spirit could be put to rest at the same time.

Sheriff's Office

Jedidiah waited patiently in the sheriff's office. He was about to ask the deputy if he could return later, after he'd found something to eat. His stomach felt like a caged beast. But before he had a chance to ask, the sheriff returned with two gentlemen in tow. One man looked to be in his sixties. His hair, mustache and goatee matched the white suit he wore. The other man was considerably younger. His curiosity about the two men ended when his stomach growled loudly.

"Sheriff, do you mind if leave? I need to find some work. I haven't eaten in two days," Jedidiah pleaded.

"I believe your problem is solved on that account," the sheriff replied. He introduced Jedidiah to Judge Gooch and Henry Welch.

The judge looked the young man over. "I don't know, Hiram," he said to the sheriff. "He's terribly young to handle such a burden."

"I'm stronger than I look," Jedidiah replied anxiously. "I just need something to eat. I'll do any task to the best of my ability." His stomach growled again.

"Don't you want to know what the task is first?" Henry asked.

Jedidiah hesitated a moment. "Just as long as it's legal, and I don't have to kill anybody."

"No worries on that account," the judge replied with a chuckle. "It's perfectly legal and the man's already dead."

"You need a gravedigger?" Jedidiah questioned. He thought that most towns in Louisiana buried their dead above ground.

"Not exactly," Henry replied. He patted Jedidiah on the back. "Mr. Lucas…

"Just call me Jedidiah," he interrupted.

"Very well, Jedidiah, come with me. My carriage is just outside. I'll make sure you have plenty to eat."

Jedidiah got in the front of the carriage with the driver, while the judge and Henry sat in the back and talked quietly. He knew the two men were talking about him, but couldn't exactly hear what they were saying. The only time he heard clearly what they said was when they made comment about an old woman wearing black, standing beside a large bell.

"What's she doing in town?" Henry exclaimed.

"She's probably going to the general store. Benjamin usually made their purchases," the judge replied.

Jedidiah looked at her as they passed. Though her black hair was streaked with white, he thought she possessed a certain timeless beauty. He noticed she kept her eyes on him, and before they passed she smiled. He returned it in kind and nodded his head, since he didn't have a hat to tip to her. He also noticed that the two men in the back of the carriage barely acknowledged her.

***

The Welch residence was just at the edge of town. The large, three-story, Victorian style house was painted light green, with dark green shutters and white trim on the first and second levels. The upper level was painted red. Jedidiah thought of his mother when he saw it looming before him. She'd showed him a picture of that style of house. Once when Mr. Bedlam was not at home, his mother pulled out an old drawing that his true father had made, and said he was going to build one for her just like it for them. Thoughts of what his life could have been like and what they actually were stood in stark contrast of each other. But things were what they were, and he tried to push the thoughts from his mind.

The carriage stopped in front of the house, and the three of them got out. They were greeted at the door by the butler.

"Fredricks, take Jedidiah to the bathhouse so he can freshen up," said Henry. He turned to Jedidiah. "Go with him, and I'll tell the cook to prepare some food."

Jedidiah hesitated for a moment. "Mr. Welch, you haven't told me what I'm to do for this measure of kindness."

"After you've washed and had a bite to eat, we'll discuss the matter," he replied. He went into the house.

Jedidiah followed the butler. Who was he to argue? He was going to have a proper bath for the first time in over a week, and he was going to be fed.

***

Jedidiah leaned back in the claw-footed tub and soaked in the hot water. He felt the tension of the past few days melt away. His stomach had even ceased to make noises, until he inhaled the aroma of a freshly baked apple pie escaping through the kitchen window. The pleasure of soaking in the hot water was forgotten, and he commenced to scrub the few layers of dirt and odor from his body.

After bathing, he was escorted to the kitchen for the promised meal. Jedidiah thought at most he would get a bowl of soup and a piece of bread of which he would have been extremely grateful for. However, his eyes widened when the cook set a plate before him with country ham, rice, a bowl of white beans, cornbread, turnip greens and to top it all off, a piece of that apple pie that smelled like it came from heaven's kitchen. He did his best to eat slowly, though his taste buds kept screaming: *Faster! Faster! More! More!*

***

Erma Welch took a peek at the boy through the kitchen door. "He's terribly young. He barely looks past twenty. Isn't there anyone else?"

"He's seventeen, Mother, and there is no one else." Henry sighed. "It's either him, or we bury Father tomorrow without."

His mother put a handkerchief to her eye. "Then it must be. I want your father's spirit to be at peace." She went back to the drawing room where her husband lay waiting a proper burial.

***

Jedidiah couldn't remember when he'd eaten so well. Afterward, he was escorted to the drawing room where Henry and Victor waited. When he was announced, Erma Welch walked up to him and put a hand on his cheek. "Bless you," she said and rushed out the door.

Jedidiah was curious as to what she had blessed him for. He hadn't done anything yet.

"Come on in, Jedidiah," said Henry. "Was the meal satisfactory?"

"More than I expected. Thank you for your kindness." He saw a coffin at the front of the parlor and walked toward it. "Who died?"

Henry joined him. "My father."

"Sorry for your loss." Jedidiah closed his eyes and thought of his mother. "Losing a parent is a hard thing."

"Your sympathy is appreciated." Henry looked upon the remains of his father. "My father is why we asked you here. There is a certain task my mother and I would like you to perform." He turned his back and walked off glancing at Victor.

"You want me to bury him?"

"No - not exactly," replied Victor. "There is a certain religious ritual that needs to be performed which may or may not be familiar to you. We'd like you to be his – Sin-Eater."

Jedidiah was a little dumbfounded. "A what?"

"Before my father's spirit can be at peace, someone must bear the burden of his sins here on Earth," said Henry.

"You're joking," Jedidiah responded with a humorless chuckle. "How can anyone take over someone else's sins?"

"We're very serious," replied the judge. "Tonight at a special service, a piece of bread will be placed on the chest of the deceased. You'll say the prayers, eat the bread and drink the wine. Then Alvin's soul will be cleansed of any transgressions, and he will be able to pass through the pearly gates of heaven."

Jedidiah was beginning to think these people were crazy. He was willing to scrub floors, dig a grave or any other task, but to eat something off of a dead man? That was just too strange in his mind. He was about to say no and offer to do any other chore that needed to be done for the feast he'd just had, when they heard a raised voice coming from the foyer.

***

Erma Welch was summoned to the front door by the butler. "Fredricks – I told you, to tell her, she was not welcome here!" She hurriedly crossed the foyer toward the front door.

"Yes, madam," replied the butler, "But she refuses to leave until she pays her respects."

Erma opened the door. "You are not welcome here, Paloma Day! Go on back to your swamp where you belong."

Paloma smiled pleasantly despite the harsh reception by Alvin's widow. "I'll not leave until I say good-bye to my husband's friend." She hesitated a moment. "Besides, I believe you'll have need of me."

"Don't be droll! No one in this town has need of you," Erma retorted.

The discussion was halted when Henry and the judge entered the foyer. "What's going on here, Mother?" Henry asked.

Erma looked at Paloma coldly. "This – person demands entrance! She says we need her."

Henry went to the door. "What can we do for you, Mrs. Day?"

"As I told your mother, I wish to pay my respects in private, before the other mourners arrive this evening. It would be less awkward. I know how everyone in this town feels about me."

Henry wondered how she knew that there was a service planned for this evening since they hadn't told anyone about it yet. But she was the town witch. What did he expect? He was about to carry out his mother's wishes and deny her entry, until Victor whispered something in his ear, and he changed his mind. Henry smiled at Paloma. "By all means, Mrs. Day…"

"Henry!" exclaimed his mother as her son escorted the woman into the parlor.

"Now Erma," Judge Gooch interceded. He put a comforting hand on her back, gently urging her off to the side to speak to her privately. "Mrs. Day's arrival couldn't have come at a better moment."

"Why in heaven's name would we need her of all people?"

"The young man in the parlor has no experience in these religious matters. Who better to give him instruction than the widow of a Sin-Eater? You do want Alvin's cleansing to be done properly, don't you?"

Erma hesitated a moment and then sighed, "I suppose you're right, Victor."

With Henry's mother consoled, the judge re-entered the parlor. Paloma was kneeling beside the coffin with Henry standing behind her. Jedidiah sat in a chair looking out the window.

After a moment of prayer, Paloma crossed herself and stood. She gave her condolences to Henry and looked to the boy. "He's your Sin-Eater I assume?"

Jedidiah stood and looked at the older woman. He just then recognized her as the woman standing by the bell. "I'm not…"

"Shhh!" Paloma interrupted abruptly. She looked to Henry and the judge. "Let me speak with him privately, if you would."

"Certainly," the judge replied before Henry had a chance to object. The two men left the room and closed the door.

"I don't know about this, Judge," Henry replied. "Leaving her alone with my father's body? What if she casts…"

"Non-sense!" Victor interrupted. "The boy was about to say no. This is a thing that has to be done willingly. We can't force him to do it. Perhaps she can convince him otherwise."

Just then there was a knock at the door, and Henry opened it to find the sheriff. "Hiram – I didn't think you were going to be here until this evening. Anything wrong?"

The sheriff smiled. "You haven't seen the New Orleans paper, I assume."

"No," both men said simultaneously.

"Is there somewhere we can talk privately?"

***

When the two men left them alone, Paloma sat next to Jedidiah and they introduced themselves.

"You're the lady I saw by the bell today, aren't you?"

"I am," she replied.

"I take it you're not well liked around here by the tone of Mrs. Welch's voice."

"I'm not."

"Why?" he asked curiously. "You seem pleasant enough."

Paloma folded her hands in her lap and grinned. "Because I'm a witch."

Jedidiah laughed and shook his head. He stood and walked to the window. "Then you're crazy too!"

"You don't believe in witches?" she asked playfully.

Jedidiah turned his head and looked at her from the corner of his eye. "No - and I don't believe that another person can eat another's sins." Then he raised his voice slightly and faced her. "It's ridiculous!"

Paloma sighed. "I totally agree, boy. But the people in this town are steeped in their forefather's beliefs and superstitions. They believe in witches, ghosts, magic and evil spirits. There isn't one person in this town who doesn't carry either a rabbit's foot, or an acorn in their pocket for good luck."

Jedidiah folded his arms and smiled. "What about black cats?"

"They're rare in this town, but if one crosses someone's path, they'll turn in the opposite direction just in case."

"And you hold with these crazy notions?"

"I didn't say that," she replied. "I said I understand them. I don't believe in them. I have two black cats that live under my porch."

Jedidiah turned and looked out the window. He didn't know what to do. He told Henry Welch he'd do anything, but eating something that was placed on the chest of a dead man made his skin crawl. It seemed to him indecent.

"The first time is the hardest," Paloma said.

Jedidiah turned around. "First time doing what?"

"Sin-Eating, of course. You don't believe, so it should be easier for you than a person who does believe. Benjamin told me, he just closed his eyes the first few times. Eventually, the strangeness wore off, and he concentrated on the prayers he said."

Jedidiah sat next to her, and she told him about how her husband came to be the Sin-Eater for Black Water. "My husband and Alvin Welch met when they served in the cavalry together as young men. Both were discharged on the same day. Since Benjamin was raised in an orphanage, he had nowhere in particular to go so he accompanied Alvin to Black Water. Unfortunately, while in the cavalry, my husband had received a severe burn to his face from an accident with gunpowder. He was severely scared and lost an eye. The people of Black Water feared his rough exterior, and he found it hard to find work. At the time, Alvin Welch had no clout to help him. When the town's Sin-Eater disappeared, Alvin had suggested that Benjamin take on the responsibility. Since the people usually avoided him anyway, he figured his life wouldn't be that much different. He bargained for a monthly ration of staples from the general store; flour, coffee, sugar and the like, so he wouldn't starve."

Jedidiah was surprised. "They just gave it to him?"

"If they wanted to keep him," she replied. "Once a man becomes a sin-eater, he's basically avoided. No one would hire him to work in the fields or anywhere else for that matter – with the exception of the undertaker on occasion when something needed to be done at the cemetery and couldn't get anyone else to do it."

"Why didn't he just move on?" he asked curiously.

"Because of his looks," she shrugged. "I'd asked him the same thing. He told me that he'd get no better treatment anywhere else. His face was too badly disfigured. By staying here, he at least stayed fed. He was also told that he could have the old Sin-Eater's shack to live in, if he could find it in the swamp. It took a bit of looking, but he found it and made it his home."

"But how did you meet him?" Jedidiah's curiosity was peeked.

Paloma smiled. "That's for another day."

"But I don't intend on staying here." He shook his head and shivered slightly. "This town is too strange. I'm moving on after this one task."

"So you've decided to do it?"

He stood, walked back to the window and shoved his hands in his pockets. "I don't see as I have a choice. I practically said I'd do it before I found out what it was they wanted me to do. I don't like going back on my word."

Jedidiah asked if there were any special prayers he needed to say when he did this thing, but Paloma told him to just say whatever he thought the Lord would appreciate listening to. She then stood. "I'll take my leave." She walked to the door. "I'll be waiting for you by the bell this evening."

"Why?" he asked curiously.

"Destiny," she replied as she put her hand on the doorknob. "You'll need somewhere to stay for the night. It's almost certain you won't find anywhere to stay in town tonight - unless you bed down in an alley somewhere. You may stay with me for as long as you like." Then she left.

"Destiny?" he repeated. "What does that mean?"

***

Jedidiah paced nervously in the small room of the servant's quarters where they said he could rest until time to perform the service. He'd put on his black suit and looked in the mirror. "What does one say for eating sins?" He shook his head and laid down on the bed. "God, help me!"

The clock on the wall finally chimed five times, and he headed for the parlor of the main house. He sat in the back of the room as instructed and watched as the mourners came to pay their respects. He saw three beautiful young ladies, who appeared to be about his age, enter the room with their parents. They looked at him and smiled. Two of them giggled when he smiled and gave them a wink. For an instant, Jedidiah had second thoughts about leaving, until the mother of one of the girls whispered something into her ear. The alluring smiles instantly turned into disgust as the word was passed on to each girl. All thoughts of staying were banished from his head.

Jedidiah saw the town's preacher standing behind the podium. He was a tall, thin, clean-shaven man in his mid-forties. Jedidiah imagined that with his pinched facial features, he might have a soft mousy kind of voice - until he started sermonizing. Hell! - Fire! - and Brimstone! spewed forth from Reverend Donner's mouth. His words would have made old Scratch himself shake in his boots.

"Damnation…!" the preacher shouted raising his fist. He then opened his hand and extended an accusing finger as he slowly swept the congregation of twenty or more mourners. "…is your reward if you do not repent your transgressions.…"

Jedidiah scanned the faces of the people in the room and could tell they were captivated by his words. Reverend Donner's eyes blazed as he shouted, "…And if you are not humbled before the Almighty, the lake of fire will rise up and wash you into the pit of eternal torment - F-O-R-E-V-E-R!"

"Amen!" he heard the people shout.

Jedidiah did his best to suppress a smile as he thought, *I bet no one falls asleep in his church!*

After a few more heated words from the pulpit, followed by a few more Amens and praises to the Lord, Reverend Donner asked for the Sin-Eater to come forth. Jedidiah felt his nervousness return. He was in the spotlight - the center of attention - and he could feel all eyes upon him. He looked at the preacher, who nodded and whispered, "Say a prayer, eat the bread and drink the wine."

All the words he'd planned on saying flew from his brain. He drew a blank. So he just said whatever popped into his head. "Hello, God? I didn't know this man, but I'm sure you do, or did. I'm going to take over his sins and…" he hesitated a moment, "…with your will be done, I'll do it by eating this bread and drinking this wine. So if you don't mind, will you open your pearly gates and let Mr. Welch in?" He hesitated again and added, "If you please? Amen."

He glanced at the Rreverend who closed his eyes and shuttered slightly. It was apparent the man didn't approve of his prayer, and he could have sworn he heard someone snicker from the seats. But it must have been good enough, for Reverend Donner gave him the nod to eat bread and drink the wine.

Jedidiah avoided looking at the dead man's face and focused on the small, round loaf of bread that was about the size of a biscuit, laying on his chest. He did as Paloma suggested and closed his eyes as he picked up the bread and small cup of wine. He hesitated a moment and thought to himself, *Just two bites and it's done!*

He took the first bite. He thought that this might be some special bread with a different taste, but it was just plain old bread. He quickly finished it off and chased it with a swallow of wine, but almost choked on it when the mourners suddenly burst into a lively rendition of, *In the Sweet By and By.*

Jedidiah stood behind the preacher until the singing was done, and everyone left their seats and started mingling with each other. Reverend Donner told him that Henry Welch wanted to speak with him and to wait in the room across from the parlor.

The room looked like an office. There was a large desk in the center with a bookcase behind it and a seating area by the window. He left the door slightly ajar and sat in a chair beside it. He listened to some of the remarks and conversations of the people who passed by or stood in the foyer just outside the room.

"I believe that was the worst prayer I ever," he heard one woman say.

Another woman responded, "I'm sure the Lord understands it was his first time. He'll surely improve in time."

Jedidiah laughed slightly and then he heard three girls talking and stood to take a peek. They were the same girls he'd seen earlier.

"I thought he was cute," said the first girl. "Too bad he's a dirty Sin-

Eater."

The second girl shuttered. "When my mother told me what he was, it sent cold chills up my spine. I flirted with him with my eyes before I found out. I instantly said three *Hail Mary's* and the *Lord's Prayer* twice."

"That should cover you, you didn't know," said the third girl. "I wonder why he did it? He looks to be our age. What self-respecting girl will look at him now?"

"I'll never look at him again," the first girl said adamantly. "Besides that witch, Paloma Day, who'd want a bow or husband who's destined to burn in hell?"

"Not me!" exclaimed the other two.

Jedidiah plopped back down in the chair and leaned against the wall. "I'm definitely not staying in this town!" he mumbled to himself.

A few minutes later, Henry Welch entered the room and Jedidiah stood.

"Thank you for doing this," said Henry. He pulled out his change purse and gave Jedidiah two nickels.

"Have a seat, Jedidiah. I have a matter I'd like to discuss with you."

But the boy had a feeling he knew what he was going to ask. "If it's about becoming a permanent Sin-Eater – no thanks. I plan on leaving as soon as I can."

"I'm sorry to hear that," Henry replied.

He walked to the door and opened it. Sheriff Wright entered with Victor Gooch following behind.

"Son," said Sheriff Wright, "I'm afraid I'm going to have to take you into custody."

"Custody!" Jedidiah replied shocked. "For what?"

"For the possible robbery and murder of the people on that stagecoach," the sheriff said as he pulled out a set of handcuffs.

"I didn't do it!" Jedidiah exclaimed. "If I'd done it, I wouldn't be here, and I wouldn't have told you about it."

"I was willing to give you the benefit of the doubt…," the sheriff replied, "…until I read about you in the New Orleans' paper. You were found guilty of murder…"

"I was acquitted," Jedidiah interrupted.

"All the same," Victor replied. "An investigation will have to be made. Protocol has to be followed."

"I find your credibility doubtful after reading this," the sheriff replied holding up the newspaper. "I don't know you."

"But I'm innocent," Jedidiah pleaded.

"Now wait a minute," Henry said evenly as he looked at the sheriff and Victor. "Isn't he innocent until proven guilty?"

"True," Victor replied. "But where is he to stay if not in jail? He can't leave town until after the inquest. Are you going to keep him here?"

Henry sighed and shoved his hands in his pockets. He turned to Jedidiah. "I'm sorry, young man. My hands are tied. You're not a resident, and it's doubtful you'll receive any type of employment here. If you have nowhere to go, I'm afraid you'll have to go with Sheriff Wright."

"Wait a minute!" Jedidiah said angrily. "I spent three years in a Yankee prisoner of war camp. I have no desire to spend another minute in a jail cell, especially when I'm innocent!"

"Can't be helped," said the sheriff as he slapped a cuff on one of Jedidiah's wrists. "Vagrancy is against the law here."

"For how long?" Jedidiah asked.

The sheriff looked to the judge. Victor scratched his chin. "An investigation will have to be made. The sheriff will have to contact the authorities in New Orleans and inquire about your character and then there's the problem of my being out of town. I have several small towns I travel to, to hear cases." He hesitated a moment. "I'd say it shouldn't be any more than six months."

"Six month!" Jedidiah exclaimed as the sheriff slapped on the other cuff. He knew he was being railroaded, but there was nothing he could do about it. "Hold on a minute. I have a place to stay." He looked toward Henry Welch. "And I've been offered a – job."

"Oh?" Victor questioned. "Pray tell, where to stay and what to do?"

"With Mrs. Day. I'm to meet her at that bell I saw earlier," Jedidiah replied heatedly. "I'll be your town's Sin-Eater – temporarily!"

"What do you think, Judge?" Henry asked.

He hesitated a moment and then looked seriously at Jedidiah. "You understand, that if you leave town before this matter is settled, I'll put a warrant out for your arrest."

"I understand," Jedidiah replied coldly.

Victor turned to the sheriff and nodded. He removed the cuffs and told Jedidiah to come with him, and he'd drop him off by the Sin-Eater's bell. When they left, Henry sat down on the sofa by the window and watched as the young man got in the back of the sheriff's wagon. Victor sat in the chair across from him.

"Did you receive an answer from the wire you sent to New Orleans about the boy?" Henry asked.

"Almost immediately," Victor replied. "The poor boy has had some hard times. Judge Harcourt replied personally as to his character – said basically he was a good boy and his stepfather deserved what he got."

"What about the stagecoach?" Henry asked.

"Hiram rode out to where the boy said it was. Everything was as he described. He recognized one of the robbers the boy shot from a wanted poster on him. There's no doubt of the boy's innocence."

"You think he'll stay?"

"Who can say?" Victor shrugged. "Hopefully, he believes our little deception and stays for the six months at least. If he does leave, there's nothing we can officially do."

Chapter 5

Emmaline Candlewick was glad to be getting back home. She hoped by being gone for so long, it might inspire Henry Welch to ask her uncle's permission to officially court her. He was a very independent man and well respected in the community, but where romance was concerned, she thought him completely backward.

"You look a million miles away," said Barbara as she looked at her young cousin. "Thinking about Henry, I bet."

"He makes me angry," Emmaline huffed. "His name is on my dance card several times at all the cotillions, and he manages to be seated next to me at all other social events. And then there are his visits to talk with Uncle Victor on some pretext, but that is just so he has an excuse to talk with me on this subject or that." Emmaline was becoming more frustrated. "But he just won't ask your father's permission to officially court me! What's wrong with him?"

"Some men are like that," Barbara replied. She took her husband's hand in hers. "Jeffrey was the same way. I thought he'd never ask my father's permission to see me. When he finally did, it took him two years to get up the nerve to ask permission to marry me."

Jeffrey laughed. "Your father is an intimidating man."

"Father is just a big, old teddy bear," Barbara replied hiding a smile. "I don't know why you'd think that."

Emmaline giggled as she listened to Barbara and Jeffrey discuss Victor Gooch. She would miss Barbara when she and her husband returned to Baton Rouge in a few days. It wasn't often that she saw her cousin since she had married, but she hoped that someday she would be just as happy and in love as they were.

Her thoughts turned back to Henry and she sighed. She turned her gaze in another direction and saw Paloma Day standing beside the Sin-Eater's bell just ahead. She had an idea and summoned up her courage to follow through with it.

"Jeffrey, could you have the driver pull over just ahead," Emmaline asked.

"Whatever for?"

"I see Mrs. Day over there. I need to ask her something."

"The witch!" Barbara was shocked. "Heavens no!"

But Emmaline wasn't going to be put off. "If you don't pull over now…" she said seriously, "…when we get home, I'll go looking for her – even if I have to seek her out in the swamp!"

Barbara sighed. She knew her cousin meant what she said. She thought Emmaline was sometimes too independent for her own good. "You may as well have the driver pull over, dear. I know that look in her eye. When she's made her mind up to do something, she's going to do it no matter how foolish it is."

***

Paloma waited patiently on the covered bench by the Sin-Eater's bell. Benjamin had put it there years ago to shelter himself from potential rain. Sometimes he had to wait for the family who had summoned him to pick him up.

She saw a carriage pass and then stop a few feet away from her. She was surprised when a young, dark-haired girl got out and approached her. Paloma smiled. "What can I do for you, girl?"

"If you please, Mrs. Day," Emmaline curtseyed. "Could you tell my fortune?"

"Do you play a farce with me, girl?" Paloma asked. Sometimes the young would tease her whenever she entered town.

"Oh no!" Emmaline assured her. "I'd be afraid to. I'm very serious. I can pay you."

Paloma looked into her eyes and smiled. "I can see that you are, child. What is it you wish to know?" She extended her hand, and Emmaline pressed a few coins in her palm. The money would come in handy.

"I want to know if I will ever have a future with a certain man."

"I should have guessed," Paloma laughed slightly. She moved over on the bench. "Have a seat beside me." When the girl hesitated, she added. "Don't worry, girl, contrary to popular belief, I won't bite you."

Emmaline summoned up her courage and did as she asked. She wasn't exactly afraid to sit next to Paloma because she feared that the woman would do something to her, she feared that Mrs. Day would be able to sense the family secret that her father had imparted to her before he died. She wasn't quite ready to know what the outcome of that secret would be just yet. Emmaline held her breath.

"Relax, child, you're too tense." Paloma took the girl's chin in her hand and looked deep into her dark blue eyes for a moment and then closed hers. "I see a marriage in your future."

"To Henry?" Emmaline was excited.

"Let me see your palm." The girl extended her hand, and Paloma traced the lines in her palm. "I see two paths." Paloma closed her eyes once more. She sensed something within this girl. The two paths she saw didn't belong to her, but to two others and it confused her. *Children perhaps?* she thought. She took the girl's other hand and traced the lines. "You may not like what I'm about to tell you."

"I won't be with Henry?" Emmaline guessed.

"The only way I see this young man in your future is – if you do the asking."

"Me!" Emmaline was shocked. "How can I? It's the man who's supposed to do the asking."

"If you do this, I see you with him. If you don't, your path will lead in another direction."

"If Henry and I are together, will we be happy?"

"Life is full of unlimited possibilities," she replied. "It's unclear." Then Paloma smiled and added, "Happiness is what you make of it."

"Thank you, Mrs. Day." Emmaline stood. "I've got a lot to think about."

"If you had the courage to sit down by me and talk, being bold with your young man should not be any more difficult."

Emmaline thanked her and bid her a good evening. She was now glad she stopped. Paloma Day didn't seem like the horrible person her Aunt Sally and all the other women in town depicted her to be. She actually thought her a likable person. She was also relieved that her secret was not discovered. At least she didn't think it was.

Paloma watched the girl get in the carriage and drive away. Something was going to happen with this girl, but she couldn't tell what. Somehow she felt a connection to her, but it was an indirect connection. Her thoughts were interrupted when she saw the sheriff coming down the street in a wagon. He stopped in front of her.

"This young man said he is staying with you, Paloma," Sheriff Wright stated boldly.

"I've been expecting him." She turned to Jedidiah. "Come along, boy. We'll just make it home before it gets dark."

Jedidiah got out of the wagon and followed her. He was still curious as to how she knew that he would be there. He didn't even know.

"Remember, you're not to leave town," the sheriff called after him.

Jedidiah didn't look back. "How can I leave town?" he mumbled to himself. "I've no horse and ten cents to my name!" Then he spoke to Paloma. "Do you know what they did to me?"

"Of course," she replied as she walked ahead of him. "I saw it seventeen years ago. The night you were born."

Jedidiah stopped for a moment and shook his head. "I'm in a town full of crazy people!"

***

Jedidiah followed Paloma through the tangle of woods. He wondered how he was going to find his way back to town. There was no clear-cut path. She made twists and turns, crossed over dead wood and pushed away branches that were in their way. "Are you sure we're not lost?"

"I believe I know the way to my own house, boy." She stopped a moment, cocked her head in his direction and grinned. "I've only been walking the woods of this swamp for thirty-eight years." Her expression suddenly became serious. "Don't move!"

Jedidiah froze in his tracks. "What is it?"

She didn't answer, and he didn't ask again when he saw her pull a knife from a sheath hidden in the waistband of her dress and pose her arm to throw it. He quit breathing for a moment and when she shouted, "Duck!" he didn't hesitate. He felt something heavy fall on top of him. He brushed it away and quickly jumped up. But as he did, his wooden leg slipped off, he lost his balance and fell backwards. He felt his heart beat wildly in his chest when he saw it. "It's a snake!"

She grabbed the wriggling snake, pulled her knife from its head and severed it from the body. "Correction – it was a snake. Now it's dinner. When you get yourself back together," she said indicating his wooden appendage, "Pick it up. We're almost home." When he hesitated, she added, "It's dead. It won't bite."

Jedidiah found a sturdy stick and picked up the creature. It looked to be about eight foot long, and was as big around as the calf of his leg. "If you think I'm eating this thing, you're crazy!"

"I don't know why not." She grinned. "It would have eaten you."

A few moments later, they entered a clearing. Jedidiah was surprised by the surroundings. He saw a nice little cottage, painted green with white trim, and a carpet of green grass surrounded the area. Flower boxes hung outside the windows and there was a vegetable garden off to the side enclosed by a fence. He saw a covered well with a bucket hanging from a rope and a fire pit with a large, black kettle hanging on an iron rod. "I thought they said you lived in a shack. You have a nice little house."

"Thank you. I like it. But years ago, before Benjamin moved in, it wasn't fit for pigs to live in," she replied as they walked toward the house. "It took him years to cut back the woods and create this little haven. If it's not tended to, it won't take long before the woods take it back."

Paloma took the carcass of the snake and threw it over a wooden rack beside the porch. When Jedidiah entered the house, he was equally impressed. It consisted of three rooms; two bedrooms and a living area. The living area had a fireplace with two padded rocking chairs before it; a spinning wheel with a basket of yarn was in the corner and yellow curtains hung in the windows. He scanned the connecting kitchen area and saw a small dining table with four chairs, a cook stove, large cupboard and small counter area for cooking preparations. Everything was neat and orderly.

Paloma led him to one of the bedrooms. "This will be your room."

The room for the most part was empty, except for a chest of drawers and a cradle in the corner. Jedidiah was about to ask if she had any children, but she seemed to have read his thoughts and answered before he asked.

"Benjamin added this room and built the cradle and chest over there when I became pregnant," she said sadly. "I lost the baby. We were never blessed again." She wiped a tear from her eye and cleared her throat. "I have extra blankets. You can make a pallet on the floor until a suitable bed can be fashioned."

He noted the hurt in her tone and sensed she didn't want any condolences on her loss by her abrupt change of subject. He replied kindly, "I can manage. This will be fine."

He watched her walk outside, and after he put his meager belonging in the chest of drawers, he joined her on the porch - she was skinning their dinner.

Paloma looked at him and grinned. "How do you like your snake? Fried or stewed?"

"I prefer it as just plain ol' dead!"

She laughed as she started deboning the meat. "It's definitely that. I'll stew it. If you don't have the courage to eat the meat, you can fill your stomach on the vegetables. But if it makes you feel better, it tastes akin to chicken."

As he watched her, he broached the subject of how she became the wife of a Sin-Eater, since the people of this town looked down upon them. Paloma stopped for a moment to gather her thoughts.

"I was born in 1831…" she said as she tossed a piece of meat into the pot. "…to a family of Gypsies."

Jedidiah raised his eyebrows. "Gypsies!" he laughed. "You don't look like a Gypsy."

"That's what I said. Now, do you want to hear the rest or not?"

Jedidiah nodded, and she continued.

"I was thirteen when my father died. We traveled from town to town. My mother and grandmother told fortunes. In most places, after we were there for a few days, we were asked to leave. However, when we came to Black Water, we weren't asked to leave. My mother couldn't really tell the future, she was just good at telling people what they wanted to hear and put on a good show for her customers by reading Tarot cards; however, my grandmother's ability and mine came naturally. I predicted mostly inclement weather when I was younger. I saved many farmers' crops from being planted too early or harvested too late. My predictions were often posted in the newspaper."

Jedidiah laughed as he peeled the carrots she'd handed him. "Then why don't they like you now?"

"Because as I grew older, I became prettier, the women became jealous and the young men lustful. My mother met many a liquored up boy at our door with a shotgun."

"So when did Benjamin come into the picture?"

"I met Benjamin before he became a Sin-Eater. His exterior was harsh, but I could see past that. He was a warm, caring person. I read his palm one evening. I told him he was going to marry a beautiful woman and live a long, happy life." Paloma stood, went into the house and dumped the snake meat in a pot of water. Jedidiah followed her.

"What did he say when you told him that?" He added the carrots to the pot.

"He laughed at me and asked who it was." Paloma smiled at the memory. "I told him it was me."

"Did he marry you right away?" He put wood in the cook stove and sat at the table to peel potatoes.

"No. I pursued him for almost year. He was much older than I, but I didn't care. I'd fallen hopelessly in love with him. By then, he'd become the town's Sin-Eater."

"Your mother didn't object?"

"He wasn't her ideal choice, but she knew how I felt. Anyway, during that year, both my mother and grandmother died in an epidemic of influenza when I was seventeen. I followed Benjamin into the swamp after he ate their sins."

Jedidiah stopped peeling for a moment. "Hey, I thought you didn't believe in that sort of thing?"

"I don't," she said with a shrug. "But the town's people feared their ghosts and insisted. Besides," she said with a grin. "It was a good way to get him to my house so I could follow him back to his. Benjamin became angry when he discovered me and told me to go home. I told him that if I went back, I would more than likely fall victim to some young buck, since I was now alone in the world. And if he didn't take me as a wife and something happened, I would be labeled a wicked woman and it would be his fault."

"So you guilted him into a marriage." Jedidiah laughed.

She thought for a moment. "No - I would say that it was more like I made him feel sorry for me," she said as she covered the stewpot to simmer. "He was also a lonely man. I filled a spot in his life." She walked to the front door and looked out. "I never gave him a moment of regret. We were very happy together until nine days ago." Paloma shook off her sad feelings and turned to Jedidiah. "Now tell me about you."

Jedidiah told her his life's story up to now. By the time he was finished, the snake stew was done. She dished out a plate and set it before him. He figured that if he could endure three years of the slop they'd fed him in that Yankee prison camp, he could at least taste the snake meat. He closed his eyes, turned up his nose and shoveled a spoonful in his mouth. He was pleasantly surprised. "Hey! It tastes like chicken!"

"Told you." Paloma laughed inwardly.

CHAPTER 6

Time went by quickly for Jedidiah. Paloma taught him many things about the swamp. Most of their food came from there. She showed him where Benjamin had his traps set, the best place to fish and catch crawdads as well as which snakes were poisonous and which weren't. Flour, sugar, salt, coffee and tea were about the only things he ever came into town for. But when he did go to town for supplies, it was usually first thing in the morning before the store opened, and he'd meet the store clerk at the backdoor.

Not counting the few cents he received from sin-eating, the only actual money Jedidiah made was from selling the snake skins they'd collected to a boot maker at Paloma's suggestion. She told him that's what Benjamin used to do, so he took over the task. When he'd asked her why the boot maker was the only man that would do business with him, she told him that it was greed. Snake skin boots, belts and wallets were very profitable for him and if it hadn't been for Benjamin, he'd have to go snake hunting himself if he wanted to make them.

During his forced stay in Black Water, Jedidiah had performed five sin-eatings, and as Paloma had told him, they'd become easier. His prayers sounded less comical, and the last time he performed the ritual, Reverend Donner actually gave him a nod of approval.

But finally, the six months had ended and Jedidiah approached Judge Gooch on the morning of the last day of his confinement to the township. The man could no longer put him off, and he was cleared of the trumped up charges. He was free to go, but was asked to stay.

When Jedidiah got back to Paloma's cottage, he saw her sitting on the porch. "I'm free, Paloma!" He was ecstatic. "I can leave whenever I want!"

She smiled as she rocked in her chair. "Good for you, boy."

"Why don't you come with me? We can go to Baton Rouge, or anywhere else we want."

"No, my place is here," she said sincerely. "It's my home. You go on.

Have a good life."

He knelt down beside her. "But why? You have no one here. What's to keep you?"

"Destiny," she replied thoughtfully. "I have this feeling that I need to stay. It's not clear to me why as of yet."

Jedidiah stood. "Destiny!" he repeated in a huff. "You're always saying something about it. Well, I believe destiny is what you make for yourself. And mine isn't in this place."

He marched into the house, threw his belongings in a bag and went back outside. "I'm leaving, Paloma. I'm not staying here."

"No one asked you to," she replied pleasantly as she rocked.

"You're not going to guilt me into staying here." He took a step off the porch.

"Wouldn't dream of it," she replied. She stood and went to the herb box that hung at the window and picked some fresh parsley.

Jedidiah was perplexed. She was an old woman. He couldn't believe she wanted to stay in a town that hated her.

She turned. "You haven't left yet? Hurry along or you'll be late."

"Late?" He thought that was the most confusing statement she could have made. "Late for what?" But he didn't wait for an answer. He knew what the next word would be - destiny. "Never mind - bye!" Jedidiah said angrily. He walked through the woods mumbling to himself. "She's the most stubborn woman that ever lived. I offer to take her out of the swamp, and she doesn't want to go." He stepped over a log and pushed a vine out of the way. "She's not going to make me feel guilty about leaving her here. I have my own life to live. I want a wife someday! Kids! And I can't get them here!"

He came to the edge of the clearing by the Sin-Eater's bell. He saw a little redheaded girl, who looked to be about six years old, about to ring it. She spotted him before she did and lowered her hand.

"Hello," she said in a business-like manner. "I saw you before when Mr. Baker died. You're Mr. Sin-Eater, aren't you?"

Jedidiah chuckled slightly and knelt down beside her. "I am, but you can call me Jedidiah." He pointed to the bell. "You shouldn't play with the bell, little girl. I wouldn't want you to get in trouble." He looked around, but didn't see an adult anywhere near. "Best you get home. I don't think you should be out here by yourself."

"I wasn't going to play with it. I need you, Mr. Jedidiah," she said innocently.

She turned and picked up a basket that was behind her. Jedidiah saw a solid white kitten covered partially with a cloth. It looked to be dead.

"This *was* my Fluffy," she said sadly looking at the kitten. "A dog got her." She looked back up at Jedidiah. "I want her to go to heaven, so could you eat her sins?" The little girl held up a coin. "I have a penny."

Jedidiah stood for a moment and turn his back, so not to laugh at her. The child was completely serious. He did his best to gather his composure and knelt back down. "I don't believe Fluffy has need of a Sin-Eater. I think kittens automatically go to cat heaven."

"That's what Mommy said. When my daddy gets home from work, he's going to bury her." She held out the penny in her palm. "But I have to make sure. I really, *really* loved Fluffy."

Jedidiah heard the sincerity in the girl's voice and saw she was about to cry. He gave her a warm smile. "Well, I guess we can make extra sure."

The little girl set the basket down. She pulled a piece of bread out of a sack she had in the basket and placed it on the dead cat. She also had a small mason jar of yellow liquid. "I'm not allowed to touch Daddy's wine. Will lemonade work?"

"For kittens – I'd say lemonade is perfect." He watched as the little girl knelt down and folded her hands. Jedidiah said a little prayer, ate the bread and drank the jar of the worst lemonade he'd ever had, but managed to keep a straight face in doing so. Afterward, the little girl sang a hymn to complete the ceremony.

"Thank you, Mr. Jedidiah." She handed him the penny, picked up the basket with the dead cat and walked off.

Jedidiah leaned up against the post and looked at the penny in his palm. He figured if he refused it, the little girl would just give him another argument. "Destiny," he said repeating Paloma's favorite word.

***

Paloma was chopping a potato at the kitchen counter. Her back was to the open door. "Put the snake on the table outside, boy," she said without turning around. "After you put away your things, go ahead and skin it, but sure you remove all the bones this time."

How does she do that! he wondered. There was no way she could have seen him from the window, and he was sure he hadn't made a sound when he stepped up on the porch. It was frustrating. No matter how many times he'd tried to sneak up on her, she'd always know he was there. He put the snake on the table and entered the cottage. "Do you have eyes in the back of your head or something?"

"Or something." She turned slightly and grinned. After giving him a wink, she turned back to what she was doing.

"You act like you're not surprised I'm back," he huffed. He threw his sack of clothing on the bed in his room.

"I'm not," she replied

"Why?"

She turned to face him. "Do you really want me to answer that?"

Jedidiah rolled his eyes. "Don't tell me – destiny!"

Paloma turned around. "So if not destiny, what made you return?"

"A dead cat," he replied with a grin.

She nodded her head as she continued chopping vegetables. "Now it makes sense."

He shook his head and laughed. "It would to you!" He went outside, skinned the snake and brought the meat back in to debone it. He sat in silence as he waited for Paloma to ask him to elaborate on his dead cat explanation, but when she didn't, he finally had to ask, "Okay! How does it make sense?"

She sat down at the table next to him with a bowl of beans and started to snap them. "I had a dream last night involving you, and a cat. It was a bit hazy though. I dreamt you left, as you did, but while later, I saw a white kitten emerge from the woods – you were following it." She looked at him and smiled. "So, why did the dead cat lead you back?"

"Finally," he replied with a laugh. "Something you don't know!" He told her about the service he performed for the little girl. "She said the one thing no one else did – she needed me. The people in town wanted me to stay for their benefit. They didn't say they needed me. When I thought about it, I wondered who else might need me." He smiled warmly at Paloma. "The only person who came to mind was you."

Chapter 7

Shadrack Community

Jedidiah stood by the bell and waited for whoever rung it to pick him up. A little over two years had passed since he'd decided to stay. He was now twenty. He'd lost count of the number of services he'd performed. The bell was rung by all levels of Black Water's society - from the very rich to the very poor.

Finally, after about an hour, a rickety wagon came toward him with a boy driving. Jedidiah thought he looked to be about thirteen. He was wearing overalls that had so many patches sewn on it, he could barely tell where the original material was. Jedidiah knew immediately he was going to the Shadrack Community.

"Well – git in!" said the boy rudely. "We ain't got all day."

Jedidiah got in the back of the wagon as was customary when someone picked him up. He never sat with the driver and no conversation took place. Sometimes the driver would tell him who needed of his services, but most of the time he didn't find out until he arrived at his destination..

Shadrack was about five miles outside of Black Water's town limits and, for the most part, skirted the waters of the swamp. The community was named after Elmo Shadrack, the leader of group of backwoods, Kentucky hillbillies. The group left the hills ten years earlier and settled there after hearing that there was good money in fishing and hunting alligators in Louisiana from a traveling salesman. Elmo was the first to become dinner for a gator.

Jedidiah thought sure that the boy had hit every rut in the road on purpose. He was glad when the wagon finally pulled into a yard and stopped. Several children, varying in age, scattered when they saw him. While he waited for someone to come out of the house to speak with him, a girl walked up and propped her arms on the side of wagon. Jedidiah thought her a wild looking thing. Her dress looked like it was made from a burlap sack that had been patched several times. She was barefoot and her brown hair looked like it hadn't been combed in a month. "Hello," he said with a smile.

"You ain't suppos'ta be talkin' to me, Mr. Sin-Eater." She was grinning from ear to ear.

"I could say the same thing about you." He got out of the wagon and stretched.

She laughed. "I ain't a carin'. My Aunt Josie says, I ain't nothin' but plain white trash anyhow, so I fig'er we're equal."

"Why would she say that?" He wondered how her relative could refer to her in that manner.

"My mama was a loose woman before she died. And bein' that I ain't got no daddy – least ways my mama told me once he could'a been anybody, the apple don't fall far from the tree. That's what my Aunt Josie says."

Jedidiah was surprised at her openness. Most people would keep information like that to themselves. "Is it your mother I'm…"

"Na'," she interrupted. "My mama died a while back. It's my cousin, Obie. Gator got him."

He noticed that her tone was indifferent. "You don't seem very upset about it."

"Why should I?" she replied with a shrug. "I had ta' hit him upside the head with a bucket once!"

Jedidiah tried not to laugh since the man was dead, but the way she said it was just too funny, and it made him curious. "How come?"

She hesitated a moment and looked around. "I don't know if'n I should be tellin' ya' this, but since yer in a way doin' the Lord's work…" She took a second look around. When she saw no one in earshot she whispered, "…he tried to – know me once, like the Good Book says. It were just pure luck I saw the bucket. I hit him upside the head three times with it before he let me be."

Jedidiah nodded his head. "I don't blame you for your feelings. Didn't you tell your family about it?"

"Good Lord a'mighty! No! It were over and done with when I hit him with the bucket. If I'd said somethin', they would'a taken Obie's side. He would'a lied and said I put designs on him, but I didn't." She frowned. "I ain't my mama. I want a right'n proper husband." Then she sighed. "But I'm an old maid now."

"You're kidding." He tried not to laugh for she seemed completely serious. She didn't look much older than sixteen or seventeen.

"I almost got married last year, but I ain't got much in the way of a dowry, so they called it off." Then she laughed. "I was glad though. Shad McCoy is a widower three times my age. His boy, Shad Jr., is older than me by three months!"

Jedidiah laughed with her until he saw an older man wearing a pair of patched overalls come out of the house. He was tall, thin and his face was covered mostly by a thick beard. "Git on away from him, girl!" he shouted. "Before I takes a strap ta' ya'!"

"I was just talkin' with him, Uncle Ennis!"

The man shook his head. "Sometimes, girl, ya' ain't got the sense God gave a goose. Ya' ain't got no business talkin' ta' the likes of a Sin-Eater. Go on!"

Jedidiah watch the girl run off into the woods. He shook the thoughts of the outspoken girl from his head when the man asked him to come inside.

He looked at the dead man in the pine box. Obie, as the girl called him, looked as if he were in his mid-thirties. If he actually believed in the eating of sins, Jedidiah would have told the family to forget it. He thought that any man who would try and violate a young girl, and a kinsman at that, didn't deserve to have his spirit put to rest. But he wasn't doing it for the man, he was doing it for the peace of mind it gave the grieving family.

When the service was done, the man paid Jedidiah with six eggs from the chicken coop, and the boy who'd picked him up took him back to the bell. As he walked home, he had a strange sensation that he was being followed. He looked behind him twice, but didn't see anything.

Jedidiah walked into the cottage and saw Paloma fixing dinner. "Got some eggs." He put them in a bowl and went to his bedroom to change out of his black suit.

"Wash up!" Paloma shouted after him. "Stew is about done."

Jedidiah went to the well and drew some water. He washed and dried his face and when he looked off into the woods, he thought he saw something. As he walked in that direction, he saw one of Paloma's cats exit the woods. He picked her up and stroked her black fur. "Was that you following me, Esmeralda?"

The cat purred and nuzzled him as he walked back into the house. He noticed Paloma setting three plates at the table. "Expecting company?"

"No, why?" she asked.

"Then what's the extra place for?"

Paloma noticed what she'd unconsciously done. "I guess we are." She looked toward the window. "I believe we have company."

Jedidiah laughed. "Another one of your intuitions?"

"No," she replied evenly. "I just caught a glimpse of a face in the window." She turned back to the stove and stirred the stew. "Show some manners and invite her in."

"Her! I knew someone was following me!" He quickly turned and went to the door. He saw the shabby looking girl who had talked to him earlier. She was about to run off the porch, when Paloma's other black cat crossed her path. She stopped dead in her tracks.

Jedidiah was surprised to see her. "What are you doing here?"

The young girl turned around. "Have ya' got a window I can crawl out of? I can't git off the porch. A black cat crossed it."

He folded his arms. "That still doesn't answer my question."

"I hear'd tell that the Sin-Eater lived with a witch. I've never seen a real witch before. My curiosity was itchin' at me. I wanted ta' see her fer myself." The girl peeked back in the window and whispered, "She don't look like a witch."

Jedidiah laughed. "What's a witch supposed to look like?"

"Old and ugly with one tooth and warts on a crooked nose," she replied. "I seen a picture once."

"Well, if you'd like to come in, I'll introduce you." He turned to enter.

She hesitated. "I don't know."

He looked back. "If it will set your mind at ease, she's not a witch. She's a Gypsy."

"Well, that's a relief," she sighed. As she followed him in, she asked, "What's a Gypsy?"

They invited the girl to stay for dinner. She started to say no, until she caught the aroma of Paloma's stew, and she said it wouldn't be polite not to stay for have a "samplin'."

She told them her name was Abigail Hicks, and until three years ago, she lived in Hazard, Kentucky. When her mother died, her grandmother said she was too old to care for her, so she shipped her off to Black Water to live with her mother's half-sister, Josie, and her husband, Ennis Hagen.

Both Paloma and Jedidiah enjoyed having Abigail as company. They never had visitors and only had each other to talk to. After two plates of stew, Abigail stood.

"I be thankin' ya' kindly. But I best be goin' home before it gits dark. You got a back window I can go out? I don't know if enough time has passed since that black cat crossed yer porch."

"No need in that, girl," said Paloma. "I have a remedy for black cat crossings." She walked to the fireplace where Esmeralda was lounging in a chair. She picked her up and handed it to Abigail. "If a black cat comes to you, it's good luck and will cancel out the bad luck."

The cat nuzzled her. "I'd be thankin' ya' agin."

Jedidiah went with her. She said it wasn't necessary, but he told her that the path leading back to town could get confusing, and he'd take her as far as the bell. He offered to walk her all the way home, but Abigail said her aunt and uncle might not like it, and she'd most likely get a 'whoopin' if they'd found out where she'd gone to.

Jedidiah and Abigail were talking and laughing with each other as they walked through the woods. Suddenly, he came face to face with two double-barreled shotguns pointed at his head.

"Jubal! Uncle Ennis!" the girl exclaimed. "What'cha doin' here?"

"Yer cousin, Jubal, here, told me he saws ya' crawl out from under the wagon," Ennis said angrily. "We tracked ya' here. What in tar'nation was ya' thinkin', girl!"

"I just wanted ta' see the witch is all, Uncle Ennis," Abigail replied. "Jedidiah was just showin' me a kindness by walkin' me ta' town so I wouldn't git lost in this here part of the swamp."

"Ha! Git lost in the swamp! You could walk this here swamp blindfolded." Ennis shook his head. "Just like yer Ma! Ya' don't go walkin' out with a man, lest ya' be betrothed ta' him."

"Nothing happened, sir," Jedidiah offered.

"You hesh up, boy! You should'a know'd better too, bein' what ya' are." He pointed to Abigail. "She can track better than most her cousins – even Jubal, here!" He pointed to the boy.

"No she can't, Pa!" Jubal objected. "I'm better than any ol' girl!"

"Hesh up!" He slapped the thirteen year old upside the back of the head. "I ain't talkin' ta' you, boy." He turned his attention back to Jedidiah. "We Hagen's ain't rich like them Black Water folks, but we ain't trash! And like it or not, Abigail is kin." He looked harshly at the girl. "There's only one thing ta' do…"

"No – Uncle Ennis!" She shook her head.

But he ignored her and starred at Jedidiah. "Sin-Eater or no – there's gonna be a weddin'!"

Jedidiah opened his mouth to object, but when Ennis and Jubal cocked both barrels and pointed their rifles at him, he closed it.

***

Jedidiah walked into the house and flopped in the chair by the fireplace. Paloma was crocheting. "You're back quickly." Then she noticed the strange expression on his face when he didn't answer. "What's wrong?"

He laughed humorously as he looked into the fire. "I'm surprised you didn't see this coming." He looked up at her. "Have you got a nice dress?"

"Yes, why?"

"We're going to a wedding next week."

"Whose?"

Jedidiah looked back into the fire. "Mine!"

Chapter 8

Gooch Residence

Emmaline Candlewick was upset. She'd just read in *The Black Water Caller,* the town's newspaper, that their Sin-Eater was to be married this Saturday.

Sally Gooch saw her niece crumple up the newspaper and throw it into the fireplace. "What in the name of heaven is the matter, dear?"

"Jedidiah is getting married," she said in a huff.

Sally shook her head and clicked her tongue. "I heard about that from Katie Longwood yesterday. I don't know what those Kentucky hill people are thinking. Having a relative marry the Sin-Eater? It's unthinkable!" She took a sip of her tea and added, "But why should that upset you so?"

"Because!" Emmaline folded her arms and started to pace. "Henry and I have been seeing each other for two years now! He hasn't once broached the subject of marriage to Uncle Victor!"

"And how would you know?" Sally asked.

"Because I asked Uncle Victor." Emmaline sat back down on the sofa.

"Emmaline!" Sally exclaimed. "That was very inappropriate!"

"I know," she sighed. "But I love Henry. I want to be his wife and mother to his children."

Sally got up from her chair and sat beside her niece. She put a comforting arm around her. "Everything works out in its own time, my dear. It's just our place to wait and hope our wishes come true."

"I suppose you're right, Aunt Sally." She agreed with her aunt just to save an argument. Emmaline thought back to when she'd asked Paloma Day to tell her fortune. She'd taken a week to think about what the woman had said and decided to take her advice. If she wanted things to happen in her life, she was going to have to take the initiative, so the next time Henry had visited she'd boldly asked him if he had any feelings for her. When he said he did, that day he'd asked her uncle for permission to call upon her. Now it seemed as if she was going to have to bring up the subject of marriage with him also.

Jedidiah's Wedding

Jedidiah had just returned home after performing the death ritual of a young boy who'd drowned. Those were the worst for him. Though he sympathized with all the families who had lost loved ones, it bothered him most when he had to perform the ritual for a child.

He'd created special prayers to say for children and tears would well in his eyes every time. He always wanted to comfort the parents by speaking of a loving God, and how the deceased child would be swaddled in His arms; whereas Reverend Donner rarely said anything that might comfort the grieving parents for their loss in his sermonizing. Even with the death of a child, he preached hell, fire, and brimstone to the living!

Jedidiah sat down in the chair by the fireplace and started reading the newspaper he'd picked up lying on the ground behind the general store. He read where Henry Welch and Emmaline Candlewick were to be wed next month. He crumpled up the paper and threw it into the fireplace.

"So what did the paper do to you?" Paloma asked as she prepared supper.

"It just reminded me that I'm getting married tomorrow!"

"Was there another article in the paper about you?"

"No!" He stood and walked over to the counter and leaned against it. "Henry Welch is going to be married to a woman he loves. I'm going to be married tomorrow to someone I don't even know!"

"Arranged marriages happen all the time."

"Yeah, but usually it has to do with wealth and status. I have neither! It's either marry or be shot!"

"Speaking of being shot," Paloma said. "Tell Jubal to wash up. Supper is ready."

He went to the window and shouted out towards the woods. Jubal had been his shadow for the past week. Ennis Hagen had told Jedidiah that if he'd left town, he'd be hunted down and brought back. Also, if he slipped through their fingers, there were kinfolk that stretched from the Louisiana Bayou to the hills of Kentucky and West Virginia they'd get word to. To ensure he wouldn't leave, the man left his son to watch him.

Jedidiah went to bed that night with a lot on his mind. He had recently started to think more about women. Before he was forced into the army, the only woman he thought about was his mother. When he was in the army, the only thing he thought of was being able to shoot straight and hit what he aimed at. The three years he'd spent in the Yankee prison camp, he safeguarded himself from becoming a surrogate woman for a few perverted men. Now he was going to be married and hadn't had the first kiss from a woman. His soon to be bride wasn't the only virgin in this union – so was he!

***

Ennis Hagen approached Reverend Donner and politely asked about a church wedding for his niece, Abigail. However, being that Jedidiah was a Sin-Eater, the preacher refused. The good reverend also refused to go to their home and perform the ceremony.

The people of Shadrack had their own preacher for Sunday go-to-meetin', but he wasn't legally ordained for hitchin' ceremonies yet. The older preacher had been snake bitten and died a few weeks earlier. But Ennis Hagen was determined. He let the refusal slide for the time being and then the morning of the wedding, he and a few other kinsmen, kidnapped the man from his breakfast table at gunpoint. It was either perform the ceremony or get shot. Reverend Donner reasoned that even a Sin-Eater deserved some trifle of happiness, and if this wretched family wanted their niece wed to him, who was he to say no?

***

Paloma did her best to ease Jedidiah's nervousness. She tried to make light of it and told him that all grooms are nervous before the wedding. She even reminded him that lately, he'd often talked about finding someone to start a family of his own with. But it didn't help. Finding someone on his own was one thing, a shotgun wedding was another - especially when he didn't do anything wrong. The girl may have been entertaining to talk to, for it was rare that anyone talked to him beyond what concerned his profession, but this girl, Abigail, looked a mess with her wild hair, potato sack dress and dirty face!

When they arrived at the Hagen's shack, they saw tables set up in the yard made up of a few planks of wood on top of sawhorses. Several women were setting out food for the celebration afterward. The ragged looking children he'd seen last week had on their Sunday best, which was only slightly better than what he'd seen them in before. The entryway of the porch was decorated with wildflowers. They also saw four men sitting on the porch tuning musical instruments; two had banjoes, one had a fiddle, and the other was blowing on a jug that had three X's drawn on it.

Paloma leaned over to Jedidiah and whispered, "At least it looks like they're going to attempt to make it a pleasant experience for the both of you."

Jedidiah was about to respond, when he saw Reverend Donner exit the house and approach them. He looked angry.

"You'll have your portion in the lake of fire, Jedidiah! You should know better than to dally with the affections of a young girl like her, especially being what you are!" he whispered harshly.

"I dallied with no one's affections, Reverend," Jedidiah gritted out. "I was just walking her home so she wouldn't get lost in the swamp. *She* is the one who followed me!"

"With these hill-type people, you may as well have bedded her!"

A few minutes later, Ennis came out of the house and approached Paloma. He wanted her to see Abigail's dowry. For even though this was a forced marriage, they still followed the same traditions.

Jedidiah pulled her aside for a moment and whispered, "If you say it's not acceptable, perhaps I can get out of this?"

Paloma whispered back, "If I say it's not, they may shoot you anyway!"

She followed Ennis into the house. He showed her a beautiful chest made of cypress wood. It contained a quilt and a pocket watch that belonged to the girl's grandfather which didn't work. The man also said Abigail had two dollar and seventy-five cents belonging to the dowry. Paloma decided to at least bargain for a few more things to add to it. Not that they really had anything that she wanted or needed, she just didn't want them to get by with this forced arrangement without them having to suffer losing something they might favor.

"Not much of a dowry," Paloma said.

"Well, that's all her ma left for her," Ennis replied.

Paloma shook a finger at him. "Shame on you for not adding to it!"

"Why should I? She ain't my youn'in." Ennis folded his arms and grinned. "I could just shoot the boy. I'd be in my rights."

Paloma nodded her head and smiled. "True, but then you'd be stuck with Abigail." She saw the smile leave his face. She knew she'd struck a nerve. "And if I'm not mistaken, you tried to marry her off before, but her poor dowry was the reason someone turned her down at that time."

"So? Your point bein'?"

"My point is – I know you have two daughters about marrying age, and if you don't add to Abigail's dowry, I'll let it be known to all of your guests how poor it was. If you send your niece out with such a poor dowry, anyone interested in your daughters will probably think you have the same pitiful dowry for them. Then you'll be stuck with two spinsters on your hands."

Ennis frowned and scratched his bearded chin. She had a point. He loved all his daughters, but two of them looked like they'd been hit with an ugly stick. "We don't have much. What do you want?"

Paloma looked around the kitchen and living area. She spotted a nice cast-iron skillet, a new wet-stone and a skinning knife. "I'll take those – and two dozen eggs."

Josie came out of the bedroom just in time to hear what Paloma had wanted as part of Abigail's dowry. She quickly went into the kitchen and pulled her husband aside. "Ennis! That's my good chicken fryin' skillet!" she whispered. "Ya' ain't givin' that away!"

"Listen, woman," he whispered harshly. "I done figer'd out a way ta' be shed of Abigail. So what'll it be? The skillet or Abigail? Besides, I'm givin' up my new wet stone. I just bought it last week!"

Josie didn't care much for her half-sister when she was alive, and the only reason she took in her daughter was that she felt it was her Christian duty. Besides, if the people in their community found out that she'd turned out her own kin, she'd be looked down upon. She took the skillet from its place on the stove and handed it to Paloma with a smile pasted on her face. "T'ain't much, but it's the least we can do for Abigail."

"You're too kind, Mrs. Hagen," Paloma replied.

***

About an hour later, the ceremony was ready to begin. Reverend Donner stood impatiently on the porch with his book in hand, wanting this event to be over with so he could go home. He glared at Jedidiah, who stood nervously before him, silently cursing their town's Sin-Eater for being so reckless.

Jedidiah could feel the good reverend's animosity toward him and hoped that some divine intervention would come about to get him out of this situation. He looked into the crowd of guests and saw Jubal, along with a few other relatives leaning on their shotguns. There were about twenty of Abigail's relatives and friends of the family who had arrived to witness the ceremony. That didn't including the countless number of children running about. He figured most of them came for the food or just to witness the outrageous fact that someone was actually going to marry their Sin-Eater.

When the fiddler started playing the wedding march, Abigail was escorted from the house by her Uncle Ennis. Jedidiah was surprised. He wondered if it was the same girl. She didn't look like the wild wood nymph from last week. He thought she actually looked pretty. *Maybe this isn't such a bad idea after all,* he thought.

Abigail wore a neat but old, blue dress that she borrowed from one of her cousins. That took care of fulfilling the tradition of having something old, borrowed and blue. As for new, her aunt bought her a new pair of shoes for the occasion. They weren't actually new, she'd bought them from a second hand store in town, but they were new to her. Her hair was neatly combed with a circle of tiny white flowers crowning her head, and she carried a bouquet of wild flowers.

Abigail looked up at Jedidiah and saw a slight smile on his face. She shyly looked down at the bouquet of flowers in her hand and thought, *Well, he may be a sin-eater, least ways he's handsome and young. Not like ol' Shad McCoy, Uncle Ennis tried ta' marry me off to!* She looked back up at Jedidiah and returned his smile.

Reverend Donner went through the ceremony as quickly as he could, skipping his usual flowery sermon about the sanctity of marriage. He just said what was legally necessary.

When Jedidiah heard, "You may kiss the bride," he gave Abigail a quick, simple kiss on the lips, which she returned. The men with their instruments started playing, and a few of the braver guests reluctantly approached the Sin-Eater and his new wife to give their congratulations. Reverend Donner ordered Ennis to immediately take him back home, which he had Jubal do right away - they couldn't bring out the corn-squeezin's with the preacher there.

During the reception, Jedidiah spent most of the time sitting alone on a log away from the guests, while Abigail mingled with family and friends. He saw the expression on a few of their faces. It looked as if they were giving her their condolences instead of their blessings.

Jedidiah looked in another direction and saw that a few people had cornered Paloma so she could tell them their fortunes. He noticed that these hill people weren't as leery of her as the town's people. The last man she'd talked to quickly ran to his wagon, jumped in and drove off. After that, she joined him.

"What was wrong with him?" Jedidiah asked.

"I told him that the sheriff was closing in on him, and he was going to jail for making and selling whisky around here." Paloma grinned. "He went to move his still."

"You actually saw that," Jedidiah stated skeptically.

"No…" She started laughing. "…I read in the newspaper you brought home the other day that Sheriff Wright was closing in on someone. Earlier, I saw him passing out jugs from his wagon that men were giving him money for. I just put two and two together."

"So much for fortune telling!" He laughed with her and then he sighed. "I'm ready to go home."

"Then go to your wife and tell her," Paloma said with a shrug.

He looked in Abigail's direction. "I thought I'd just wait until she's ready to go."

Paloma saw a look of nervousness in his eyes. She chuckled slightly. "Why Jedidiah! You're a virgin!"

The young man opened his mouth to deny it, but who was he kidding? She'd know he was lying. "So – what if I am!"

"There's nothing wrong with that," she reassured him. "Only men are critical of other men who are virgins. I think Abigail will appreciate the fact that you are." Then she stood. "I think I'm ready to go also."

Jedidiah watched as she walked up to Abigail and whispered in her ear. A fleeting thought entered his mind. *I hope she isn't telling her what I am!* A moment later, both joined him and he stood.

"Paloma says she's tuckered out and wants ta' go. I'm guessin' I'm ready ta' go too," sighed Abigail.

Jedidiah breathed a sigh of relief. He really didn't think Paloma would tell her of his innocence, but he couldn't help where his thoughts went.

Abigail bid her aunt and uncle good-bye. Ennis told them he would bring her dowry chest, along with her other things, to the bell tomorrow at noon. The three of them got into the Hagen's rickety wagon, and Jubal took them to town and dropped them by the entrance to their part of the swamp.

Jedidiah and Abigail started toward the path that led home, but noticed Paloma wasn't following them.

"Aren't you coming?" Jedidiah asked.

"I've business in town," she replied with a smile. "I'll see you tomorrow." She turned and headed toward the hotel. This was Jedidiah's and Abigail's wedding night. They didn't need an old woman around to add to their nervousness.

She walked into the hotel to register for a night's lodging. Maurice Shaw, owner of the hotel, was just about to tell her that they were full, until a man and woman came in behind her. If they'd heard him tell her that, they might walk out. He had no choice but to let her have a room.

Paloma took her key and turned toward the stairs. She accidently brushed against the middle-aged woman behind her. "Please excuse me."

"No harm done," the woman replied kindly.

But just from that slight touch Paloma immediately sensed a future even in the woman's life and asked, "When are you due?"

The woman and man gave her a puzzled look. "Due for what?" she asked.

Paloma laughed slightly. "Why, your baby, of course."

"I'm not pregnant," the woman replied. She placed her hand on her stomach. "It must be this dress. I told my husband I thought it made me look fat." The woman sighed. "Though, it would be nice if I were."

"I'm afraid you must be mistaken," the husband added. "We've been trying for the past ten years." He took his wife's hand. "We've given up hope."

"Maybe, but life is full of surprises, and surprises often come when we least expect them." She took a couple of steps toward the stairs and turned back to the couple. "Just a piece of advice. Keep a wastebasket by the bed tonight. You might have need of it." She went upstairs.

The couple turned toward the hotel manager. "Who was that strange woman?" the man asked.

"Her name is Paloma Day," Maurice replied. "She's the local..." he was about to say witch, but caught himself and said, "...fortune teller. She's descended from Gypsies."

"Really?" The woman put her hand to her stomach. "Can she really tell the future?"

Maurice gave them their key. "Well, let me put it this way. If you have need of the wastebasket tonight, I'd say you'll have your answer."

The Swamp

Jedidiah and Abigail walked in silence as they made their way through the woods, until they spotted a rabbit nibbling on a plant unaware of their presence. "There's dinner!" both whispered simultaneously. They looked at each other and smiled.

Jedidiah pulled the knife he always carried with him. He never knew what he would run into in the swamp. He was posed to throw it, when Abigail stopped him and pointed in another direction. There were three baby rabbits close by.

"We can't take their mama," Abigail said. "It wouldn't be fittin'."

Jedidiah agreed with her. That broke their silence as they talked about hunting, trapping and what their favorite foods were. Jedidiah said his favorite thing used to be chicken until he tasted Paloma's snake stew. Abigail told him he hadn't eaten anything good until he'd tasted her gator jambalaya.

When they reached home, Jedidiah opened the door for her to walk through first, but she didn't go in. "What's wrong?"

"I can't walk in there on my own!" she exclaimed.

"Why?" he asked curiously. "You walked in before?"

Abigail rolled her eyes. "Don't ya' know yer post'a carry a new bride over the threshold?"

"I've heard of it, but I don't know why."

He swept her up in his arms, and she put her arms around his neck. "It's 'cause of evil spirits. If'n I walk in on my own and fall, it'll be bad luck for our family."

Jedidiah laughed as he carried her in. He still held her in his arms after they entered. "Can I put you down now?"

"You can until it's time for the weddin' night," she said somewhat shyly. "Then yer' post'a carry me through that threshold too." She nodded to his bedroom.

"More evil spirits?"

"No – a new bride is 'post'a be shy on her weddin' night." She coyly looked away.

Jedidiah's nervousness disappeared as he carried her through the bedroom door. He gently lowered her to her feet and pressed his lips to hers for a first, real kiss.

When their lips parted, Abigail looked into his eyes. "I didn't lie, I am a virgin. My Aunt Josie told me it ain't much fun the first time. She says it'll take some practicin' before the fun starts."

Jedidiah laughed lightly. She was delightfully funny in her innocence. "We have all night to practice. Do you think we could start now?"

She put her arms around his neck and grinned mischievously. "Well, the way I sees it, if we gits the part that ain't fun done with, then we can start the fun part!"

Jedidiah now thought marrying her might be a good thing. She was talkative and outspoken, they had similar things in common and she didn't mind living in a swamp. The other good thing, he didn't have to leave Paloma by herself in his search of feminine companionship. He had developed an affection for the old Gypsy woman, similar to that of a son for his mother. He now had the start of a life!

The Hotel

Maurice Shaw had just taken over for the man who had watched the front desk at night. The couple he had checked in yesterday approached him.

"I hope you had a pleasant stay with us," Maurice said politely.

"Actually, I didn't," the woman replied happily. "I was ill last night. It came over me suddenly."

"Is that Gypsy woman still here?" the man asked.

He looked on the hook for the key to her room. "No, it looks like she's already checked out. Why do you ask?"

"I have an establishment in Baton Rouge. She'd be a wonderful attraction at our hotel. Do you know where she lives?"

"I'm afraid not," he replied. "She lives in the swamp. No one knows where."

"Too bad," the man sighed. He pulled a card from his pocket. "The next time you see her, have her contact me. It could be profitable for both of us."

Maurice watched them leave and looked at the card. He'd never thought of their local witch as being an attraction. It gave him a wonderful idea. He immediately went to the general store, the only place their Sin-Eater frequented, to leave word for Jedidiah that he wanted Paloma to contact him about an employment opportunity to benefit both of them.

Chapter 9

A year had passed. Paloma delighted in her new family. Jedidiah and Abigail were like the son and daughter she'd always wanted. They filled the space that had been empty for so long. She only wished her beloved Benjamin was still alive to complete her family circle. But she didn't dwell upon his death. She knew he was in a better place and one day she'd join him.

As for Jedidiah and Abigail, their mutual regard for each other blossomed into love. There were many things they had in common as far as their likes and dislikes. Hunting was one of their favorite things to do together. Jedidiah wasn't the least bit jealous that she was a better tracker than he. In fact, he was delighted. It provided them with more meat in the stewpot.

Another thing they talked about was starting a family. They both wanted children, but it was the number in question. Abigail asked Jedidiah if he would mind keeping the number down to ten. Her uncle told her it was a woman's place to give a man as many sons as she could bear. She said her Aunt Josie had a baker's dozen, seven boys and six girls, and at the end of the day, she was "plum tuckered out." Jedidiah told her he wanted to be a little more conservative than that, and one would do to start with. Abigail was relieved. She told him that with so many "young'ins" to care for, it might take all the fun out of being in bed with him. Jedidiah said he didn't want to decrease her fun.

The Hotel

Paloma walked into the Black Water Hotel. She had now been telling fortunes there for the past three months. Maurice had left message after message for her to contact him. She'd finally decided to do it after she'd dreamt about it. Whether it was premonition or a desire to earn a little extra money for her newly acquired family, she didn't know; however, since

Jedidiah and Abigail were starting to talk about children more frequently, she decided to the take hotel manager up on his offer.

The price for a reading was fifty cents which Paloma and Maurice split. The first time he placed an advertisement in the newspaper, she'd only received two or three locals, but those who'd stayed at the hotel from out of town lined up for the novelty of having their fortunes told by Madam Paloma – Gypsy Queen – as Maurice had billed her.

Paloma went into one of the back rooms to change into her fortune teller's costume. It consisted of a black skirt, red blouse, gold-colored scarf for her head and a few bangles and beads to wear around her neck and wrists. She thought she looked ridiculous, but Maurice insisted, saying that it made her look authentic – as if he knew what authentic was. She then took her place at the table in the corner of the lobby. She enjoyed meeting the different people she told fortunes to. It was refreshing to talk to someone who didn't refer to her as a witch. The other thing she enjoyed was the extra income. The past three sessions had profited her a total of seventeen dollars and twenty-five cents, after Maurice took his cut.

For the most part, her predictions were about the gender of babies, finding love or lost articles. Some of the old local farmers, who knew her in her younger days, asked her about the weather conditions for planting crops. However, on one occasion, a man sat before her and extended his palm. He appeared to be a gentleman of quality, for he was impeccably dressed in a businessman's attire and spoke intelligently to a few men standing in line about business ventures. But as soon as Paloma touched his hand, she sensed he wasn't the gentleman he appeared to be. She'd closed her eyes. Images of him stealing a few pieces of jewelry from Browker's Jewelry Store entered her mind. Other flashes of him picking pockets also came into her visions. She'd smiled at him and told him he was going on a trip to an unexpected place. After the man left, Paloma immediately told Maurice what she'd suspected, and he promptly informed Sheriff Wright. The man was detained from leaving town and the jewelry plus a few wallets were found among his possession. He went to trial, was found guilty and sent to prison.

A few minutes after Paloma sat down at her table, Maurice approached her with a box. "I have something for you, Paloma."

"What's in it?"

He laughed. "I thought you might already know."

Paloma shook her head and smiled. "I tell other people's fortunes.

Not mine." She opened it and found a glass ball mounted on a black, wooden base. She broke out in laughter. "Really, Maurice, a crystal ball?"

"I thought you Gypsies used them?"

"Perhaps the ancient Druids, Viking seers, or Merlin, the sorcerer, might have used them, but not me."

"You mean I spent three dollars for nothing!" He was agitated. "I ordered it all the way from New York!"

Paloma shrugged. "I wouldn't say for nothing. Just consider it decoration." She jingled the jewelry around her wrists. "Just like you've decorated me, it will add to the atmosphere of the readings." She watched him walk away, muttering to himself about wasting almost a third of his profits.

***

Emmaline Candlewick Welch entered the lobby of the hotel with one of her friends to have lunch in the restaurant. She glanced around the room and saw a short line of people waiting to have their fortune's read by the town's witch. "Look over there, Charlotte."

Her friend shook her head. "I can't believe Mr. Shaw is allowing her to do this!"

"If it involves money, Mr. Shaw would bargain with the devil himself!" Emmaline and Charlotte both giggled.

As the two headed for the restaurant, Emmaline put a hand to her abdomen and stopped. She turned to her friend. "What do you say we be a little adventurous and have our fortunes told?"

Charlotte looked toward Paloma and shook her head. "I don't know. I'm not that adventurous. When I was a little girl, I think I saw her flying on her broomstick one Halloween night."

Emmaline rolled her eyes and shook her head. "My Aunt Sally used to tell me stories like that all the time. I don't believe a word of it! I've talked with Mrs. Day before, and she seems to be a very pleasant person. She gave me some very good advice once on how to get my Henry." She grabbed her reluctant friend's hand. "Come on! Afterward, I'll buy lunch."

The two girls only had to wait a few minutes until it was their turn. "Good afternoon, Mrs. Day." Emmaline curtsied.

Paloma smiled and nodded her head. "I read about your marriage in the newspaper last year."

"I have you to thank for it. Your advice was very helpful." She got down to the business at hand and pulled a dollar from her purse. "My friend and I would like our fortunes told, if you please."

Paloma smiled. "Who's first?"

Emmaline urged Charlotte to have hers told first. Paloma saw a look of fear in the girl's eyes. "Don't be afraid, girl. I rarely bite." She extended her hands. "Put your hands in mine."

The reluctant girl summoned up her courage and did as asked. "I would like to know…"

"Shhh …" Paloma interrupted as she closed her eyes. A moment later, opened them and looked at the girl's palm. She smiled. "I see something very good. You'll like it."

"Really?" Charlotte's fear was replaced by curiosity. "What is it?"

"I can't tell you," Paloma replied. "It will spoil the surprise and could change the outcome if I told you."

"If you can't tell me, then how am I to know if you really knew my fortune?" Charlotte asked.

Paloma took a piece of paper, wrote down her prediction and handed it to Emmaline. "You may see, but don't tell until it comes to pass."

Emmaline looked at the paper and drew a deep breath. She put a hand to her chest. "Charlotte! I'm so envious!"

"Oh, please, can't you tell me!!!!!" Charlotte begged.

Emmaline turned to Paloma. She was excited for her friend. "When will she find out?"

"I'd say in the next day or so. It's not clear. But the time is drawing near," Paloma replied.

"It's not fair!" Charlotte pouted. She was dying to know, but neither did she want to jinx whatever it was either.

"Me next!" Emmaline urged Charlotte from the chair. She sat down and extended her hands.

Paloma took them and closed her eyes. She heard crying. "You're pregnant."

"That's right. I'm only a little over a month," Emmaline confirmed. She closed her eyes also and hoped her most fervent hope. "Boy or girl?"

Two images formed in Paloma's mind, but it confused her. The first image she saw was Emmaline standing on a porch calling a girl's name. "Evelyn," she said aloud. But it was the second image that seemed out of place. She saw Jedidiah pushing a little girl on a swing in their swamp. She was about to say the name he called the child when her thoughts were interrupted.

"So it is a girl!" Emmaline was ecstatic. "That's the name Henry and I decided on last night for a girl – Evelyn. It's what we both wanted." She hesitated before getting up as a past memory of something came to her mind. "Do you see only one child?"

Paloma closed her eyes again and the same vision came to her. She opened her eyes. "It's unclear," she replied. "But the name of Evelyn is very predominant in your future."

Both girls curtseyed and bid her good-day. Emmaline looked at the paper again. It read: *Going to Mardi Gras.* If it came true and Charlotte went to New Orleans for Mardi Gras, it was fairly certain she would have the girl she was longing for. She also had a slight worry in the back of her mind about having twins. Though she would love to have them, the possibility of the second child surviving was slim in her family. Her own twin brother died at birth, and her father's twin died a few days after.

When the girls were out of sight, Paloma's smile disappeared. The name of the girl Jedidiah called out was Hattie. But she couldn't understand why she'd see Jedidiah's child in Emmaline's future?

***

After telling Emmaline's fortune, the same vision kept replaying over and over in Paloma's dreams. Jedidiah would be pushing the shadowy form of a little girl on a swing. He called her Hattie. She would also see Emmaline with a girl she called Evelyn. The old Gypsy woman tried to reason what it meant, but it was beyond her.

There was also the other dream which was most unnerving. The sound of a baby's cry echoed in her unconscious mind. Sometimes it startled her awake, but the only sounds that came to her ears were the usual noises of the night coming from the swamp.

As the months passed, Paloma's dreams of the crying child worsened. The baby's simple cry gradually escalated into screams, the screams would then go silent and she'd feel as if she was suffocating. Sweat would be dripping from her forehead when she woke. She'd tried every sleeping remedy she knew to cause her a deeper sleep so she could go beyond the dreams and those heart-wrenching scream, but nothing helped.

One evening, Paloma was sitting on the front porch enjoying the night air, dreading sleep. Jedidiah and Abigail joined her.

"Paloma, are you alright? You haven't been yourself lately," said

Jedidiah.

"Just tired," she replied. She didn't want to burden them with her unfathomable nightmares.

"Well, we got somethin' ta' tell ya' that'll perk ya' right up!" Abigail said as she took Jedidiah's hand. "What'da' ya' think about bein' called Granny?"

Paloma smiled. "I'd like that very much." She stood and gave them both a hug.

"I'm surprised you didn't tell us?" Jedidiah laughed. "You generally know things before we do."

"Maybe I just wanted you to have the pleasure of telling me." But in truth, she hadn't known. Normally she could tell right away when a woman was pregnant, whether she showed or not, just by a simple touch of the hand. But even with hugging Abigail, she couldn't sense anything about her condition. She thought perhaps it might have been due to her lack of sleep.

"Does ya' think ya' kin tell us if it'll be a boy or girl?" Abigail asked.

Paloma sat back down in her chair. Abigail knelt in front of her with Jedidiah at her side. The old woman extended her hands. "Put your hands in mine and we'll see." She closed her eyes and concentrated as she usually did, but she saw nothing. After a few more moments, she opened her eyes and sighed. "I'm sorry, girl. I guess I'm just too tired." She stood. "I think I'll just go to bed."

Jedidiah and Abigail watch Paloma go into the house. "I'm worried about her," said Jedidiah. He stood and leaned against the porch post. "I hope she's not getting sick."

"She's been actin' a might strange," Abigail replied. "I snuck up on her yesterday. That's the first time she didn't know I was behind her. Ya' don't suppose she's losin' her witchin' ways do ya'?"

He laughed and shook his head. "How many times do I have to tell you, she's not a witch. There's no such thing."

Abigail folded her arms and looked at him from the corner of her eye. "All right, Mr. Smarty Britches, tell me how she knows what she knows?"

Jedidiah hesitated for a moment and scratched his head. He'd been trying for years to figure that one out himself, but he had to tell his wife something. An idea struck him and he grinned at her. "Heaven sent intuition!"

Abigail giggled and put her arms around him. "Think that if'n ya' want. I'd rather be thinkin' of her as a witch."

He chuckled and brushed a strand of hair from her face. "Why?"

"It's more fun, silly! Like ever' now and agin, tellin' ghost stories 'round a fire under a full moon and gittin' all goose pimply." She shivered slightly in his arms. "Only we have our very own witch – a good witch. It'll be somethin' our youn'ins can tell their youn'ins."

Jedidiah laughed. "I guess I can go along with that." He kissed her and then added in a lustful tone, "Speaking of fun, what do you say we retire ourselves?"

"Why, Jedidiah!" she exclaimed raising her eyebrows. "Ya' must be part witch too?"

He cocked his head and looked at her curiously. "And why do you say that?"

"'Cause ya' must've been a readin' my mine." She took his hand, led him into the house and to their bedroom.

***

A month had past and Jedidiah made his usual trip into town to pick up his monthly allotment of supplies. He sat in the back room of the general store early one morning waiting for Mr. McGuire to finish with his other customers. They always came before he did. He'd asked Abigail if she wanted to accompany him, but she told him she was feeling poorly and decided to stay home.

The store was unusually busy for this time of morning. He enjoyed listening to some of the customers talk about what was going on in their lives while they shopped around the store. When he'd first become the Sin-Eater, he tried joining in on a conversation once, but the people quickly departed and Mr. McGuire forbade him from mingling with his paying customers - it was bad for his business.

That was another thing about this town Jedidiah hated. Black Water Township may have been a quiet, clean and a fairly rich town, but their obsession with silly superstitions, religious rituals that made no sense to him, non-existent witches and their treating him like the plague is why he desired to leave it. But until Paloma was willing to leave, he had to stay for her sake. He wouldn't leave her alone.

As he peeked through the door of the backroom to see if Mr. McGuire was finished haggling with a man over the price of a few eggs, he saw Sally Gooch and Erma Welch talking by the yard goods. "Look at this adorable pink, polka dot material," he heard Mrs. Welch say. "I think I'll purchase some of this to have a gown made for Emmaline's baby. There's not that many weeks left until the stork arrives."

Sally studied the pink material for a moment. "Are you sure it'll be a girl?"

"Emmaline insists it will be," Erma shrug. "I asked her how she could be so sure, and she told me it was because her friend Charlotte Hamilton went to the Mardi Gras this year. What that has to do with the price of eggs, I haven't a clue."

"I bet you anything that she went to see Paloma Day at the hotel!" Sally said harshly.

"You're probably right," Erma agreed as she looked through other bolts of material. Then she added, "Speaking of babies, I heard a few weeks ago that the Sin-Eater's wife is expecting a child also."

"Really!" Sally shook her head. "Can you imagine what sort of child will be produced from that union? He carries the weight of all those sins and has an illiterate, hillbilly wife to boot."

"Plus! They live with that witch! I shudder to think of it," Erma added.

When Jedidiah heard that, he became angry. Not at the remarks about him, but those toward his wife and unborn child. He was about to go out and give them a piece of his mind, when Mr. McGuire approached the two women.

"Ladies, I can fill your order now."

Jedidiah hesitated going out for a moment, until after Erma Welch ordered the pink polka dotted material and Mr. McGuire had cut it; then he left the back room and approached the three of them.

"Mr. McGuire," Jedidiah said. "While you're cutting that material, I'd like a yard of it too." He glared at Erma. "Mrs. Welch is right. I think it will make a nice gown for a baby, and my child will look beautiful in it." His gaze turned toward Sally. "My hillbilly wife is excellent with a needle and thread when given the opportunity and material to sew with."

"Yard goods aren't included in your lot of supplies," said the older man, "Can you pay for it?"

"Not at the moment," Jedidiah replied. "But be assured I'll be back for it." He really didn't want the material he just wanted to subtly let the two old biddies know that he didn't approve of what they'd said.

The two women realized that their Sin-Eater had been ease-dropping on their conversation. Erma Welch cleared her throat. "Mr. McGuire, I've changed my mind about the material."

"I've already cut it!" the storekeeper said angrily. "All sales are final on cut yard goods."

Sally whispered in Erma's ear, and she turned to the storekeeper. "Mr. McGuire, I've decided to make this material a gift to – him." She nodded toward Jedidiah. "After all, he does provide a valuable service to our town. I'll pay for it. Just put it on my account." The two women quickly departed.

"The nerve of him listening to our conversation!" Sally exclaimed. "That was absolutely rude."

"What can you expect from trash like that," Erma replied. "But you know, Sally, you were absolutely right. Giving him that material would constitute as a charitable act. Surely, the good Lord will smile down upon us."

"My thoughts exactly," Sally replied. "After all, it's better to give than receive. Besides, if he had come back for the same material, what if a child of his was seen in the same gown my grand-niece and your grandchild was wearing?"

"Shudder the thought!" Erma shivered.

***

Jedidiah walked through the woods carrying a sack with his normal allotment of coffee, tea, sugar and flour in one hand, and in the other hand, he carried the polka dotted material. He knew how much Erma Welch liked that piece of material by the tone of her voice when she spoke of it. He also knew that she wouldn't want it, if she thought that he was going to buy some of it. It shocked both him and Mr. McGuire when she just let him have it. The two women were renowned for their charitable actions, but only when it benefited them in some way and was very publicly announced. Jedidiah was hoping for more of an argument between Mrs. Welch and the shopkeeper to sooth his bruised feeling, but with the gift of the material, he considered his family honor avenged.

Jedidiah was anxious to get home and present Abigail with the material. As he exited the woods, he saw Paloma come out of the house to greet him.

"Look what I have for the baby." He showed her the cloth. "If we have a daughter, I think she'll look pretty in it." But when he looked into his friend's eyes, he saw she'd been crying. "What's wrong?"

Paloma wiped a tear from her eye. "It's Abigail. She lost the baby."

Jedidiah dropped the sack and the material to the ground. His heart pounded in his chest. "Is she alright?"

"Physically, yes - but her heart is broken. She's lying down."

Paloma watched Jedidiah as he ran into the house. For weeks she'd tried to sense the gender of their child. She thought it was because her nightmarish dreams made her so tired. Now she knew why she couldn't sense the child. It was because the baby didn't have a future. But even if she'd known this was going to happen, there would have been no way she could have told them. A thought then crossed her mind. If the child in her dreams wasn't this child, who was the little girl Jedidiah was pushing on the swing?

Chapter 10

Welch Residence

It was three o'clock in the morning, and Henry Welch paced outside the bedroom door hoping for word from Dr. Jackson that he was a father. He was fearful for the life of his beloved wife and their unborn child. Emmaline had been in the throes of labor for the past two days. Her screams of pain tore at his heart. He felt helpless. The only thing he could do was pray for both of them.

Sally and Victor Gooch stayed with them after they were informed that it was Emmaline's time. Her Aunt Sally refused to leave until she knew all was well, and Henry was glad to have them there. Sally may not have been able to ease Emmaline's pain, but she and his mother comforted each other. Victor had been his rock while they waited.

For the moment, Henry waited alone for news – any word one way or the other about his wife's progress. Victor had to force his wife to get some rest before she keeled over from exhaustion and worry. They'd retired a few hours ago. Henry's mother went downstairs to have a fresh pot of coffee made.

Many times Henry wanted to go to his wife as her screams reached his ears, but he was told to be patient. Suddenly, the hallway was silent. Emmaline's crying had ceased. Henry's heart pounded in his chest as he waited for another cry - the cry of a newborn. The minutes of waiting in the silent hallway seemed like an eternity. "Please, please, just a little cry," he murmured. "Just a little cry." He listened intently, and a brief, sweet little voice finally reached his ears.

Dr. Jackson opened the door. "Henry," he whispered. "Come in."

He entered and saw his wife lying in the bed, motionless. "My wife – is she…"

"She's fine for the moment," he whispered. "She passed out just as the baby was delivered."

"What about the baby? I don't hear it crying?"

Dr. Jackson picked the child up from the bassinette that was beside the bed. "It's a girl. She had a rough time of it and is just as exhausted as her mother. For a moment, I didn't think she was going to breathe for me. But she's fine and fast asleep."

Henry smiled as he took his new, sleeping daughter in his arms. "Has Emmaline seen her yet?"

"No," he said seriously. "But we have a problem. There's another baby, and your wife is too exhausted to deliver it. The child itself isn't making any progress. I'm going to have to operate and take it."

Henry put the baby in her bassinette and knelt beside his wife. He wiped the sweat from her forehead. "Is it dangerous?"

"I won't lie to you. It's very dangerous. Emmaline could die. If we wait, both could die. She won't be able to handle another arduous delivery like the last." He was silent for a moment. "Wake the family and you might…" he cleared his throat, "…want to send for the Sin-Eater."

The Swamp

Jedidiah woke to the sound of Paloma screaming. He and Abigail jumped out of bed and entered her room. They saw her tossing and turning and clutching her throat as if she couldn't breathe. He sat at her bedside and shook her awake. Paloma sat up. Her eyes were wide and a panicked look was etched on her face. "I'm not dead! I'm not dead!" they heard her shout.

Jedidiah shook her again, for it seemed as if she were still in a dream state. "Paloma! Wake-up!"

A moment later, they heard the Sin-Eater's bell. "Someone's dead or dyin'," said Abigail as she turned her head toward the door. "Maybe that's who she's dreamin' 'bout."

Paloma woke from her dream state at the sound of the bell. "I'm fine," she said as she swung her legs over the side of the bed and quickly got up. She went to the cupboard and pulled out a pouch of herbs. "Build me a fire, Jedidiah!"

He left the house and did as she asked. Abigail was both frightened and excited. She was finally going to see Paloma do some witchery. She'd asked once what the herbs were for, and the old Gypsy woman told her that they were for seeing things more clearly.

When the fire was built, the three of them sat down on the log and watched the flames as they crackled. There was no moon, but the stars dotted the sky with light. Paloma took a pinch of the herbs from her pouch and threw them into the flames.

"What'da ya' see, Paloma?" Abigail asked as she pulled her shawl tightly around her shoulders.

"It's not what I see – it's what I feel and don't see." Paloma closed her eyes. "Everything is dark around me. I've been abandoned." She put her hand to her throat. "Can't breathe."

"We'll never abandon you," Jedidiah said in a comforting tone.

Paloma opened her eyes and looked at Jedidiah. "Even though it feels like I'm the one experiencing these feelings, it's not me. I don't know whether it's happening now or is going to happen sometime in the future."

"Do ya' know who?" Abigail asked in a whispered tone.

Paloma threw another pinch of herbs into the flame. After a moment, she shook her head. "I don't know. All I see is darkness." She closed her eyes. "I'm feeling the terror this person is or will feel."

"Is there anything we can do for you, Paloma?" Jedidiah asked. He was greatly concerned for her. He and Abigail would often hear her moving about during the night.

Paloma decided to tell them part of her dream. She thought that maybe in the telling, she could finally get peace. "For months I've heard the sound of a baby screaming. Tonight was the worst. I felt as if I was being buried alive, but it wasn't me." She was going to tell them the second part of her dream, about Jedidiah pushing a child on a swing, but with their recent loss, she decided to keep that part to herself. Abigail was still trying to come to terms with it, and as of yet, she still hadn't told her kinfolk about the loss.

They heard the bell ring again. Normally, they'd ring the bell once then pick him up the next day around noon. "Someone is anxious," Paloma said. "You'd better go. You're probably ministering to the living."

"I don't want to leave you in this state," Jedidiah said concerned.

Paloma smiled. "I'll be fine." She took Abigail's hand. "I've got Abigail to see to me."

***

It was dawn when Jedidiah arrived at the bell. Someone was waiting for him in a carriage. He recognized the man as being a servant of the Welch household. "Who died?" he asked as he got into the carriage.

"No one yet," the man answered. "But Mr. Welch's wife had a baby tonight, and she's not doing well."

The Welch Residence

The mood of the Welch household was solemn. There should have been cheerful sounds of gladness bursting from the hearts of everyone at the birth of a child. But the joyous birth of one child was overshadowed by the death of the other, and it was uncertain whether or not Emmaline would survive.

Dr. Jackson was just as exhausted as the rest. He hadn't left Emmaline side since her labor started. The second child had taken a solitary breath of life and breathed no more. He tried several times to get the child to cry. He took out his stethoscope and listened for a heartbeat, but heard nothing. He turned his attention to Emmaline. She'd survived the surgery, but she'd lost a lot of blood, and he wasn't sure if she was out of danger. When she was stable, he told the family that he was going to get some sleep, but said he'd return later in the day to check on her.

Henry was beside himself with grief. He looked toward his mother who coddled baby Evelyn, while Sally sat at Emmaline's bedside putting compresses to her niece's forehead. He looked down in the small box where his other daughter, the one who hadn't survived was laid. A tear trickled down his cheek and a lump formed in his throat. He reached down and touched her little fingers. They were still warm from her birth, but they would soon be cold.

Victor put a hand on his shoulder. "I'm sorry, Henry."

"I don't know how I'm going to tell Emmaline." He looked back at his wife. "If she survives this, and learns she had twins and one didn't live, it will devastate her."

Victor was quiet for a moment to gather his thought before he spoke. "Come outside with me."

They left the room. Henry watched Victor as he looked up and down the hallway. It seemed as if he was making sure no one was around. "What is it, Victor?"

"Listen. I know my niece, and you're right. Her grief for the lost child will overshadow the life of the one that lived. When she comes to visit us, all she does is talk about the baby." He looked around again and whispered, "I say we don't tell her. Don't tell anyone! The Sin-Eater is on his way. We'll have him take the body and secretly bury it in your family's crypt."

Henry was incensed. "Victor, you're out of your mind! That's my child you're talking about!"

"Shhh! Keep your voice down. And no - it was your child. Your child is in the Lord's hands. That's just the shell of who she would have been."

Henry turned his back. "I can't believe I'm even listening to this."

Victor sighed. "I know it sounds like I'm a heartless, insensitive bastard, but to the contrary. I'm thinking about the happiness of my niece and your daughter that survived. Sally and I love Emmaline as much as we love our own daughter." He hesitated a moment. "We men are different. We didn't carry the child for nine months. We grieve, but not like a mother. If you want to deal with Emmaline's grief, you're a better man than I am."

Henry was about to reply when Sally came out and joined them. "Is there any change?" Henry asked.

"She's still the same." Sally put a handkerchief to her eye. "Emmaline will be heart sick when she finds out one of her children didn't live."

Victor turned to Henry. "It's your choice, son."

Henry didn't answer, but went back into the room. His mother put Evelyn in his arms, and he walked over to the child in the box. "I would have loved to see the two of you play together." He turned back and looked at his wife, who was just barely with him. Victor was right. His wife's grief would cast a shadow over Evelyn's childhood. He turned to his mother and told her to go outside and talk to Victor, that he had something to explain to her.

A few moments later, Henry put the baby in the bassinet and went in the hallway to discuss the matter with his family. Henry told Victor he would go with what the majority thought. Sally agreed that Emmaline would be devastated and it might affect Evelyn's life, but neither did they want to hide the child away as if they were ashamed of it.

They decided to seek the council of Reverend Donner and sent someone for him. During their conversation, they heard the baby let out a very weak, solitary cry. Sally went in and checked on the child. "Huh? She's fast asleep." Then she had a thought. She went to the box where they'd put the other child. It lay still, but she could have sworn the child's head was in a different position than it was before. "Could it be?" She had to be sure. She went to Emmaline's dresser, picked up a mirror and put it before the infant's mouth and nose – but there were no signs of breath. Sally felt foolish and was glad no one was in the room to see what she'd done.

She figured that maybe when Henry was grieving over her, he must have touched her face which changed its position. She went back to Evelyn and picked up the sleeping child. "You must have been dreaming."

Chapter 11

Jedidiah arrived at the Welch residence and was told to wait in Henry's office until Reverend Donner arrived. He still wasn't told who had died, and he was fairly sure he might be eating the sins of Emmaline Welch.

The room brought back unpleasant memories of being forced into becoming the town's Sin-Eater. He shook off the memory and pulled a book from the shelf to pass the time. "*Hamlet - A Shakespearian Tragedy,*" he read. He let out a sardonic laugh. "Perfect. My whole life has been a tragedy!" As he read through the pages, he came to Polonius's advice to his son Laertes: 'This above all: to thine own self be true....' He closed the book and leaned back in the chair. He wondered if he was being true to himself by staying in Black Water. But then there was Paloma's favorite word she liked to throw at him every so often – destiny. Was it his destiny to keep doing a thing he didn't believe in just to appease the religious superstitions of these people? How was that being true to himself?

His thoughts were interrupted when Henry Welch and Reverend Donner entered the room. There was no apology for keeping him waiting – there never was. As they entered, the reverend got down to the heart of the matter. "Your duty is two-fold," he said stiffly. "Mr. Welch's wife is gravely ill from child birth. I feel it will aid in her recovery to be released from the burden of her sins while she's still living."

"My best wishes for her speedy recovery," Jedidiah said to Henry.

"Your sentiments are appreciated," he replied.

The preacher continued. "The second duty is to Mr. Welch's child. One of a set of twins is waiting to rest in the Lord's hands."

Jedidiah closed his eyes and bent his head. It reminded him of his own loss, only he had no one to share his pain with. He was the Sin-Eater. No one would listen and more than likely they would tell him it was for the best; a child of a Sin-Eater would be a child to be despised. He shook the thought and gave his condolences.

Reverend Donner led him upstairs to where Emmaline lay. There was a small gathering of about ten, including family members and close friends who had come to see how the new mother was fairing.

Jedidiah folded his hand and poured his heart into his prayer. It was very seldom that he actually prayed for a living soul that needed the Lord's intervention. He empathized with the pain she was going to feel *when* she woke from her deep sleep and learned of the child that died. He knew the depth of Abigail's pain at the loss of their child.

After he ate the bread and drank the wine placed on Emmaline's chest, the next duty was to the infant that lay so still in the small box. A tear streamed down his face when he looked upon her. His throat ached from the lump that formed in it. His heart ached for the mother that bore her, and he was again reminded of Abigail's pain. He bowed his head and a pray came forth:

I hear crying, but not the sad weeping coming from this child's father and their friends. The sound I hear is the cry of rejoicing from the Angel's of the Lord for the return of this little one. For when she joined us here for just a brief moment, heaven wept and the Lord decided he wouldn't be separated from this beautiful child. We should be comforted that she sleeps in the arms of the Lord.

Jedidiah wiped his eyes as the people in the room said, "Amen." He'd asked the Reverend earlier how an innocent babe could have sin for this was the first newborn he'd ever said prayers for. The preacher told him that since the child died before baptism, he would be taking away the Original Sin of Adam and Eve.

As he looked at the bread that lay on the infant's chest, he thought his eyes were playing tricks on him. He could have sworn he saw the piece of bread move slightly up, then down. He closed his eyes and looked again, but as he stared at it a little longer, it didn't move. It was another one of those illusions. There had been several other times when he'd looked upon the dead and thought he'd seen the same thing. He chalked it up to a trick of the eyes or wishful thinking.

When Jedidiah was done, it was Reverend Donner's turn to speak. At first, he thought it was going to be the same hell, fire and brimstone sermon he usual gave. But this time it was different.

"Friends," he started out by saying. "A lie is a hurtful thing, and all liars will have their portion in the lake of fire. But now I'm asked by the family of Henry Welch to encourage you to hide a truth." He turned his head toward Emmaline. "Our Sister Emmaline lies there twixt life with her living child, and death, joining the child who has gone to the Lord. The family charges you not to tell our sister of her lost one, for it may prey upon her too heavily and life with her living child will not be as fulfilling for thoughts of the other."

Jedidiah, as the others in the room, was shocked. The friends of Emmaline started mumbling amongst each other. He also wondered how they could keep something like that from her, and Reverend Donner agreeing with it? A moment later, the preacher raised his hand and all was quiet.

"Friends, I ask you to search your hearts. Will the truth be comforting to our sister that she bore a dead child? Or will the lie protect her from the sorrow she would otherwise experience if she wakes from her fateful sleep. If she knows the truth, will she wallow in grief for the lost instead of enjoying and sharing the life of the one who lived? I for one am willing to take the chance that the Lord will reprieve me from the scorching flames of the liar's pit to give Sister Emmaline a happy life with her living daughter, Evelyn. The family of our Sister Emmaline will abide by your decision, for it is a silence everyone will be bound to keep."

All were silent for a moment and then one by one, each person in the room, from Emmaline's friends and family to the servants of the household, swore an oath they'd be silent upon the subject. Jedidiah also said he would be silent, but in his heart he knew it was wrong. He had faith that Emmaline Welch would recover and believed she also should have had a chance to grieve over the lost one, instead of the child's existence being unacknowledged.

When all was said and done, the small box was closed and gingerly carried downstairs to a waiting carriage to be taken to the family mausoleum. Henry Welch went along with Victor's suggestion, except for having the Sin-Eater spirit her away. He wanted to say good-bye to her for both himself and Emmaline. There was no funeral procession. Only the family and a few servants went to the cemetery so as not to draw attention from the other residents of Black Water. The fewer people who knew about it, the easier the secret would be to keep. The servant who had picked Jedidiah up earlier dropped him off by the sin-eater's bell and he started walking home.

The Swamp

Paloma sat in her rocking chair on the porch, watching Abigail pick beans from their garden. She closed her eyes and thought about the lost child. She knew Abigail was doing her best to hide her grief from Jedidiah, but the girl was still hurting.

It didn't take long for sleep to overcome Paloma. Her nights for months had been anything but restful. A dream came upon her. It was the same dream about Jedidiah pushing the little girl on the swing - only this time it was different. The fuzziness was gone. She saw the back of the child's head this time. Her hair was long and dark. She could hear her laugher as Jedidiah pushed her.

"Higher, Daddy!" she heard the child say.

Jedidiah had responded by asking, "Who's Daddy's best girl?"

It was then Paloma saw the little girl's face for the first time when she tilted her head back to look at Jedidiah as she went high in the air. But it wasn't the face of a little girl she saw; it was the face of Emmaline Welch! Paloma's pleasant dream melted away into the same horrible feelings she'd been having for months. She was being buried alive - she couldn't breathe - she screamed!

Abigail turned with a fright at the sound. Paloma was clutching her throat and crying, but it wasn't the sound of an adult's scream – the gasping sound she made almost sounded like a baby's cry of terror. The young girl fought back her impulse to run away from this strange sort of witchcraft Paloma was making in her sleep. She ran to the porch to wake her from her day-mare.

Paloma's eyes sprang open. She now knew what her dream was about. All the bits and pieces from the two times she looked into Emmaline's palm fell in place. She gasped for breath as she clutched Abigail's arms. "We've got to go! She's not dead!"

"Who ain't dead!" Abigail exclaimed as she trembled with fright in the old woman's grasp. "Where we goin'?"

Paloma got up from her chair and left the porch. "To the cemetery – to save Hattie!"

***

Jedidiah took his time walking home. He saw a plump rabbit sitting on a log unaware of his presence. It was an easy target and would have made an excellent addition to the stew pot, but he wasn't in the mood for hunting. He couldn't get his mind off the day's event.

His thoughts were shaken by the sound of something making its way through the woods. He pulled his knife and hid behind a clump of brush just in case it was some sort of wild animal coming toward him. He relaxed, but was surprised to see Paloma and Abigail. He stood and went to greet them.

"Where are you two going in such a hurry?" he asked.

Paloma stopped and panted heavily. She wasn't used to moving so quickly these day, but she felt time was running out. She grabbed her young friend's hand. "Was a child buried today?"

"Yes," he replied sadly as he lowered his head. "It was the child of Henry and Emmaline Welch. Twins were born. One lived - the other died."

"The child isn't dead!" Paloma exclaimed frantically.

"That's not funny, Paloma," Jedidiah said harshly. "I saw the child. It didn't move. It wasn't breathing."

"I'm telling you, she's not dead!" Paloma insisted.

Jedidiah was about to shake his head no, but wondered how the old woman knew it was a girl child? He also remembered what he thought was an illusion when he saw the bread on the baby's chest move up and down slightly. Could it be true? If it was, how is it that the doctor didn't know and pronounced the child dead?

He was about to ask, when Paloma interrupted his next words. "We've got to hurry! There's no time!"

As they made their way through the swamp toward the cemetery, Paloma finally told both of them about the other dreams she'd been having about Jedidiah and the little girl on the swing.

The Cemetery

Henry stood before door of the mausoleum where his daughter lay. His mother, Victor and Sally waited for him at the carriage. He wiped a tear from his eye. "May the Lord forgive me for not telling your mother about you."

As he started to walk away, he heard a noise coming from high up in a tree. He shielded his eyes from the sun. He saw an owl. It hooted once then took flight. Henry cringed slightly. It wasn't a good sign. It was bad luck to see an owl in the sunlight. Henry joined his family in the carriage, and they headed for home.

When they arrived, they found Dr. Jackson by Emmaline's bedside. "Any change?" Henry asked.

Dr. Jackson smiled slightly. "She stirred only a moment ago. She's not completely out of danger, but I think she has a chance."

Henry breathed a sigh of relief. He pulled the doctor aside and spoke in low tones. "How are we to explain the surgery? I didn't think about it before, but wouldn't she remember that she had a regular birth?"

"Not necessarily," Dr. Jackson said as he cleaned his spectacles. "She had two hard days of labor. She was practically in a state of delirium from pain and lack of rest just before Evelyn was born. I don't believe she'll doubt that I had to take Evelyn surgically."

They heard Emmaline call out from her bed. "Henry…"

He quickly went to her bedside and knelt down. "I'm here," he said lovingly. "Don't talk, you just rest."

"The baby…" she said wincing in pain. "…I had a bad dream …"

"We have a beautiful little girl," he interrupted. He went to the bassinette, picked up the sleeping child and put her in her mother's arms. "Our daughter has been waiting for you to wake."

Emmaline smiled and kissed her baby. "My beautiful Evelyn." She looked up at Henry. "Just one?"

Henry wondered if she knew. He choked back the truth. "Just one."

Emmaline sighed and smiled lovingly at her daughter. Part of her was disappointed that she didn't have twins - then again, another part of her was relieved.

After a few moments of enjoying her daughter, Emmaline asked the doctor why she still hurt so. When he finished explaining, it was just as he'd told Henry - she believed him. The doctor had Henry take the baby and gave Emmaline something for her pain and to make her sleep.

***

Paloma held on to the cemetery gate as she took a few breaths. "Jedidiah…" she panted. "Look for the Welch Family mausoleum – hurry!"

Luckily the gate was unlocked. Abigail stayed with Paloma as Jedidiah went from burial house to burial house. They didn't have to worry much about anyone interrupting them - the fear of evil spirits lurking about the graveyard kept everyone away. When residents passed the cemetery, they'd hold their breath and turned their head so as not to accidently breath in an unwanted spirit if any were about. The only time people came to the cemetery was when someone died or on Sundays to pay respects. They believed evil spirits were kept at bay on the Lord's Day. Abigail too was somewhat leery about being there, but decided that with the rabbit's foot in her pocket and a good witch at her side, she was fairly safe.

"I think I found it!" Jedidiah called.

It was a large stone building with the name Welch carved into the stone and a statue of a warrior angel on top, as if it were guarding the place. The two women joined him. Paloma entered, but Abigail stood in the doorway.

"I don't hear any screaming," Jedidiah said quietly as he looked along the wall at the chambers. Some of the vaults had names carved into the stone slabs and some didn't. "Which one is she in?" He counted. "There are twelve nameless chambers."

Paloma closed her eyes and ran her hand across the stone slabs of the nameless vaults. She stopped before one of them. "This one!"

Jedidiah took a deep breath and let it out to calm his nervousness. He removed the stone covering and saw the small box. "Are you sure, Paloma? I don't hear anything. If you're wrong, we're violating this family's…"

"I'm not wrong," she interrupted. "Open it – quickly!"

He removed the box and set it on the stone table in the middle of the room. Jedidiah crossed himself. *God forgive me*, he said inwardly as he opened the lid. He looked down at the child that lay there so still.

Paloma put her hand in the box and touched the child. She sighed, "We aren't too late."

"What do you mean? She didn't move and hasn't made a sound even when I pried open the lid."

Paloma smiled as she picked up the baby. "Touch her. She's warm. If she wasn't alive, she'd be cold by now."

Jedidiah hesitated a moment then did as she asked. The child was warm and as soon as he touched her, she made a slight sound. He was stunned. "How can this be?"

Paloma placed the child in his arms and put her ear to the infant's chest for several seconds. "Her heart beats, but it is extremely slow."

"I still don't see how the doctor missed it!" he said angrily as he coddled the child.

"God only knows," she replied. "Perhaps this child's heart stopped and started several times unbeknownst to all of them."

Then Jedidiah laughed slightly. "Now I know she's alive." He looked back at his wife. "She just wet my arm!"

Abigail was still standing by the door. This was magic way beyond what anyone has ever told her about. She was hesitant about going near the child. "This ain't right!" she said wearily. She looked at Paloma. "Did you make this happen?" A tear rolled down her cheek. " If ya' did, why couldn't ya' help me keep my baby?"

Paloma put an arm around the sad, frightened girl. "This isn't my doing." She looked toward the child. "The baby's heart is just not working right. She could still die."

When the child started to cry, Jedidiah came toward Abigail. "You want to hold her?"

Tears were streaming down Abigail's face. "I can't!" She ran out the door.

"Abigail!" Jedidiah shouted after her.

"Leave her be," Paloma said.

Jedidiah gave the baby to Paloma. He put the empty box back in its place and replaced the stone. After he shut the door to the mausoleum, he turned to the old woman. "How are we going to explain this to the Welch's when we take her back?"

"We don't," Paloma replied. "You raise her."

Jedidiah was surprised. "Me! This child belongs to the Welch's. How can we do that?"

"You forget. The child was pronounced dead. You told me they were going to keep her existence a secret from the child's mother. How are you going to explain her return?"

Jedidiah shook his head. "I don't know."

"All those people who attend her service thought the child dead. As superstitious as this town is, this child would be despised and feared," she said emphatically. "Even more than you and I are. To them, she'd be coming back from the dead, and they would hang the three of us for witchcraft."

Jedidiah took the baby in his arms and smiled at her. "She's a pretty baby. Look at those big, deep blue eyes."

Paloma laughed slightly. "She's smiling back at you, Jedidiah. I think she likes you."

"It's probably gas," he replied as he rocked the child in his arms. He then remembered what Sally Gooch and Erma Welch had said in the store about the child Abigail had carried and wondered if the town would shun this child as they did him. Jedidiah was about to express his concerns when Paloma spoke again.

"I know what you're thinking, boy," she said. "It's just a chance we'll have to take."

Jedidiah shook his head. *How does she do that!* he thought. She always seemed to know what he was going to say before he said it.

The baby started crying. "Come on, let's go home. She's probably hungry. We'll talk about it on the way," said the old woman.

Paloma gave several other reasons why they should keep her instead of giving her back to the Welch's. She told him that if they returned the child, the lie Henry told Emmaline could severely jeopardized their love relationship. There's also the other child to consider. If this child was despised by the town, how would it affect her twin? The last comment she made hit home. She told him that with them, this child would be loved and cared for. If they dropped her before the steps of someone's home to be fostered, who's to say that she wouldn't become someone's household servant or a stepchild to be ridiculed and treated with cruelty?

With that, Jedidiah remembered his own stepfather, Homer Bedlam. He nodded his agreement. She was right. There was no other choice. They would raise her as their own. He just hoped he could bring his wife around to accepting her.

Chapter 12

Jedidiah hoped that Abigail would be waiting for them when they returned home, but she wasn't there. Paloma said she'd look after the child while he went to look for her, although he had a fairly good idea where she might be. When she was angry with him, or upset about something, she would always go to small clearing in the swamp to think.

***

Abigail sat on the bank by a small pool of water and stared at the lily pads floating on top. Her eyes then caught sight of a small water snake weave between the cattails and reeds in the water. She didn't worry about it, for she knew it wasn't the poisonous kind and as long as it left her alone, she wouldn't bother it.

Abigail's mind was filled with thoughts. She didn't know what to do. She loved Jedidiah, and though she thought Paloma a witch, she'd always been a good witch in her mind. But now there was this child brought back from the dead. Everything she'd been taught or heard of from her people was that once a person died they didn't come back and if they did, they would surely be possessed by evil.

"Penny for your thoughts?"

Abigail looked up and saw Jedidiah. "Go away!" She turned her face back toward the floating flowers on the water.

He sat down beside her. "How can I leave the woman I love alone, especially when she's upset?"

"You're plannin' ta' keep that child, ain't ya'?" Her tone was bitter.

"It would be the best thing for her," he replied gently.

Abigail stood abruptly. "How can you!" she yelled. "She was brought back from the dead! She'll be evil!"

Jedidiah became angry. "Superstitious nonsense!" he yelled back. "That's an innocent baby with an ailment that doesn't make her heart beat right. That's all! The people buried her by mistake!"

He could tell by Abigail's silence that he had to take a different tact with her. He calmed his tone, gathered his thoughts for a moment and then asked, "You believe in, Jesus, don't you?"

"'Course I does! Ya' can't go ta' heaven lest ya' do," she replied sharply.

"Do you remember the part in the Good Book when Jesus made Lazarus rise from the dead?"

"I remember. My Granny told me that story when I was a little girl back in Hazard." She picked up a pebble lying by the pool and skipped it across the water.

Jedidiah smiled as he watched the rock skim the water three times. "Good one," he said commenting on her skill. He got back to the subject. "Was Lazarus evil?"

Abigail thought for a moment. "Not that I recollect Granny sayin'."

Jedidiah picked up a pebble and skimmed it across the water. It was also a three skipper. Then he asked, "Was Jesus evil for bringing back Lazarus?"

Abigail's chin dropped and she stood, planting her fists at her hips. "Jedidiah Lucas! 'Course he weren't! Them is sinful words! Ya' better bend a knee and say a prayer for forgiveness!"

"There was no sin intended in my question," he replied chuckling lightly. "Answer me this. Who's to say that it wasn't the Lord telling Paloma where to find the baby when those people from town made such a terrible mistake by burying her?"

She thought for a moment. "It's possible." She picked up a pebble and threw it. This time it was a four skipper.

"Who do you think is more likely to give a dream to point Paloma in the right direction to find that innocent baby – the Good Lord – or the devil?"

Abigail flopped down on the bank and started to cry. "I'm feelin' right shameful with my thinkin'." She threw a pebble in the water and it sunk to the bottom. "I guess I ain't over the loss of our baby."

Jedidiah took her in his arms and held her. He told her why he and Paloma decided to keep the child. He then suggested that it could have been the Lord who led them to find the baby because he knew they'd love her unconditionally.

Abigail wiped her eyes and smiled after that. "Maybe he gave her ta' us in place of our own?"

"Maybe," he replied. "He probably knew you'd be a good mother."

Abigail stood and picked up a pebble. "I promise I will!" She threw the pebble and it skipped seven times across the water.

Jedidiah put his arms around her. "Any woman that can make a pebble skip seven times will make a great mother!"

She kissed him. "Let's go home. I wanna see our little Hattie."

Jedidiah was surprised that she wanted to name this baby after his mother. That was the name they'd chosen to call the child they'd lost if it was a girl. But Abigail told him that Paloma had named the child before they met up with him to go to the cemetery. She said by naming her Hattie, it would do both his mother and their lost child honor.

***

The next few weeks with Hattie were difficult. The three of them took turns watching over her while she slept both day and night. Her little life balanced on a thread. Several times it seemed as if she'd stopped breathing and her heart stopped beating. When it did that, they'd pick her up and pat her gently on the back, and it would startle her back to life.

On the fourth week, Jedidiah had to go into town for supplies. He took a collection of snake skins to sell to the boot maker for extra money to buy things they needed. Next, he went to the general store. It was empty of customers that morning, so the storekeeper was able to wait on him right away.

"Do you carry cigars, Mr. McGuire?" Jedidiah asked.

"Tobacco is listed in your monthly allotment, but not cigars." The older man looked at him oddly. "I didn't think you smoked?"

"I don't," he said with a smile. "I want to buy one for you. I'm celebrating. I became a daddy."

He'd forgotten that his hillbilly wife was in the family way. The shopkeeper cleared his throat. "Congratulations," he said evenly to be polite, but inwardly he didn't think a sin-eater had any business being married, and bringing a child into the world was unheard of. "I don't smoke either." He turned his back to gather the usual supplies.

"Suit yourself." Jedidiah shook his head. He was slightly peeved. The man didn't ask if it was a girl or boy, or what they named her. He pulled out a piece of paper that had a list of things Abigail said they needed. "I also need some yard goods for diapers, a baby's bottle, diaper pins…"

"Those are not in your monthly…"

"I have money. I can pay!" Jedidiah cut off the man's next words.

With each item Jedidiah called out, Mr. McGuire announced the price of it and informed him of the running total. When they came to the table with the bolts of cloth, he ordered a few yards for diapers. He also spotted some material with blue and pink flowers that he thought would make into a lovely dress for Abigail and asked how much of it he would need for one.

"That's terribly expensive for you. It came from New York. At fifty-cents a yard, you'd need at least three dollar's worth. Are you sure you have…"

Jedidiah's frustration was quickly changing to anger. He shoved a hand in his pocket, pulled out twenty dollars and slammed in on the table. "Listen, McGuire! Don't tell me what I can afford and what I can't. I have a lovely wife and a beautiful daughter to spend my money on. What I buy for them with it is my business!"

The storekeeper felt like ejecting Jedidiah and hated the fact that he had to supply him with necessities, but he was a necessary evil to Black Water. If it wasn't for him, the town would be full of unsettled spirits and someday he might even have need of the Sin-Eater for himself. He was about to measure out the flowered material when the bell on the door jingled. "You'll have to wait. I've got real customers."

Jedidiah rolled his eyes. "Certainly," he said sarcastically. "Heaven forbid my business would cause them to have to wait a couple of minutes!" He went into the back room and waited - as usual.

Emmaline Welch entered the store pushing a baby carriage. Her mother-in-law and friend, Charlotte, accompanied them.

"Good morning, Mr. McGuire," Emmaline said politely.

The storekeeper smiled pleasantly. "Good morning, ladies. What a pleasure to see you this fine morning." He walked to the carriage and peeked inside. "What a beautiful little girl. Evelyn, isn't it?"

"Thank you, Mr. McGuire," Emmaline replied. "You're too kind."

"How can I help you today?"

"I'm needing some material to have a gown made for Evelyn's christening and a dress for myself," Emmaline replied.

"Right this way," he said.

Though he couldn't see who came in, Jedidiah listened as Mr. McGuire talked about the different materials. He never once told them the price. He heard one of the women make a comment about wanting some yardage of the pink and blue flowered cloth. He peeked through the crack in the door and saw him holding up the same material he'd wanted.

"I agree with you," said Mr. McGuire. "I think it would make a lovely dress."

He rolled out the cloth and cut off what they wanted. While the ladies continued to shop, Mr. McGuire decided to take care of Jedidiah and get rid of him. He went to the back room. "Do you have all you need?"

"Except for the material," he replied.

They went to the cutting table and looked at the bolt. "There isn't enough. You'll have to pick something else out."

"There was before! You knew I wanted that material," Jedidiah shouted angrily. "You sold it out from under me!"

"This is my store!" McGuire shot back. "I supply you because I have to. My regular customers come before you. Do I make myself understood?"

"Perfectly!"

Emmaline and her companions couldn't help but hear the shouting and saw their Sin-Eater arguing with the storekeeper.

Erma Welch smiled. "Serves him right!"

"How so, Mother Welch?" asked Emmaline.

"I'd picked out some material a few months ago that I thought would make a pretty gown for Evelyn, trusting it would be a girl, and that dirty Sin-Eater had the nerve to pick out the same material I wanted for his - issue," she said haughtily. "Naturally, I couldn't buy it after that. Mr. McGuire wouldn't take the piece I had cut back so I was forced to give it away. It would have been awful if that hillbilly wife of his had brought her child into town wearing the same thing as our Evelyn."

"The very nerve!" Charlotte shook her head agreeing with Erma.

Emmaline was furious with her mother-in-law and not too happy with Charlotte at that moment either. She didn't have the same take on Jedidiah as the rest of the people. He performed a wonderful service for the people of this town. The servants of their household had told of the beautiful prayer he said over her, asking the Lord to heal her.

Emmaline took the flowered material from her mother-in-law's basket and walked over to the table where Jedidiah and Mr. McGuire were arguing.

"Emmaline!" Erma exclaimed in a half-whispered voice. "What do you think you're doing?"

But she paid no attention to her mother-in-law as she approached the two men. "Pardon me."

"Go on to the back," McGuire said to Jedidiah. "Have a little courtesy."

"No!" Emmaline said curtly. "It's you who needs to show a little courtesy, Mr. McGuire." She walked up to Jedidiah and presented him the material. "This is for you with my compliments."

Jedidiah felt embarrassed. If he'd known it was Hattie's true mother who'd purchased the material, he would have kept his big mouth shut. "That's not necessary. I'll pick another." He glared at Mr. McGuire. "It was the principal of the thing anyway."

"I hear your wife is going to have a baby?" Emmaline asked pleasantly.

Jedidiah cleared his throat. "She's here already. She came early." He hated to lie, but there was no other way around it. "We named her Hattie."

"My congratulations, Jedidiah," Emmaline said sincerely. "Please, it would hurt my feeling if you didn't take this. I believe that if it wasn't for your prayers when I was in a bad way, I wouldn't be here today."

Jedidiah accepted it graciously and left the store. He leaned against the building momentarily and closed his eyes. He felt guilty and heart sick for Emmaline Welch. She had a daughter she knew nothing about. He was obliged to keep it a secret because of this idiotic town's superstitious non-sense, but for the sake of Emmaline and Henry's happiness and the welfare of the child, the lie had to stand.

Chapter 13

The months of sleepless nights and days trying to keep Hattie alive soon turned into a year. With Jedidiah's and Abigail's constant vigilance along with some of Paloma's remedies, her weak little heart improved and her spells of not breathing became few and far between. By her second birthday, Hattie slept during the night as peacefully as any other child her age.

Jedidiah was completely happy with his family. The only dark spot in his life was Black Water Township. Abigail didn't mind living there. She said that for the first time in her life she felt completely loved and was better off now than she'd ever been. Paloma's reasons for staying were a complete mystery - even to her. But she also told him that he could take his family and leave and she would completely understand, but Jedidiah wouldn't leave her. So - he made the best of things.

***

Nine more years passed and Hattie turned eleven. Paloma watched as Jedidiah pushed the girl on a swing. She heard Jedidiah say to Hattie... "Who's Daddy's best girl?" ...and then she saw Hattie tilt her head back as she went high up in the air and reply, "Hattie is!" The sight was a familiar one from a dream long passed.

Abigail came out on the porch drying her hands on a cloth. "Come and git it!" she shouted. "Supper's on."

Hattie jumped from the swing as it was on its way back up, and as she started to pass Jedidiah, he scooped her up and swung her atop his shoulders for a ride to the house. The four of them sat down at the table and joined hands for a prayer.

"Lord," Abigail started. "We be thankin' ya' for our family and for the gator caught in this here swamp that allows me ta' make this fine, Gator Jambalaya! Amen."

"Don't forget the snakes, Mama," Hattie added, "Granny Paloma makes awful good snake stew."

Abigail smiled and added, "We be thankin' ya' for the snakes too."

"Where'd you get the gator meat?" Jedidiah asked, as he spooned a good portion on his plate.

"Uncle Ennis came by whilst you was huntin'," Abigail replied. "Some big city gents talked ta' him. He's got a big contract for as many gator hides as he can git." Then she laughed. "Seems the ladies in Californy and New York fancy gator hand bags of all things."

Hattie shook her head. "Now that's plum silly! Why would anybody wanna carry 'round a gator ta' put their doodads in?"

"That's them big city folk for ya'," Abigail replied. "They's full of peculiar notions!"

Jedidiah laughed. "So what did Ennis want? I know he just didn't give you the gator meat for nothing."

"He wanted ta' know if I'd help him like I used to when I was a youn'in. He said he'd give me a share for all the gators I help him catch. I told him I'd think on it." She picked up a piece of bread and took a bite.

"You're not seriously thinking about it are you?" he asked concerned.

"'Course not!" She then replied with a mischievous grin. "'If'n I'd flat out said no, he'd a never left the gator meat."

Jedidiah was relieved. During their first year of marriage, Abigail had gone with Ennis once while he was performing a sin-eating. It had scared him half to death when Paloma had told him what she was doing. When she returned, she'd promised never to do it again.

"Can I learn ta' hunt gators?" Hattie asked.

"No!" Jedidiah and Abigail exclaimed simultaneously.

Hattie sighed and continued eating her dinner.

Paloma listened to their conversation. She'd been waiting for the right time to broach a touchy subject. She thought that now was as good a time as any. "Speaking of learning, I believe school starts next month."

"School!" Hattie's eyes widened with excitement. She looked from one parent to the other. "Am I really goin' ta' school?"

Jedidiah gave Paloma a hard look. She knew his feelings on the subject. He turned to Hattie and forced a smile. "Eat your supper. We'll talk about it."

***

Jedidiah and Abigail tucked Hattie into bed. Afterward, they joined

Paloma outside by the fire so they could talk privately without being overheard if the girl wasn't asleep.

"How could you blurt that out in front of Hattie like that? You know my feelings on the subject of school." Jedidiah paced back and forth. "She can already read and write." He turned to Paloma. "You and I have taught her the important things."

"She needs more than that, boy." Paloma stared into the flames. "There's the world to learn about." She looked at him from the corner of her eye. "You're not ashamed to send her to school are you?"

Jedidiah frowned. "You know better than that! It's me! She'll be ridiculed or shunned."

"They don't have ta' know," Abigail added.

"You too? I thought you'd be on my side!" He turned and sat down on the log by the fire.

"I have my worries too, but Paloma's right," Abigail said gently. "Back in Hazard, when I was her age, a boy told me 'bout an animal what had a nose as long as a man was tall. He called it a elephant. I thought he was tellin' a whopper till he showed me a picture. He called me a dumb girl." She looked lovingly into Jedidiah's eyes. "I don't want Hattie ta' be just a dumb girl like me."

Jedidiah put his arm around her. "You're not dumb," he said softly as he gave her a hug. "You can track better than most men. You're a good hunter and a great mother."

Abigail grinned. "I am, ain't I."

Jedidiah sighed. "I know both of you are right, but the two of you seem to be forgetting one major problem with sending her to school – Evelyn!"

The three of them discussed the matter long into the night. Jedidiah agreed that it would be best for Hattie to go to school, but first they needed to make sure that the two girls didn't look alike. Jedidiah hadn't seen Evelyn since she was an infant, and no one from Black Water had ever seen Hattie. Though she often asked her father to take her, Jedidiah refused for just that reason.

The only children their daughter ever played with were kinfolk from the Shadrack community when Abigail took her visiting. The children of Black Water didn't associate with the children of Shadrack and none of them attended school.

The next concern Jedidiah expressed was about Hattie being ridiculed or treated badly because he was the Sin-Eater. But Abigail told him that being called names was just a part of living. She said she'd been called white trash all her life because her mama had been a loose woman. She also said that if they gave Hattie the proper kisses and hugs at home, she'd be right as rain.

The last problem was money – there was very little extra to spend on luxuries. The boot maker quit buying snake skins temporarily, and Paloma quit telling fortunes at the hotel after Hattie came to them.

Jedidiah was sure the things they needed were not in his monthly budget at the general store. Hattie would need a dress and proper shoes. The only thing she wore was hand-me-down overalls from her cousins, and she stayed barefooted most of the time. She'd also need chalk, a slate board, paper and pencils to name a few items if the school didn't supply them. School would be an expensive undertaking.

Paloma told Jedidiah that the clothing was a minor concern. She was sure they could acquire an old dress from one of Abigail's relatives and remake it for her. The issue of her being the Sin-Eater's daughter and her feelings being hurt, Paloma said they would cross that bridge when they came to it. The most important thing they had to find out was – did Hattie look like her sister? Paloma told him she'd go to town tomorrow and find out.

When the discussion had ended they retired for the night. Abigail's mind was buzzing with thoughts after she'd kissed Jedidiah good-night and turned over. Both had hoped to give Hattie a brother or sister, but she never conceived again. She considered Hattie a gift from heaven just as a child she would have given birth to. She wanted her little girl to be better than she was.

Abigail made up her mind. It had been a long time since she'd gone with her uncle to hunt gators. He'd promised her three dollars for everyone she helped catch. *Hattie's gonna look like a right'n proper young lady,* Abigail thought. *No hand-me-downs, no made over dress with patches and old shoes for our daughter.*

Suddenly, a familiar sound echoed through the swamp and both sat up. Someone had rung the Sin-Eater's bell. When it didn't ring a second time they laid back down.

"Can you press out my black suit in the morning?" Jedidiah asked with a yawn.

"Sure enough," she replied. Then she added, "I thought me'n Hattie would visit Aunt Josie tomorrow. She might have some leftover material for a dress. Does ya' mind?"

Jedidiah turned over and leaned on his elbow. He gave her a stern look. "I know a dress isn't what you're going to your aunt's for."

Abigail worried he saw through what she'd planned to do. "Oh? And what might'n that be?"

He laughed and kissed her quickly. "You plan on a going to your Aunt Josie's for a little – ratchet-jawin' as your Uncle Ennis calls it."

Abigail was relieved. She gave him a smile. "Uncle Ennis is one ta' talk about ratchet-jawin'. When he and Uncle Hannibal pull a cork, they can talk the ears off a deaf man!" She kissed him good-night again and turned over to hopefully get some sleep. Her mind was still buzzing. She hoped she was still up to the task of gator hunting.

***

Abigail was up with the sun and fixed the morning coffee before anyone else got up. She took her cup and went out to the porch to greet the morning. This was her private time to gather her thoughts before getting on with the activities of the day. A light breeze rustled the leaves on the trees, and the scent of honeysuckle was in the air. She took a deep breath, hoping the scented air would calm her spirit. She was feeling anxious about the decision she'd made to go gator hunting with her uncle. It wasn't that she had any doubts about doing it, but it was breaking the promise she'd made to Jedidiah that got under her skin like a chigger. She closed her eyes. "Lord," she prayed. "It's just a little lie. And it's for Hattie. It ain't hurtin' nobody. I just knows ya' wouldn't want me ta' send the little girl ya' gave us ta' school lookin' like a rag-a-muffin. She'd be picked on an' poked fun at." Her prayer was interrupted when she heard the door open. She saw Hattie rubbing the sleep from her eyes.

"Mornin' Mama," Hattie yawned.

Abigail put a loving arm around her. "Mornin' sweetpea." She kissed her on top of the head.

Hattie smiled. "Did you and Daddy decided if'n I'll be startin' school?"

"We's thinkin' on it still. We'll let ya' know tonight. Go wash up, now. After breakfast we're goin' ta' Aunt Josie's."

"Really!" she said excitedly. "Last time we paid visit, Cousin Caleb told me Uncle Ennis was gonna fix up the old tree house for him. Maybe it's finished."

"Could be. Hurry on now."

Hattie kissed her mother on the cheek and headed for the well to draw her wash water.

"Lord," Abigail continued her quiet prayer. "Forgive this lie and I promise I won't do it again." She went into the house to press Jedidiah's black suit. When breakfast was done, Abigail and Hattie left.

***

Jedidiah and Paloma started toward town and arrived just before noon. A wagon was waiting to take Jedidiah to where he needed to go, and Paloma had a good feeling as to where she might find Emmaline and her daughter today.

Last year, *The Society for the Betterment of Black Water*, one of the women's committees, had convinced the town council that the children needed a place to play and suggested that a park be built. It not only served as a place for children, but a place for social gatherings and concerts on Sunday after church. The park was finished about two months ago.

Paloma sat on a bench under a tree with her knitting. It was a lovely day, and she enjoyed the sunshine as she watched the children play on the swings. There were several women with their children in the park. No one seemed to pay much attention to her. It had been quite a while since she'd been in town, so either they didn't recognize her or they were too involved with their own conversations to notice her. This suited her fine.

Over an hour had passed. Emmaline and her daughter still hadn't appeared. Paloma was disappointed. A casual meeting in a public place would have been the easiest route. But if Hattie was to go to school, she had to find out if the two girls were identical or not. She decided to casually check the stores in town to see if they might be there before venturing to the Welch residence on some pretext as a last resort. But just as she was about to leave, a carriage pulled up.

***

Henry Welch kissed his wife and daughter before they exited the carriage. "I'll be back in about an hour," said Henry. He snapped the reins and drove off.

"You heard your father, Evelyn," said Emmaline. "When his council meeting is over, we're going to visit, Aunt Sally."

Evelyn sighed. "Do I have to visit Aunt Sally? Can't I go over to

Carry-Ann's house instead while you visit?"

Emmaline shook her head. "Evelyn, your Aunt Sally loves you very much. Why don't you ever want to go see her?"

"Because she's always pinching my cheeks and says she could just eat me with a spoon!" the young girl said sharply. "Mother, I'm almost twelve. Do you know how embarrassing that is when she says it in front of people?"

Emmaline smiled. "I know. She used to do the same thing to me when I was young. It's just her way. One of these days when you're older she'll stop."

"I hope so," she sighed.

"Go and play. I'll be on the bench by that tree," her mother pointed.

Emmaline spotted an old woman dressed in grey coming toward her. It took her a moment before she realized who she was. She smiled and curtseyed. "It's a pleasure to see you again, Mrs. Day. It's been a long time. I almost didn't recognize you."

Paloma smiled. "The years have added a few more wrinkles to this old face."

"But Father Time has still treated you kindly," Emmaline complimented and then asked, "What brings you to town today?"

"I read about this new park. It's such a beautiful day, I just thought I'd come see it." She looked around. "It's quite lovely," Paloma replied. She then redirected the conversation to her true interest. "Was that the little girl I predicted you'd have?"

Emmaline looked toward her daughter. "That's my Evelyn."

"Would it be presumptuous of me to ask an introduction?"

"Actually, I think she'd like that. My mother-in-law and Aunt Sally still tell her stories about you being a witch."

Paloma laughed and shook her head. "Still jealous after all these years!"

"Jealous?" she questioned. "If you don't mind me asking, what does that have to do with you being called a witch?"

"Before I married Benjamin Day, I turned the heads of many men in this town, including Victor Gooch and Alvin Welch, though I did nothing to encourage them. Their fiancés or wives said I bewitched their men. The fact that I was able to predict certain events didn't help my situation. Thus, I'm a witch."

Emmaline shook her head. "How silly. You've always seemed nice whenever we've spoken."

Paloma grinned. "Were they any sillier than a young girl seeking advice from this supposed witch on how to acquire the man she loves?"

"Point well taken." Emmaline laughed. A moment later, she called her daughter.

Paloma watch as the little girl ran toward them. Her mind was now at ease on the matter of the child's looks. Evelyn stood in stark contrast to Hattie. Except for some similar facial features, Evelyn looked to be slightly taller. She had blonde hair and light blue eyes. Hattie's hair was dark brown, and her eyes, thought blue were a deep blue.

"We're not leaving yet, are we?" Evelyn asked when she reached her mother's side.

"Do you remember your grandmamma telling you about the witch who lives in the swamp?" Emmaline asked.

"Sure! Aunt Sally told me about her too." She then added in a spooky tone, "She said she flies on her broomstick on Halloween night!"

Paloma did her best to contain her laughter.

Emmaline suppressed a smile. "Evelyn, I'd like to introduce you to Mrs. Day. She's who everyone calls the swamp witch."

The little girl's eyes widened. "Honest! You're the swamp witch?"

Paloma gave her a smile. "That's what they say, but what I truly am, is a Gypsy. I can sometimes tell the future."

"And she doesn't fly on a broomstick either," Emmaline added.

"Oh," Evelyn said disappointedly. "I was hoping you were a witch."

"Why?" her mother asked.

"Because if she could really fly on a broomstick, I was going to ask if she could teach me how."

Emmaline shook her head. "Go on and play!"

The little girl curtseyed. "Nice to meet you anyway, Mrs. Day." Then she ran off again.

Emmaline sighed and looked back at Paloma. "My apologies."

"Not necessary. She's a delightful child." Paloma smiled. "Hopefully, my fame in this town will slowly fade into obscurity with this younger generation, as it is…."

Suddenly, Paloma stopped talking and Emmaline saw the older woman almost swoon. She caught her, just before she fell. "Mrs. Day! Are you alright?"

Paloma regained her equilibrium. "I'll be fine. I just had a strange sensation wash over me."

"Do you need a doctor?"

The old woman patted her on the hand. "I'll be fine, girl. I'll just be on my way."

Emmaline suggested that she wait with her until Henry came back so they could drive her to the bell instead of her having to walk the distance back. But she declined and bid Emmaline good-day. Paloma walked quickly. She felt something wasn't right, and she needed to get home. When she arrived at the bell, she saw Jedidiah waiting for her.

Paloma grabbed his arm. "Is everything alright?"

"Fine as far as I know," he replied, "Except for old Horace Reidly. He passed on."

"We need to go home!" she said urgently.

"What's wrong?" Concern laced his voice.

"I don't know. I just have this terrible feeling."

Jedidiah knew better than to ignore Paloma's feelings. He may not have believed she was a witch, but she did have a powerful sense of perception. They made their way through the swamp as quickly as they could. When they reached the edge of the clearing, they saw Abigail's cousin, Jubal, sitting on the front porch.

"'Bout time you's got home!" Jubal exclaimed as he ran to meet them. "It's Abby. She's hurt. We sent fer Doc Jackson."

"Is Hattie alright?" Jedidiah asked as they made their way through the swamp.

"She ain't hurt, but I can't say if'n she's fine," Jubal replied.

As they went through the swamp, Jubal started to tell them what happened. "Abby left Hattie with Maw..." Jubal started, "...whilst she went with Paw, me and Uncle Hannibal to go huntin' for gators."

"She told me she wasn't going!" Jedidiah yelled.

"Don't ya' be blamin' me!" Jubal yelled back. "I can't hep' it if'n she changed her mind!" Then he continued. "Anyway, we found a good spot for trollin'..."

"What's that?" Jedidiah asked.

"Paw and Uncle Hannibal would tie a rope around us and then we'd go into the water. When a gator took after us, Paw and Uncle Hannibal would reel us in and shoot the gator in the head."

"You were used as bait!" Jedidiah couldn't believe his ears. He knew Abigail said she went with them and helped occasionally, but she didn't tell him how she helped.

Jubal laughed. "Gets the blood a pumpin' sure 'nough! We got five gators 'fore Abby got hurt."

Paloma and Jedidiah looked at each other then rolled their eyes.

"How did Abigail get hurt?" Paloma asked.

"I was gittin' ta' that, if'n you's quit interruptin'." Jubal continued. "Anyway, me an Abby just got out of the water. Then we hear'ed Hattie callin' fer her Mama. My little brother, Caleb, was with her. How she found us, I ain't got a notion. Paw asked Maw…"

"Get on with it, Jubal!" Jedidiah yelled. He was becoming frustrated. "What – happened – to – Abigail!"

"Ya' don't have ta' yell, I's gittin' ta' that," Jubal shook his head. "Anyhow, when we hear's Hattie callin' fer her Mama, Abby stops for a minute. She really shouldn't a stopped, she know'd better'n that. We been trollin'…"

"Jubal!" Both Paloma and Jedidiah yelled. "Get on with it!"

Jubal frowned and said quickly, "When Abigail stopped the gator we was trollin' fer come out of the water and grabbed her by the leg. It were just lucky Paw and Uncle Hannibal killed it afor it took her under. That would'a been three dollars of my earnin's swimmin' away if'n we lost that gator. There! Ya' satisfied!"

"What about Hattie, is she hurt?" Jedidiah asked.

"Na, just sad," Jubal replied. "She keeps a sayin' it were her fault. It were ya' know. I told her it were too! We could'a got a bunch more gator ta'day if it weren't 'cause of Hattie! Maybe even five more." Then he held up his fingers and took a few minutes to calculate. "That would'a been – twelve more dollars for me if'n we got five more!"

Jedidiah rolled his eyes. If there was another word for idiot, it would have been Jubal! "That would be fifteen, not twelve."

"Really!" He counted on his fingers again.

When they finally arrived at the Hagen's home, Jedidiah burst into the house with Paloma following behind. Abigail was laying on one of the beds in the main room. Her leg had clean white bandages wrapped around it. He went to her side and knelt down.

"Are you alright?" Jedidiah gently stroked her hair.

"I been better?" she replied. She looked into his eyes. "Ya' ain't mad at me are ya'?"

"Mad at you?" he repeated softly, then kissed her on the forehead.

"I'm furious." He gave her a smile. "I could have lost you. Why did you do it, Abigail?"

"'Cause I want our Hattie ta' walk in that school house lookin' like all them other fancy dressed younin's. I wanted her ta' have a new dress, new bonnet and a new pair of shoes. I want her ta' be smart with a fancy education. I don't want her ta' be a loose woman like my mama or trollin' for gators like me." A tear ran down her cheek.

A moment later, Doctor Jackson came back into the house. He opened his bag and gave Jedidiah some packets. "Mix this with water and give it to her to drink twice a day."

"Will she be alright?"

"The animal punctured her leg in several places, and I've stitched up the gashes. She's lucky she didn't lose it. If the wounds are kept clean she should be fine, but if infection sets in she could still lose it."

Abigail giggled. "Then we'd match, Jedidiah. We'll have one leg apiece."

"Don't mind her," said the doctor. "I gave her something for the pain just before you came in. She'll be a little fuzzy-headed until she falls asleep."

"I'll make sure her leg is kept clean," Paloma said.

"Good. I want her off of it for at least a week." Then he looked at Abigail. "No more alligator trolling for you, young woman!"

"No more trollin'," she said groggily. "It weren't as fun as it used to be when I was a young'in. I'll be an old woman next month. I'll be twenty-nine, Doc."

"Make sure you remember that if you want to see thirty!" The doctor put his instruments away and left.

In concern for his wife's well-being, Jedidiah had momentarily forgotten about Hattie. Paloma said she would stay with Abigail while he went to look for his daughter. Josie told him she'd climbed up Caleb's tree house and pulled the rope up after her.

When Jedidiah left the house, he saw Ennis and his brother, Hannibal, coming through the woods. He clenched his fist and marched up to them. His eyes were focused on Ennis.

"Now wait a minute, boy!" Ennis exclaimed holding up his hands motioning him to stop. "I didn't make her do it!"

But Jedidiah didn't listen. He pulled back his fist and connected a solid right to Ennis's jaw, and he fell to the ground. Hannibal was about to grab

Jedidiah, but Ennis waved him off.

"You should never have asked Abigail to do such a thing. She's a wife and a mother! Not bait!" Jedidiah shouted and then walked away to find his daughter.

"How come ya' let him hit ya' like that, Ennis?" Hannibal asked.

"The boy were right. I shouldn't a asked. Abigail's gittin' too old fer gator trollin'. She'll be twenty-nine next month."

"True," Hannibal replied. "But she sure could bring in the big gators!"

"Come on," Ennis said as he got up. "Grab Jubal. We can still get a few more ta'day."

***

Caleb brought Jedidiah to the tree house, and he called up to his daughter. "Come on down, Hattie!"

"No!" she shouted as she looked over the edge. "I ain't comin' down – ever!" Then she started to cry. "It's my fault Mama got hurt!" She moved away from the edge.

Jedidiah cursed Jubal in blaming Hattie for Abigail's injuries. He didn't want to scold her for disobeying him in not coming down, he knew she felt bad enough already. He thought for a moment and then said, "You can stay up there forever if you want, Hattie, but if you do, who's going to take care of me until your mama feels better?"

"Granny Paloma!"

"No, she has to stay here and take care of your mama," he said gently. "You want me to be all alone?" When she didn't answer, he sighed loudly and shoved his hands in his pockets. "Well, I guess I'll just have to be alone."

"You can come up here with me, Daddy!"

"Now, Hattie, you know I can't climb a tree anymore! Remember the last time? My wooden leg fell off!" He heard an involuntary giggle come down from above.

A few moments later, the rope was thrown over the side, and Hattie climbed down. Jedidiah knelt down, and she put her arms around his neck and cried. "I'm sorry, Daddy, I didn't mean to get Mama hurt."

He patted her on the back gently and rocked her in his arms. After a moment, he looked into her deep blue eyes and wiped away her tears. "I don't care what Jubal told you. It wasn't your fault. Your mama was doing something dangerous. She took a risk and got hurt. You understand that?"

She nodded her head and sniffed back a few tears. Jedidiah hesitated a moment then asked gently, "I'm curious. How come you went looking for your mama?"

"Caleb and me was drawin' pictures in the dirt. I started drawin' a picture of Mama, but when I finished, I'd draw'd her bein' eaten by a gator. I got scared, so me and Caleb went ta' look for her."

"How did you know where to look?"

"I don't know," she shrugged. "I just found her is all."

Jedidiah was puzzled. Abigail had started teaching Hattie how to track, but didn't think she was that good at it yet. He gave her a smile. "Well, the way I look at it, Jubal was wrong. You probably saved your mama. She may have been hurt, but she didn't get eaten, did she?"

"No." She wiped away a stray tear.

"What if it was the next gator that would have eaten your mama? So, you see, you probably saved her."

Hattie smiled and hugged her father around the neck. "Can I see Mama now? They wouldn't let me earlier."

He brushed a strand of hair from her face. "She's probably asleep, but we can sit with her."

Chapter 14

After three days at her aunt's house, Abigail was ready to go home. For short visits, she got along fine with her aunt and they enjoyed each other's company, but now they were starting to get under each other's skin. She told Jedidiah and Paloma that if they didn't help her, she would crawl home.

There was no arguing with Abigail, so they put her in her uncle's rickety wagon and took as far as the bell and the entrance to their part of the swamp. Jedidiah had made some crutches for her so she could make her way through the woods without putting undo weight on her injured leg. He would have carried her home, but with the distance they had to travel, he was afraid of tripping over something if his wooden leg got caught on something and fell.

Hattie had stayed home waiting anxiously for her mother's return. She'd picked several bouquets of wildflowers to put around the house so it would smell sweet when she arrived. She still had some feelings of guilt even though both of her parents said it wasn't her fault.

She wanted to do something special for her mother but couldn't think of what to do besides the flowers. She went outside on the porch to wait for them to return, and as luck would have it, she saw a large, fat rabbit nibbling in their garden. She pulled the slingshot from her back pocket along with a large pebble, took aim and she hit her target with the first shot. She ran to the garden and picked the rabbit up by the ears and smiled. "Mama's gonna love you! Next ta' gator jambalaya, fried rabbit is her favorite."

Hattie had just finished skinning her catch when she heard her mother calling. She looked up and saw her appear at the edge of the woods with her father and Granny Paloma. She ran to greet them and started to cry as she wrapped her arms around her mother.

"Now, now," said Abigail in soft tones. "What's all these tears for? I ain't dead."

Hattie laughed slightly as her mother wiped away a tear. "Are ya' feelin' better, Mama?"

Abigail kissed her on the forehead. "Now that I'm home with you."

When they entered their small cottage, Abigail praised Hattie for the beautiful wildflowers and even more so for the rabbit she'd caught for their dinner. That was another reason Abigail was glad to be home. She preferred Paloma's cooking to her aunt's ten times over.

Later that evening when Hattie was tucked in bed, Jedidiah built a cozy fire outside so the three of them could discuss the child's schooling a little more. This was the first chance Paloma had to tell them about Hattie's twin, Evelyn. She informed them that though there were some facial similarities, no one would recognize them as twins. Jedidiah and Abigail were both relieved. The decision was finally made that Hattie would go to school.

***

Under Paloma's care, Abigail's leg healed quickly. It had been two weeks since the incident with the gator, and Abigail was becoming increasingly frustrated that her uncle hadn't given her the share of money for the gators she did help catch. She was determined to send Hattie to school looking just as proper as the others, but without the money she was promised, they couldn't afford to pay for the things they needed. Though Jedidiah wanted Abigail to wait a little while longer until her leg was completely healed to see her uncle, she told him that she was afraid that if they didn't act now, they wouldn't see a nickel. So -- the next day they went for a visit.

Just as Abigail had suspected he would, Ennis tried to back out on paying her for the five alligators she'd helped catch.

"Ya' didn't give a full day's work, so the way I sees it, I owe ya' nothin'," Ennis said smugly.

Abigail folded her arms and glared at him. "That ain't what we agreed on, Uncle Ennis. I was ta' be paid by the gator, not by the day."

"You's just better be lucky I ain't chargin' you!" Ennis shot back.

"For what!"

"For the fine care we give ya' whilst ya' was ailin'. I say that them gators ya' helped catch will just about cover it."

"Fifteen dollars for three days! I could'a stayed at the Black Water Hotel for near on a month for less than that." She put her hands to her hips. "Besides, I'm yer kin. It were yer Christian duty ta' care for me."

"And bein' kin," Ennis replied, "It's only fittin' that ya' not mooch off yer kinfolk neither. We had some hard times. Don't ya' think ya' owe us for all that time we raised ya' before ya' married?"

Abigail saw she was getting nowhere in this argument. But she had already planned for that event. "You ain't seen hard times yet, Uncle Ennis!" Abigail looked around for a moment and saw what she was looking for - a dead branch lying on the ground. She picked it up, pointed it to the north, east, south and west. She closed her eyes, mumbled something that no one understood and walked back to her uncle. She drew a circle around him with the point of the stick. She then walked toward the house, did the same ritual and drew a circle around it. She walked back toward Ennis and grinned.

"What in tar'nation are ya' doin', girl?" Ennis asked, confused at what she was doing.

"You'll see," she replied and walked toward Jedidiah.

Jedidiah was leaning against a tree at the edge of the woods watching and listening to his wife argued with her uncle. He'd planned on negotiating with Ennis himself, but when the man pointed a shotgun at him and told him not to come any closer, he had no choice but to let Abigail do the talking. As he watched and listened, he too had no clue as to what she was doing. When she approached he asked, "What was all that about?"

"You'll see." Again Abigail did the same ritual with the stick, but this time she drew a large circle on the ground in front of Jedidiah instead of around him. "If I say so, I want ya' ta' step in this circle."

"What for?"

"You'll see." She grinned and gave him a wink. Next, she drew a line from the circle in front of Jedidiah to the circle she drew around Ennis.

"What kinda stupid game are ya' playin', Abigail," he said as he stepped out of the circle.

"Ain't no game," she said seriously. "And it don't matter if yer in the circle or not now. I already said some of the words."

"What words?"

"The words to the curse," she replied.

Ennis laughed. "You ain't no witch. How can you do a curse?"

"This is not a witch's curse. It's a Gypsy's curse and that is worse than a witch's curse."

"You ain't no Gypsy."

"But Paloma is. She taught me the words ta' say in case ya' didn't pay what ya' owed me." Abigail pulled a pouch from the pocket in of her overalls. She opened it up, took some pinches of yellow powder, sprinkled it in the breeze and in a tone that made her words sound mysterious she said, "Ora lo pongo mi scolo per dormire, io prego il signore la mia anima per mantenere!"

Ennis was starting to worry. Those definitely sounded like words of a curse. He frowned. "What did you just do?"

She glared at him. "If ya' don't pay me the money ya' owe me, all I have ta' do is tell Jedidiah ta' step in the circle I drew on the ground in front of him, and all the sins he carries will be put upon you and everyone who's in that house!" she pointed.

"You can't do that," he replied. But he wasn't exactly sure that she couldn't.

Suddenly, Abigail's Aunt Josie came running out of the house. She'd been listening and watching from the window. "Ennis, will ya' just give her the money! Ya' know she earned it." Then she whispered, "Besides, yer cousin, Dora Lee is in the house, and she heard every word. If she even suspects we been cursed, she'll tell everyone and we really will be cursed!"

Abigail gave her aunt a sad smile. "Sorry, Aunt Josie. I didn't want ta' do it, but Uncle Ennis is tryin' ta' cheat me. But if he gives me the money he owes, Paloma also taught me a Gypsy blessin', which I will gladly say to bring ya' good luck."

Josie frowned at her husband. "Ennis…."

"All right!" he shoved a hand in his pocket and pulled out a roll of bills. Abigail held out her hand and he counted out the fifteen dollars.

"What about the blessin'?" Josie asked.

Abigail smiled, sprinkled more of the yellow powder in the breeze and said in a soft, prayerful tone, "Se muoio prima che mi svegli, prego il signore la mia anima per prendere. Amen!" She looked at her aunt and smiled. "Just wait and see, Aunt Josie. Good luck is now on yer doorstep."

Josie sighed in relief and bid her niece good-bye. Abigail and Jedidiah heard Josie scold Ennis for not only trying to cheat her niece, but putting them in the situation of being cursed.

Jedidiah laughed when they were out of hearing range. "I thought you told me you were not going to lie anymore?"

Abigail gave him a puzzled look. "Lie? What lie?"

"A witch's curse and a gypsy's curse? I keep telling you there is no such thing."

"Just because you don't believe in somethin' don't mean I don't. And I didn't lie," she giggled.

He was puzzled. "If you didn't lie, what was all that with the circles and the strange words?"

"The circles was just circles. Paloma taught me them words one night when we was saying Hattie's prayers. Sometimes Hattie and I say them like that."

"Prayers," Jedidiah laughed. "What kind of prayers are they?"

"Paloma said it's a language called I-talian. She said her daddy taught it to her when she was a little girl. The first part I said was - Now I lay me down to sleep, I pray the Lord my soul to keep." Abigail laughed again. "And the second part, which I said was the blessin' was…."

Jedidiah rolled his eyes. "Don't tell me let me guess. If I die before I wake, I pray the Lord my soul to take."

"Amen!" Abigail finished.

"And what was the powder?"

"Dried mustard. Made for a good show, don't ya think?" She grinned. "Uncle Ennis tried ta' cheat me, and I just played a little game. My aunt and uncle believe in curses and witches' spells and all that. Just like you don't believe in sin-eatin' but ya' do it anyway. So, I didn't lie, I just played a game same as you."

Jedidiah laughed and kissed her on the forehead. "You, my love, are a very shrewd woman!"

Abigail smiled. "I might not have fancy book learning, but I does have a few smarts in my head."

Chapter 15

"Hold still, Hattie!" Abigail laughed as she pulled a brush through the girl's hair.

"I can't help it, Mama!" This was going to be her first day of school and she was excited.

Abigail was just as excited. With the money she'd received from her uncle, she was able to purchase all the doodads, as Hattie called them, that she'd need to look like a proper young lady.

She was relieved Mr. McGuire didn't recognize her when she entered the general store. On occasion, she had accompanied Jedidiah when he went to acquire their monthly allotment of supplies, but she was usually dressed in overalls or the old brown dress that had more patches on it than the original material. The storekeeper barely acknowledged her at those times, however, this time she'd entered through the front door dressed in her fine, pink and blue flowered dress that she'd made from the material Jedidiah had brought her years ago. She only wore it on special occasions.

Abigail laughed inwardly as the shopkeeper fell all over himself by being overly polite to her. She wondered what he would say if he realized that she was the Sin-Eater's wife. He suggested all manner of things for her to spend her fifteen dollars on. It was tempting to buy several things that caught her eye; a doll for Hattie, a new knife for Jedidiah and new fancy hats for Paloma and herself. But she resisted temptation and just bought the material and other notions to make Hattie a couple of dresses and bonnets to match. She also brought a tracing of her daughter's feet so she could purchase some brand new shoes. She thought about buying some school supplies, but decided to wait to see if the school provided them for free.

Abigail put a green bow in Hattie's hair and stepped back to take a look. She motioned for her to turn in a circle and then nodded. "Ya' look right perty, Hattie." She looked over the green dress that she'd trimmed with white lace to make sure there were no flaws. She'd spent days carefully hand-sewing each stitch to make it look like the dresses done on a fancy treadle machine.

"Do I look right'n proper fer school now?" Hattie asked.

"I hope so," she gave her a smile. "Go show yer daddy."

Hattie opened the bedroom door and walked out, clicking her new, fancy buttoned shoes on the floor. Jedidiah and Paloma were sitting at the table drinking their morning coffee.

"My! My! Who have we here?" Jedidiah exclaimed. "Where did my Hattie go?"

She laughed. "Ya' know it's me, Daddy." She walked to his side and put her arm around him and then turned to Paloma. "Mama made a right perty dress, don't'cha think?"

Paloma gave her a smile. "I'd say it looks even prettier because you're wearing it, baby girl."

A moment later, Abigail joined them dressed in her best also. "We better git goin'. Ya' don't wanna be late yer first day."

Paloma stood on the porch and waved good-bye as the three disappeared into the woods. The smile left her face as she thought about the strange dream she'd had last night. It wasn't a bad dream, or a good one for that matter - it was just odd. She'd dreamt about the weather - something she hadn't done since she was a child forecasting for the farmers of Black Water Township. She'd dreamt about rain. Perhaps it meant nothing – perhaps it did.

***

Jedidiah walked with them as far as the bell. He knelt down and spoke seriously to Hattie once more about how important it was for her not to tell anyone that her daddy was the Sin-Eater, or that Paloma was her granny. He told her if they did find out, they probably wouldn't let her stay in school and the other children might not want to be friends with her.

Hattie told them she'd remember. She loved her daddy dearly, and could never understand why people didn't like him, especially since he was doing everyone a favor by eating all those sins. Even though she was taught as Jedidiah and Paloma believed, that each person was responsible for his or her own acts in life, she was also taught to respect the beliefs of others, for her mother still was not sure that sin-eating wasn't necessary because of her own upbringing.

The schoolhouse wasn't far from the entrance to their part of the swamp. It was just a good twenty-minute stretch of the legs. The building was white-washed with a green-painted roof. Abigail saw several carriages in front of the building and some just arriving.

Before they went in, Abigail whispered to Hattie, "Remember, if anyone asks, your daddy's name is Jed Lucas, and he's a hunter."

"Ain't that a lie, Mama?"

She hesitated a moment then answered, "Not really. Jed is the first three letters of yer daddy's name. Kinda' like some of my cousins call me Abby even though my right'n proper name is Abigail. And about him bein' a hunter – he does more huntin' ta' put food on the table then he do sin-eaten, so it ain't a lie neither. Ya' understands?"

Hattie nodded. "Yes, Mama."

They entered the building. Abigail thought it strange that there weren't many children in the three-room schoolhouse. Classes for ages seven thru twelve were supposed to start at eight o'clock according to the newspaper Jedidiah read several weeks ago. But when she asked one of the mother's, she learned that there was a misprint, and they left out the word – registration. That's what today was for.

Abigail and Hattie took a seat at the back of the room. She looked about as others meandered around the room talking with each other. There were about twenty children accompanied by their mothers or fathers and a few were accompanied by both. When the clock struck eight, an announcement was made for all the children to accompany a woman named, Miss Barton, to one of the other rooms and for all the parents to find a seat. Abigail saw a woman, who looked to be in her mid to late thirties, start writing on the chalkboard. She was tall, thin and wore a pair of spectacles.

Abigail could read a word here and there and could write her own name, but she had a hard time trying to figure out what the teacher had written and was glad the woman turned and actually said who she was.

"I'm Miss Pearl-Lee Pickletta," the woman said pleasantly. "It's good to see so many new students registering today. An education is a doorway to your child's future. Even if farming is your child's ambition, without the proper education, who's to say that some unscrupulous businessman won't try and take advantage of them when they bring their harvests to market. Being able to read, write and do arithmetic will give your sons and daughters an edge in the ever changing ways of the world."

Abigail thought the woman made perfect sense, and she began to wonder if her Uncle Ennis had gotten a fair price on all those gator's he'd made a deal on. He could neither read nor write.

After Miss Pickletta finished her speech, she asked everyone to pick up a registration form from the desk and fill it out, as well as the list of school supplies they would need. Abigail was a little embarrassed when she sat back down with the paper and pen. As she looked around the room, she couldn't see where anyone was having trouble filling out the paper – even the men wearing overalls didn't seem to have any trouble.

Abigail took a quick glance at the paper of the woman sitting next to her, but the woman caught her. "I weren't cheatin'," Abigail whispered, not knowing what else to say.

The woman then leaned closer to Abigail and whispered, "These new fountain pens took me forever to get used to. A pencil, in my opinion, is much easier to work with. Would you like me to help you with your form?"

Abigail smiled. "I'd be much obliged." She handed the woman her paper and gave her the information the form requested. She was relieved when the woman didn't bat an eye after she told her Hattie's father's name was Jed Lucas. But when she asked where they lived Abigail hesitated a moment. "Why does they want ta' know that?"

"Just in case of an emergency," the woman replied. "They need to know where to reach you."

"Our place is kind'a hard ta' find," Abigail replied.

"Then a relative?"

"Ennis and Josie Hagen, in Shadrack," Abigail replied as she watched the woman write it down.

"There – all done," she replied, and then added, "I believe your daughter is the first student we've had from the Shadrack Community."

Abigail sighed. "My relations don't think much of schoolin', 'specially for girls. They think all a girl is good for is marryin', havin' babies, cookin' and cleanin'. My husband and I want better for our Hattie."

The woman gave her a smile. "You're a wise woman."

Abigail laughed then whispered, "If'n I was wise, I would'a learned ta' read and write better so's I could'a filled out this here paper myself."

The woman put a finger to her lips. "It'll be our secret!"

A few minutes later, Hattie came back into the room with another girl by her side. She was slightly taller, had blonde hair and light blue eyes.

"Mama, this is my new friend. Her name is Evelyn," Hattie said with a smile.

The little girl curtseyed. "It's a pleasure to meet you, Mrs. Lucas."

Abigail's heart pounded in her chest and she swallowed hard. "It's — it's a pleasure meetin' you too, Evelyn."

"Well, I declare!" exclaimed the woman who helped her. "Our daughters have become friends." She looked Hattie over. "What a beautiful little girl you have, Mrs. Lucas."

"I'm a thankin' ya'. You're Evelyn is right perty too," Abigail cleared her throat again. "What did ya' say yer' name was?"

"Oh, silly me! Where are my manners? I completely forgot to introduce myself. I'm Emmaline Welch."

"Mrs. Henry Welch - the mayor's wife?" Abigail asked to confirm it was the same Emmaline and the same Evelyn.

"The very same," she replied then laughed. "Please, don't hold that against us."

Abigail wanted to just grab up Hattie and run from the room. With her worry about it being discovered that Hattie's father was the sin-eater, she'd completely forgotten that they may encounter her true mother and sister.

"What's wrong, Mama?" Hattie asked. "Ya' don't look so good."

"You do look a little pale, Mrs. Lucas," Emmaline noticed.

Abigail fanned herself with the registration form. "Just a little warm, is all. Is this all we do today?"

"That's it," Emmaline replied. "Just turn in the form. Classes start officially the day after tomorrow."

Evelyn turned to her mother. "Mother, can Hattie come over and play today?"

"Can I, Mama?" Hattie pleaded.

"Maybe another time," said Abigail. She wanted to leave as soon as possible.

"She's right, Evelyn. We've a lot to do before school starts," said Emmaline. She turned to Abigail. "Perhaps this weekend?"

"We'll see," Abigail replied. "I'd be thankin' ya' agin, Mrs. Welch." She took the paper to the front and ushered Hattie out of the room quickly.

***

Jedidiah came home with a couple rabbits he'd caught and saw Hattie in the garden picking beans. "I thought you had school today?"

"It were just a registerin' day is all. The newspaper got it wrong," Hattie replied.

"I'm not surprised." He went into the house and saw Paloma snapping some of the beans Hattie had already picked.

"Where's Abigail?"

"By the pond. She wants you to meet her there."

Jedidiah noticed the concern in her voice. "Is there something wrong?"

"Best you talk to her about it. It'll watch Hattie."

Jedidiah hurried to the pond and found Abigail sitting on a fallen tree trunk. "A penny for your thoughts."

Abigail stood, put her arms around him and cried. "Hattie's ours, ain't she? Tell me she's ours through and through." Her tear filled eyes looked into his.

"You saw her birthmother, didn't you," he said softly.

"Hattie and Evelyn found each other. I didn't think I'd feel this way. When she told me who she was, I had such a feelin' of guilt wash over me. I thought I'd die!"

Jedidiah brushed a tear from her eye. "We have nothing to be guilty of. They thought her dead. We saved her. If we had taken her back you know what would have happened. We talked about this a long time ago."

"I know." She sniffed back a tear. "I just needed ya' to tell me agin. If I lost Hattie, I don't know what I'd do."

Jedidiah held her close. "We won't lose her."

When she had calmed, Abigail told Jedidiah what happened at the schoolhouse and how Evelyn and Emmaline requested Hattie come to their house the up-coming weekend. They prayed about it and talked about it. They decided that it would be wrong to keep the two sisters apart if they wanted to be friends, and it was only fair for Hattie's true mother to get to know what a fine girl her daughter was becoming under their care.

Chapter 16

It was Friday and the last day of the first week of school. Miss Pickletta's class consisted of twenty students who ranged in ages between ten and twelve years. Those younger than ten were in Miss Barton's class and those above the age of twelve were in Mr. Evan's class.

It was the last hour of class, and Miss Pickletta had her class put away their McGuffey Readers. She smiled as she addressed the class. "Most of you have done exceptionally well this first week. Learning the basic skills to get you through life are necessities. However, creativity inspires invention. So, though it is not part of the school's curriculum, art is on my agenda."

Hattie's seat was in the back of the room, and she sat next to Evelyn. She leaned over and whispered, "I like our teacher, but sometimes I ain't got a notion 'bout what she says. What'd she say?"

"She means drawing pictures," Evelyn whispered back. "Actually, most everyone thinks it's just to keep us busy while she grades our papers so she doesn't have to do them at home over the weekend."

"I like drawin'. Me and Cousin Caleb draw pictures in the dirt sometimes," Hattie replied.

Their teacher passed out paper and colored pencils to each student and instructed them to draw a picture of a happy thought. They spent about thirty minutes creating their masterpieces. Afterward, Miss Pickletta had the students show and describe what their picture was about. The boys went first. Several of them drew pictures of themselves fishing or climbing trees. One boy drew a picture and said it was Susie Wheeler kissing a frog. Susie had a wart on her lip. Everyone laughed, and Miss Pickletta promptly made him stand in the corner.

The girls were next. Most drew themselves picking flowers. Mary-Beth Coulter drew a horse, and Evelyn said her picture was she and Hattie playing on the swings at the park. Hattie was last. Her teacher looked at the picture and was surprised. It wasn't the usual stick drawing that the others made. She could tell the girl had a genuine talent, though raw, and if encouraged she would become better with more practice. "It looks like you've drawn a picture of a wedding ceremony. Is it yours some day?"

"No ma'am," Hattie replied with a smile. "I was thinking of you."

The class started to laugh. Miss Pickletta clapped her hands and they silenced. Hattie was made to stand in the corner, but she didn't understand why. A few minutes later, the bell tolled for school to be dismissed.

Hattie walked out still not understanding why her picture was so upsetting. Robbie Harp, the boy who was also made to stand in the corner, ran past her. He turned for a moment as he continued running backwards and shouted, "Good joke on ol' Pickle, Hattie! See ya' Monday!"

"Joke? What joke?"

Evelyn joined her. "I thought you liked Miss Pickletta?"

"I do," she replied.

"Then how come you drew the picture?" she asked curiously. "Didn't you know she's a spinster? She's never had a bow in her life."

Hattie sighed. "I didn't know. I didn't do it ta' be mean. It just popped in my head. I best go say I'm sorry."

Hattie went in and apologized. She told her teacher that the happy thought she had was being here in school and the next thing she knew she'd drawn the picture. Miss Pickletta sensed the sincerity of her words, and in turn, she apologized for making her stand in the corner.

As Hattie turned to leave, Pearl-Lee took another look at the picture and smiled. It was a happy thought after all, and she giggled slightly. Before Hattie walked out the door she called to her. "Who is it I'm supposed to be marrying?"

Hattie stopped at the door. "I don't know," she said with a shrug. "I'll see ya' Monday, Miss Pickletta."

Pearl-Lee started to throw the picture away, but just couldn't do it. As she walked out of the schoolhouse and started to cross the street, she couldn't take her mind off of the silly notion that she would ever be married. She was simply just too plain and too shy to attract any man, and she'd resigned herself to that sad fact. She stared at the picture a little more closely. She hadn't noticed it before, but the woman in the picture did somewhat resemble her. There was also a familiarity about the man in the picture, but who was he? Suddenly she stopped in the middle of the street and gasped. She recognized who it was. "Mr. Burnham – the apothecary?" She looked at it a little more closely. "Why would she imagine him with me?" She knew it was completely ridiculous, albeit a pleasant notion. Mr.

Jonas Burnham was a fairly handsome widower with sandy hair and green eyes. He also had a delightful thirteen-year-old daughter named Carrie-Ann. She had the girl in her class for two years, but this year she'd moved into the Mr. Evan's class.

Pearl-Lee's attention was still focused on the picture as she continued crossing the street. She hadn't noticed the carriage coming toward her. She was suddenly snapped out of her contemplative state by the whinny of the horse when the driver had to rein it in quickly to keep from running her down. She fell backwards on the ground and barely escaped being trampled on by the horse.

The man quickly jumped out of the carriage to help her up. "I'm so sorry, Miss Pearl-Lee!" he exclaimed. "Are you alright?"

"I'm unharmed," she replied. It took her a moment to gather her senses, but when she looked up she saw Mr. Burnham - the man she'd just been thinking about.

"Thank the Lord," he sighed. "I shouldn't have been driving so fast."

"It's quite alright, Mr. Burnham. It was completely my fault. My attention was distracted."

"Please, let me make it up to you. My daughter and I always have dinner at the hotel on Friday evenings. It would be my honor if you'd joined us."

Pearl-Lee was practically speechless. She'd never been invited to dinner by anyone. "I – I don't know."

"Please, if you say no, I'll feel guilty for the rest of my life," the man said sincerely. "Besides, Carrie-Ann has always considered you her favorite teacher. It would please her – both of us greatly if you said yes."

Pearl-Lee smiled brightly. "Then I dare not say no!"

"Good. We'll pick you up at the boarding house at five." He walked with her across the street to make sure she was truly all right. When she assured him she was fine, he went back to his carriage. Before he drove off, he spoke once more. "Miss Pearl-Lee, you have a beautiful smile." He snapped the reins and the horse trotted off.

Pearl-Lee stood there stunned as she watched Mr. Burnham's carriage trot off. She slowly raised the picture and looked at it once more.

The Swamp

It was Saturday morning. Hattie got up extra early to do her chores. She moved from task to task and when she was finished, she asked her mama what she could do to help finish her morning chores. Abigail knew what spurred her on to get done. All Hattie talked about was visiting Evelyn today.

When everything was done, Abigail had her bathe and put on her best pair of overalls. She didn't want her to wear her school dresses and take the chance on tearing them in play. After she finished putting Hattie's hair in braids, they started for the Welch's residence.

Welch Residence

"Evelyn!" Emmaline laughed. "You are absolutely going to wear a hole in the carpet going back and forth to the window."

Evelyn was excited. "Do you think her mother will let her come?"

"I don't see why not." Emmaline took a sip of tea.

Erma Welch clicked her tongue and whispered sharply to her daughter-in-law, "Why in the world you allowed her to play with one of those – Shadrack people is beyond me! There are so many other proper children for her to associate with."

"Mother Welch, Mrs. Lucas and her daughter, Hattie, are very nice people," Emmaline scolded. "Do you want Evelyn to grow up being – a snob?"

"Associating with the right people isn't being snobbish! It's being prudent," her mother-in-law snipped.

"She's here!" Evelyn shouted.

She started to run to the door, but her grandmamma stopped her. "Come here at once, young lady! Answering the door is the butler's duty. That's what we pay him for."

Emmaline rolled her eyes, but said nothing. Evelyn pouted as she came back to her seat and sat next to her mother.

A moment later, the butler came into the parlor. "Excuse me, Mrs. Lucas and her daughter, Miss Hattie, have come to call on Miss Evelyn."

"Show them in," Erma Welch said in her usual tone of superiority.

Abigail went over in her mind as to how she would talk to these rich folks. She didn't have fancy words. She then decided that she would act the same to Evelyn's mother as she did when taking Hattie to visit one of her friends in Shadrack. She wasn't a fancy person, so there was no sense in acting like she was one.

"How'do, Mrs. Welch," Abigail said pleasantly to Emmaline. "I'm a pleasured ta' meet ya' agin."

Abigail had barely spoken her greeting when she heard Erma Welch exclaim, "What on earth is that child wearing!"

"Oh, don't worry, Mrs. Welch. They's clean," Abigail said brightly. "Ya' knows how youn'ins is when they play. It ain't proper for a girl ta' climb a tree in a dress, if they have a mind ta' do so. 'Sides, her dresses is fer school anyhow."

Erma rolled her eyes. "Climbing trees is improper for a young lady to do at any time!"

"I don't know 'bout that, ma'am," Abigail disagreed. "Knowin' how ta' climb a tree comes in handy when yer bein' chased by a wild dog or some other critter."

Emmaline snickered slightly and grinned at her mother-in-law. "She's quite right, Mother Welch. In that area, I've been sorely lacking in Evelyn's education."

Abigail smiled. She knew Emmaline was poking fun, but not toward her - towards her mother-in-law. She looked at Emmaline. "Hattie can show her how. She can shimmy up a tree faster than her Cousin Caleb."

Erma Welch pretended to ignore what she said, but was quite displeased with her daughter-in-law and decided to speak to her son about this association this evening.

Evelyn turned to Hattie. "Come on, let's play in my room."

Abigail kissed her daughter on the forehead. "Ya' mind yer manner, Hattie, ya' hear? And do what Evelyn's mama says. I'll be back in a couple a hours."

"I will, Mama."

When the girls started to leave the room, Erma cleared her throat and gave Evelyn a stern look. "Manners, Evelyn!"

The girl curtseyed and asked permission to leave the room. When granted the two left and headed up the stairs.

Evelyn's Room

"Wow!" Hattie exclaimed. She'd never seen such a large, fancy room. Evelyn had dolls and stuffed animals in every corner. There was a desk and a small, round table with two chairs that was set with cups and plates. She looked at the bed. "You share this room with anybody?"

"No," Evelyn shrugged. "This is my room."

Hattie when over to the large bed and pushed on the mattress. It was fancied up with pink and white coverings and a canopy over top. "You kin sleep three across or five the other way!"

Evelyn laughed. She was about to say something when the butler arrived with milk and cookies and set it down on her tea table. The two talked about their likes and dislikes and then the subject of their teacher was mentioned.

"Did you hear about Mrs. Pickletta?" Evelyn said as she picked up another cookie.

"No, did somethin' happen to her?"

"Did it! I heard my mother and grandmamma talking this morning to Mrs. Caraway when she stopped by earlier. Miss Pickletta was seen coming out of the hotel's restaurant with Mr. Burnham and Carrie-Ann last night. And then someone saw him kiss her hand outside the boarding house where she lives."

"So?" Hattie finished the last of her milk and wiped her mouth on her sleeve.

"So!" Evelyn jumped up from her chair. "Hattie, don't you see? The picture you drew. It might be coming true!"

Hattie laughed and stood also. "That's silly. It were just a picture. Come on. Let's go outside and play."

Chapter 17

A month had passed since Hattie had started school. Miss Pickletta's class anxiously looked forward to Fridays. Not only because it was the end of the week, but it was the day when their teacher would have them develop their artistic abilities. They didn't care what they drew, but most everyone wanted to see what Hattie would draw next. It appeared to them that everything she drew came to pass.

The class had thought it funny when she'd drawn the wedding picture of their teacher, but now for the past several weeks, Miss Pickletta had been seen in the company of Mr. Burnham and his daughter. The second week she'd drawn a picture of her classmate, Bobby Brown, fishing with his father. After class, Bobby told her that he wished his father would go fishing with him, but he never did because he was too busy. However, the following Monday, the boy spread the word that Hattie's picture had come true. His father had finally taken him fishing, and he'd caught a ten pound catfish.

The third week Miss Pickletta had them draw pictures with an animal in it. Hattie drew a picture of a Collie sleeping on the schoolhouse steps. When they were released from class, they hesitated at the door when they saw the dog in the exact position where Hattie had drawn it.

This was now the fourth week and their teacher wanted them to draw something from nature such as trees or flowers. Hattie started to feel apprehensive about drawing. It seemed that whenever she began to draw, her mind would go blank until what she was drawing was finished.

Every day at recess that week, everyone, except Evelyn, had asked her to draw his or her picture. At first it was fun because she always drew something good, until Robby Harp asked her to draw one of him the day before. But instead of drawing him, she drew a woodshed. Why she drew it - she hadn't a clue. She tried drawing him a second time, but it still came out as a woodshed. The next morning when he came back to school, he told her he knew why she drew the woodshed. His father had taken him in there and walloped his backside for chasing his little sister with a dead garden snake.

Hattie decided to draw a tree for the project that day. Before she started, she closed her eyes and thought, *Just draw a tree! Nothing else, just a tree!* She put her pencil to the paper. When she had finished, she'd drawn a tree, but there was also someone falling out of it. Who it was, she didn't know. Why she drew it, she didn't know that either. She scribbled over the picture and turned her paper over to draw on the back. *Tree only!* She thought, but she had drawn the same thing.

Hattie was feeling sick. She didn't want anyone to see this picture. She raised her hand and asked if she could go home early, but no such luck. The teacher said there was only an hour left and she wouldn't feel any better by leaving early. Then she had an idea. She folded her paper in half and carefully tore the portion of the paper where the boy was falling. When it was her turn to show her picture, she just showed the half with the tree.

When class was finally dismissed, she crumpled up both halves and threw them in the trash when she thought no one was looking. But Robbie Harp, who'd spent most of the day in the corner, had seen her throw it away. He went to the trash, picked the crumpled halves and put them together when Hattie left. He quickly ran outside and called to those who hadn't left the school grounds to look at the picture. It didn't look like any of them that they could tell.

"Anybody thinkin' about climbing a tree today?" Robbie asked.

"If I was, I ain't now!" said another boy.

Welch Residence

Hattie walked home with Evelyn. She was given permission to play with her for a couple of hours before she went home. They talked about the picture Hattie drew, and she expressed her concerns, but Evelyn just told her not to worry, that it was just a picture like she'd said before.

When they reached her house, they put their books down and headed to the back yard to pick clover and tie them into bracelets and necklaces for their mothers.

Erma Welch looked out the window at the two. She just couldn't understand how Emmaline could be so fond of that child from hillbilly stock when there were so many other girls Evelyn could associate with.

Henry entered the room. "What are you looking at, Mother?"

"Her!" Erma replied.

Henry looked out the window and saw Hattie. "Why? What's wrong with her?"

"She's not the right type of person for our Evelyn to be associated with, and Emmaline just can't see it!"

Henry laughed. "She's just a child. I've only met her a time or two, but she seems polite enough."

"Polite isn't the point! She's giving Evelyn ridiculous ideas. Do you know that she asked the other day if she could have a pair of overalls so she could climb a tree! And she's starting to imitate her. She said ain't the other day, and she's starting to drop the 'g' off some of her words when she speaks!"

Henry grinned. "Now ain't that just terrible! I'm thinkin' I'm just gonna have ta' speak ta' Emmaline 'bout that!"

His mother frowned. "That's not funny, Henry! Don't be rude."

He laughed. "I'm sorry, Mother, but she's just a little girl. If Evelyn likes her, so do I."

Erma turned and left the room abruptly. Her son listened to her no more than Emmaline did on the subject. Henry looked out the window and saw the two girls laughing and playing together. He smiled momentarily, until a memory filtered to his consciousness about the child of theirs that had died. He remembered thinking how he would have loved to see his twins play together. He couldn't watch anymore. He went to his study and locked the door.

***

"I wish you didn't have to go, Hattie," said Evelyn as they walked toward the house to gather her friend's books.

"Mama worries about me if I'm gone too long," she replied. "Besides, I got chores."

"Grandmamma says that chores are servants' work."

"My granny says, if a person doesn't do chores that means they's lazy," Hattie replied; then as an afterthought added, "I don't mean nothin' against you'n yer ways, mind you."

Evelyn smiled. "I know you didn't. That's just our grandmothers' talking."

They started walking toward the edge of the Welch's property line and then Evelyn asked curiously, "How come you never invite me to your house?"

Hattie hesitated a moment. She'd like nothing better than to have Evelyn over, but she remembered what her parents said. If anyone found out that her daddy was the sin-eater, they probably wouldn't like her anymore, and she didn't want to lose Evelyn as a friend.

"I'd like to, but I live in the swamp. I'm thinkin' yer grandmother would have a – apoplexy," Hattie said using one of the big words she'd learned in class.

Evelyn laughed. "She would."

A moment later, they heard the sin-eater's bell in the distance. They listened to hear if it would ring again, which it did.

"Someone's dyin'," Hattie said. "I hope they don't."

"I hope they don't either, but if the Sin-Eater says some good prayers, maybe they won't. That's what my mother says. She believes that it was his prayers that saved her when I was born."

Hattie felt a sense of pride wash over her about what her father does. But then she became curious. "What do you think about the Sin-Eater?"

"I don't rightly know," she said honestly. "Grandmamma and Aunt Sally say he's a man to stay away from because he's full of sins and is destined for – hell." Evelyn crossed herself hastily after saying the "H" word and continued. "My mother says he does the town a favor, and my father says he's a necessary evil," she finished. "How about you?"

"Me and my family, except for my cousins, don't believe in Sin-Eatin'," she replied. "My daddy says a person owns their own sins and only the Lord can forgive them. He just does what your mama says – he does the town a favor for their own piece of mind..." then she caught herself. "...I mean that's what the Sin-Eater does. It's the prayin' what helps."

Evelyn shook her head. "It's confusing."

They reached the edge of the property and the girls said good-bye. Hattie ran down the street and crossed a field to take a shortcut home. She found the overalls she'd left behind a large tree and changed into them so she wouldn't ruin her dress. She climbed over the wall that separated the town from the swamp and made her way home.

The Swamp

Paloma put supper on the table. She stepped out to the porch and saw

Abigail pushing Hattie on her swing. She called for them to wash up and come in. She said there was no sense in waiting for Jedidiah. He could be back in a matter of minutes or hours, depending on where he was called to go.

They had just sat down at the table and joined hands to give praise, when Paloma looked toward the door. "Good – he's right on time." She gave Hattie a wink.

The girl jumped up from the table and hid behind the door. She loved it when her granny told her in advance when her father was about to enter the house.

Jedidiah opened the door and saw two of his loved ones sitting at the table. He had a feeling he knew where the third one was. He quickly turned around and caught his playful little girl in mid-flight as she attempted to jump on his back – again. "Gotcha!" he said as both of them laughed.

"How did you know I was there?" she giggled. "Are you a Gypsy too?"

"No! It's called experience."

He kissed her on the forehead and both sat down at the table. The blessing was said and Paloma started dishing out plates of stew.

"So, where did you go?" Abigail asked as she passed Hattie the bowl of greens.

"The Owens Farm on the other side of Shadrack." Jedidiah took a piece of bread from the plate.

"Mr. Owens sometimes hires my uncle durin' harvest time," Abigail said. "Other than that, I can't say as I knows'em well. Who passed?"

"Hopefully, no one," he replied. "Their twelve year old son had a bad accident this afternoon."

Hattie was just about to take a bite of her stew and stopped. She felt her heart beating rapidly in her chest as she remembered her drawing. "Did he – fall out of a tree?"

"I think that's what I heard. You know how it is. No one goes out of their way to converse with me any more than they have to." Jedidiah saw his daughter's face turn almost ashen and tears started to form in her eyes. "What is it, Hattie? Do you know him?"

"It's my fault!" she shouted. She jumped up from the table. "I made him fall!" She went to the door, opened it and ran outside.

Jedidiah and Abigail looked at each other in shock and then at Paloma.

"Don't look at me!" she said just as surprised as they were. "I didn't see that coming."

The three of them went to the door and saw Hattie sitting on her swing crying. Jedidiah and Abigail went to her. It had taken a few minutes, but they'd finally gotten her calmed down enough to tell them what she meant. Hattie explained about the pictures she'd been drawing at school, and how everything she drew happened. They tried their best to convince her that she didn't do anything, but nothing they said changed her belief that it was her fault.

Paloma had been standing in the background listening. She thought to herself, *Could it be possible?* She walked toward the sad faced, teary-eyed girl and gave her a smile. "You just might be," she said aloud.

"Might be what?" Jedidiah asked as he stood.

"I'll tell you after supper, I'm starving," she said as she turned.

"I ain't hungry!" Hattie exclaimed sniffing back a tear. "I caused Mama ta' be hurt by the gator and that boy ta' fall out of the tree."

"Of course you did," Paloma said agreeing with her.

"Paloma!" Jedidiah and Abigail said simultaneously. They were astonished she would say something like that. Hattie also looked up at her in surprise.

"You want to know more?" Paloma turned and walked toward the house. "Finish supper first."

Jedidiah motioned for Abigail to follow. He knew his old friend was toying with the child's mind. She'd done that so many times to him when he'd first come to live with her. She'd agree with him and then subtly change his way of thinking. They left Hattie on the swing and went into the house.

Hattie sat there and looked down at the ground. She wanted to cry some more, but all her tears seemed to have all dried up. She just knew she was responsible for what happened to the boy, but she wondered why her granny thought she did too and wanted to know what else she had to say about it. She felt a rumbling in her stomach. Her appetite was back, but not only for supper, for information from Granny Paloma.

***

When the dishes where cleared away from the table, cleaned and put in their proper places, Paloma sat down with her family to prove what she suspected about Hattie. She asked the girl to get her slate board, some paper and a pencil to draw with. At first the child was afraid because she never had much control over what she might draw. But Paloma told her not to be afraid. They were going to play a type of guessing game.

Paloma closed her eyes for a moment. She took the slate board, wrote on it and handed it to Jedidiah telling him to keep what she had written to himself. She then turned to Hattie. "I want you to draw me a picture of the chair by the hearth."

Hattie thought it harmless so she picked up her pencil and started drawing. When she'd finished, she'd not only drawn the chair, but their cat jumping into it, though she didn't know why she did. She showed it to her family.

"Very good picture, Hattie." Abigail was impressed by her daughter's artistic ability.

A few moments later, their black cat, Esmeralda, entered the house through the open window, walked to the chair and jumped into it. Jedidiah's eyes widened as he looked at the picture and what was written on the slate board.

"See!" Hattie exclaimed. "Look what I made the cat do."

"I don't think so," her father said as he turned the slate board around.

Hattie looked at the writing. It read - cat jumps in chair. "Did we both make her do it?"

"No," Paloma replied. "We both predicted she'd do it. You, baby girl, I believe are a seer, or fortune-teller as I am. We can foresee the future to some extent. I can sense things. Yours comes to you through your drawings."

"But how do you know we aren't causin' things ta' happen?" Hattie asked.

Paloma thought for a moment to consider what the child could draw that would never happen. "I want you to draw Esmeralda sitting on this table. You know, that she knows better than to do that."

Hattie took another sheet of paper and drew the cat sitting on the table, but she also drew her mother knocking over a cup of water. She turned her head to look at the cat, and saw her nestled comfortably in the chair ignoring them. Abigail couldn't see if the cat was moving so she leaned forward a bit and overturned the cup of water. Hattie then showed her artwork. The only thing in the picture that didn't happen was the cat jumping on the table. Paloma explained that if Hattie had shown her mother the artwork before she leaned forward, she would have moved the cup first, which would have made the outcome of the picture false.

Paloma had the girl draw several things that could happen, but more than likely wouldn't. They all laughed when she'd told Hattie to draw her father standing on his head. She also had her draw an alligator by the fireplace, a snake crawling through the window and snow falling outside. In most of pictures she drew, there was some small element that did happen in them. The picture with the alligator, showed the cat licking her paw, which it was doing. The one with the snake had a butterfly sitting on the windowsill. It landed there for a moment and fluttered off. The picture of falling snow showed a rabbit nibbling in the garden. Seeing that, Abigail quickly ran outside and chased it out. The final picture with Jedidiah showed nothing out of the ordinary and he said he had no compulsion what-so-ever to stand on his head.

Hattie was relieved that she didn't cause the things she drew to happen, but she told them she was concerned about having to draw things in class on Fridays and tell about them. She didn't mind drawing good things - it was the bad things she worried about. But Paloma told her, that if she drew something that wasn't good, such as the boy falling from the tree, it could be a warning for that person not to do something, thus changing the outcome of the picture. On the other hand, if she drew something good and she told that person, it could also change the outcome and the good thing wouldn't happen. She said with the gift of being able to see the future comes the responsibility of when to tell it and when not to, and she would have to use her best judgment on that.

When Hattie went to bed that night, she prayed that if she drew anything else that looked into the future, it would only be pleasant things. But even though she prayed for that, she doubted it would happen.

***

Paloma couldn't sleep again for the third night in a row and got up. She went outside and sat in her rocking chair on the porch to listen to the sounds of the night. The rustling of the leaves in the breeze, the crickets chirping throughout the woods, and a lone bullfrog croaked somewhere in the swamp, blended together in a harmony that not many people would appreciate. She closed her eyes hoping the symphony of the night would bring on sleep. Rain had saturated her dreams on and off for the past two months. She was becoming concerned. It was just about harvest time for the local farmers. She wondered if she should warn them about it or not.

If they harvested too early, their crops would be worth less. If it rained too much before the harvest their whole crop could be ruined. But this dream of rain was not the same as what she'd dreamt in her youth. It could mean something totally different. She decided it best to think about it.

Chapter 18

Hattie had a lot to think about when she went to school the following Monday. By this time, all the students knew about the boy who fell out of the tree, and Robbie Harp had spread the word that Hattie had drawn it before it happened. Students from all three classes, except Evelyn, asked her if she'd draw their picture. But this time she said no. She didn't want to take the chance that she would draw something else bad. But then Friday finally arrived and unfortunately Miss Pickletta's art assignment for the day was to draw pictures of classmates. She had no choice.

She closed her eyes and said to herself, *Come on Hattie, just draw something normal!* She already knew who she wanted to draw - Evelyn. She never seemed to draw anything about her future. As she started drawing, she planned to just draw her face, but her pencil seemed to have a mind of its own and for a few moments she seemed to go blank. When she'd regained her senses the picture was finished. She looked at it. She'd drawn Evelyn alright, but she was standing on the school house steps with Robbie Harp and Billy Tate. Why she drew them, she didn't know, but it seemed a harmless enough picture. After she presented it to the class as usual, she asked Evelyn if she wanted it.

Evelyn said she would be glad to have it, but she'd like to edit it a little. She took the picture and tore off the half with the two boys. She showed Hattie the half with just her in it and grinned. "What do you think?"

She snickered. "Looks much better without them two eye sores in it."

When class was over, Hattie said a quick good-bye to Evelyn and ran out of the building before anybody had a chance to ask her to draw something again.

Evelyn crumpled the half with the boys on it and tossed it in the wastebasket. As soon as she started down the schoolhouse steps, Robbie and Billy called to her and she stopped. "What do you want now?" They were always asking her if she knew where Hattie lived.

"Look," Robbie said holding the crumpled paper. "This is us. We are in the exact spots she drew us on, and I'm holding this paper in my hand just as it is in the drawing."

"So," she shrugged. "Everybody saw that picture. You're just being a copycat." She started walking away, but the two followed her.

"Come on, Evelyn, you're her best friend. How come you don't know where she lives? Aren't you even curious?" Robbie asked.

"It doesn't matter if I am or not. You know she lives somewhere in the swamp. My parents and grandmamma wouldn't let me go there even if I did know."

Robbie stopped and laughed. "Miss Goody-Goody Two Shoes. I bet you do everything your parents tell you to do."

Billy nudged Robbie and added, "Yeah, and I bet when she gets home she sits on a pillow like a little princess!"

Both started to swagger and said together, "Little Miss Muffet, sits on her tuffet, eating her curds and whey…."

Evelyn turned abruptly and put a fist on her hip. "I do not! As a matter of fact, I climb trees sometimes with Hattie even though my grandmother tells me not to!" But internally she knew they were right. She rarely, if ever disobeyed, and she only climbed a tree once.

"Then prove it!" Billy dared. "Help us find out where she lives."

"Why should I want to help you two corner dwellers?"

"She's hiding something - that's why!" Billy exclaimed. He pointed a finger at her. "And you can't tell me you're not curious."

She knocked his hand away and thought for a moment. He had her on that point. She was curious, and she actually followed Hattie once to a certain point before she entered the swamp – but went no further. Black Water Swamp was a fearsome place. Even the grown-ups avoided it and talked about it with gloom and doom. "If I decided to help you – and I'm not saying I will – where do I come in on your plans? Why don't you just follow her yourselves?"

"We've tried for weeks!" Robbie exclaimed. "But she runs too fast and we can't keep up. She goes to your house after school sometimes. We figure that when she leaves, she won't be running, and we can follow without her knowing. We just need you to tell us what day she's coming over."

Evelyn raised her eyebrows. "You're actually going to follow her into Black Water Swamp?"

Robbie and Billy looked at each other. Their curiosity about Hattie overwhelmed their fear of it. "That's the plan," Robbie replied. "So will you do it?"

"I'll think about it." Evelyn turned and walked away.

Welch Residence

Evelyn walked into the house and heard voices coming from the parlor. She was about to enter when she caught a glimpse of her Aunt Sally sitting next to her grandmother on the settee and her Uncle Victor in a chair across from them. She didn't mind her uncle, but she was tired of her aunt treating her like a five year old. She started to tip-toe passed when she heard them mention the name – Hattie. She decided to keep her presence hidden and listened.

"I'm telling you, Sally, that Hattie is going to be the ruin of our little Evelyn," Erma Welch said and then took a sip of tea. "I don't know why Emmaline insists on letting her come for visits."

"Well, let me tell you what I heard," Sally returned. "I was talking to Mrs. Barnaby this morning. She said that Mrs. Tate told her that Mrs. Harp's son, Robbie, said that Hattie drew a picture of a boy falling out of a tree. She said she didn't think anything of it, until she read in the newspaper that the Owens boy actually did fall from a tree."

"I read that story," said Victor. "The boy is expected to live, though it's doubtful he'll walk again. But what has that got to do with that little girl?"

"According to Mrs. Harp," replied Sally, "Robbie says the girl draws pictures that come true all the time."

"Strange, Evelyn has never mentioned it," replied Erma. She hesitated a moment. "You don't think that swamp girl has bewitched her, do you?"

Victor laughed. "You women and your obsession with witches! You labeled Paloma Day, and now you're trying to label a child."

"Mr. Gooch!" Sally said stiffly as she contradicted her husband. "Paloma Day has mysterious ways about her and you know it. What if that child, Hattie, is cut from the same cloth? Suppose she caused that boy to fall from the tree with her drawing?"

Victor rolled his eyes and stood. "That's ridiculous! And I don't want the two of you starting any rumors about the child."

Erma sighed. "I don't intend anything of the sort. All I want the two of you to do is talk some sense into Emmaline and Henry. When it comes to Evelyn's choice of friends, by whom I mean that swamp girl, they turn a deaf ear to me. She's a bad influence."

Sally took Erma's hand in hers. "You can count on me talking to Emmaline." Sally turned to her husband. "Will you talk to Henry, Mr. Gooch?"

"No, I won't," Victor replied abruptly. "As a matter of fact, I know why he won't do anything to discourage Evelyn's friendship with the girl." He walked to the window and looked out. "He told me that when he sees them together it reminds him of what it could have been like if the other had survived."

"Victor!" Erma scolded sharply. "That's a subject not to be mentioned in this house or anywhere!"

He looked back at Erma and his wife. "You asked! I told you. Leave me out of your witch hunt." He pulled out his pocket watch and checked the time. "Mrs. Gooch, I'll be back for you at five o'clock after the council meeting." He walked to the door and then turned back to the two women. "Take my advice. Just leave Henry and Emmaline to raise Evelyn as they see fit." He walked out the door and closed it behind him.

***

Evelyn had just ducked around the corner and was relieved her uncle hadn't seen her. She was furious with her grandmother and Aunt Sally. *There's nothing wrong with Hattie,* she thought. *She may be poor, but she's fun to be with and never asks a thing except to be friends.*

As she walked upstairs to her room, she thought about what Robbie and Billy had asked of her. She decided she'd help them, but she was going also. Not necessarily to satisfy her curiosity, but to make sure Robbie and Billy didn't make up something and start some wild rumor about her themselves.

She sat down at the desk in her room and opened one of her study books, but then she thought of the comment she'd heard her uncle make. *What did he mean by – the other?* She wondered if she'd had a brother or sister who'd died that no one told her about.

Chapter 19

Welch Residence

Evelyn sat at the breakfast table staring into her bowl of rice and raisins as she slowly pushed a raisin around with her spoon. The weekend was over too soon, and she was nervous about how she was going to respond to Robbie and Billy. One moment she was going to do it and the next she'd change her mind. It was an invasion of Hattie's privacy.

"Evelyn, quit dawdling, you'll be late for school," said her grandmother as she sipped her morning coffee. But her granddaughter was still in a daze. "Evelyn!"

She snapped out of her revere and took a bite.

"What are you in such deep thought about, dear?" asked her mother.

"Oh, just contemplatin'," she replied.

Her grandmother rolled her eyes. "Heaven's child, there is a G on the end of that word!"

Henry and Emmaline covered their mouths with a napkin to hide their amusement when their daughter repeated the word over emphasizing the -ing.

"About what?" her father asked after overcoming his amusement.

Evelyn was at a loss as to what to say. She didn't want to lie, but neither could she tell the truth. "Oh, just kid stuff," she replied with a shrug. "You know how it is. May I be excused? I'm gonna be late for school."

"Going to!" her grandmother corrected again. "Evelyn, you don't live in a swamp. You go to an excellent school and young ladies should always speak properly."

"Yes, ma'am!" She was about to leave the room, but her grandmother called her back and turned her head for the usual morning good-bye kiss on the cheek. Evelyn really didn't feel like kissing her. She was still angry with her grandmother over the things she'd overheard her say about Hattie to her aunt and uncle a few days ago. But she kissed her anyway and left the room.

Erma shook her head. "You see what I mean! That swamp girl is going to be the ruin of Evelyn. Her speech is becoming atrocious."

"Mother, if you will remember, I was worse when I was her age," Henry replied.

"Never-the-less, you were a young boy. It's natural. Evelyn is a proper young lady. There's a difference."

"It's just a phase, Mother Welch," Emmaline defended her daughter.

Henry gave Emmaline a quick wink and said to his mother, "Does that mean I can start droppin' my G's? It's easier sayin'."

Erma frowned. "That was not one bit funny, Henry."

Both he and Emmaline, laughed lightly and stood, bidding his mother good-day. Henry was leaving for a council meeting, and Emmaline was going to her morning sewing circle.

Erma sat back in her chair. Paloma Day almost ruined her life, and she wasn't about to let some swamp girl ruin her little Evelyn. "I'll think of something," she mumbled.

School

Evelyn entered the classroom and saw Hattie sitting at their desk. She sat down beside her.

Hattie saw a pained expression on Evelyn's face. "What's wrong? Ya' don't look so good."

"I've got an upset stomach," Evelyn replied. She didn't exactly lie, for she felt like she had nervous knots balling up inside her.

"Peppermint tea," Hattie recommended. "That's what my granny gives me when I'm feelin' poorly."

"I'll see if we have any when I get home," she replied.

Hattie had planned on visiting with Evelyn at her house this afternoon. "Maybe I should wait another day ta' come over."

"That would probably be better," Evelyn replied. Today she had to give the two boys her answer. She hated what she was about to do. She figured eventually Robbie and Billy would discover where Hattie lived. She just didn't want them to tell some wild story about her if they did.

A moment later, Mrs. Pickletta tapped her pointer on the desk for the students to come to order. "Class, today we will start with a geography lesson." She picked up a book. "This is a picture book of Australia...."

***

When class was over, Hattie told Evelyn that she hoped she felt better tomorrow and ran out the door. Evelyn giggled slightly as she watched Robbie and Billy take off after her, but even in a dress, Hattie could still run like a jackrabbit. When she saw her friend disappear behind one of the buildings, she started for home. A few moments later, Robbie and Billy caught up to her.

Robbie grabbed her by the arm and turned her around. "I thought you were going to help us?" he asked angrily. "She was supposed to go home with you today."

Evelyn jerked her arm away. "I said I would think about it!"

"So you've decided not to?" Billy asked.

"I didn't say that," she replied. "But I'm going to do it on my terms. I'm going with you."

Robbie folded his arms and laughed. "You're going into the swamp."

"But you're a girl!" Billy joined in with his friend's laughter.

Evelyn pursed her lips. "So is Hattie. And she lives in the swamp." Evelyn grinned. "Besides – do either of you know how to track?"

Robbie and Billy looked at each other and shrugged. "No," Robbie replied. "What's that got to do with anything?"

"Then how do you expect to follow her without her knowing? If she found out that you were behind her, she could lead you in a circle and lose you in the woods if she had a mind to," Evelyn shot back.

"And you know how to track," Robbie said in a sarcastic tone.

It was Evelyn's turn to grin. "As a matter of fact, I do know a little about it. That's one of the games Hattie and I play. Every time we played hide-and-seek, she'd find me instantly. She told me she tracked me to my hiding places. That's when she started teaching me how."

"So what are we waiting for? Let's do it now!" Billy exclaimed.

"No," Evelyn replied. "I'm not dressed for it. We'll wait until tomorrow. This is what I have in mind…."

The Swamp

Abigail was tending to the garden when she heard Hattie call her name. "Hi, sweetpea. I thought you was goin' ta' Evelyn's ta'day?"

"She was feelin' poorly," Hattie replied. "Where's daddy?"

"He just left a few minutes ago ta' go frog giggin'." Abigail heard her sigh in disappointment. She smiled and added, "Put yer things up. If'n ya' hurry, ya' might catch up ta' him." Abigail laughed lightly when her daughter took off like a shot into the house. A moment later, she flew out again and disappeared into the woods.

Paloma came out on the porch. She looked toward Abigail. "Was that Hattie or a breeze that blew in then out of the house so quickly?"

"A little of both, I suspects. I told her she could go frog giggin'."

"That girl does love to hunt with her daddy," Paloma replied. She sat down in her chair on the porch.

Abigail joined her, leaned against the rail and looked toward the trail that Hattie took. "Ya' know, Paloma, I was hopin' I could'a give Jedidiah youn'ins from me. 'Specially a son. All men wanna boy ta' go huntin' and fishin' with." She looked back at Paloma. "But I don't fret about it no more. With Hattie, we got the best of both. I kin dress her up and comb her hair at night and talk mother daughter things. But with Jedidiah, she goes huntin', fishin' and don't bat an eye at skinnin' a snake or batin' a hook. Most girls shy away from that sort'a thing." She looked back down the path. "She's a blessin'."

"That she is, girl. That she is." Paloma saw a contented smile come across Abigail's face. She remembered a time when the young woman used to cry on her shoulder because she remained childless after she'd lost the only child she'd ever conceived. Hattie had filled a space in all of their hearts - including hers.

***

Hattie and her family sat down at a bountiful table of plump frog legs that were fried to a golden brown, oven baked taters and a mess of black-eyed peas. After thanking God for all they had, they passed the plates and talked about their day.

"Tell your mama what you learned about in school today, Hattie," said her father.

"We learned 'bout a place called Australia."

"I hear'd 'bout it. Ain't it on the bottom side of the Earth?" Abigail asked.

"They call it down under, so I guess that's right," she replied.

"Tell her about the animals," Jedidiah added as he passed Paloma the peas.

Hattie's eyes widened. "They's got kangaroos, walla'bees what look like kangaroos, and koala bears and wombats."

Abigail raised her eyebrows. "What kinda animals are those? I never hear'd of them before."

"I can draw ya' some pictures. Ya' wanna see?"

"After supper," Paloma suggested.

***

When they'd finished eating and cleared away the dishes, they gathered around the table and watched Hattie draw her pictures. Hattie was just glad that when she drew them, that was all she drew and nothing that predicted the future. She explained each one as she drew them. Abigail picked up the picture of the animal she'd called a wombat.

"That don't look like any bat I ever seen! It ain't got no wings, and it looks more like a groundhog if ya' asked me." She looked at her daughter from the corner of her eye and smiled. "You ain't fun'in us are ya', Hattie?"

She laughed. "No, Mama. I didn't think ya'd believe me so I asked Miss Pickletta if she'd let me borrow the book with the real pictures. She said I could tomorrow. Shelly Hanson borrowed it today."

They talked and laughed about the animals she'd drawn for a few more minutes, and then they went about their normal routines before bedtime.

***

The next morning when Hattie arrived at school, she noticed that Evelyn was missing. Robbie and Billy were missing as well, but that was nothing unusual. When class was over, she borrowed the Australia book and started for home.

For once, she was able to take her time walking since she didn't have to worry about getting away from Robbie and Billy. She still weaved between some of the building to mask her direction, as she always did, until she came to the field she usually crossed to take the short cut through the woods to get home. She thought about going to Evelyn's house to check on her, but if she was sick, her grandmother probably wouldn't let her in anyway, and she would have made the trip for nothing.

Earlier that Morning

Evelyn left home as she normally did that morning, but instead of going to school, she met Billy and Robbie at their favorite fishing hole.

"Did you bring them?" Evelyn asked. Robbie handed her a rolled up pair of overalls. They didn't smell very good. She looked at him and frowned. "These are dirty!"

Robbie grinned. "You just said bring a pair. Ya' didn't say in what condition. Besides, beggars can't be choosers."

Both boys snickered as she went behind a tree to change. Robbie thought about giving her his clean pair, but decided it would give him a good laugh. He'd only worn the pair he gave her for a week anyway.

Evelyn cringed as she put on the soiled overalls. They smelled disgusting, and she truly thought she was going to throw-up. There was only thing to do. She took off her shoes and ran from behind the tree. "Last one in is a rotten egg!" She dove into the pond hoping to wash away some of the stink. It was better to be wet for most of the day as opposed to smelling like Robbie Harp. The two boys followed her in.

As the hours passed and school was about ready to be dismissed, Evelyn took the two boys to the spot where she believed Hattie would make her way to the woods. Robbie sent Billy to keep an eye on the school and watch to make sure Hattie was actually there. He and Evelyn waited in a field of tall wheat a few feet away from a huge tree by the wall that separated the field from the woods.

It wasn't long before Billy came running back. "Hide!" he shouted. "She's coming!"

They ducked down among the tall shards of golden wheat. They were glad the harvesting hadn't begun, or they wouldn't have had a place to hide unless they climbed the wall and hid in the woods. They were nervous enough about going in there anyway.

They watched as Hattie made her way through the field. When she reached the tree, they saw her look around and start to undress. Evelyn saw Robbie elbow Billy in the side. Both had silly grins on their faces. She popped both of them on top the head. "Avert your eyes now, or I swear I'll stand up and call to her!" she whispered harshly.

"Spoil sport!" Robbie huffed as he and Billy put their heads down.

***

Hattie changed into the overalls she'd hidden behind the tree that morning. She folded her dress neatly and climbed the wall. As she walked through the woods toward home, a few times she thought she heard voices behind her. She wondered if she was being followed. She turned and retraced her steps. She also pulled her slingshot and a stone from her back pocket just in case it was something she could bring down and take home for dinner.

***

"Are you sure you know where you're going!" Robbie whispered.

"You better not get us lost!" Billy added.

"I know what I'm doing." Evelyn bent down and looked at the impressions in the ground. It had rained lightly the night before, which made her imprints a little deeper and easier to follow. "This is her shoe print." Then she thought, *At least I hope it is!*

A moment later, the three of them heard something coming toward them. "What's that?" Billy asked.

"I don't know, but it's getting closer," Evelyn said.

"Quick! Hide!" Robbie whispered.

The three darted in different directions and hid behind large trees. They saw Hattie coming back toward them. Their hearts beat wildly in their chests. They scarcely breathed or twitched a muscle.

Hattie looked around and smiled. She spotted something. "I see you!" she said as she pulled back on her slingshot and let her stone fly. "Gotcha!"

Evelyn put a hand over her own mouth so she wouldn't make a sound. Hattie had brought down a squirrel that had climbed the tree she was hiding behind, and it landed just a few feet away from her. She carefully inched her way around the other side so as not to be seen. She heard Hattie approach. She dared not breathe and plastered body as close to the tree as she could.

Hattie bent down and picked the squirrel up by the tail and looked at it. "I bet when you woke this mornin' ya' didn't think ya'd be squirrel stew tonight." She turned and went on her way.

Several minutes past before Evelyn and the boys came out from their hiding places. They wanted to make sure Hattie was well out of earshot.

"That was close!" Robbie sighed when they finally gathered together.

"Can you believe she's gonna eat that squirrel!" Billy exclaimed. "Yuck!"

"I can't believe she hit it!" Robbie added.

Evelyn was just glad she wasn't spotted. "Come on, let's go."

The two boys now trusted Evelyn's tracking skill where once before they were in doubt. They kept their talking to a minimum. They didn't want to take the chance that Hattie would double back.

***

Hattie exited the woods and saw her mother and Granny Paloma shucking corn on the porch.

"How was school today?" her mother asked as Hattie kissed her on the cheek. "Learn anything new?"

"Just the same things…" she shrugged, "…readin', writin' and 'rithmetic." She held up her catch. "I got a squirrel."

"It's a nice'n," Abigail said. "Put it on the table yonder and put yer things up."

Hattie put her school books in the house, except for the picture book of Australia which she took back out to show her mother and granny. "See Mama, this is a Kangaroo and that's a wombat."

Abigail took the book, looked at it and shook her head. "Well, I declare! It's a real picture." She turned the book around, showed Paloma and added, "God sure did create some strange creatures in that Australia place."

Paloma laughed slightly as she handed the book back to Hattie. "I'm sure the people in Australia say the same thing about possums and armadillos."

"What's so strange about them?" Abigail said as went to the table to tend to the squirrel. "They's just ordinary, everyday creatures."

"Where's Daddy?" Hattie asked. "I wanna show him."

"At a sin-eatin' in Shadrack," Abigail replied. "He should be home any time now."

Paloma stopped shucking corn and closed her eyes for a moment. She looked back at Hattie. "I think you have company coming."

"Me?" Hattie questioned. "You know I wouldn't bring anybody home."

"Nevertheless…" she nodded toward the woods. "I think – over there."

***

"It sure is small," Robbie whispered as he peeked through the opening of the woods into Hattie's yard. "Our wood shed's almost as big as her house."

Evelyn grinned. "You should know. Your daddy takes you in there enough."

Robbie stuck his tongue out at her as she and Billy snickered. "Come on. Let's surprise her," Robbie said. They were just about to exit the woods and make an appearance, when Hattie came to the edge of the clearing.

"All right, Robbie Harp and Billy Tate!" Hattie folded her arms. She knew it had to be them. They were the only two interested enough in where she lived to chance following her into the woods. "I know it's you two in there. Come on out!" The two boys stood. "I thought so." Then a third person stood and Hattie was shocked. "Evelyn!"

The three of them exited the woods. "Surprise!" Evelyn said meekly and gave her a small wave. The expression on her face was half smile and half embarrassment. She didn't quite know what else to say.

"I told you we'd find you out sooner or later," Robbie said sarcastically.

"Yeah," Billy added. "I don't know why you wanted to keep where you live a secret anyway. It's a small house, but better lookin' than some of those in Shadrack."

"I got my reasons." Hattie was nervous. Her daddy could be home at any time. "Just go home."

Billy looked toward the porch. "Is that your mama and granny?"

"Yes! You've seen where I live, now just go!" Hattie insisted. If her daddy got there before they left, her secret would be out. Not many people in her class knew what her grandmother looked like, but everyone knew who the Sin-Eater was.

"Since we're here, why don't you introduce us to your family," Robbie said as he and Billy walked past her toward the porch.

Hattie looked toward Evelyn. "You brought them here?"

"I didn't have a choice." Evelyn felt guilty. "They were going to follow you anyway. I didn't want them to come back and start some type of bad rumor about you. You know how they are."

Hattie sighed. "I know."

As Evelyn started toward the porch, she recognized the woman sitting next to Hattie's mother. She stopped in her tracks. It was Paloma Day – the witch as everyone called her. She remembered her mother introducing her when they were at the park. Her mother said she was a nice person, but everyone else had a different story to tell. Evelyn then put two and two together. If this was Hattie's grandmother, and it was said that the Sin-Eater lived with her, that meant only one thing – her best friend's father was....

"What's wrong, Evelyn?" Hattie asked when she saw the strange look on her friend's face.

Evelyn unconsciously backed up a few steps toward the woods and shook her head. "No! You couldn't be!"

"What is it, Evelyn?" Hattie asked. But she had a feeling she already knew what the problem was.

Suddenly, Hattie saw her father exit the woods and Evelyn bumped right into him. The girl turned quickly and looked up at the Sin-Eater. He had a rabbit and two snakes thrown over his shoulder. Evelyn screamed and ran back into the woods. When the two boys heard her, they turned and recognized the Sin-Eater also. They likewise screamed and followed Evelyn.

Jedidiah stood there stunned as Evelyn and the boys ran passed him. He was struck speechless for a moment and then looked at his daughter questioningly. "Hattie..." but that was all he got out. He saw tears stream down her face as she turned and ran into the house.

Abigail joined her husband. She would see to Hattie in a moment. "Ya' better go after them just in case they get lost and we get the blame!"

"What happened? Did Hattie bring friends home?" he asked as he handed her the rabbit and two snakes he'd caught for dinner.

"I'll explain when ya' get back." She turned and headed toward the house.

Jedidiah followed them through the woods as fast as he could with his wooden leg. They were younger and faster; however, as he tracked them, he could tell that they were headed in the right direction. When he got to the wall where Hattie usually climbed over, he could see the three running through the wheat field with Evelyn leading the two boys. He headed for home and when he got there, he saw Paloma on the porch skinning one of the snakes.

"They followed her home," Paloma said before Jedidiah had a chance to ask. "She didn't know they were behind her."

Jedidiah went into the house and saw Abigail in the rocking chair with Hattie on her lap. He bent down beside them and stroked Hattie's hair. "I'm sorry they found out about me."

She looked at him and wiped her eyes. "It don't matter." She put her arms around his neck. "You, Mama, and Granny Paloma are all that matter."

Jedidiah hugged her tightly. When the word got around that she was the Sin-Eater's daughter, he imagined they would shun her as they do him - if they allowed her to stay in school at all.

"I told her she don't gotta go to school tomorrow if she doesn't want to," Abigail said.

"That's fine," he replied. He wiped away a tear from her eye. "You don't have to go back."

"But what about the book?" Hattie replied.

"What book?" he asked.

She got up from her mother's lap and went to the table to retrieve it. "Miss Pickletta let me borrow it so I could show you the pictures. I'm supposed to bring it back tomorrow."

"I'll return it for you," Abigail volunteered.

Jedidiah opened the book and looked at the picture. He noticed how well Hattie's drawings resembled the ones in the photograph. She'd learned so much since she started school. She was reading well and speaking a little more properly. It would be a shame for her to leave. "No," he said as he closed the book. "She has to go back tomorrow."

"Jedidiah!" Abigail scolded. "Surely yer not gonna make her go back. Ya' know how mean some kids can be."

"Okay," he said thoughtfully. He opened the book again and showed her the picture of the Kangaroo. "We laughed at it and said how funny looking it was. It's so different than anything we've ever seen. If we saw one up close, we'd probably be afraid of it. Do you think that Kangaroo cares one way or another what we think of it?" She shook her head, and he continued. "Hattie, I'll make it your decision." He then added in a gentle tone, "Are you ashamed of me because of what I do?"

"No, Daddy, I love you. You do God's work," she replied. "You pray for people who die and help them go to heaven."

"If you're afraid, you can stay home and hide yourself in the swamp or…" he hesitated, "…you can go back with your head up and be proud of who you are."

Hattie thought for a moment. "I ain't a coward." She dried her eyes on her sleeve. "I'll go back."

Jedidiah smiled. "Good. That's my brave girl." Then he opened the book. "What do you say I read to you about these strange looking Kangaroos after supper tonight?"

Hattie laughed as she wiped away a tear. "I was hopin' ya' would. I gotta tell about it in class tomorrow. I was gonna listen while I did my other homework when you read it to Mama."

He looked at her from the corner of his eye. "So you were going to have me do your homework for you, ay?" She nodded her head and he smiled. "Well, that's okay. I would have read it anyway."

Later that evening when Hattie went to bed, Jedidiah and Abigail sat out on the porch looking at the stars.

"You've been quiet this evening," said Jedidiah. "Are you mad at me for insisting Hattie go to school?"

"No," she sighed. "I'm right ashamed of me. I wasn't thinkin' when I said she could stay home. By doin' that, I pert near was sayin' that she should be ashamed of you." She looked into his eyes. "I'm sorry."

Jedidiah kissed her gently and replied, "I never once thought that. At first, my instincts were the same as yours. We just want to protect her. But we can't protect her from life."

Abigail put her arms around him. "How did I get so lucky ta' get hitched to a smart man like you?"

"If I'm so smart, why am I living in a swamp?"

She thought for a moment. "If ya' hadn't been livin' in this here swamp, ya' would'a never met me, we would'a never been hitched and we would'a never gotten Hattie. So I think it was a right smart thing to do."

Jedidiah pursed his lips in thought. "You know what? I think you're right. This swamp isn't so bad after all." They laughed and said good-night to the stars as they went inside and headed to bed.

Chapter 20

Evelyn had no problem making her way through the woods to get back to the wall. She just kept her eyes on the tracks that she and the boys had made in the soft ground. She heard the boys behind her yelling to "wait up," but she didn't stop. Neither did she bother going to the spot where she'd left her dress earlier that day. When she reached home, she entered through the front door and saw her mother and grandmother in the foyer. Her mother's eyebrows raised and her grandmother had a horrified look on her face.

Her grandmother gasped. "Evelyn! What in heaven's name are you wearing?"

"I don't want to talk about it!" she shouted. She ran passed them and went upstairs to her room.

Erma frowned. "It's that Hattie! I warned you that she was a bad influence. Emmaline, I must insist you put a stop to that relationship."

Emmaline kept her thoughts on that subject to herself. "Right now, I don't want to discuss it. It's obvious my daughter is upset about something. I'm going to have a talk with her to find out what's wrong."

Erma nodded her head. "You're right. We need to find out what she's been up to."

Her mother-in-law started to follow, but Emmaline turned on the stairs and gave her a stern look. "Mother Welch, if you please, I'd rather talk to her alone."

"Well!" Erma turned and went into the drawing room.

Emmaline didn't care what her mother-in-law thought. Sometimes she felt like asking Henry to build them a house of their own. But Henry loved his mother dearly, and she couldn't ask him to leave her alone. She didn't want to put him into a situation where she would have to choose between her and his mother. It wasn't that Erma was that bad to live with, it was just her constant interference with the way she wanted to raise Evelyn that bothered her. She resigned herself to deal with it the best she could.

Emmaline knocked on her daughter's door. When there was no answer, she tested the knob and found the door to be unlocked. She entered and saw Evelyn lying on the bed with her arms wrapped around a pillow. She sat on the bed next to her and stroked her hair. "What is it, sweetie?"

"I don't know if I can talk about it," Evelyn cried.

Emmaline looked at the dirty overalls she was wearing and took a guess. "Does it have something to do with Hattie? Did the two of you have a fight?"

Evelyn sat up. "I found out something about her today." Tears formed in her eyes. "Hattie and I can't be friends anymore. Tomorrow everyone at school will know about her. Robbie Harp and Billy Tate will tell!"

Emmaline hesitated a moment. "So – the three of you found out a secret about her, and you've decided not to be friends with her?"

"Of course not!" She wiped away a tear. "When Grandmother finds out about it, everyone in town will know who Hattie Lucas really is." She looked down. "I'm afraid you and Papa won't like it either."

Emmaline smiled. "Would that secret be that Hattie is our Sin-Eater's daughter?"

Evelyn was stunned. "Did Robbie and Billy already come over and tell you?"

"No," she said in an even tone. "I've known since the first day I met her mother at school. No one really remembers what our Sin-Eater's last name is. It's been years since anyone has heard it. They've either called him Jedidiah or Mr. Sin-Eater. I don't think your papa and Uncle Victor even remember, and they're the ones who recruited him."

"How come you remember?" Evelyn dried her eyes.

"You remember me telling you how well Jedidiah prayed for me the night you were born. Do you think I could ever forget his full name?"

Evelyn was surprised. "And you still let us become friends?"

Emmaline was silent for a moment. She had her own family secret. Her Aunt Sally didn't even know about it. She took her daughter's hands in hers. "I, least of all, should condemn anyone for their parentage or ancestry. I've debated on whether or not to tell you our family secret now or wait until you got older."

Evelyn forgot her troubles for a moment. "What is it, Mama?" She added in a hushed tone, "What kind of secret?"

"A secret that you will have to swear that you will not tell a living soul. Especially - the people in this town. Do you swear?"

Evelyn crossed her heart and held up her right hand. "I swear!" Her curiosity overshadowed her sadness.

"Have you ever heard of the Salem Witch Trials in Massachusetts that happened back around 1692?"

"Of course I have. All of us kids know about them. It's in our history books and, every Halloween Mr. Johnston tells us stories about the witches from there."

Emmaline kept her amusement in check. Mr. Johnston basically told stories fabricated from his own imagination. "Now you know that my maiden name is Candlewick," she started. "A Candlewick family used to live in Massachusetts. During that time, one of our ancestors was accused of-- practicing witchcraft!"

Evelyn drew a breath. "Really! Why? What did she do?"

"Not a she - but a he. Adam Candlewick was like Paloma Day in the sense that he could foretell the future - by drawing it. A neighbor, who coveted his property, somehow found out about his ability and accused him of witchcraft."

Evelyn was entranced. "What did they do to him?"

"They were going to hang him. He just barely escaped with his life."

Evelyn's eyes grew wider. "How!"

"Adam had a wife and "twin" sons. He was afraid the town's people would harm them as well, so as soon as the accusation was made, he sent his family away to hide with his "twin" sister, Evelyn. When Evelyn found out that her brother was in trouble, she came up with a plan to rescue him.

"Wow!" Evelyn said in a whisper.

Emmaline continued. "No one knew his sister there. One evening, she baked a pie and brought it to the guards of the prison where her brother was held. She told them it was a gift to thank them for guarding a dangerous witch."

Evelyn was confused. "Why would she do that?"

"I'm getting to that." Emmaline continued. "She had mixed very powerful sleeping powder into the pie. When they were asleep, she let him out. Adam took his family and left Massachusetts. Since Evelyn was widowed with no children, she went with her brother."

Evelyn smiled. "You named me after her, didn't you?"

"Yes. Because she was brave and saved her brother whom she loved."

Emmaline continued with the rest of the Candlewick history. She told her daughter that there has always been a Candlewick who had the artistic ability to draw, not only pictures, but the future as well. She also said that in every generation, the first born were always twins, but most of the time the second child rarely survived. She added, "My own twin brother died a few days after he was born. My father's twin sister died at birth."

Evelyn told her mother she was sorry about her brother but was curious about one point. "Can you draw the future?"

"No," she replied. "Perhaps it was my brother that would have been able to if he had lived."

"Then how do you know there was always someone in our family who could? All I can draw is stick people."

"My father could." Emmaline remembered fondly. "He was a wonderful artist. He also could draw the future like Adam Candlewick. When I was a child, we used to make it a game. I would point to something and he would draw it, but something extra was always in the picture. It had always tickled me pink when I saw his pictures come true." She became serious. "He said I could never tell anyone, except the twins I might have one day." Emmaline also told her that though he could draw the future for just about anyone, he couldn't for himself or members of his family. She said if he could have done that, he would have foreseen his and her mother's deaths.

Evelyn hesitated for a moment. "If everyone in the Candlewick family had a set of twins, how come I don't have a twin or brothers and sisters who are twins?"

"I don't know," she said thoughtfully. "Perhaps the chain of twins and fortune telling artist in our family has been broken. Perhaps it is my inability to have any more children." Emmaline smiled and kissed her daughter on the forehead. "But you, my sweet, are all I could ever want. You are my joy."

Evelyn thought about telling her mother about Hattie's ability to draw the future. She wondered if it might be possible that somewhere along the line, Hattie was related to the Candlewick family. But she was an only child also. She decided to keep her thoughts to herself and returned to the subject of her friendship with Hattie. "So you don't mind if she comes over and we continue being friend?"

"I didn't mind before. Why should I mind now?" But Emmaline's curiosity was peeked about her manner of dress. "How is it that you are wearing overalls?"

Evelyn hesitated a moment about telling the truth, but figured she'd find out about it anyway from Robbie Harp's mother. So she told her. Her mother scolded her severely for such a dangerous undertaking. She said that when her father got home, a suitable punishment would be discussed for her venture into the swamp and for skipping school as well. Evelyn already considered that possibility before she went into the swamp. Her main concern was that Hattie would be at school tomorrow so she could apologize for what she did and explain the reason why she ran away.

School

The next day, Hattie walked up to the steps of the schoolhouse. Normally, she was one of the first one' there, but today she was the last. She took a deep breath expecting the worst as she stepped through the doorway of her classroom.

"You were almost late, Hattie," said Miss Pickletta. "Hurry, take your seat."

She was surprised that her teacher didn't act any differently toward her. She walked up the aisle to return the book on Australia to Miss Pickletta's desk and then turned to go to her seat. No one gave her anything but a casual glance. A couple even smiled at her. She looked around the room and saw Robbie and Billy in their seats whispering to each other, but they didn't look her way - and then there was Evelyn. Her eyes were forward as she sat down beside her. Hattie was wondering if anyone knew. She didn't think that Evelyn would tell anyone, but why didn't Robbie and Billy? A moment later, Evelyn passed Hattie a note when the teacher's back was to them. She took a quick look. It read:

I'm sorry for yesterday. No one knows – yet. I still want to be friends. We'll talk later.

Hattie was relieved. Evelyn gave her a smiled. Now she was glad she had come to school. She didn't care what Robbie or Billy thought, but she would have been heart-broken if she had lost Evelyn as a friend. A moment later, Miss Pickletta called Hattie to the front of the class to give her oral report about Australian wildlife.

***

It was finally recess time, and as usual when the bell rang, students quickly headed out the door - except Robbie Harp and Billy Tate. They were banned from recess for excessive talking during class and were made to eat their lunches inside as well as cleaning the erasers after school.

Evelyn and Hattie sat under a tree away from the other children who were either sitting on the porch steps or playing on the swings. They pulled their sandwiches from their lunch pails and Evelyn extended hers. "You want to trade?" she asked to break an awkward silence.

"Sure." Hattie accepted her offer.

"I want to apologize for my behavior yesterday. It was uncalled for," said Evelyn. "When I saw your grandmother, I guessed who your father was. My mother introduced her to me at the park a while back, and everyone knows that the Sin-Eater lives with Paloma Day." She took a bite of the sandwich. She wondered if it was chicken.

"Once we became friends, I should'a been honest with ya' and told ya' who I was." Hattie looked down toward the ground. "But I was afraid that if ya' found out, we wouldn't be friends anymore." She took a bite of Evelyn's sandwich. It was definitely roast beef.

"I could never give you up as my friend," she said with a smile. "Mostly, I was afraid that my parents and especially my grandmother would keep us apart. But my mother already knew about you before I told her." She took another bite. "Is this chicken? It has an unusual taste."

Hattie giggled slightly and took a bite of her sandwich to avoid the question. "My daddy told me to tell you he's sorry for spookin' ya'."

"It wasn't exactly your daddy that scared me." She shuttered as if a cold chill ran down her spine. "I detest snakes! I guess I'm more afraid of snakes than anything. I'm surprised I just didn't faint dead away when I saw them hanging over your daddy's shoulder." She took another bite. "You want to trade sandwiches tomorrow?"

Hattie started giggling almost uncontrollably. She wondered if she should tell Evelyn that she was eating a snake sandwich. "Sure!" she cackled.

"What's so funny?" Evelyn couldn't understand what was so hilarious about trading sandwiches.

"I don't know," Hattie replied. "I guess I'm just happy."

Evelyn then became serious again. "But your problem still isn't over."

"Robbie and Billy," Hattie guessed. "Why didn't they tell anyone?"

"I don't know," she shrugged. "They were talking by themselves this morning when I got here. I guess we'll find out when class is over." Evelyn looked back toward the schoolhouse. They saw Miss Pickletta come out on the front step. She was about to ring the bell for class to resume.

The Swamp

Abigail paced back and forth across the porch. She was anxious about what had happened at school today. Hattie didn't return home early so she knew they didn't expel her for being the Sin-Eater's daughter.

"Abigail, you're going to walk a hole in the porch!" Paloma laughed. "She'll be home soon."

She stopped her pacing and sat down in the rocking chair. "Are ya' sure ya' don't have any feelin's 'bout her?"

"If I did, I'd tell you," Paloma replied shaking her head. That was only the fourth time today she'd asked. A moment later, she got up from her chair and started down the steps.

"Where ya' goin'?" Abigail asked eagerly. "Did ya' feel something? Are ya' gonna meet Hattie?"

Paloma rolled her eyes and glared at her. "Yes, I felt something, and no, I'm not going to meet Hattie!" She turned her back on Abigail and headed toward the outhouse.

Abigail sighed and walked to the edge of the woods where Hattie normally came out. She debated on whether or not to go after her. She'd wanted to walk with her to school that morning, but Hattie insisted that it was something she had to face by herself – and Jedidiah was no help! He agreed with Hattie.

"I should have followed her this morning!" Abigail mumbled to herself. She started to pace again. "She's probably in the woods somewhere just cryin' her little eyes out." The more she thought about it - the angrier she got. She looked in the direction of town. "Them uppity-up town's people! They don't appreciate what Hattie's father does for them! And their youn'ins ain't no better!" She turned her back on the woods and started walking back toward the porch. "Hattie's a good girl. They shouldn't shun her like that! I have a mind ta'…" suddenly she felt two arms snatch her around the waist and pick her up. Abigail squealed from the surprise.

"You have a mind to what?" Jedidiah asked.

"Put me down, Jedidiah Lucas! I'm madder than a wet hornet at you!"

He raised his eyebrows. "Me! What for?"

Abigail extended her arm and pointed to the woods. "Our daughter is out there by herself to face…"

"…Nothing!" Jedidiah interrupted with a laughed. "You're getting yourself all worked up for nothing." He picked up the box of supplies he'd set down for a moment and went into the house.

"And how do ya' know that?" She followed him in.

"Simple. When I went to the general store, I couldn't resist sneaking a peek in the schoolhouse window. And before you say anything, no one saw me."

"Was she all right?" Concern was etched in her voice.

"It looked like a normal day at school," he said with a shrug. "She was sitting next to Evelyn, and it looked like they were studying something together. No one was staring at her or pointing fingers."

Abigail sighed. "That's a relief."

Jedidiah put the supplies on the table, turned and put his arms around her. "So see, there was nothing to worry about." He kissed her.

Just as he did, Hattie came busting though the door and slammed it afterward. She also slammed her books on the table and flopped down in the chair.

Abigail looked at her husband and frowned. "All right, ay?" She went to the table and sat next to her daughter. "What's wrong, sugar?" She put her arm around her. "Was they mean ta' ya'?"

"Nobody knows – yet!" Hattie replied in a heated tone. She put her elbows on the table and propped her chin on two clinched fists. "If I could make things happen with my drawings, I'd draw Robbie and Billy tied by their ankles and dangling from a tree over a pit of snakes or a hungry gator!"

Jedidiah was surprised by her sudden desire to hurt someone. "Why – what did they do to you?"

Hattie stood and paced the floor. "It ain't what they did, but what they want me ta' do! They want me ta' draw pictures of the future for the kids at school and charge a penny a picture. Then they want me ta' give the money ta' them! If I don't, they'll tell. I've got till tomorrow ta' decide."

"Why those little carpet baggers!" Abigail exclaimed

Hattie looked at her questioningly. "What's a carpet bagger?"

"Someone who profits off the misfortune of other," Jedidiah explained. He was just as agitated.

Hattie sat back down and looked to her parents for an answer. "I don't know what to do?" Her voice cracked as she tried to keep from crying.

Jedidiah and Abigail looked at each other. They didn't know what to tell her. By not doing what they asked, it could put her in the position of being shunned. To do what the two boys suggested was wrong also. They had no answer to give.

Paloma had just entered the house as Hattie explained her predicament. When neither Jedidiah nor Abigail could give her an answer, she had one her own. "Tell me, baby girl – how many children at that school actually consider you a friend?"

"Nobody – except Evelyn," she replied with a shrug. "One or two might say a word now and again, but mostly they call me the Shadrack girl since they think that's where I live. The only time they really talked to me is when they wanted me ta' draw a picture of them."

"How does Evelyn feel about the situation?"

Hattie smiled. "She don't mind. We're still best friends. She says her mama knew all along, and she don't mind neither!"

Paloma grinned. "Are you proud to be their daughter?" She nodded toward Jedidiah and Abigail.

Hattie went to her father and sat down on his lap. Abigail kissed her on the forehead. "Ya' know I am."

"Then I tell you what to do. Put everything you just told me together. I want you to go to your special place with your drawing things. You think on it and draw pictures. You'll figure out what to do."

Hattie was a little puzzled. She looked toward her parents, but her daddy said to go on and listen to Granny Paloma. She was hoping she would get an answer, but she still had the same problem she started with – what was she going to do? Hattie sighed, picked up her drawing paper and pencils and headed to her favorite place to be by herself.

When Hattie left, Jedidiah chuckled and shook his head. "I didn't even think of that."

Abigail was just as puzzled as Hattie. "I don't see what ya'll find so funny?"

"It's simple, my love." Jedidiah kissed her on the forehead. "We were so worried that she would be teased and ignored because of me, we didn't even think about what the town's people thought of the folks from Shadrack. In their eyes, they're just barely a few steps above me."

Abigail thought for a moment and rolled her eyes. "Well, butter my bottom and call me a biscuit!" She sighed. "Except for Evelyn, she's bein' shunned anyhow." She looked toward Paloma. "How come ya' just didn't tell her?"

"If we made everything easy for her, she wouldn't learn to think for herself," Paloma replied. "She's a smart girl. She'll figure it out." She headed for the door. "You two get the supper ready. I'm going to sit on the porch and enjoy the breeze."

Paloma left them to their chores and relaxed in her rocking chair. She closed her eyes. Her dreams of late were veiled with rain. Wind had also been added to the mix lately. She tried to picture what it meant. It had rained on an off for weeks in Black Water, but nothing of any consequence. She laughed inwardly. *My bones creak, my skin is wrinkled and my dreams are shrouded.* A moment later, the cat jumped in her lap. She stroked her black fur that now had hints of gray mixed in. She chuckled lightly. "Esmeralda, we're both old." The cat meowed as if it agreed.

Hattie's Shack

Hattie went to her little place in the woods. It was an old shack she'd found a few months ago. Her parents started letting her explore some of the swamp without them since she'd become quite adept at being able to track her way home. When she'd first found it, the small place had a table, two chairs, two broken down cots on either side of the room and a large, old copper kettle with twisted piping coming out of it. She'd recognized it as being a still. She and her Cousin Caleb had followed her Uncle Ennis to his. She remembered her uncle whoopin' the daylights out of Caleb when he'd spotted them, and he'd given her a tongue lashing that she'd never forget, saying the he'd darn near shot at them.

For fear of being shot, Hattie had quickly gone home and asked her granny if anyone else had lived close by. Paloma had told her that her husband, Benjamin, had a small place in the woods where he liked to go to once in a while with Alvin Welch, Evelyn's grandfather, and the still had probably belonged to them. But to be sure, her daddy checked it out, and when he was satisfied that it hadn't been used in years, he took the still apart and allowed Hattie to use the shack. She'd cleaned out the cobwebs and animal dropping, decorated it with pictures she'd drawn of her family and hung dried flowers to make it smell good. She called it her special place.

Now she had some serious thinking to do. She sat down and started drawing pictures. She started with her parents. They were getting supper ready. Her granny was sitting in a rocking chair on the porch with the cat in her lap.

She thought about what would happen if her teacher found out the secret, but all she did was draw another wedding picture. She tried again. This time thinking about what would happen if she didn't find out - she'd drawn the same thing.

She thought about a few of her classmates and started drawing pictures with the two different scenarios. Some of the pictures changed slightly, and some of them didn't. She thought about Evelyn, but all she drew was her face. There was nothing that told her of some future happening. She drew a picture of Evelyn with her parents. They were just ordinary pictures as well. Hattie thought it strange. Her drawings could predict future happenings of everyone except for herself and her best friend and her best friend's family.

The last picture she drew was of Robbie and Billy. She grinned from ear to ear as she drew it. She had them dangling from a tree with a gator underneath with its mouth wide open. But when she'd finished, she'd noticed that she'd also drawn a woodshed in the background. She remembered drawing the same woodshed before. She figured sometime soon, Robbie would be visiting it – again!

After looking at all her drawings, and thinking about her granny's words, she'd made a decision. Most of the pictures she'd drawn were of good things. Why should her classmates have to pay Robbie and Billy for them? Suddenly, she understood. If she let those two force her into something she didn't want to do, she was no better than they were. Also, if she gave into them for this, there was no telling what they would have her do next. If people found out she was the Sin-Eater's daughter, she didn't care. She loved her daddy. Hattie gathered up her pictures and went home.

When Hattie came through the door with a smile on her face, Paloma, Jedidiah and Abigail knew she'd made up her mind about the situation. Hattie told them what she'd figured out. They all sat down to the supper table, joined hands and prayed to God for what they had and the courage to do what was right in the face of adversity.

***

Hattie barely slept that night. Dawn had not yet broken, and she lay in bed listening to the crickets chirping outside. She turned over. An owl and then a bullfrog chimed in as well. She tried wrapping the pillow over her ears but that didn't work either. The once soothing sounds that she could sleep so well too, suddenly turned into just a bunch of noises. She could have sworn that the bullfrog kept croaking, "Get up, get up, get up!"

And the owl would answer, "Who you, who, you, who you." She tossed and turned but could sleep no longer. She got up and started to tip-toe out of the bedroom so as not to wake her granny, but noticed she wasn't in her bed. She didn't see her in the main room either, but when she looked outside she saw her sitting by the fire and decided to join her.

There was a slight chill in the air, and Paloma drew the girl next to her. They shared a blanket as they sat on the log and listened to the crackling of the small blaze. "Are you nervous about today?"

Hattie shrugged. "A little, I guess." She hesitated a moment and then asked, "Did you tell fortunes a lot when you were my age?"

"No, I didn't realize my ability until I was little older than you. But when I did start telling them, I did it quite often. That's how my family and I survived." She looked down at the girl. "You don't like predicting the future, do you?"

"They scare me a little. Especially when I draw somethin' that's bad. A couple of times I drew people in coffins. The next day, or there abouts, the Sin-Eater's bell would ring."

"Is that why you don't draw much at home?"

Hattie nodded. "Do you ever see anything like that?"

Paloma decided to be honest with the child. She needed someone to guide her who'd had similar experiences and feelings. She threw some herbs into the flames and they crackled in the fire. "I saw many bad times in my dreams. I even saw the death of my husband."

"That's what scares me. I used to like to draw. But now I'm afraid I might draw somethin' that shows Mama and Daddy gettin' hurt." She looked down toward the ground. "I don't like drawing anyone getting hurt." Then she thought, "Well - maybe Robbie and Billy…" She measured an inch with two fingers. "…but just a little bit. A trip to the woodshed would be good." Both of them laughed.

"I had your same feelings when I was young. Even now sometimes I wish I could turn off my visions," Paloma replied. "But I'll tell you what my grandmother told me. We have a special gift that I believe to be God given. To ignore it would be a waste of His gift." She then told her a story. "When I was a young girl here in Black Water, my weather dreams saved many farmers from losing their crops. One time, two great twisters came through Black Water. I'd dreamt about it three days before it happened. I saw crops destroyed, as well as houses being blown apart by the swirling winds. My mother and I gave warning to the town council and they spread the word.

The farmers' crops were for the most part ready to be harvested, but if they'd waited about a week more, they would have had a very profitable year. Those farmers that listened to my warning started harvesting early and saved the majority of their crop. Those that didn't heed my prediction lost everything. Some even lost their lives." When she finished, she looked down at Hattie. "What do you think would have happened if I'd kept that knowledge to myself?"

"Everyone would have lost everything?" she replied.

"The town of Black Water would have died. Those who harvested early helped those who didn't and the town survived. There were also a few lives saved."

Hattie was silent for a moment. "So you think I should start drawing pictures all the time?"

"No…" she replied, "…just at your discretion when you think it's necessary. Sometimes if a prediction is made, by telling it, the outcome could be very different."

"How?"

Paloma thought for a moment. "Say Robbie Harp asked you to predict what he was going to get for his birthday, and you tell him. He then brags to everyone that he knows what he's getting. Now say his parents find out he knows. To teach him a lesson about being nosey, they might decide not to give him that present and get him something else instead or nothing at all. The picture you drew then becomes false. If you'd not told him, he would have enjoyed the thing he was supposed to get. Does that make sense?"

Hattie nodded. "If anybody asked me to draw something like that, I wouldn't draw it. But…" She grinned. "…considerin' it was Robbie who'd asked me - I'd tell him."

Paloma laughed. "In his case, I wouldn't blame you." She kissed her on the forehead.

They talked until the sun started to rise. Hattie asked questions and Paloma answered them the best she could, until it was time for her to get ready for school. She wanted to be early.

School

Evelyn paced in front of the schoolhouse awaiting Hattie. She racked her brain all night trying to think of how she could help her friend with this predicament, since she felt it was partly her fault. She couldn't get Robbie and Billy out of her mind either. At that moment, she wished she was a boy so she could beat them both to a fine pulp. As of now, the only thing she could do was give Hattie moral support.

A few minutes later, she saw Hattie coming down the road. She ran to greet her. "I didn't know if you were coming or not."

"Why shouldn't I!" Hattie held her head high. "I got nothin' ta' be ashamed of."

Evelyn saw she brought some pictures with her. "Are you going to do as they want?"

"Yes – and no." She handed the pictures to Evelyn. "I drew these yesterday. I'm going to give them away to those who want them. They're all mostly happy pictures."

They saw a carriage pull up in front of the school with Mr. Burnham and Miss Pickletta sitting next to him. He kissed her hand and she got out. The three of them watched him drive away.

Miss Pickletta turned to the two girls. "Good morning, young ladies!" Her tone was overly enthusiastic. She took a deep breath and closed her eyes for a moment. "This is such a glorious morning. Don't you think?"

Hattie and Evelyn looked at each other. Their teacher was basically pleasant, but she was never this giddy in the morning. They both responded with a "Yes, Ma'am," and she turned to enter the schoolhouse.

"Oh, Miss Pickletta," Hattie said as she thumbed through her pictures. "I drew something for you last night."

The teacher looked at the wedding picture and sighed. "How did you find out? I planned on making a surprise announcement during class this morning."

Again Hattie and Evelyn looked at each other. "Find out what?" they asked together.

Her eyes twinkled with delight. "I'm to be married next month to Mr. Burnham."

The two girls congratulated her and promised they wouldn't say anything. Their teacher went inside, and they waited for the others to arrive. The first was Mary-Beth Coulter. Her father, Braden Coulter, was the banker and one of the men on the town council. Hattie gave her a picture. It depicted her riding a horse as it was jumping a hedge.

"I don't have a horse," she sighed. "Every time I ask my father for one, he keeps saying no."

"Who knows?" said Evelyn. "Maybe he'll change his mind."

Mary-Beth smiled. "It's a nice thought though – and a good picture." She entered the building staring dreamily at the artwork.

Orin Katts was the second to arrive. She gave him two pictures that showed him with a monster of a fish at the end of his pole. One depicted him catching it - the other showed the line breaking.

"So which is it?" His tone was harsh. "My brother and me are goin' fishin' after school."

Hattie shrugged. "I don't know. I just draw them." She'd thought about not giving them to him. His desk was behind hers, and he sometimes called her stupid Shadrack trash whenever Miss Pickletta asked a question that she had answered wrong. She watched him go inside.

Hattie continued handing out pictures. One girl was giving flowers to her mother. The girl said she'd given them to her last night – it was her mother's birthday. Each picture depicted something simple that they had either done the previous day or were planning to do. Most everyone was excited over them, and Hattie was actually glad she had drawn them.

It was just about time for class to start, and Hattie had handed out all the pictures except for one - the one with Robbie and Billy. They hadn't arrived yet, but they were generally the last to get there anyway. As they sat on the porch waiting for them, Hattie pulled out the pictures she drawn of Evelyn and her parents.

"Sorry," Hattie said. "I tried ta' draw your future, but just an ordinary picture came out."

Evelyn sighed and gave her a smile. "That okay. They're very good pictures anyway."

The girls were about to go inside, when the boys finally arrived.

"Okay, Hattie, hand it over." Robbie extended his hand.

"Hand what over?" Evelyn spoke up.

"He wasn't talkin' to you," Billy answered. "But we're talkin' about the money."

Robbie sneered at the two girls. "We were watchin' from over there..." he nodded, "... we saw you handin' out pictures."

"I gave them out for free," Hattie stated boldly and then added, "The two of you wanna see your futures? Here!" She let the picture slip from her fingers and a slight breezed carried it away.

The two girls watched as the boys chased after it. It was all Evelyn could do to keep a straight face. Hattie showed and explained it to her earlier while they were waiting for everyone to arrive.

Hattie and Evelyn took their seats and a few minutes later, the boys entered and took their seats as well. The girls saw them whispering to those sitting behind and in front of them. One by one, heads turned in Hattie's direction. Chins dropped and eyes widened in astonishment.

Evelyn whispered in Hattie's ear. "It won't be long now. Everyone will know."

Hattie looked down. She saw the looks on some of their faces. It was the look of loathing. A couple of them took the drawings she'd given them and crumpled them up. She knew what it might mean to Evelyn if she remained friends with her. She whispered, "If you want to pretend not to be friends with me, I'll understand." She looked in Evelyn's eyes. "If you like me, they won't like you."

Evelyn thought for a moment about the story her mother told her about their ancestor who was almost killed for being accused of witchery. If she denied Hattie, she was no better than those witch hunters of Salem. "No more of that kind of talk. We're friends, and I won't hide it."

Before the news was circulated through the whole room, Miss Pickletta called the class to order. She was so excited about her upcoming marriage that she could barely contain herself. She didn't feel like teaching. She walked in front of her desks and laced her fingers daintily. "I have an announcement to make...."

Predictions: Mary-Beth Coulter

Mary-Beth was happy for Miss Pickletta when she made the announcement that she was getting married. The excitement doubled when her teacher declared it a holiday and class was dismissed with no homework. Her joy dwindled when Robbie Harp and Billy Tate pulled her and others aside to tell them the news about Hattie. She was horrified. Her seat was right in front of the Sin-Eater's daughter. She wondered if some of the sins he carried could have been passed on to Hattie, and with her being in such a close proximity to the girl for all this time, could they affect her? She thought that would be a question for Reverend Donner to answer, but she was just as afraid of him as she was of the Sin-Eater.

She started to walk home, but decided that it might be best to talk to her father first. Her mother was very superstitions about religious matters and would probably have her on her knees praying for the next couple of hours. She'd learned her lesson on that the first time her mother caught her in a lie. She had to kneel for an hour and pray her soul wouldn't burn in the lake of fire when it was her time. Her father would have just take her to the woodshed - she preferred the woodshed.

As she walked, she pulled out the picture Hattie had given her. Most everyone crumpled up their papers and threw them away. She started to, but she just couldn't. She'd wanted a horse too badly and thought that if she'd thrown it away, it might be bad luck. It would be like throwing away a dream.

***

Braden Coulter just finished having breakfast with some of the men on the council as was his custom on Tuesday morning. He looked at the clock. There was enough time for one more cup of coffee before opening the bank. He sat back in his chair slightly aggravated. The topic of conversation centered on their children. Everyone bragged about things they'd done. Elias Mayfield gloated that his son brought down a ten-point buck. Cal Bayens sang his daughter's praises when she won a blue ribbon for her strawberry-rhubarb pie in the Baton Rouge fair last week. Even their Mayor, Henry Welch, went on about how his Evelyn was at the top of her class and won the class spelling bee three times in sucession.

One man after another had something extra-ordinary to say about his child. But what could he say? Mary-Beth was an only child, and even though he loved her with all his heart, there was nothing at all remarkable about her. He tried to fashion her after that famous female sharpshooter, Annie Oakley, who'd he'd seen in Buffalo Bill's Wild West Show one time, but she didn't like guns and his wife bent his ear about it when she'd found out he'd tried. Her grades were average and even though her mother was attempting to teach her how to cook, it was all he could do to eat it and keep an approving smile on his face as he choked it down.

His thoughts were interrupted when a boy peddling newspapers came into the restaurant. He purchased one and quickly scanned the articles until his eyes came across some bold print that read:

Girl wins Junior Equestrian Event

He read where the proud parents were quoted as saying that their fourteen-year-old daughter had been training for two years. "More proud parents," Braden grumbled quietly.

"Papa…"

Braden looked up from his paper and saw his daughter. "What are you doing out of school?"

"Miss Pickletta gave us a holiday." She explained why.

"Ah yes." He smiled. "I heard that this morning." His daughter set her books on the table. Hattie's drawing just happened to be on top. Braden saw it and picked it up. "What's this?"

"Hattie drew it for me," she replied. "That's what I want to talk to you…"

"This looks like you?" he interrupted. "She's a very talented artist."

"It is me. Now about what I wanted to say…"

But a light had just shined on an idea. "Of course!" Braden looked at the picture and smiled. "Say no more, Mary-Beth. I know exactly what you are going to say."

"You do?" Her eyes widened in surprise.

Braden stood. "Sweetie, I've got some work to do." He kissed her on the forehead. "You go on home. Tell your mother I'll be home in about three hours."

"But Papa! I…" Her words fell on deaf ears. Mary-Beth sighed. Her question would just have to wait until he came home.

Braden strutted briskly across the street with thoughts of Junior Equestrian Events foremost in his mind. He decided to give in to a request Mary-Beth had been making for a long time. He was going to buy her a horse and pay for her to have riding lessons. He opened the doors to the bank, did some quick paperwork and told his clerk he would be out for the rest of the day.

***

A couple of hours later, Mary-Beth heard her father's voice calling her and her mother to come outside. When she got to the door, she saw a young colt tied to the back of her father's buggy. Her eyes widened and her heart pounded in her chest until he said the words she'd hoped he would say. "He's yours!"

The question she had about Hattie disappeared from her mind, until she was getting ready for bed. She picked up the picture and looked at it. Her dream came true at last. She wondered, *Maybe Hattie's being the Sin-Eater's daughter isn't bad. Did she make this happen?* There was no way she was going to say anything about Hattie. If she did, her mother might have her father take the horse back. Especially if she found out that the Sin-Eater's daughter had predicted it. If her parents found out about Hattie, it would be from someone else! Not her!

Predictions: *Orin Katts*

Orin Katts was thirteen. He should have moved out of Miss Pickletta's class that year, but was forced to repeat it again due to his bad grades the previous year. He'd crumpled his pictures and tossed them in his desk when he'd gotten the word about Hattie. He wasn't going to keep anything that came from – *her!* He thought it bad enough that they allowed one of those Shadrack kids in school anyway. His father, Ezra Katts, was the blacksmith. He always said that the people from Shadrack were lazy, good-for-nothing, white trash and Orin was of the same mind. Now to find out that Hattie was the daughter of the Sin-Eater - it was a revolting idea!

He went home to get his fishing pole. If his father knew he was out of school early, he'd make him work at the blacksmith shop with him and his brother Kyle. He thought about waiting for his brother, but decided to go without him. Kyle was always putting in his two cents anyway, giving him advice about fishing whether he wanted it or not. Orin was jealous of his older brother. His father was always holding him up to Kyle. This time he was determined to get the praise for bringing home a good catch.

Orin arrived at his favorite fishing bank and dropped in his line. It felt good to be out of school. He'd like to quit, but his father wouldn't allow it. He said he needed to better himself; however, Orin didn't see the point. He knew he was going to work in the blacksmith shop with his father anyway, and who needed an education for that!

It proved to be a good morning for fishing. He'd already caught three decent size bass, but they were nothing to brag about. "Monster fish my eye!" he mumbled as he thought about the pictures he crumpled up earlier. He figured that all he needed were two more and it would be good eating tonight! It would also probably take the sting out of the scolding he would get when his father found out he didn't help him at the shop - after all, it was food on the table.

It was starting to get late, and he was down to his last night-crawler. All he needed was one more fish. He picked up his catch and moved a little further down the bank. He threw in his line. A moment later, he felt it tug -

then a strong jerk. He struggled with it, and a fish leaped out of the water. It was the monster! It was Ol' Ned! Kyle and others talk about hooking and losing it every time they fished. Now he had him. To catch him would give him bragging rights for years! He could see this giant bass mounted and hanging on the wall now!

As he fought with it, he accidently kicked the stick that was holding the string of fish he'd already caught in place. He saw them float downstream, but he didn't care about them. This was the prize! "You're mine!" he said as he reeled him in. Orin took one more tug on the line. Suddenly, the line broke, and he fell backwards on the bank. Ol' Ned was gone. When he regained his senses, he looked downstream for the other fish, but they were gone too.

He thought about the pictures Hattie had drawn and went back to the schoolhouse. The door was still unlocked. He went to his desk and pulled out the crumpled pictures. He examined them more carefully. The sun was drawn in the morning position where he'd lost the fish. He also saw the string of fish floating way, where he hadn't notice it before. The other picture showed a different location, with the sun in the late afternoon position. He then realized that if he'd waited and gone with his brother, he would have caught the fish. He became angry. "It's all Hattie's fault! She caused me to lose that fish!"

Predictions: Pearl-Lee Pickletta

Pearl-Lee was struck almost speechless when Hattie and Evelyn approached her and told her the truth about Hattie's parentage. They told her she would find out about it eventually, and wanted to tell her themselves before she heard it from other sources. Hattie had asked her if she would now be expelled from school and Evelyn pleaded for her. The teacher didn't have an answer for them.

When the girls left, Pearl-Lee sat back in her chair to think about it. Hattie was a good girl, and even though she was the daughter of their Sin-Eater, she found it hard to believe that his profession would affect her in any way. But she wasn't that religious minded, and it would be something for the good Reverend to figure out.

Her thoughts were interrupted when Mrs. Sheryl Corinth, one of the other teachers, entered the room. She was an older woman who was substituting for Mr. Evan's while he was out of town for a week.

"What happened, Pearl-Lee! I heard all the noise. Where did the children go?" she asked concerned.

Pearl-Lee stood with a smile that stretched from ear to ear. "I declared a holiday. I'm to be married!"

"That's wonderful! I'm so happy for you." The older woman gave her a great hug. "You stay right here. I'm dismissing my class also. We're going shopping!"

For the moments, thoughts of Hattie were put from her mind. Pearl-Lee and Sheryl had a wonderful day. They looked through catalogs in Mr. McGuire's store and found a wedding dress that they could have Mrs. Turner, the best seamstress in Black Water, make a copy of.

When their day of shopping was done, Pearl-Lee went to her room at Mrs. Logan's boarding house. She thought of how it wouldn't be long before she would have a home of her own, tend her own flower garden and be a wife to a wonderful man and mother to a girl she was very fond of. Her thoughts were shaken to the present when Mrs. Logan's calico cat jumped into her lap. How often had she sat in this room alone with nothing but the cat for a companion? "Too often," she answered her own thought.

She got up from her chair and went to her desk to revise her lesson plan for tomorrow. She opened her book and found the pictures Hattie had drawn. She smiled as she saw her image in the wedding dress - then something struck her as familiar about the dress. She examined it a little more closely. She pulled out the picture that she'd torn from the catalog to give to Mrs. Turner. It was the same dress. She dug through her papers and looked for the first picture Hattie had drawn for her months ago. It was the exact same dress. Mr. McGuire said that the catalog she'd taken the picture from had just come in. "How did she know?" Pearl-Lee said aloud. Everyone knew that the Sin-Eater lived in the woods with Paloma Day – the witch! She looked from one picture to the other and wondered, *Is Hattie cut from the same cloth? Is she responsible for my upcoming marriage?*

Predictions: Robbie Harp and Billy Tate

After Robbie and Billy told all their classmates about Hattie, they grinned with delight. "That'll teach her to cross us!" Robbie announced.

"Yeah!" Billy agreed. He pulled out the picture Hattie had drawn of them hanging upside down over the open mouth of a gator. He looked at

Robbie. "You don't suppose this is really gonna happen to us, do ya'?"

"Na!" he laughed. "There hasn't been a gator leave the swamp in years since they built the wall and the dam. And who's going to tie us upside down like that anyhow?"

Billy sighed in relief. "I suppose you're right. Now what are we gonna to do?"

"Who are the two biggest gossips in town?" Robbie asked with a grin.

He thought for a moment and grinned also. They both said at the same time, "Our mothers!"

The boys went to Robbie's house first and saw his father chopping wood, as was his custom in the morning before it got hot. They snuck past him. If they'd been spotted, Robbie knew he'd be put to the task.

They went into the house and saw Billy's mother sitting at the kitchen table. Robbie nudged his friend in the ribs and whispered, "Two birds with one stone." They ran to the table.

"Guess what we found out!" the boys exclaimed.

"What are the two of you doing out of school!" shouted Vera Harp.

They first had to explain about their teacher, and then they told their mothers' about Hattie.

"Really!" Robbie's mother exclaimed. "And how did you find out?"

"Yesterday, Billy and me followed her into the swamp and..." Robbie started.

But both mothers jumped up from their chairs. "You what!" shouted Robbie's mother. She grabbed Robbie by the ear and he squealed in pain. "How many times have I preached and preached and preached to you about the dangers of that swamp!"

"Likewise, young man!" Billy's mother latched on to his ear as well.

The two women pulled their sons out the back door. "Ralph! Ralph." Robbie's mother shouted to her husband.

Ralph Harp put down his axe and looked to the house. He knew that tone of voice, especially when he saw his son being towed outside by the ear. "Will that boy ever learn to behave!" he mumbled to himself. It was going to be another trip to the woodshed.

His wife explained where the boy's had gone. This time, he was in agreement that a trip to the woodshed, plus extra chores was in order. He'd also had lectured his son many times about that swamp. Mrs. Tate asked him if he would mind doing her a favor and give Billy a little education in the woodshed as well, since her husband was out of town. He was more than happy to oblige.

Welch Residence

Evelyn went up in her room. No one was at home when she arrived except for the household servants. She felt sorry for Hattie. A few kids from her class used to be pleasant to her on occasion, but who would be that way to her now?

She pulled out the pictures that Hattie had drawn of her and of her parents. *She is so talented*, Evelyn thought. "It's too bad she couldn't draw something from our futures." She laughed slightly. "It would have been curious to see if it came true." Another thought crossed her mind. The conversation about how her mother's father could draw the future. She wondered if somehow through the generations, Hattie might be related to the Candlewick family. *Perhaps we're cousins?* Her thoughts were interrupted by voices coming from downstairs. She went to the stairway and saw her mother and grandmother enter the drawing room – arguing. She went downstairs and listened.

"I told you that girl was no good!" Erma Welch insisted. "Didn't you even listen to what Vera Harp and Tilly Tate said?"

"There is nothing wrong with Hattie!" Emmaline returned. "She's a sweet child, and Evelyn loves being with her."

"That child is the Sin-Eater's daughter!" Erma yelled. "Who knows what sins might have been passed on to her through his copulation with that Shadrack woman. Those people are nothing but trash!"

Emmaline folded her arms. "That's a horrible thing to say! First of all, Jedidiah Lucas is married to Abigail, and though she may be uneducated, she's a nice woman who just wants her daughter to better herself. Secondly, I think it's a ridiculous thought that the sins her father carries could ever be passed to his child."

This time Erma was undaunted. "I'm putting my foot down! This is my house, and that swamp girl isn't setting foot in it!"

At that point, Evelyn couldn't take it any longer. She was angry. She ran into the drawing room. "No, Grandmother! You can't stop me from seeing Hattie!"

Erma wasn't going to be swayed by her granddaughter's words either. "Evelyn, it's for your own good whether you believe me or not. You'll understand when you're older. That's my last word on the subject. That swamp girl is not to set foot on my property again!"

"Fine!" Evelyn yelled with tears streaming down her face. "Then I won't be here either! I'm going to stay with Hattie!" With that she ran out the door.

Emmaline glared her mother-in-law. "See what you've done!"

Erma laughed. "I wouldn't worry. She won't go into the swamp. It's just a threat. She'd get lost, and she knows it."

"You're wrong, Mother Welch!" Emmaline replied. Though she told Henry about their daughter's venture into the swamp, they both decided not to tell his mother. "Evelyn knows exactly where she lives. Hattie taught her how to track. She went into the swamp yesterday!" She turned her back on Erma and ran out the door. She got as far as the porch and saw her little Evelyn running down the street. She started after her, but a moment later, her daughter was out of sight. When she reached the spot where she last saw her, she'd disappeared completely.

Chapter 21

The Swamp

Paloma sat on the porch watching Jedidiah push Hattie on the swing that hung from a tree at the edge of the woods. She laughed at the memory of the day he'd put it up there. Hattie was five years old at the time, and Jedidiah was determined to hang it for her when she'd asked for one. He'd made it up the tree and got the swing tied with no problem, but was startled by a snake slithering across a branch when he'd turned around. He'd grabbed the creature and slung it out of the tree, but in the process his wooden leg came loose. It dropped through the branches and hit the ground. Hattie had picked it up and yelled, "Daddy, your leg fell off!" At hearing the child say it so nonchalantly, as if it were a common thing to happen, she and Abigail had laughed until they wouldn't see straight. It didn't help matters any with Jedidiah yelling back that it wasn't funny. It had taken several minutes before Abigail could stop laughing long enough to climb up with his leg so he could reattach it and climb down. That was Jedidiah's last venture up a tree.

Paloma's attention was drawn to the other side of the woods. She had a strong sense that they were about to have company. A moment later, the Sin-Eater's bell rang. Abigail came out of the house drying her hands on a towel.

Jedidiah stopped pushing Hattie and looked in the direction of the sound. Another moment later, the bell rang again. That meant they wanted him to come now. He kissed his daughter on the head. "Sorry, sweetie, I've got to go." He went in the house to change into his black suit and then stepped back out on the porch.

"Ya' want us ta' wait supper 'til ya' get back?" Abigail asked.

Jedidiah kissed her. "You all go ahead and eat. No telling when I'll be back."

The three of them watched him disappear into the woods. Hattie sighed as she stepped upon the porch and leaned against the post. "What's for supper?" she asked, but didn't really care.

"Leftovers," Abigail replied. She'd asked Hattie how things went at school, but she didn't say much about it except that her teacher didn't know if she would be allowed to continue going to class or not. It was up to the Black Water school board. Abigail and Paloma figured that if Hattie came home from school early tomorrow - they'd know. Abigail put her arms around her daughter and kissed her on the cheek. "How 'bout comin' in and helpin' me finish gettin' the supper ready?"

The two started to go in when Paloma suggested, "You better add to the pot, and set another place."

Abigail looked at her questioningly. "Why – is Jedidiah coming back so soon?"

"No." She nodded in the direction Hattie normally took to go to school. "I believe Hattie is going to have a guest."

"Me?" Hattie was surprised. She hoped it wasn't going to be those two boys again coming to taunt her on her home ground. If it was, she decided one of them was going home with a black eye! They were all surprised when Evelyn appeared in the clearing. The front of her yellow dress was dirty and torn where it looked like she'd fallen. "Evelyn!" Hattie called out.

Both Abigail and Hattie ran toward her. Her hair was disheveled, her face was dirty and her eyes were filled with tears.

"Child! What on earth are ya' doin' here?" Abigail asked as she knelt down and dried the girl's tears with the towel she had in her hand.

"I thought I heard something chasing me through the woods. I thought it might be a snake or gator," Evelyn cried. Her courage had been padded the first time with the two boys with her, but going through the woods alone was another story entirely. "I tripped over a tree root." She held out her hands and showed her skinned palms.

"Gator's don't come this far in," said Hattie. "And you'd never hear a snake. Most likely it was a rabbit or deer."

"But why did ya' come here?" Abigail repeated since the girl hadn't answer her question. "Don't tell me yer' mama let ya' come."

"Oh, she knows I'm here. I told her."

Somehow that didn't ring true, but she needed to get her cleaned up anyway. She had Hattie fetch water from the well for Evelyn to wash her face, hands and skinned knees. Afterward Abigail took her into the bedroom and gave her a pair of Hattie's overalls in place of her torn dress. When she came out of the bedroom, Paloma applied a poultice to her hands and knees while Abigail brushed out the leaves and twigs that were tangled in her hair. Hattie straddled a chair and watched them care for her friend.

"Are ya' stayin' for supper?" Hattie asked.

"If I'm invited," Evelyn replied looking first at Paloma and then to Abigail.

"You're invited," Abigail answered. "If ya' don't mind eating leftover sna…"

"Chicken stew," Hattie interrupted quickly. She didn't want to see Evelyn go running from the kitchen at hearing they were having the standard meat for supper – snake.

Paloma and Abigail looked at each other and smiled. When they finished tending to Evelyn's needs the girl stood next to Hattie. Abigail took a deep breath.

"The two of you go outside and play. I'll let you know when it's time to eat," Paloma said.

The girls ran outside, and Abigail sat down. "Did you see?"

"I saw."

"Dressed alike as they are now with their hair in braids, they're close ta' bein' two peas in a pod. If it weren't for their hair and eye color and a little difference in height…." Abigail shivered at the thought. "Do ya' reckon that the person who rang the bell was one of Evelyn's parents?"

"That would be my guess," Paloma agreed. "Better throw a couple of extra potatoes and carrots in the pot. I believe we might have more company."

Abigail was thinking the very same thing, and she wasn't even a Gypsy fortune teller.

***

Jedidiah walked through the woods and hoped he didn't have to go all the way to Shadrack. His stomach started to rumble. Now he wished he'd grabbed a quick bite before he left. It wasn't that he didn't feel any compassion for the one who was possibly dead or dying, but the last time he went to a sin-eating before dinner, his stomach gave an embarrassing roar during Reverend Donner's prayer. If looks could have killed, the good Reverend would have sent him straight to hell!

When he arrived at the bell, he saw Henry and Emmaline Welch. Jedidiah wondered if something was wrong with his mother.

"There he is!" Emmaline exclaimed.

Henry grabbed Jedidiah by both shoulders and looked him in the eye. "Is my daughter at your house?"

Jedidiah was momentarily thrown into a state of shock. First, no one ever touched the Sin-Eater. Secondly, that was loaded question. His mind instantly went to Hattie. There was no way he could answer without lying since Hattie was also his. "Ahm - your daughter?"

"Evelyn ran away from home," Emmaline cried. "She said she was going to see Hattie."

"She wasn't when I left," Jedidiah replied. "But that doesn't mean she isn't there now."

"Please," Emmaline pleaded, "Could you take us to your house?"

Jedidiah was slightly relieved, but was also worried about Evelyn. "Come with me."

Henry did his best to dissuade his wife from coming, but she wouldn't hear of it. They followed Jedidiah through the woods. As they walked, Henry couldn't believe that his daughter found her way through the tangle of these woods the other day when Emmaline informed him of what she'd done. He hated these woods. He remembered when he was a child looking for the house of the witch, Paloma Day. It was by accident that he and his friend found the place and pure luck that they made it back out. He tried to look for familiar landmarks, just in case Evelyn did this again, but he saw nothing he could pinpoint with any certainty.

Henry didn't know who to be angry at: Evelyn, for running off like that; his mother for antagonizing his daughter; or himself for ignoring the conflict between Evelyn's desire to have Hattie as a friend and his mother's complete hatred of that little girl. Something had to be done, but he didn't know what.

***

Hattie pushed Evelyn on the swing. "So, why did you really come here?" Hattie asked when they were alone.

"My grandmother made me angry. She said things I didn't like."

"About me?"

"Do we have to talk about it?" Evelyn asked as the swing went high in the air.

Hattie sighed. "It was about me. I know she doesn't like me." She walked over to the log by the fire pit and sat down.

Evelyn stopped swinging and joined her. "It doesn't matter. I like you and my mother likes you. If I have to run away every day, my grandmother isn't going to stop us from being friends."

"I don't want you to get in trouble," Hattie replied, but she was also delighted that Evelyn would risk the possibility of seeing snakes and punishment to come and see her.

"I've always done whatever my parents and grandmother told me to do. My grandmother is always telling me what I can or can't wear, which parties I can or can't go to and a lot of other silly etiquette stuff she says a lady should know. How to sit, how to walk and even how to drink tea!" She then pretended to hold a teacup and demonstrated how a lady should drink from it. Both of them laughed and then Evelyn became serious again. "But she is not going to tell me who I can be friends with. I'm putting my foot down!" she exclaimed using her grandmother's own words.

The girls talked for a while longer and decided to drop the subject of Evelyn's grandmother and play. Hattie asked permission to show Evelyn her special place but was told no. They decided to climb trees since Evelyn was now dressed for it.

***

"We're here," Jedidiah said as they entered the clearing.

Paloma came out on the porch when she sensed the expected company. She saw Henry and Emmaline coming toward the house. "Yes, Evelyn's here," she answered before they asked.

Emmaline was relieved. "Where is she?"

Paloma nodded toward the tree. "They're up there."

The two turned around and looked up. "Evelyn!" Henry shouted. "You come down here this instant!"

"No!" she shouted back.

Henry was at a loss for words. That was the first time his daughter had ever disobeyed him or talked back to him before.

Emmaline put a hand on his shoulder. "Don't be cross with her, Henry. You'll never get her down that way."

Henry nodded and replaced his harsh tone with a soft one. "Evelyn, honey, I'm not angry with you. I want you to come down so we can talk and straighten everything out." But the answer that came back was still no.

Emmaline also tried pleading with her daughter to come down, but the answer was a polite, "No Mama."

Henry turned to Jedidiah. "Do you have a tall ladder?"

"Sorry, you'll have to climb it," he replied. He would have ordered Hattie to come down, but he had a feeling her answer would have been the same in support of Evelyn.

Henry started to peel off his coat, vest, and tie.

"You're going up?" Emmaline asked.

"I don't see as I have any choice in the matter." He headed toward the tree.

Abigail came out of the house and joined them. She looked toward Emmaline. "I'm sorry for all the trouble, Ms. Welch."

Emmaline gave her a smile. "I'm just relieved that she's here and not lost in the woods." And then she added, "Please it would do me honor if you would call me Emmaline. Mrs. Welch is my mother-in-law."

"Why'd she run off like that, if ya' don't mind me askin' - Emmaline?"

"An argument between her and her grandmother," she sighed.

"About Hattie, I reckon. She don't like her."

"Truthfully, dislike is too light of a word for it," she answered, as she watched her husband struggling to climb the tree. She looked back at Abigail. "But it's not my feeling or Henry's. We both think Hattie is a delightful child."

Abigail shook her head and thought, *If the elder Mrs. Welch only knew she was a hatin' her own grandchild!*

Evelyn watched her father climb the tree. She hoped he wouldn't fall.

"Has he ever climbed a tree before?" Hattie asked.

Evelyn shook her head. "Not as I ever remember."

"Last time my daddy climbed a tree his wooden leg fell off!"

Evelyn and Hattie both laughed just as Henry made it to the branch where they were sitting. He pulled a handkerchief from his pocket and wiped the sweat from his brow. "Did I look that funny coming up?" he asked relieved that he'd made it.

"No Papa," Evelyn replied. "I'm just glad your leg didn't fall off." Both girls giggled.

Henry didn't quite understand the humor behind her statement. He turned to Hattie. "Do you mind if I have a private word with my daughter?"

Evelyn gave Hattie a nod, and she climbed down leaving the two of them up there. Henry turned back to his daughter once he saw Hattie was safely down. "I think we have some issues to discuss."

"Hattie isn't an issue, Papa, she's my best friend," Evelyn said seriously. "Grandmamma says she can't come over anymore."

"She has her reasons, and it is her house."

"Can we move?"

Henry smiled. "It's not that simple. If we left her, she'd be in that house all alone."

"So?" Evelyn replied in an angry tone.

Henry thought for a moment. "Let me put it this way. If I died and you were married with a little girl who was angry with your mother, would you leave your mother alone in that big old house?"

Evelyn looked down. "No. I love Mama."

"Well, I love my mother also. I love both of you."

She looked into his eyes. "But what about Hattie?"

"I'm not saying you have to give her up as your friend. What do you say we go home and work it out?" He gave her a smile. "Besides, it's almost dinner time, and I'm getting hungry. Cook made your favorite dessert – Pecan pie."

Evelyn thought for a moment. "Okay – but Hattie invited me to stay for supper. Can we stay?"

Henry hesitated for a moment. He didn't relish the idea of dining with the Sin-Eater and his family, but if Evelyn was willing to discuss a compromise, he'd make this one concession for her - this time. Besides, he was anxious to get out of the tree. There was a broken limb poking him in the back.

Emmaline was relieved to see them finally come down. She went to Evelyn, gave her a hug and told her never to scare her like that again.

Abigail had gone into the house to stir the pot of stew and returned to the doorway. "Supper's ready. Yer' all invited."

Emmaline was surprised that Henry graciously accepted. They entered the house and sat down at the table. Jedidiah brought in a bench from outside for extra seating, letting their guests have the good chairs. They joined hands and Jedidiah said grace. Afterward, Abigail brought the stew pot to the table and lifted the lid.

"It smells delicious!" Emmaline said honestly, as a portion was ladled onto her plate.

Henry took a bite and nodded his head. "Very good. The meat has an unusual flavor. What kind of stew is it?"

Jedidiah grinned. "Actually, its sna…"

"Chicken!" Hattie, Abigail and Paloma said at the same time, cutting off his next word.

Henry had the strangest feeling that it wasn't chicken, but he figured he was better off not knowing!

Chapter 22

The word spread quickly through Black Water Township that Hattie was the Sin-Eater's daughter. Those who didn't have children in school found out through Vera Harp, Tilly Tate, Erma Welch or Sally Gooch. For the past three days, Reverend Donner had parents knocking on his door asking if their children were in any danger of contracting sins by being in such close proximity to the child, Hattie. He told them he would pray on the matter and let everyone know on Sunday during service.

The preacher hadn't a clue what to tell them. If he told them she was a danger to their children, he wouldn't put it past some of the more fanatical members of his church to do harm to the child in the name of the Lord. If he said their children were safe in her company, it may cast doubts upon his spiritual teachings, their religious beliefs and it would be saying that it was all right to keep company with a Sin-Eater. Reverend Donner mentally cursed Jedidiah for marrying, begetting a child and causing him this headache to figure out.

The following Sunday there was barely standing room in church. It seemed the whole town showed up to hear his say on the matter – even those who hadn't set foot through the doors in years. He gave his usual hell, fire and brimstone sermon, yet he still didn't know what he was going to say about the daughter of their Sin-Eater – until he spotted a woman coddling her infant, and it came to him.

He looked across the congregation and smiled. He began. "And Jesus said, *'Suffer the little children, and forbid them not, to come unto me: for to such belongeth the kingdom of heaven.'* This is from Matthew 19:14. Children are a gift from God." He hesitated before he continued. The room was so quiet that if a pin dropped at the front of the room, it could be heard in the back. He scanned the room and studied the faces of the parishioners. They were hungry for an answer. "You asked me if there is reason to fear for the sake of your children. All of you have heard the prayers said by our Sin-Eater. Many of you are moved by his words of compassion at the passing of your loved ones as he takes on their sins." He raised his voice an octave higher. "It takes a strong man to carry his heavy burden, knowing that his only reward will be to burn in hell when it is time for his passing." He then made a fist and held it up in the air. "Our God is a vengeful God!" he shouted, and then his voice softened to almost a whisper as he lowered his hand slowly to the podium. "He is also a merciful God. Is it not beyond God to give our Sin-Eater some small token of joy in his life before he burns in hell? Would God permit a child to be born of a Sin-Eater without immunity? Are your own children not protected from your life's sins when they are born? I say to you search your own hearts and the answer is there."

He hesitated a moment to scan the room. There were a few people nodding, a few scratching their heads and some with blank expressions still waiting for him to say a positive, yes or a definite no. He knew more had to be said. "Pray with me, my friends." He put his hands together and closed his eyes. "Lord, hear our prayer. We pray you guide our hearts and our minds. We pray that through your goodness, mercy and unyielding power that evil shall not befall our community. Your signs are everywhere, Lord. We pray we have the wisdom and courage to face and stamp out any evil that may be put upon us, as well as knowing and protecting the innocent. Amen!" The congregation repeated in kind and then he added, "How many times have we read in the Bible where God puts tests and trials before his people to see if they will do what is right. If we do the wrong thing, we could be punished just as Sodom and Gomorrah. If we do the right thing, reward could be waiting for us in the everlasting eternity. Abraham walked perfect in the light of the Lord, and he was blessed."

When he was finished, he look again at the faces of the people. This time there were no questioning looks or blank expressions. Almost everyone nodded their head or was sighing with relief. His own relief remained hidden. He'd answered their question, without really answering their question. But then there was the one person who just had to ask, "Reverend? So does that mean we kick her out of school or not!"

Welch Residence

Henry and his mother arrived home from church. No matter how hard he and Emmaline pleaded Evelyn's case to allow Hattie to come for visits, Erma Welch wouldn't budge on the issue even though Reverend Donner basically said the sins her father carried didn't pass on to his child.

"You may have heard one message," Erma said. "But he also said to have the wisdom to recognize evil as well."

"That child is not evil!" Henry responded.

Erma marched into her drawing room and rang for tea to be brought in. "It doesn't make sense to me, Henry! How could you allow your child to go into the swamp like that today? And to the home of the Sin-Eater of all people!"

"Because I promised Evelyn," he replied. "Besides, Emmaline went with her."

"That doesn't make it any better! The two of you give into that child to easily," she scolded. "Children should listen to their elders – not the other way around."

Henry smiled. "It doesn't have to be like that, if you'd give in."

"I should say not! You may not care about our social standing in this community, but I do! It was bad enough when it was just thought she was Shadrack trash..."

"Mother!" It was Henry's turn to scold. "Don't let Evelyn hear you say that, or she'll never speak to you again. Hattie is a sweet, beautiful child. Evelyn showed me pictures she'd drawn of us. She has quite an artistic talent. How can you be so hateful toward a child?"

"A rose is beautiful and has a wonderful scent. But it has thorns!" The butler walked in and put the tea on the table. When he left the room she continued. "It's as if that girl has all three of you bewitched. And what about those pictures? Some say her drawings predict the future just like that witch, Paloma Day does. Look what happened to that boy who fell out of the tree a while back. Some say that swamp girl caused it."

Henry walked to the window and looked out. "Don't be ridiculous. She didn't cause it."

Erma sighed. "Then what is it about that girl with the three of you?"

"I don't know. There is something I see in her when I look at that sweet face. Maybe it's because Evelyn adores her like a ..." He couldn't finish the sentence.

"Like a sister?" Erma finished harshly. "Well, she's not her sister. Her sister is..."

Henry turned around and glared at her. "Don't say it, Mother!"

"But it's the truth. You're trying to replace something that's buried."

"What if I am! Sally and Victor said how hard it would be for Emmaline if she knew a second child of hers had died during birth. Don't you know how hard it's been on me? I'm not even aloud to share my grief with my wife because she doesn't know about it! I can't morn my daughter's death. I curse myself every time I think about what I agreed to." He started to walk toward the door. He didn't want to talk about it anymore. "So forgive me, Mother, if I bandage my grief with a child of the living whom my - *living child* - has attached herself too." With that he walked out and slammed the door. If he was a drinking man, and this town had saloon, he would be bellying up to the bar right now to drown his sorrow!

Erma Welch closed her eyes and shook her head. A moment later, Sally Gooch was brought into the room by the butler.

"What's wrong with Henry? I passed him on the steps, and he acted as if he didn't see me. Not so much as a good-afternoon."

Erma invited her to have a seat and poured tea. "We've had the same argument again."

Sally shook her head and poured a little cream in her tea. "You all left church a little early this morning. I came to inform Henry that Victor has called a town meeting in the morning to decide whether or not to let - *that child* - continue in our school."

"Well, I think I know how Henry and Emmaline will vote. I'm telling you Sally, my son and your niece are blind!" She dropped three lumps of sugar into her cup.

Sally took a sip. "I've tried my level best with Emmaline. She refuses to see that Hattie is just not in the same class as our Evelyn. Especially now - the Sin-Eater's daughter - I shudder to think." She took another sip. "What is to be done? Reverend Donner all but said there was nothing wrong with the child."

Erma thought for a moment. "But he doesn't know about the pictures. If that child's witching ways are recognized for what they are, perhaps it will change his mind." She grinned. "We just need more proof."

"But how do we get it?"

Erma stood and paced a moment. Suddenly an idea struck her and she smiled. She turned to her friend. "Sally – I'll tell you how…."

***

Evelyn impressed her mother by showing her how well Hattie had taught her to read signs as she led the way out of the swamp. However, Hattie and Abigail accompanied them just to make sure they went in the right direction. When they reached the Sin-Eater's bell, Emmaline and her daughter waved good-bye and waited on the bench for Henry to pick them up at the appointed time.

Emmaline sighed. "I wish your grandmother could see past her prejudice and hatred. Abigail and Mrs. Day are very nice people."

"I think so too," Evelyn replied. "Why is everyone afraid of Mrs. Day? Even Papa said she makes him nervous."

She hesitated for a moment. "You know the stories they tell at Halloween about the witches of Salem? Someone started a wicked rumor, and it grew out of proportion. That's the same thing that happened with Mrs. Day."

With that said, another question was brought to mind. "Mama, do you think that Hattie could be some kin to us through the Candlewick family?"

Emmaline laughed slightly. "Why would you ask that?"

Evelyn was quiet for a moment. "Because she can draw pictures like you said your father could. She can draw the future too." She wasn't going to bring up the subject, but more and more kids at school were taking about Hattie's drawings, and she figured her mother would hear about them eventually.

"I've heard some talk about that. Surely her pictures are just coincidences."

"No Mama, I've seen the things she draws come true."

Emmaline thought for a moment. *Could that be the reason Hattie looks so much like Evelyn?* She'd noticed the striking resemblance for the first time the other day when they stood side by side dressed alike in overalls. Though their heights, hair and eye color were different, there was something in the face. *Could Hattie's looks come from the Candlewick generations? Evelyn looks more like a Candlewick than the Welch side of the family.* "I suppose it's a possibility," she replied. "It's not known where all of our relations moved to throughout the years."

Evelyn smiled. "Wouldn't it be wonderful if Hattie was a distant cousin? Maybe if we tell Grandmamma, she might like her better?"

"Heavens no!" Emmaline exclaimed. "If you told her that, you'd have to explain why. You would then have to reveal our family secret. Your father doesn't even know about it. It has to remain that way. This town has way too many superstitions." Emmaline grinned. "The next thing you know, they'd be accusing us of being witches."

Evelyn laughed. "I forgot. But it would still be nice if she was."

Emmaline put her arm around her daughter. "We'll just keep that happy thought between us."

A few minutes later, Henry arrived with the carriage, and they headed for home. When they arrived, they received the shock of their lives. Henry's mother relented. She said she would allow Hattie to visit once per week on the condition that Evelyn didn't make it public. Hattie's visits were to be in secret. If they had unexpected company, Hattie would either have to go home or remain hidden until the company left.

Henry and Emmaline asked her why the change of heart, but she wouldn't explain. They decided to accept it as it was - a compromise. One doesn't look a gift horse in the mouth, and that meant they didn't have to venture into the swamp again. But on the other hand, was that gift horse a Trojan horse? Was there a hidden motive behind her gesture?

Town Hall

"Order! Order!" Judge Victor Gooch banged his gavel on the podium. "I can't hear a blessed thing if everyone speaks at the same time!"

After Sunday service was over, Victor was bombarded with questions from the town's people on the steps of the church. When Silas Connor asked Reverend Donner if Hattie should be expelled from school or not, he promptly answered that it was a school board decision. He only advised on spiritual matters - not governmental issues. Since Victor was also the head of the school board in Black Water, it was his matter to settle. To prevent an argument in the street, he cancelled school for Monday so the problem could be discussed in a civil manner. All teachers, board members and parents who had children in school were to meet at eight o'clock in the morning at the town hall, if they had an opinion to express and wanted to cast a vote.

The next morning, every seat in the hall was filled. Victor expected his wife and Henry's mother to be sitting in the front row, since they did nothing but harp on the issue that Hattie shouldn't be allowed to associate with anyone in Black Water. But to his surprise, they didn't come. Both had strangely come down with headaches.

When everyone had quieted, the meeting began. "Listen, people," said Victor. "Our town has never been in this situation before. There has never been a Sin-Eater in our midst who's had a school age child before. I will listen to all opinions one - at - a - time!" He looked at Henry. "The chair recognizes Henry Welch to speak first."

Both Henry and Emmaline stood. "My wife and I would like to state that the child in question is our daughter's best friend. When she has come for visits, she's been well behaved, well mannered and has never shown us anything but respect. We see no problem with her staying in school."

"No problem!" Vera Harp stood. "My Robbie and Mrs. Tate's son, Billy, were lured into the swamp by that girl. I'm sure she has some evil in her." She pulled out the picture that Robbie had given her. "She's drawn our sons in a picture with an alligator getting ready to eat them. I felt guilty for having my husband take him to the woodshed after he gave me this."

Braden Coulter stood. "I could say the same thing about your Robbie, Mrs. Harp! He by no means is an innocent boy. Last year, your son put live crawfish in my daughter's lunch pail and threw a dead snake at her!" Everyone in the room laughed. Victor banged his gavel and when everyone quieted, Braden continued. "Hattie was no where around then, so you can't say that she ever coerced him into doing that! I think he was just being a boy satisfying his natural curiosity and followed her into the swamp of his own accord." Braden didn't relish the idea of the Sin-Eater's daughter sitting behind his child in school, but he did realize that it was Hattie's drawing that inspired him to get Mary-Beth a horse. After talking with her instructor, the man told him that she had a natural way with horses and thought she'd be ready for her first competition next month. He finally had something he could brag on Mary-Beth about. Braden cleared his throat. "I say the girl should stay in school."

"What about this picture?" Vera yelled as she held it up.

Miss Pickletta stood. "Mrs. Harp, during our art appreciation hour on Fridays, your son has described his drawings depicting events of a similar nature. The only difference is, Hattie is artistically inclined and Robbie, shall we say, artistically challenged."

Vera sat down in a huff and another woman stood. "She's the granddaughter of that witch, Paloma Day! Who knows what she's teaching her!"

"Why would we want the Sin-Eater's child near our children!" said Tilly Tate. "Really, it doesn't seem right at all. I even heard that Hattie's mother was born from a - fallen woman. The apple doesn't fall to far from the tree you know!"

"Trash begets trash," Ezra Katts added. "That's all those Shadrack people are. Even before we found out who her father was, she should'a never been allowed to associate with decent folk anyway."

Emmaline jumped to her feet. "That's a horrible thing to say! Especially of a child! The only thing indecent is your attitude!"

Ezra sneered. "If the shoe fits...."

"And if you don't like the shoes, you get another pair!" Emmaline shot back. "They want better for their daughter! Hattie should have the same opportunity as all the other children." There were split mumbles of agreement with her statement and an even number of people shaking their heads no.

Pearl-Lee Pickletta stood. "I could teach the child privately."

"Why should she get special treatment?" replied another.

One person after another stood and stated an opinion.

"What if that witch, Paloma Day, seeks revenge for not letting her grandchild stay in school? Did anyone think of that?"

"If we don't allow her to attend school, what if the Sin-Eater doesn't answer the bell when we need him? That's something to consider!"

What if.... What if.... What if! Victor realized that they were getting nowhere fast. He listened until his head felt like exploding. The room was divided. In some cases, the opinions of husbands differed from their wives. Some didn't want her in there at all, some were afraid of retaliation from Paloma or Jedidiah and only a handful called all their worries non-sense. Victor wondered if King Solomon felt this way when two mothers argued over one child. Although in this case, except for Henry's and Emmaline's opinions, the town's people would probably think it in their best interest if the child was split in half.

When all opinions were stated, Victor called for a vote by way of a secret ballot. A show of hands wouldn't work. By doing that, it may force someone to vote either no or yes whether that was the way they truly felt or not. Also, though women generally didn't vote on town issues, he felt that since their children were involved, he would have a riot on his hands if they weren't included. It was either yes to keep Hattie in or no to expel her. There were to be no undecided marks put on the ballots. Everyone agreed to abide by the majority decision. When everyone put their ballot in the box, Victor felt lucky. Just as Pontius Pilot washed his hands in that grave decision, he was able to abstain from voting. Fifty-seven ballots were stuck in the box - there wouldn't be a tie.

Chapter 23

When Monday came, Hattie took her normal path to school, and saw Evelyn waiting for her at the wall. She told Hattie that school was cancelled so a decision could be mand on whether or not to expel her. Evelyn also informed her that her grandmother finally compromised, and as long as her visits were kept secret, she could come over. Hattie was glad of that. It was much easier for her to come to Evelyn's house than it was the other way around.

Since there was no school for the day, Evelyn invited Hattie to come to her house for a couple of hours to wait on the decision. That way she wouldn't have to make another trip tomorrow if they decided against her. Hattie agreed and accompanied Evelyn home. When they arrived, both girls were shocked that Evelyn's grandmother invited them in for tea.

The girls sat properly beside each other with their tea cups in hand and a small dish with a few cookies on a table before them.

Erma took a sip from her cup. "You look nice today, Hattie."

"Thank ya' - ahm. Thank you, Mrs. Welch," she corrected herself. Hattie had walked through the woods in her overalls as usual and carried her good dress, but even though there was no school, Evelyn told her it might go better with her grandmother if she put it on anyway. She was now glad she did. Mrs. Welch never had anything nice to say to her. Hattie took a bite of a cookie.

"Are the cookies to your liking?"

Hattie nodded and replied after she swallowed. "I like shortbread cookies. Mama makes them now and again for me."

Erma pasted a smile on her face but thought, *It's once in a while, not now and again, you half-witted child!* She took a sip of tea and continued. "I have a favor to ask of you, Hattie."

"Yes ma'am?"

Evelyn was suspicious of her grandmother. She wondered why she was being so nice to Hattie all of a sudden. They had learned a couple of new words in school and this was a perfect example of it. Her grandmother had an *ulterior motive*! She was anxious to hear what that favor was.

Erma took a sip of tea and continued. "Evelyn and her parents continually sing praises about your artistic capabilities. I've seen the pictures you've drawn of my granddaughter, and though your talent is raw, they are none the less still note worthy."

"Thank you, Mrs. Welch," Hattie replied.

That's the second compliment, Evelyn thought. *What's her - ulterior motive?*

"Our town's annual Halloween Mask is in about two week at the town hall," Erma continued. "I'm chairwoman on the decorating committee, as usual, and I'd like to recruit you and Evelyn to help with some of the decorations. Will the two of you help me?"

Evelyn thought it odd. In the past, her grandmother always wanted her out of the way when it came to decorating for this party. She had always offered to help and even had suggestions, but they were always rejected.

"If I can," Hattie replied. Evelyn responded similarly.

"I would like the two of you to draw scary pictures that I can post on the wall. You know, black cats, jack-o-lanterns, scary witches and maybe some pictures with the guests in them." Erma pulled out a list of names. "Take this."

Hattie went to Mrs. Welch's chair, took the list and sat back down next to Evelyn. The two girls looked at the list of people. Hattie whispered to Evelyn, "I don't know about this. What if I draw something bad? I can't always control the things that I draw."

"We can just throw away any pictures you don't like," Evelyn replied. She tried to figure out what kind of scheme her grandmother had, but nothing came to mind. She concluded that her grandmother was making an effort to accept Hattie. "Maybe if we do this for her, she'll continue to be nice to you."

Hattie thought for a moment. She had a point and nodded her head in agreement. "It'll take me a while ta' draw all these people."

Erma pasted a contrived smile on her face. "I'll appreciate your efforts," she replied. "But I'd like the two of you to keep this project a secret between the three of us." She looked at Evelyn. "You know how I like to surprise everyone with my decor every year."

The door to the drawing room was open and they heard Henry and Emmaline in the foyer. Erma turned to the girls. "Remember, this is between us." The girls nodded.

Henry and Emmaline entered the room and were shocked to see Hattie in the same room with Evelyn's grandmother. Both were tempted to say something witty or sarcastic but thought it better to keep their thoughts private.

"The tea is still warm. Have a seat and tell us what the verdict is," Erma said.

"No thank you, Mother, I have to leave momentarily," Henry replied. He looked toward Hattie and Evelyn. "It was a close vote, and a couple of concessions had to be made with it."

Emmaline sat next to Hattie. "The decision went your way by two votes. You can stay in school."

Hattie instinctively hugged Evelyn's mother. "Thank you!"

Emmaline hugged her back. Something felt so right about Hattie being in her arms. It felt as if that is where she should be - just as it felt right with her Evelyn.

Evelyn was just as excited, and a moment later, the two girls quickly rose from their seated positions and jumped up and down.

"Girls, if you would, show a modicum of control," Erma said. The girls sat back down and she turned to Henry. "What are the stipulations?"

Henry cleared his throat. "Hattie can stay in school on the condition that her desk is away from the other children and positioned in the back of the room. That's also including sitting apart from Evelyn. Hattie is to sit by herself."

"That seems silly," Evelyn replied.

"None the less, those are the stipulations," her father replied.

"It don't - I mean, doesn't matter," Hattie replied. "At least I get to stay in school. Mama and Daddy will be happy about that. So am I."

The grandfather clock in the foyer struck the eleventh hour and Hattie announced that she had better be getting home. Henry offered to take her to the bell in his carriage, since he was going that way, but Hattie said she was going to take a shortcut.

"Perhaps you can come tomorrow, Hattie," Erma said. "I'm sure Evelyn would love to have you over."

"If it's alright with Mama," Hattie replied.

Henry and Emmaline were still stumped at his mother's drastic change in attitude, but they were glad to see it. Evelyn, on the other hand, knew why her grandmother invited her back again. It was so she could draw the secret pictures. But why were black cats, jack-o-lanterns and witches such a big secret?

***

When Hattie returned home, her parents were concerned about

her early return, and she told them of the decision the town had about her staying in school. They were glad that she was able to continue her education, but were surprised that the vote was so close. They thought it would have been a landslide "NO" vote. But they weren't surprised they segregated her from the rest of the class. Hattie said it didn't bother her. As long as she had Evelyn as a friend, no one else mattered. The next surprise was when she told them of Erma Welch's change of heart about her visiting Evelyn. When Hattie asked if she could visit with Evelyn after school tomorrow, they didn't refuse.

***

The next morning, Hattie went to school as normal. The other children ignored her - as normal - and Robbie and Billy were just as obnoxious to her - as normal. Miss Pickletta still called on her the same as she normally did to read orally when called upon. The only difference was her location. Her desk was in the very back of the room, and she was now at the opposite end from where Evelyn was seated. She also saw faces of parents peering into windows throughout the day. One parent actually came into the classroom to see where her child was in conjunction to Hattie's seat. Satisfied, the mother left without a word spoken.

When school was out, Hattie went home with Evelyn as planned. They had totally forgotten about the favor Evelyn's grandmother had asked them to do until the older woman reminded them as they were about to go into the backyard. So instead of playing on the swing, they resigned themselves upstairs to Evelyn's room.

The two girls sat down at the desk. "This seems like an awful waste of our visit together," Evelyn sighed. "Besides, I can't draw very well at all. You'd be doing all the work."

"Well, if it puts me on your grandmother's good side, it'll be worth it. But I tell ya' what. I'll draw and you can color in the pictures."

"That works for me!" Evelyn said with a laugh.

A few moments later, Erma peered through the open door of Evelyn's room and saw them quietly at work with colored pencils in hand. She grinned deviously and thought, *Let's see what you conger up with your drawings – young witch!*

***

Hattie drew several pictures of cats, pumpkins and witches for Evelyn to color. It surprised her that she didn't added any future happenings to them. Next she took a better look at the list of names. "I don't know hardly any of these people. How do I draw someone I don't know?"

Evelyn thought for a moment. "You drew the boy who fell out of the tree. You didn't know him."

"I was thinking of a tree. The boy just happened," she replied pursing her lips. That picture still bothered her every time she thought about it.

"Well, think of the party. Think of the town hall." Evelyn looked at the list. "Draw the Sheriff first. You know him." She went back to her coloring.

Hattie nodded and closed her eyes. She pictured the party and Sheriff Hiram Wright in her mind as she put her pencil to the paper and started to draw. Her hand moved quickly around the paper, and her eyes became fixed on her artwork, picking up one colored pencil then another. She could see what she was drawing, and it started to frighten her, but she couldn't stop. It felt as if someone else was using her hand to make her draw this horror. When she finished, she jumped up, knocking the chair over as she backed away and grabbed on to the tall post at the foot of Evelyn's bed.

Evelyn's eyes widened when she saw the terrified look on her friends face. "What's wrong?"

Hattie couldn't speak for a moment and then she pointed at the picture. "That's why I don't like to draw!"

Evelyn picked up the picture and looked at it. Sheriff Wright was lying on the ground with a piece of jagged wood stuck in his back. Hattie had even drawn and colored in the blood flowing onto the ground. She shook her head. "Dead as a doorknob! Who'd want to kill the Sheriff?"

Hattie started to pace. "I don't care if yer grandma hates me for the rest of her life. I can't draw anymore pictures like that!"

Evelyn continued to study the drawing ignoring Hattie's words. "Such detail you've drawn here. He didn't even draw his gun. It's still in the holster." She pondered a moment. "Did someone sneak up on him?"

Hattie put her hands on her hips. "Are you listening to me?"

Evelyn looked at Hattie with a gleam in her eye. "Sure I am. Look at this picture."

"I drew it. I already know what's there!"

Evelyn ignored her comments and became excited. "Somebody is going to kill the Sheriff. If you draw another picture, we can find out who kills him before it happens, and we can warn him. Don't you see!"

Hattie walked tentatively back to the desk and sat down. She took the drawing from Evelyn and looked at it. She wondered if it were possible that she could solve a crime before it happened.

Evelyn put a comforting hand on her shoulder. "Look at it and concentrate. Think about who kills Sheriff Wright." She took the picture from Hattie's hand and gave her a blank sheet.

Hattie closed her eyes for a moment. She picked up the pencil and started to draw again. Her eyes transfixed once more in that concentrative stare. When she was done, they looked at the drawing and were confused by it.

Evelyn scratched her head. "Why did you draw that?"

"Heck if I know," Hattie replied.

The picture was of Robbie and Billy smoking in some room wearing Halloween costumes. Evelyn gave Hattie another piece of paper. "Try again. Think of Halloween night."

Hattie concentrated and started drawing again. When she finished, Evelyn picked up the paper. It too made no more sense as to who killed the sheriff than the last picture. "What is that?"

"I ain't got a clue!" Hattie shook her head.

The picture was a scribbled mess, but in that mess were boards, chickens, people and what looked like a roof from a house and odds and ends of farm tools.

"Were you concentrating on that night when you drew it?" Evelyn asked.

"I'm pretty sure I was. But I told ya', I ain't got no control over what I draw most of the time."

"Try again." Evelyn gave her another sheet of paper. "Think of Halloween night."

Hattie tried again. She closed her eyes and concentrated. She thought of the party; she thought of the people on the list; she thought of the town hall where it was to be held; she thought of the Sherriff. She picked up her pencil and started to draw.

Evelyn watched her in amazement as people, places and things started to take shape on the paper. When Hattie finished one drawing, she grabbed another sheet of paper and started drawing again. Hattie didn't say a word as she made her sketches, and Evelyn didn't interrupt her trance-like state. Five pictures later, Hattie shook herself into reality and put down her pencil.

They studied the first picture. It looked like the dividing wall between Black Water Swamp and the town. A large portion of it was destroyed. The rocks it was built with were scattered all about.

"It looks like it was blown up!" Evelyn exclaimed.

"Who'd want to do that?"

Evelyn shook her head and went to the next picture. There was a house that was partially destroyed and next to it was a man draped over the branch of a tree.

"Do you know who it is?" Hattie asked.

"It looks something like the Hamilton's house. That might be Mr. Hamilton in the tree. I can't see a face." Evelyn looked at the third picture. There were bodies scattered everywhere on the ground. "These look like some of the guests invited to the party." She couldn't tell if they were dead or just lying on the ground. The fourth picture was of the town hall. It looked blown-up as well. The last picture was of the Sheriff again. It was exactly the same as the first picture.

"Hmm," Hattie said in thought. "It didn't change."

"What do you mean?"

"We said we would warn the sheriff. If we had warned him, the picture should have changed. Granny Paloma says that sometimes if a person finds out their future it might change what they do."

Evelyn plopped down on the edge of the bed and sighed. "That means he didn't believe us."

"I bet cha' he'll think it's a Halloween trick if we tell him. What adult is going to believe us anyway?"

Evelyn stood and paced the floor to think and then the idea struck her. "Your grandmother! She's the witch – ahm sorry, I mean she can tell the future too."

Hattie grinned. "That's okay. We joke about that all the time."

Evelyn gathered the pictures together and on a blank piece of paper wrote a few words. "Come on – let's go!"

"Where we goin'?"

"Your house."

Hattie stood. "Won't ya' get in trouble if your parents find out?"

"Probably," she replied with a slight laugh. "My life was boring until we met. I'm finding that getting in trouble once-in-a-while isn't that bad."

They quietly went downstairs and saw the butler in the foyer with a tray that held Erma Welch's tea. Evelyn held a finger to her lips when the butler was about to say something to her. "Mr. Fredricks, give these to Grandmamma," she whispered and put a few pictures on the tray. "Hattie and I have some urgent business to take care of."

The butler smiled. "Very good, Miss Evelyn," he whispered back as he watched the two tip-toe past the drawing room and out the front door. He didn't blame the two girls for wanting to avoid his employer. He thought that if it were up to her, Erma Welch would have Evelyn sitting on a satin pillow doing needlepoint instead of outside playing and enjoying her youth.

The butler entered the drawing room and set the tray on the table before his employer. He picked up the papers and handed them to her.

"What are these?"

"From Miss Evelyn. She said that she and Miss Hattie had urgent business and left."

Erma looked at the note Evelyn had written.

Grandmamma,

Here are the pictures you requested. I'll be back before dinner.

Evelyn

Erma smiled momentarily until she saw the pictures: pumpkins, black cats and witches. There were no pictures of any of the guests. She was hoping that Hattie would draw pictures of what their guests were going to wear to the party. She would then have proof when she accused her of being a witch like Paloma Day. She wadded up the papers and threw them in the wastebasket next to her chair. "Somehow I'll prove to Henry, Emmaline and everyone that Hattie is no good!"

Chapter 24

Paloma sat on the porch in her rocking chair. She hadn't felt right all day. None of her headache remedies seemed to help. She looked toward the woods. This was the perfect time of the year. The hot summer days were gone, and the leaves on the trees were starting to turn the brilliant reds, oranges and yellows of the autumn months. She just wished she could enjoy it a little more today.

Abigail put the stewpot on the stove to simmer and went outside to relax before supper. She noticed Paloma had been quiet most of the day, and she looked a little pale. "Are ya' feelin' poorly, Paloma?"

The old woman gave her a smile. She didn't want to burden her family with the aches and pains women of her age normally have. "I'm fine," she lied. "I've just been sitting here thinking. If the town's people could see what I see from this porch, they would probably take a different view of the swamp."

Abigail looked around, closed her eyes and took a deep breath. "And the smell of pine in the breeze." She opened her eyes and picked up her sewing. Hattie needed a new coat for the colder months to come. Jedidiah had started trapping mink for the fur, and she started piecing the pelts together.

Paloma turned her eyes toward the woods. "Someone's coming." A moment later, Hattie and Evelyn emerged. They ran toward the porch and collapsed on the steps breathing heavily.

Abigail was surprised to see them. "What in heaven's name!" She gave her daughter a stern look. "Hattie, ya' know better than ta' bring Evelyn here without her mama!"

"We – had to come!" Evelyn panted.

Hattie took a couple of deep breaths. "We ran all the way here. Somebody is gonna blow up Black Water!"

"And kill the Sheriff!" Evelyn added. "And a lot of other people on Halloween!"

Abigail shook her head and laughed. "There ain't any war goin' on now. Why would ya' think that?"

"I drew pictures," Hattie replied. "We figured the only one who'd believe us would be Granny Paloma. The town's people will believe her more than me."

Hattie and Evelyn approached the older woman and handed her the drawings. Abigail saw the seriousness on the girls' faces and stood behind Paloma to look at the pictures as well. They presented them in the order that Hattie had drawn them.

Abigail put her hand to her chest and took a deep breath when she saw the first picture. "Oh, my!" she exclaimed seeing the board embedded in the sheriff's back. "That's the sheriff alright. He's deader than ta'day's dinner!"

Paloma carefully examined all the pictures. She couldn't glean anything from the picture of the two boys, but the picture she went back to was the scribbled mess with the objects drawn in it. "What were you thinking when you drew this?"

"Halloween night and who killed the sheriff," Hattie replied.

"We were hoping we could solve a crime before it happened," Evelyn added. "But this came out."

Paloma had a feeling she knew what it was, but she wanted to be sure. She put the pictures down and extended her hands. "Hattie, put your hands in mine and concentrate on Halloween night."

Hattie did as she asked, and Paloma closed her eyes. Evelyn stood beside Abigail, her eyes wide with wonder. Evelyn whispered, "What's she doing?"

"I ain't rightly sure," Abigail whispered back. "But I think she's tryin' ta' see the future through Hattie."

"Wow!" Evelyn mouthed the word silently. She was excited and wondered if her mother felt this way when she watched her father tell the future through his drawings.

Hattie concentrated hard. She thought about the pictures she drew, but she couldn't see past them. However, for Paloma it was different. As soon as she touched Hattie's hands, she could see the devastation as if it was happening now and she was in it. She saw a funnel cloud of swirling winds eat through the field taking the rock wall with it. She watched as the twister skimmed the top of the Hamilton's house and take off the roof before it touched the ground. She saw the Town Hall blow apart, but somehow it didn't seem associated with the swirling winds. She saw the board impale Sheriff Wright. Hattie's pictures had come to life in her visions. She then saw a glimpse of something in Hattie's future. She broke the connection suddenly and gasped.

"What did ya' see?" Abigail asked. She noticed a concerned expression on her face.

"There's a storm coming," Paloma replied. "Hattie drew pictures of the devastation it will cause." She stood. "The two of you take Evelyn home."

"What about the people who might die?" Evelyn asked. "We have to do something."

"I'll go to town, and see what I can do," Paloma answered. "People used to heed my warnings of bad weather when I was younger, but that was a long time ago, and I haven't had a prediction of that nature since. A new generation leads the town now."

Abigail worried about Paloma going into town by herself. "Why don't ya' wait till I git back, and I'll go with ya'."

"Why?" Paloma grinned. "Do you think I'm getting to old to go places by myself?"

"No – it's just…" But Abigail didn't really have a response, for that is just what she was thinking.

"I can go with you," Hattie jumped in.

"No, it's best you stay out of it," Paloma replied. "You go on with your mama and Evelyn."

When the girls left the porch, Paloma whispered in Abigail's ear, "I'll talk to you and Jedidiah this evening."

Abigail had a feeling that something more serious than a storm was heading their way, but figured Paloma didn't want to alarm the girls.

***

Paloma headed toward town. Her head felt as if it were going to explode, but she had to do her best to give the town's people warning of the impending danger before she and her adopted family left Black Water. Though she loved her little corner of the swamp, she knew Jedidiah would never leave without her. As she walked down the street, no one really gave her a second look. It was apparent no one recognized her. But most of the people she passed were of a younger generation. Whereas once she turned heads because of her beauty, now she was practically invisible. Paloma laughed inwardly at the thought.

She went to the Sheriff's Office first, but learned from the deputy that Sheriff Wright was out of town and wouldn't return until the party Halloween night. The only other logical place to go was the newspaper office. *The Black Water Caller* used to always publish her weather predictions when George Tyler Sr. managed the paper. But he died years ago, and his grandson was now the editor.

She opened the door and the bell above jingled. She went to the counter and saw a young man, of about thirty, placing letters in his typesetting machine. *Spitting image of his grandfather,* Paloma thought noticing his profile. "Excuse me, young man."

"I'll be with you in a few moments, Ma'am," George Tyler III said politely as he concentrated on his work. "If you'll have a seat, I'm just about finished putting the final touches on tomorrow's paper."

"Take your time." Paloma sat down. The trip into town paid a toll on her and thought that maybe she should have waited for Abigail to accompany her after all. A shooting pain went through her temple. She leaned her head back against the wall and closed her eyes. A few moments later, her headache seemed to just disappear. *Maybe it was just eyestrain,* she thought.

George put the last letter in the typesetter. "There! I'm all done," he said aloud. He wiped the printer's ink from his hands and went to the counter. An elderly lady was sitting in the chair apparently asleep. She didn't look familiar, and he thought he knew everyone in Black Water. He cleared his throat. "Ma'am, may I help you?" But she didn't stir. He laughed slightly. *I didn't think I was that long to have her fall asleep on me.* He came around from behind the counter and gently touched her on the shoulder, but she still didn't open her eyes. "Ma'am," he said again and gave her shoulder a slightly firmer shake. She slumped sideways in the chair. "Oh my God!" He backed away. "She's dead!" He ran from the building shouting, "Doctor Jackson!" But as he headed for the doctor's office, he was thinking, What a story! Headline: *Woman drops dead in newspaper office!*

A few minutes later, George returned to his office with the doctor in tow. The physician's eyes widened when he saw her. "Why it's Paloma Day!"

"The Swamp Witch!" he exclaimed. *Even better story,* he thought. *Swamp witch drops dead in newspaper office!*

***

Evelyn had talked Hattie's mother into letting Hattie stay at her house for a few more hours, but Abigail told her daughter to be home by supper time. Two hours passed. Abigail started to worry, but not about Hattie. Paloma should have returned by now. She came out of the house and looked toward the woods for the third time.

"Settle down, Abigail," said Jedidiah as he skinned a rabbit. "I'm sure she's all right."

"She's been gone for better than two hours. She looked kind'a poorly today."

"I tell you what. As soon as I finish with this rabbit, I'll go into town and look for her."

"I gotta better idea. I'll finish the rabbit and you go now!"

Jedidiah handed her the skinning knife. "How about I go now." He stood and was about to leave the porch when he heard the bell ring. A few moments later it ran a second time. "Duty calls."

Abigail went to the well and drew some water so Jedidiah could get cleaned up. He told his wife that he would keep an eye out for Paloma as he headed to town, and he would check with the sheriff's office to see if she'd been there before he went to where ever it was he was going.

As Jedidiah walked through the woods, he called Paloma's name a few times, but there was no response. As he emerged from the woods, he saw George Tyler standing by beside the bell. "Hmm - I wonder who he's come about." The young newspaperman was single, and his grandfather and both parents died years ago.

George saw the Sin-Eater approach. He instinctively took a few steps backward as he neared. After his return from the University of Pennsylvania, he had his doubts about the roll a sin-eater played in the cleansing of a person's soul after death. But old habits die hard and some of the teachings from his youth were still ingrained. "Jedidiah, I need you to…"

"Before I go anywhere," Jedidiah interrupted, "I need to go by the sheriff's office first to see if he has seen…"

"Paloma Day?" George finished his sentence anticipating his next words. "That's why I rung for you. Mrs. Day is at the newspaper office. Something happened to her."

Jedidiah was worried. "What happened?"

"I don't know. She came into my office, I asked her to have a seat and the next thing I knew she keeled over in the chair. Dr. Jackson is with her now."

Jedidiah followed the man as quickly as he could. Though his wooden leg made it possible for him to walk with no problem, running was a different story. The last time he'd tried running, his appendage came off and he fell and broke his arm.

They arrived at the newspaper office and saw that a crowd had formed at the front of the building. Upon his approach, Jedidiah heard someone shout, "He's coming!" and the people quickly made room for him to pass. None of them wanted to be touched by him in case some of the sins he carried might be transferred to them. He went inside and saw Paloma lying very still on the floor. The doctor was sitting in a chair next to her. Jedidiah swallowed hard. "Is she…"

"No, she's not dead," Dr. Jackson interrupted. "I just checked her vital signs a moment before you came in. Her heart rate, pulse, and breathing are fine. I've also checked her extremities for possible signs of paralysis. Her reflexes also respond normally."

Jedidiah knelt down beside her. "What's wrong with her? She looks like she's sleeping."

The doctor stood and cleaned his spectacles. "It's a possibility she is suffering from some sort of apoplexy."

"Is there anything I can do for her?" Jedidiah wiped a tear from his eye.

"If this was a large city with the proper medical facilities, I'd say maybe. There are new treatments for the disorders of the brain. But I'm just a simple physician. I deliver babies, set broken bones and perform minor surgeries. But when it comes to the brain - that's beyond my skills. What I suggest is for you to take her home and care for her the best you can until the inevitable."

Jedidiah looked up at the doctor. "But how am I to do that? I have no means to get her there, and I can't carry her by myself."

"All I can say is ask someone," Dr. Jackson pointed toward the door. "I have a litter you can borrow."

Jedidiah stood and approached the door, but most had heard what the doctor said and had started to scatter before they were asked. He stepped out on the sidewalk. "Please, can someone help me?" But those still standing nearby turned their backs and walked away also. "You hypocritical bastards!" Jedidiah shouted. "You claim to love the Lord, but you hate your neighbor!" He watched as the people quickened their paces or entered stores closing the doors behind them. He stepped off the walkway and stood in the middle of the street. "All these years, I've prayed for the souls' of your loved ones, and now I need a little help with my loved one and you turn your backs?" But his words still fell on deaf ears - the street was empty. "Damn all of you to hell!" Jedidiah hung his head and closed his eyes. A tear streamed down his face, and then he felt a hand on his shoulder. It surprised him. No one touched the Sin-Eater.

"I have a buckboard around back. I'll go to the livery and get my horses," said George Tyler. "I'll help you get her home."

Jedidiah looked at him coldly. "Aren't you afraid you'll be contaminated by helping me?"

George understood the reason for his sarcastic response and didn't blame him for it. He laughed slightly. "I became contaminated when my grandfather sent me away to college years ago." He remembered the argument his grandfather had with Reverend Donner about the evil of big city schools and how some of the required theological classes were contradictive to their religious beliefs. But his grandfather had great admiration for Benjamin Franklin's achievements, the founder of the school, and sent him to the college anyway.

Jedidiah sighed. "I apologize for my rudeness."

"Not necessary. I'll be back in a few minutes."

George went to the livery stable to retrieve his team of horses. He looked around for the stableman and heard the distinctive sound of snoring. When he didn't see him, he shouted, "Wake up, Elvin! I need my team."

The elderly man was startled. He removed the newspaper that was draped across his face, got up from the pile of hay where he'd been napping and brushed the evidence from his clothing.

"I ain't asleep, and I ain't deaf, so quit yer shoutin'!" He came around from behind the hay bales. "I'm a busy man. What'cha say ya' wanted?"

George chuckled slightly. "I can tell." He pulled a couple of straws from the toothless, old man's scruffy beard. "I need my horses."

"You young whipper-snapper," he grumbled hiding his amusement and then he smiled. "Where ya' off to, Georgie?"

"Nowhere. Just going to help get Paloma Day home. She suffered some sort of episode in my office."

"Ya don't say!" The old man shook his head. "She were a looker in her day. Before she married up with Benjamin Day, t'weren't a man here in Black Water that didn't turn his head ta' look at her when she walked by." He cackled slightly. "Tried ta' court her myself once. Her granny met me at the door with a shotgun."

George laughed. "I don't blame her! If I'd seen someone who looked like you come to court my granddaughter, I'd'a shot ya'!"

"Now don't let these here whiskers fool ya', sonny," he said as he put a harness around one of the horses. "I were a fine lookin' man in my prime. Once upon a time, there were two young beauties what had a knockdown, drag out fight over me, claimin' I was her bow. Ta' keep peace amongst the women folk, I decided ta' grow these here whiskers ta' hide my charm from 'em. I could tell ya' stories..."

"Maybe another time," George interrupted, before Elvin started telling another one of his personal fairy tales. As he led the horses down the street, he saw a group of women approaching him, and by the looks on their faces, he could tell they were women on a mission. Mrs. Gooch, Mrs. Petty-John, Vera Harp and Tilly Tate were the biggest gossips in town and more often than not, by the time he printed a news story in the paper - it was *old* news.

"You don't mean to help that witch, do you? Why your grandmother would turn over in her grave," said Sally Gooch.

"Well, what do you propose I do with her, Mrs. Gooch? She's lying in the floor of my newspaper office. Jedidiah can't manage her by himself, and it seems no one else is volunteering."

"I say let him do it himself. She is his responsibility. Besides, didn't you hear him put a curse upon us in the street!" added Mrs Petty-John.

"I say that whole family is evil," added Vera Harp. "Why my Robbie says that child of his, Hattie, coerced him into that swamp by means of magic."

"My son, Billy, also," Tilly Tate added. "He would never go into that swamp. He's such a timid child. He must have been compelled."

"Why, even Erma Welch has told us that the child Hattie has bewitched her granddaughter," said Mrs. Petty-John.

George was getting perturbed. "Poppycock!" He saw the ladies draw a deep breath, shocked at his language. "The only evil in this town are your wicked tongues. Now if you'll excuse me, ladies." He pushed past them and then as an afterthought he added, "And speaking of curses, he didn't put a curse on you, you did it yourselves. I suspect that the next time the

Sin-Eater's bell rings, it won't be answered." He turned his back on them and continued on his way.

The four women stood and watched as he led his horses. "Ladies," said Sally Gooch. "We need to call an emergency meeting of the Women's Committee."

***

Jedidiah rode in the back of the buckboard with Paloma. She still looked as if she were sleeping. He cradled her head in his lap and stroked her white hair. "Come on, old woman, it's time to wake up."

As George drove down the street, he saw people whispering with each other and shaking their heads. Socially this may have not been a wise move on his part, but he didn't really care. He was ready to shake the dust of this town from his feet and move to greener grounds. All he waited for was a response to his queries from one of the big city newspapers. His grandfather's small paper gave him credible experience for his resume. He listened to Jedidiah as he spoke to Paloma. "She means a lot to you."

"She's been like a second mother. She's the reason my family and I still live in Black Water. Even though the people treat her like the plague, she was compelled to stay."

"Do you know why?" He was curious not only from a personal standpoint, but it also reeked with potential for a story.

Jedidiah shook his head. "Not a clue."

They reached the bell, and George got out of the wagon to help Jedidiah with the stretcher. From that point on they would have to walk. The path through the tangle of woods was too narrow for a wagon.

George tried to note landmarks to find his way out, but one tree or vine looked the same as any other to him. He had a slew of questions to ask Jedidiah as to why Paloma came to see him in the first place, but every time he was about to ask a question, a strange noise would draw his attention elsewhere, so he decided to wait until they got where they were going to satisfy his curiosity.

When he was a child, his parents put the fear of God in him about the swamp as well as the infamous witch who lived there. Now, as an adult, maybe the woman didn't scare him, but the swamp still made the hairs on the back of his neck stand on end.

***

Abigail paced the porch, anxious for Jedidiah or Paloma to return. Finally, she heard the distinct sound of voices coming from the direction of town. Just as she stepped from the porch, she saw Jedidiah and another man exit the woods carrying Paloma on a litter. "I knew something was wrong!" she exclaimed as she ran toward them. "What happened?"

"She just collapsed," Jedidiah told her. "The doctor said there was nothing he could do. It's some type of apoplexy. He said all we can do is make her as comfortable as possible."

They carried the old woman into the house and put her in her room. Jedidiah and George exited and closed the door so Abigail could see to Paloma's personal needs.

"Thank you again for your kind assistance." Jedidiah asked George to have a seat so he could answer the newspaperman's questions. He poured both of them some coffee and sat down at the table.

"Do you know why she came to my office?" George took a sip from his cup.

"Paloma came into town to give a warning. Apparently, she had a premonition of a major storm heading this way Halloween night."

George chuckled slightly. "My grandfather told me stories of her predictions. I thought he was making them up to sell papers."

"I wouldn't laugh," Jedidiah replied. "I don't understand it, but she does have a way about her. If she said something bad was going to happen, I'd believe it. She saw a twister in her premonition. With all those people attending the celebration on Halloween night, many will either be killed or seriously injured." He hesitated a moment as he remembered seeing the picture that Hattie drew. "Sheriff Wright was one of those killed."

George put down his coffee cup. "How?"

"A board impaled him in the back."

The newspaper man saw the seriousness of the Sin-Eater's expression. "This isn't a prank? She really saw all that."

"My hand on the Bible," Jedidiah swore.

They saw Abigail exit the bedroom. She told him that Paloma was resting comfortably. She looked at George. "Mister, I hear'd watch'a been talkin' about. Ain't no lie. Everybody calls Paloma a witch, includin' my people. But she's a good one. So if ya' don't print in yer paper what she come ta' tell ya', then her bein' like she is now will be fer nothin'."

George stood. "I'll print the story. I don't know about printing the possible death of the sheriff, but as to the destruction of the town, I'll do the story right. But I can't guarantee that the town's people will believe it."

"That's all we ask," said Jedidiah.

George then begged his pardon and asked Jedidiah if he would lead him back to town so he could work on the story for the next edition.

Earlier - Welch Residence

Evelyn and Hattie discussed the premonition that Paloma had as they sat on the swing in the gazebo at Evelyn's house.

"I say we have to do something," insisted Evelyn.

"You heard what my granny said. She said we needed ta' stay out of it."

"But we just can't! What if they don't listen to your grandmother?"

Hattie shook her head. "I don't know."

"Could you live with yourself knowing that you could have helped someone and didn't?"

Hattie sighed. "No. But what can we do? No grownup is gonna listen ta' us."

"The same thing we did earlier. You draw pictures."

Hattie raised her eyebrows. "Of everybody in Black Water!"

"That would be a little much," Evelyn agreed. "Then how about just the kids at school? I know they don't like you much, but some of them are my friends. I'd like to make sure that they won't get hurt."

Hattie was quiet for a moment. Her granny said to stay out of it. But Evelyn was right too. She also remembered her granny saying that her ability was a gift, and it was a responsibility to do the right thing with it. "I guess I'll do it."

"You're doing the right thing." She smiled. "Come on. Let's go up to my room and…"

"Evelyn! Hattie!" The girls' heard Evelyn's mother call and saw her running toward them.

"What is it, Mama?" Evelyn figured it was something urgent. Her mother rarely ran.

"Hattie needs to go home…"

"Don't tell me!" Evelyn interrupted, pursing her lips. "Grandmamma changed her mind about Hattie coming over - again!"

Emmaline stood next to Hattie and stroked her hair. "Your Grandmother has become very ill. She collapsed in town a short while ago."

Hattie didn't wait to hear any more. She didn't even say good-bye. She turned and ran in the direction of home.

Evelyn put her arm around her mother and sighed. "Mama, it seems like everything is just piling up on her. She's had nothing but bad luck lately."

"It would seem so, sugar," Emmaline replied. "Come on. Supper is almost ready. Your father should be home shortly." She changed the subject to lighten the mood. "After dinner, how about we try on your Halloween costume. I picked it up from the seamstress this morning. It's adorable!"

Evelyn hesitated a moment before answering. "Mama, about Halloween...."

Chapter 25

Welch Residence

Erma's mood changed considerably after learning what happened to Paloma Day from a few of her friends. She'd been upset with Evelyn and Hattie for not drawing the pictures that she really wanted. They had put a crimp in her plan. She'd considered reneging on her word about letting the child come for visits - be they secret or not. However, the more she thought about it, the more she considered it would probably be better if she continued to allow it. If it were known that Evelyn and her mother were visiting the shack of the Sin-Eater, it would be more of an embarrassment than if someone had seen the girl at her home. But she wasn't going to let that spoil her mood.

When the butler announced that dinner was ready, Erma went into the dining room with an unusually cheery demeanor. She saw that Emmaline and Evelyn were already seated. "Everything smells wonderful!"

The cook and the butler looked at each other. Erma Welch never complimented the help. If she said anything, it was mostly derogatory. The food would be too hot, too cold, too spicy or not spicy enough.

"Thank ya', ma'am." Martha, the cook, curtseyed.

Henry entered the room a moment later. He kissed his wife on the cheek and sat next to her.

"Did you have a good day, Henry?" his mother asked.

"I had an interesting day." He thought his mother's tone uncharacteristically pleasant. "You seem to be in a good humor, Mother."

"Emmaline and I heard some surprising news this afternoon," she replied.

Henry put his napkin in his lap. "And what would that be?"

"Why, about that witch, Paloma Day, of course. You were in town. I'm surprised you didn't hear about it." She dipped a spoon in her bowl of soup and took a sip. "Very good, Martha."

The cook was becoming uneasy. She was beginning to wonder if her employer was ill. But she thanked her again.

"I wasn't in town today. Victor and I visited Bill Harrington this afternoon. He installed a water closet in his house."

"What's that, Papa?"

Henry chuckled. "That's a device that means no more trips to the - outside facilities on a cold or rainy night. I'm thinking about having one installed here."

"Henry!" his mother scolded. "What an absolutely horrendous topic for the dinner table!"

Evelyn snickered. "Did you try it out?"

Henry winked at his daughter. "I did, but I used it after your Uncle Victor." He grimaced. "If I decide to install one, I will definitely have a window put in as well..." He cleared his throat. "...for ventilation."

"Henry!" his mother admonished again as Evelyn and Emmaline giggled.

"I think I'll have to agree with your mother," Emmaline tried to control her amusement. "I believe after dinner would be a more appropriate time to discuss the matter for the digestion's sake."

Henry smiled and gave his daughter another wink, which she returned. He tasted his soup and looked to his mother. "So, what news do you have to tell us about our resident witch today?" he said light-heartedly. But when Emmaline nudged his leg and saw her shake her head, he knew that whatever it might be was nothing to joke about. He also noticed his daughter eyeing her grandmother with displeasure.

Erma continued. "She collapsed today in the newspaper office. There was quite a scene, so I heard."

"Maybe this should also be left for another time," Emmaline interrupted and glanced at Evelyn.

"Non-sense. Henry's the mayor. He should know these things. Anyway, when Jedidiah showed up to collect her, would you believe he had the audacity to ask someone to help him! Then he cursed the whole town when no one would. He should know better, cursed as he is himself. I knew one day that servant of the devil would come into her own. Help her? I should say not."

"No one helped him?" Henry looked at Evelyn and saw her brow start to knit.

"That young George Tyler did, I'm told." Erma shook her head. "His grandmother would turn in her grave if she knew that."

"Mother, Emmaline's right. Maybe we should discuss this later."

"Why? This is happy news!" Erma's smile brightened. "Black Water could shortly be rid of that horrible woman."

Evelyn had her spoon gripped tightly in her hand. With that last comment, she slammed it down on the table and stood.

"Evelyn! Mind your manners!" exclaimed her grandmother. "Sit down!"

"Mother!" Evelyn exclaimed through gritted teeth. "May I be excused? I'm not hungry."

Erma was about to object, but Emmaline quickly interceded and Evelyn stormed out of the room.

"How could you do that, Mother Welch!" Emmaline scolded.

Erma looked at her with an air of innocence. "Do what?"

"You know very well what! Now if you will excuse me, I've also lost my appetite!" Emmaline left the room and followed Evelyn.

Henry felt caught in the middle. Should he leave and follow his wife and daughter or stay and have dinner with his mother, who seemed to absolutely gloat. He decided to stay, but at the moment, he wasn't too happy with her. After having had dinner with the Sin-Eater and his family that one evening, Henry was not as leery of Paloma Day as he once was. He found her to be very pleasant and an interesting person to talk to. And, if Jedidiah hadn't been the town's sin-eater, he could have been a very likable man. He felt a tad guilty for having been instrumental in coercing him into that position.

Later that Evening

Henry and Emmaline readied for bed. Emmaline had a long talk with Evelyn. She'd listened to her daughter rant about how mean *her* grandmother was being towards Hattie's grandmother. Emmaline also talked more about what Hattie predicted might happen on Halloween night. She said it might just be best to let nature take its course and say nothing. She warned her that if she got involved, as superstitious as the town was, they might accuse her of dabbling in something evil. Emmaline hoped she would heed her words.

"Is Evelyn alright?" Henry asked as he got under the covers.

"I just don't understand why your mother hates Mrs. Day that much. I know there was an issue of jealousy, but this is way beyond that." Emmaline said as she sat before the mirror and brushed her hair.

Henry hesitated a moment. "There *is* more to it."

She turned her head and looked at her husband. He was grinning as he pulled back the covers inviting her to come to bed. She put down her brush and quickly hopped in bed beside him anxious to hear a very old story.

"So, what happened?"

Henry put his arm around her and pulled her close. "Once upon a time…"

"No fairy tales, dear, I want the cold hard truth." She snuggled up next to him.

Henry smiled. "First, let me tell you, that my father loved my mother - but - before he married her, he was completely smitten by Paloma, and if it hadn't been for Benjamin Day, he probably would have married her instead of my mother."

Emmaline was shocked. "How did you find this out?"

"Victor told me this afternoon. We were discussing Paloma and her granddaughter and the subject of my mother's hatred of the woman came up." Then he warned, "What I'm about to tell you, stays completely between us."

Emmaline crossed her heart. "I swear. Tell me more."

"As you've been told, just about every man in Black Water was infatuated with Paloma when she was a very young woman. Her grandmother met several young men at the door with a shotgun. The old woman told them that her granddaughter was not allowed to have gentlemen callers until she was sixteen. My father *quit* seeing my mother for a while and persistently called on Paloma, though he was never allowed past the front door. He wanted to let the old woman and Paloma know that his intentions were sincere and completely honorable. When Paloma turned sixteen, her grandmother died and she was left alone. My father thought he had his chance. But Paloma disappeared. The next thing everyone knew, she was married to Benjamin Day - the former Sin-Eater. Benjamin and my father were good friends. Though he was the Sin-Eater, he visited the two quite often. Eventually, my father did marry my mother and catered to her every whim. Victor told me, that my father told him, Paloma never had eyes for him. She only had eyes for Benjamin. Apparently, Paloma had seen him at a funeral, and for her, it was love at first sight." Henry grinned. "I don't know why though, Benjamin Day was pretty hideous to look at."

"You know what they say, love is blind," Emmaline replied.

Henry chuckled lightly. "So there's the reason for my mother's complete hatred of Paloma Day. Since my mother was and still is a very popular woman, all the other women in town follow her lead. The fact that she thought she'd almost lost my father to Paloma, plus the woman's uncanny ability to forecast the future was the perfect catalyst to bestow the title of witch on her. Since then, the rumors intensified, multiplied and became exaggerated through the years. The true reasons for Paloma's label as a witch has most-like been forgotten."

Emmaline sighed. "It's a pity. Paloma's beauty sabotaged her life."

Henry stroked the side of Emmaline's cheek. "Well, let's quit talking about other women. I'd much rather talk about your beauty." He kissed her neck.

Emmaline laughed. "How about we just quit talking?" She leaned over and blew out the lamp and pulled the cover over both of their heads.

Chapter 26

Three days passed, and Paloma's condition hadn't changed. Every once in a while, she would make sounds as if talking in her sleep, but they couldn't understand what she was saying.

Abigail took care of her bodily needs, and though Paloma couldn't eat, they discovered that she could swallow. They gave her water and fed her broth through small, hollow reeds Jedidiah had gotten from a pond in the swamp.

Hattie stayed home from school and did what she could to help her granny. She would talk to her or read to her from one of her books, but on the fourth day, Jedidiah and Abigail decided Hattie should go back to school and suggested that she go for a visit with Evelyn afterward. They thought that Paloma's condition was weighing on the child's mind, for she seemed sullen and unusually quiet.

Though Hattie was worried about her Granny Paloma, it was the drawings she'd been making that bothered her. She kept them a secret from her parents, figuring they had enough to worry about. At first, she'd changed her mind about drawing them, but then she thought of how she wished she'd drawn something that would have given them warning Paloma's illness was coming on. If she had, her granny might have been able to take one of her remedies to prevent it.

The next morning, Hattie gathered her drawings and went to school. Evelyn was the only one who'd asked about her grandmother and expressed best wishes. No one else welcomed her back. There were just the usual stares and whispers from the students. The substitute teacher barely acknowledged her. Miss Pickletta had taken off to prepare for her wedding that was to take place in two days.

During recess, Hattie and Evelyn sat down under a tree together. Evelyn told her that her father read in the paper where Paloma predicted a twister devastating Black Water on Halloween night. She said her grandmother didn't believe it - that it was just a lie Paloma had invented to scare everyone and ruin her Halloween party.

Hattie then pulled out the ten pictures she'd drawn so far. She said she did the same thing as before. She thought about Halloween and a person.

Evelyn studied the pictures. Some of the pictures were difficult for her to tell what was going on and some were obvious. Some were good and some not so good. One showed their classmate, George Canapple, with a broken arm. Ezra Katts, the blacksmith, was by a pile of bricks and looked as if he were throwing them off the pile. There were also group pictures with people lying on the ground and other people kneeling over them. Reverend Donner was in one of those. When Evelyn came to the picture of Mary Beth Coulter, she smiled. "She's holding a blue ribbon. I bet she's going to win that horse competition her father entered her into. She'll be out of town during Halloween." She looked at Hattie. "You wanna tell her she's going to win?"

Hattie hesitated before answering and thought about some of the scenarios her granny told her. "No - it'll be best not to. If she knows, she might get too nervous and lose, or not be nervous enough and lose."

"I suppose you're right." Evelyn scanned more pictures. She'd drawn the same picture again of Robby Harp and Billy Tate smoking, but then she came to the one that bothered her the most.

Hattie pointed at it. "That's what I drew when I thought of Miss Pickletta - a gravestone with Carrie-Ann's name on it."

"Yesterday, Carrie-Ann told me she's going to stay with the Hamilton's while Miss Pickletta and her father are on their honeymoon. They won't be back until after Halloween."

They heard the school bell ring which indicated that recess was over. Evelyn collected the pictures and stood. "We've got to tell her. Carrie-Ann can't stay here. She has to go with them."

"But we don't know if her staying here is what causes this, or her goin' does," Hattie replied. "It's just a gravestone. It don't tell us nothin' more than that."

Evelyn pursed her lips and thought. "You'll just have to do some more thinking and drawing. Can you come over today?"

"My mama already said I could."

"We've got today and tomorrow to figure out about Carrie-Ann and nine days to figure out the rest of it and decide what to do." They heard the bell ring a second time and Evelyn sighed. "Uh, oh! We're late. You know what that means."

"Dang!" Hattie exclaimed as they picked up their pace. "I hate cleanin' the erasers after school."

Welch Residence

After cleaning the erasers, and being teased by Robby and Billy for having to do it instead of them, Hattie walked with Evelyn to her house. They went straight up to her room. Evelyn's grandmother saw the two, but said nothing as they passed.

Their first order of business was to figure out what to do about Carrie-Ann. Evelyn thought of different ways of telling her friend that she might die, and Hattie tried drawing pictures. But in every scenario Evelyn thought of, Hattie still drew a gravestone.

Evelyn picked up the picture and flopped backwards on her bed, draping the paper over her face. "This is frustrating!"

Hattie turned in her chair and propped her chin on the back of it. "Tell me about it! I think I thunk about it so much, my head is gonna split'n two pieces!"

Evelyn sat up. "The only way I see it, is we've got to tell her."

"Tell her what!" Hattie exclaimed. "That my drawin' says she's gonna die! How do ya' tell someone somethin' like that? We don't even know if it will happen on Halloween for sure."

"I don't know. I'll think about it." Evelyn stood, walked back to the desk and pulled a list out of the drawer. "I wrote down the names of all the kids in all the classes at school. "Are you up to some more drawing?"

Hattie turned back around in her chair. "Maz'well, that's one of the reasons I come over ta'day." She picked up a pencil, closed her eyes and concentrated. She opened them again, and as before, she started drawing.

Evelyn sat in amazement as she watched her. Her hand flew around the paper as people and things took shape. Hattie said nothing as she drew. When she finished one paper, she went right to another. She never looked at the list of names again, but people who were on it appeared, and if it wasn't one of their classmates on the paper, it was one of their parents or a brother or a sister. After an hour, Hattie put the pencil down.

"I'm done," she sighed as she dropped her head to the desk. "My hand hurts and my brain hurts."

"I don't wonder," Evelyn said as she looked at the drawings. "I declare, Hattie, your drawings keep getting better and better."

"If ya' call disasters better," she replied as she stood and stretched. "I best be gittin' home. Ya' mind if I leave the pictures here? I don't want Mama and Daddy ta' find'em. They got enough worries."

"I'll study over them and see if I can figure out what we can do about them. Can you come tomorrow?"

"Depends on what Mama says."

Evelyn put the pictures in her desk drawer until she could look them over later, and walked with Hattie to the edge of their property line. After waving good-bye, she ran back to the house and headed upstairs to her room. She was surprised to see her grandmother coming out.

"There you are, Evelyn," said her grandmother. "I came up to see if you and Hattie would like to come downstairs and have some cookies and milk."

"Hattie already went home."

"Maybe another time." Erma smiled and walked back downstairs.

Something didn't set right with Evelyn about her grandmother's niceness. She entered in her room, closed the door and had a horrible thought. "The pictures!" She quick opened the drawer and sighed with relief. They were all still there, but she didn't want to take any chances. She hid them in her secret place. If her grandmother had found them she didn't know what would happen.

***

Erma walked down the steps grinning from ear to ear. The girls had been unusually quiet the whole time Hattie had been there. She'd gone upstairs to listen at the door, but there were no sounds for a long time. She'd quietly opened the door and peeked in. Hattie was sitting at the desk and Evelyn's back was to the door. She closed it and went back downstairs and waited anxiously. When the girls left, she started to go back upstairs to see if she could seek out what the two were so engrossed in doing, but she was interrupted by the cook with some trivial incident in the kitchen that she had to attend to. With that done, she went up to Evelyn's room and looked around the top of the desk. When she opened the desk drawer, she found the pictures, but didn't have enough time to look at them. She shoved them back in the drawer when she heard someone coming up the steps. Though she didn't get a good look at them, she knew they would be evidence against the granddaughter of her enemy.

Erma went back to her drawing room. She sipped on her tea as she thought, *Soon, witch-child, you won't be corrupting my little Evelyn. You're as wicked as that grandmother of yours.*

Chapter 27

The next morning, before Evelyn went to school, she folded the picture of the gravestone with Carrie-Ann's name on it and put it in one of her books. She and Hattie were going to figure out how to tell her about the picture, but Carrie-Ann wasn't at school, and Hattie said she had to go straight home. Her daddy wanted her to go with him to catch crawdads after school, which was one of their most favorite things to do together. If she'd turned him down, he would have asked her why, and she didn't want to lie to him about it. *Crawdads!* Evelyn shivered at the thought. She didn't even like to see them on the plate when their cook fixed them for her father.

When school was out, Evelyn went to the Burnham residence to see Carrie-Ann. She was invited into the drawing room and saw her friend standing on a stool with the seamstress kneeling on the floor with pins between her lips.

"Hi, Evelyn!" Carrie-Ann said.

"Hold still, Carrie-Ann," the seamstress mumbled. She removed the pins from her mouth. "Or your hem will be uneven! This has to be ready by tomorrow, and I still have to go to your future mother's house for the final fitting of her dress."

"Sorry, Mrs. Campbell," the girl apologized.

The woman turned to Evelyn and smiled. "Hello, dear. Have a seat. I'll be finished in just a minute."

Carrie-Ann smiled brightly. "Doesn't that sound wonderful, Evelyn? My future mother. I'm so glad Daddy asked Miss Pickletta to marry him."

"I'm happy for you," Evelyn replied. But in her mind she was wondering if Carrie-Ann would survive to be able to have a mother, according to the picture drawn by Hattie.

The seamstress put the final pin in the dress and told Carrie-Ann to be careful when she took it off. When the girl returned from changing, she and Evelyn went outside and walked toward her swing.

"You'll be at the wedding won't you?"

"Of course I will, but…"

"Wait till you see everything," Carrie-Ann interrupted. "The flowers are beautiful. I got to help pick them out."

"That's great, but Carrie-Ann…"

"And the cake. It's going to be three tiers with a bell on top. It's chocolate cake, with white icing and chocolate roses. I just love chocolate. I think Miss. Pickletta chose that flavor just because I like chocolate. Don't you think that was sweet of her?"

"Yes, but…"

"Miss Pickletta…" Carrie-Ann said her name in a dreamy tone. "Just think, after tomorrow I won't be calling her that any more. I've been trying to decide what to call her. Mama, Mother, just plain ol' Mom. I'm too old to call her Mommy," she laughed. "What do you think?"

This time Evelyn didn't even have a chance to get a word out before Carrie-Ann answered her own question.

"I think Mama. Mother is too formal and like I said, Mom is too plain…"

"CARRIE-ANN!" Evelyn shouted as she stopped walking. Then she blurted out, "If you don't stop talking about the wedding and listen to me a moment, you may not be around to call Miss Pickletta anything!"

Carrie-Ann tilted her head and looked at Evelyn curiously. "What do you mean by that?"

Evelyn felt like kicking herself. Her words didn't come out as subtly as she'd wished, but the girl's excessive glee and constant interruptions caused her to spit them out. But now it was out there, and she had to explain it.

"Did you hear about the storm that was predicted by Paloma Day in the newspaper for Halloween night?"

"Sure," she shrugged. "Because so many people were upset about it, an emergency council meeting was called this morning. Your father called it." She hesitated a moment. "But I guess you didn't know about it since you were probably in school. My father thinks it's just a Halloween joke by Mr. Tyler. But what has that got to do with me?"

"It's no joke." Evelyn pulled out the picture and gave it to her. "Hattie drew this."

Carrie-Ann looked at it and shrugged her shoulders. "So, it looks like my tombstone. "What of it?"

Evelyn thought she'd be upset. "Don't you see? It's a prediction that you might…" she hesitated. "…die!"

Carrie-Ann laughed.

"I don't see what's so funny. I don't what you to die!"

"Come with me," she said.

Evelyn was confused, but she followed her friend to a small fenced area with some wooden boards that were painted gray and stuck in the ground with names on them. She saw Carrie-Ann's name, her father's, Miss Pickletta's, *her own* name and a few other of Carrie-Ann's friends. There were ten grave markers in all.

"This is my Halloween cemetery," Carrie-Ann said. "I put me and my family's plus my best friends' names on each marker."

"Why would you do that?" It was unnerving to see her name on a makeshift headstone.

"To fool the evil spirits, of course. I was told that if you put your name on a gravestone before Halloween, the evil spirits would think you're already dead and bad luck will pass you by. The opposite of bad luck is good luck."

"Who in the world told you that?"

"Robby Harp and Billy Tate," she replied. "They said they make one every year, and they always have good luck on Halloween. They get lots of treats."

"And you listened to them?" Evelyn rolled her eyes. "Did you consider the source? Robbie and Billy get into more trouble than any two people I know. They're idiots!" Evelyn looked at the picture again. It didn't look like a simple wooden headstone. It was fancy looking. She looked at her own name in Carrie-Ann's graveyard again. "I appreciate you wanting me to have good luck, but I don't think putting your name on a tombstone at any time is good luck until you're really dead, and that is not good luck. You can keep your name in there if you want, but please take mine out. I have enough problems to deal with now."

Carrie-Ann looked at her cemetery. She was beginning to have second thoughts about what she'd done. "They were so serious when they told me about it."

Evelyn liked Carrie-Ann, but sometimes under all that pretty blond hair was an empty space. She spoke to her again. "Please, I want you to do me a favor. You're one of my friends. Don't go to the Halloween party. I'm not going. Something very, very bad is going to happen. If you're still going to stay with the Hamilton's on Halloween night, please sleep in their storm cellar."

"How do you know? Did Hattie tell you?"

Evelyn hesitated a moment. Hattie's predictions carried some weight with some students, but not enough. "Actually, I heard it straight from Paloma Day herself."

"The Swamp Witch!" she exclaimed and added in a hushed tone, "Wow. Maybe I should start sleeping in their cellar when I get there."

"I think just on Halloween night would be good." Evelyn tried not to laugh.

Carrie-Ann asked Evelyn if she would help her take down her cemetery. She decided she'd never had any bad luck on any other Halloween nights, so why tempt fate just in case Robbie and Billy played a trick on her, and it was really *bad* luck to put your name on a tombstone. After the task was accomplished, Evelyn started for home. She hoped she'd done the right thing.

Chapter 28

Henry Welch just left a meeting with the farmers and a few others at the town hall. Everyone was in an uproar over the storm predicted in the newspaper that George Tyler had written. The farmers were worried about their crops and wondered whether they should start harvesting now or wait until after Halloween was over when their crops would be at their peak. George had also been there to assure everyone that the story wasn't something he'd fabricated for a joke. The only thing Henry could tell the people was to use their own best judgment about their crops. The people left the meeting still in a quandary as to what to do. Some decided to go ahead and start harvesting whereas others decided to take their chances.

Henry walked down the street and entered the general store. The last time he and Emmaline were in there together, he'd noticed her ogling a particular hat that Mr. McGuire had in the window. He thought he'd surprise her with it and get some rock candy for Evelyn as well. As he entered, he heard the shopkeeper arguing with Jonas Burnham.

"I'm not paying for something I didn't order!" shouted Jonas. "I wanted two boxes of fireworks for the wedding celebration, not four."

"Look at this order sheet," said McGuire. "It says four boxes!. I can't return the other two."

Jonas looked at the paper. It looked like someone had written over his number and turned it into a four. "All I know is I only wanted two."

Mr. McGuire's delivery boy, Jimmy Johnson, came into the store. "Mr. McGuire, Mr. Baxter is out of town. His wife said she won't take delivery of that box of dynamite until he comes back to handle it. She said he'll be back next week."

The shopkeeper rolled his eyes. "That's just great! What am I going to do with a box of dynamite? I can't keep it in the store!"

"Dynamite!" Henry exclaimed. "What did he order that for?"

"He has a couple of large tree stumps and boulders on a section of property that he wants to clear. He said he's tried digging them out and pulling them out, but they won't budge. So he's going to blow them up."

"You make sure he informs the sheriff before he uses that stuff. We don't want some child wandering around in the area."

"That still doesn't solve my problem as to what to do with it," the shopkeeper grumbled.

"What about my problem?" Jonas said. "I'll pay for two boxes of fireworks only!"

"Perhaps I can solve both of your problems," said Henry. "How about I take the other two boxes of fireworks for the Halloween party? The children will love to see another display. As far as the dynamite, the town hall will be empty until Halloween night. You can store your box of dynamite in the storage room since the weather is cooler. No one will bother it there."

Both men were relieved. Mr. Burnham didn't have to pay for something he didn't order, and Mr. McGuire wouldn't lose the profit he was going to make from the fireworks or have to keep the sticks of dynamite in the store.

Henry made his purchases and left. He thought that the shopkeeper would have given him a discount on the hat he'd bought for his wife, or at least not charged him for the rock candy for solving his problems. But Mr. McGuire was not a man known for charitable acts or doing anything that didn't benefit him in some way. If someone did him a favor, that didn't mean he had to return it.

The Swamp

Jedidiah and Hattie walked along the stream carrying their buckets. "There's some big ones by that rock!" Hattie pointed.

"Good eye." Jedidiah pulled the baited strings from his pouch and handed them to Hattie as he got the net ready. He watched as she lowered the bait into the water and when the crawdad latched on, he scooped it up and dropped it in the bucket. "If you can get a couple more, we'll have plenty for supper."

Hattie dropped her line two more times. The last one took a little coaxing to take the bait, but she finally caught it. She looked at the number of crawdads she had in her pail and sighed. She'd told her daddy how Evelyn said she cringed to just looking at one of those creatures on her father's plate. "If she would only try crawdad fishin' just once, I think she'd like it."

"Not all girls are like you, Hattie," Jedidiah chuckled. "Your mother and I taught you things that most parents wouldn't teach a daughter. It's all a matter of what you are introduced to. We've been taking you with us to go crawdad fishing since before you could say the word crawdad. I believe you were four years old when you caught your first one."

Hattie sat down on the bank. "I think I remember." She held up her left index finger. "I think it pinched me."

He laughed as he sat beside her. "As a matter of fact, it did. I remember that you cried, looked at the creature that did the deed and told it that you were going to eat it when you got home to teach it a lesson for pinching you."

Hattie laughed and then she became quiet. Jedidiah noticed that her happiness of a few moments ago slowly disappeared and the smile turned into a look of concern. "You're worried about Granny Paloma, aren't you?"

"Do you think she's going to die?"

"God only knows, sweetie. It's up to Him."

"I hope she don't. I'd miss her somethin' terrible."

"So would I. But if she does, you know she will be in a good place."

Hattie smiled and gave him a hug. When she first learned of her granny's illness, she'd tried drawing a picture to see if she could predict her getting better, but all she did was draw her as she was now - sleeping. But Paloma wasn't the only person on her mind. With the storm that was coming, she was worried about Evelyn and her parents. Try as she did, she just couldn't draw anything futuristic about them. She also tried drawing pictures of her own parents on Halloween night, but they seemed to be normal pictures. Her mother was sewing and her father was reading a book. She wondered if that meant they were going to be safe from the storm.

***

Jedidiah, Abigail and Hattie joined hands and said grace. They thanked God for the bountiful "mess" of crawdads He allowed them to catch for supper, and they also prayed for the well being of Paloma.

Jedidiah was about to dig in, when they heard the sin-eater's bell ring. He waited for it to ring a second time - it did. But this time, he ignored it. He continued to fill his plate.

"Are ya' goin'?" Abigail asked.

"No!" he said adamantly. "They expect me to come after what happened in town? I don't think so."

"But what if it ain't town folk? What if it's Shadrack folk?" Abigail asked. "They weren't in town."

Jedidiah put down his fork. He saw the look of concern on his wife's face. Even though the people from Shadrack didn't have a lot to do with her, some of them were her relatives. He reached over, took her hand and gave it a little squeeze. "I'll go…" he picked up his fork. "…but I'm going to eat first!"

When dinner was over, he dressed in his black suit and left. Hattie and Abigail stood on the porch and watched as he disappeared into the woods.

"How come Daddy didn't want to go?" Hattie asked.

"He's still angry 'cause the town folk wouldn't help him with yer granny."

"Is he going to quit being a sin-eater?"

"I don't know. It's up to him."

***

Jedidiah walked through the woods muttering to himself. "If it's anyone except someone from Shadrack, I'm just going to turn around and go back home!" As he marched through the woods, stewing in his anger, he didn't see the tree root before him and the foot of his wooden leg got caught. It detached from the stump of his leg and he fell. Fortunately, he only suffered scrapes on the palms of his hands. He turned over, retrieved his leg and examined at. "Just lovely!" he huffed. The wooden appendage had a crack in it. "I was hoping I could get a little more mileage out of you!"

He looked around and found some vines lying on the ground. He stripped some of the strands and started wrapping the damaged appendage, hoping that it would hold together until he could make a new one. This was the fourth one this year that went bad on him. Usually he could get by with only making two or sometimes three a year. This was the first year he had to make five. He reattached the leg and stood. He tested it as he put his weight on it, and it seemed like it would hold. He continued on his way, but this time a little more carefully. He purposely limped to keep as much weight off the damaged leg as he could.

He finally reached the edge of the woods and saw a young, red-headed woman standing by the bell. She looked to be in her mid-twenties. He was determined. This was not a person from Shadrack. She was nicely dressed, and the carriage she'd come in had a well dressed driver. "I'm just going to apologize and tell her no," he mumbled as he approached her.

The red-headed woman turned and gave him a smile. "Hello, Mr. Jedidiah."

"Hello, I'm sorry Miss, but…"

"You don't remember me, do you?" she interrupted.

"No, I can't say as I do. But I've seen so many people over the years, and most don't have any more conversation with me beyond telling me who passed or who's ill."

"My name is Jessica Trainor. I was six years old the first time we met, and I've never forgotten the service you did me."

Jedidiah scratched his head and tried to remember what service he did for a six year old. "I'm sorry, but I don't remember."

"Perhaps you'll remember the circumstances. I had a little white kitten…"

"Fluffy!" Jedidiah interrupted. It was many years ago that he did a little red-headed child a favor by eating the sins of her dead cat. "That is one sin-eating I will never forget. It had a definite impact on my life."

Jessica smiled sadly and looked down. "I didn't think you would come after the incident in town, and I wouldn't blame you if you didn't come with me now. I heard what happened and thought everyone treated you badly. If I'd been there, I would have at least tried to help you."

Jedidiah sighed. He couldn't say no to this young woman. "How can I be of service?"

"My little boy is very sick. He's only ten months old. His father is in the cavalry and is currently in Texas. I came for a visit so my parents could meet their grandchild." Her voice crackled as she tried not to cry. "I don't know if he's going to make it or not. Could you come and pray for him? Your prayers are always so beautiful, that I'm sure the Lord will listen to you if you ask him to let me keep my son."

"I'll come," he answered in a soft tone. "I don't know if my prayers are any better than the heartfelt ones of a grieving mother, but I'll pray with you."

Jessica thanked him and extended her hand. Jedidiah was surprised, but he took her hand in his and squeezed it ever so gently and then got in the back of the carriage with her. He was feeling somewhat guilty about wanting to deny people who wanted the comfort his prayers gave them. He remembered a passage in Matthew 5:39, *"...but I say unto you, resist not him that is evil: but whosoever smiteth thee on thy right cheek, turn to him the other also."* Jedidiah thought about some of the things he tried to teach Hattie. Forgiveness was one of them. How could he expect his daughter to forgive people, if he couldn't do the same thing?

Chapter 29

The Wedding

The town was excited about the wedding of Pearl-Lee Pickletta and Jonas Burnham. It was going to be one of the biggest social events of the year. Pearl-Lee didn't have the money to spend on anything but a simple ceremony for herself. She had no family, being raised in an orphanage, and was groomed to become a teacher. Though she told Mr. Burnham that she was fine with a small, intimate celebration, he wouldn't hear of it. He wanted her to have all the trimming that the younger brides had and more. The ceremony was going to be at three o'clock. Afterward, it wasn't just going to be cake and punch for the reception, there was going to be a barbeque at the Hartford Mansion. Later, a fireworks display to start off a formal dance to be held that evening.

Pearl-Lee had told Mr. Burnham, as she still called him, that he was being overly extravagant on her behalf, and it would take him years to recuperate all the money he was going to spend on her. But he told her that unknown to everyone in Black Water, he had more money than any twelve of the richest men in town put together. Not even the town banker knew what he was truly worth for he kept the majority of the money at a bank in Baton Rouge to keep his financial affairs private from nosey neighbors. He told her that his uncle had struck it rich in California during the gold rush, and when the man died he'd inherited everything, including some property he hadn't decided what to do with.

Pearl-Lee looked in the mirror and didn't recognize herself. The face staring back at her wasn't that of ol' Miss "Pickle" - a nickname the boys in her class secretly called her. She felt like a princess - a dream that she had longed for had come true. As she readied herself for the walk down the aisle of the church, she hoped that if all this was a dream, she never wanted to wake up!

***

Evelyn sat in the church with her parents, anxiously waiting for the doors to open and the bridal procession to begin. She looked around at the decorations. There were red and white roses everywhere as well as large, white bows hanging at the end of every pew. She had never seen the church decorated so beautifully. She saw Mr. Burnham standing at the front with Reverend Donner waiting for the bride. Mrs. Zackabee was sitting at the organ ready to play when the preacher gave her the nod.

When the music started, two men unrolled a white cloth down the middle of the aisle and opened the doors after it was unfurled. One by one the bridesmaids entered escorted by groomsmen. Evelyn didn't particularly care for the green dresses the bridesmaids were wearing. She thought that lavender would have been a much prettier color and decided if she ever got married, that's what her bridesmaids would wear. She saw Carrie-Ann enter after the bridesmaids. She looked like a miniature bride herself, dressed in white. She walked through the door carrying a basket of red and white rose pedals, dropping a few at a time on the left side of the aisle and then the right.

Evelyn smiled brightly when her friend gave her a little wave. She was happy for Carrie-Ann. Her friend had been without a mother for a long time. Now she would have a good one - if - she lived! Evelyn was still not completely sure her friend would be safe in Black Water. She couldn't get the picture of the gravestone out of her head. She was going to be staying with the Hamilton's, and she knew from Hattie's drawings the roof of their house was going to blow off.

Evelyn watched as Miss Pickletta walked down the aisle next. She barely recognized her. She was dressed in the prettiest, white satin dress she had ever seen. Her hair, which was usually knotted in a bun, was loose and flowing down her back. Her facial features were painted lightly with colors and the lip rouge she wore just intensified her smile. She didn't look like the plain ol' Miss Pickletta she was used to seeing - she actually looked beautiful. As she took her place beside Mr. Burnham, Evelyn thought they looked like the perfect couple.

When Reverend Donner *finally* quit sermonizing and got to the part where he said, "You may kiss the bride," everyone stood and clapped. As the happy couple left the church, everyone followed behind - except for Evelyn. She asked her parents if she could have a private moment to say a prayer before they went to the barbeque. All during the ceremony, she still couldn't get her mind off of Carrie-Ann, and she decided something else besides taking down that cemetery had to be done. Her parents said it would be a little while before they left, so when the church was empty, she started her prayer. She knelt down and folded her hands.

"Dear God," she started. "You probably already know I have this problem because you know everything. I'm very worried about my friend, Carrie-Ann, so I might have to do something I don't like to do, but I'll be doing it for a good reason. I might have to tell a fib! I'll do my best not to if I can. I know all liars will burn in hell, but since I'll be doing it to help someone, I hope you will give me leniency like Uncle Victor sometimes does when he judges criminals at court. So that's why I'm telling you in advance. Sincerely, Evelyn Welch. Amen." When she finished her prayer, she joined her parents and they headed for the reception.

The Hartford Mansion

The long carriageway going toward the Hartford Mansion was lined with Magnolia trees. In front of the two-story mansion was a huge fountain. Twelve roman style columns supported the covering over the front porch. The grounds were landscaped beautifully with gardens and fountains. There was a play area for the children as well as gazebos dotting the premises where people could shade themselves from the sun to sit and converse. The owner of the mansion, Shelby Hartford, almost lost his home due to back taxes after the war, but came upon the idea of renting out his home to host lavish social events since it was the largest home in Black Water. The idea worked, he paid his taxes and kept his head above water. As the years went by, the farm attached to the property became profitable, and he again lived comfortably.

***

Evelyn walked around the grounds looking at all the fountains. It seemed that the whole town came for the reception. There were tables and tables of food. Everyone brought some type of dish. Her mother brought her specialty, bread pudding. There were all types of barbeque: pork, beef, chicken, deer and rabbit. She tried everything, except the rabbit. She just couldn't bring herself to eat a bunny.

Evelyn did her best to try and get her teacher alone so she could talk with her, but one adult after another kept grabbing the bride's arm an escorting her to another group of people. She shadowed her everywhere to catch her by herself, and when Evelyn finally saw her alone and started to approach, she heard a voice behind her.

"There you are, Evelyn!" said Carrie-Ann. "I was beginning to think you weren't here. I've been looking for you everywhere."

"I was just getting ready to…"

But Carrie-Ann grabbed her by the arm and dragged her off. "Come on! You're my partner in the three-legged race. First prize is a box of chocolates. You know how I love chocolate!"

Evelyn went with her, hoping that sometime before her family was ready to leave, she would be able to talk with Carrie-Ann's new mother.

***

Henry and Emmaline walked down the path of one of the many gardens at the Hartford Mansion. "Beautiful place," said Emmaline as she looked at the variety of flowers.

"Speaking of beautiful, I barely recognized Pearl-Lee," said Henry. "It was like the ugly duckling turned into a swan."

"Henry!" Emmaline scolded and gave him a little slap on the arm with her drawstring purse. "That wasn't very nice."

"What did you hit me for?" he chuckled. "I thought I was being nice. All I'm saying is, why did she hide her looks like she did? If she'd made herself up like she is today, she probably would have been married years ago."

"I guess that's just how she was raised. You know she lived in an orphanage. She's just a quiet person."

"Speaking of quiet, Evelyn's been very pensive lately. I know she's not very happy with Mother, but it seems like it's more than that," said Henry.

"It's about Halloween night."

"Don't tell me," Henry sighed. "That damned article in the newspaper. It's caused a real stir. Mother swears up and down that it's either Jedidiah's or Paloma's way of ruining her big event next week."

"None the less, Evelyn says she is not going, and she doesn't want us to go either."

"Well, if she doesn't want to go, I'm not going to make her, but we have to attend. All I can say, is she's going to miss a lot of fun including a closer view of the fireworks." He chuckled a little. "Mother was absolutely ecstatic when I told her that I bought two boxes."

"Your mother has been a very happy woman these last few days."

Henry looked around. "Where is she anyway? I haven't seen her since we left the church."

"She's cloistered somewhere with her women's group."

He nodded his head. "Ahhh, the battle-axes of Black Water - Mrs. Petty-John, Tilly Tate, Vera Harp and…"

"…Sally Gooch," Emmaline continued when Henry stopped short before mentioning her aunt's name. "Henry Welch!" She suppressed her smile. "You are not being very nice today at all! First you call the bride an ugly duckling and your mother and my aunt battle-axes!"

He grinned. "Would Harpies be a better word?"

"Oh you!" She started slapping him with her purse as both of them giggled.

Henry then grabbed her around the waist. "I give up!" He looked in her eyes as she put her arms around his neck. He kissed her.

***

Erma Welch sat in a gazebo with her women's group. A servant brought them a tray of sweet tarts and a pitcher of lemonade. After pouring each of them a glass, the servant departed. Erma took a sip and continued the conversation now that they were alone. "I still say she should have gone with orange or brown dresses for the bridesmaids to be more in line with the season."

"I couldn't agree with you more, Erma," said Mrs. Willa-May Petty-John. The heavy-set, gray-haired woman picked up a tart from the tray. "I told Pearl-Lee that she should have sought your advice in arranging this affair."

"Absolutely," added Sally Gooch. "Green for a bridesmaid dress is fine for spring but for autumn…" She shook her head. "…a seasonal blunder."

Erma sighed. "Well, what's done - is done. At least the venue is appropriate. I've always loved this mansion." The women nodded their heads in agreement.

"I still can't figure out why a handsome man like Jonas Burnham would want to marry a mousey thing like her anyway," said Tilly. She took a sip of lemonade and mumbled, "I make better lemonade than this." She took another sip.

"Maybe it's guilt? I heard he almost ran her down in the street. Maybe

232232232232232

23223223223223232

232

she played a sympathy card," said Sally. "You know he paid for everything when it is supposed to be the bride's responsibility. You never know about those quiet ones."

"I would say he married her out of necessity," said Vera. "He probably just wanted to provide his daughter with a mother. The child should be entering womanhood shortly, and she'll need some motherly advice. Carrie-Ann may be a sweet child, but God knows she's not very bright." She picked up a tart, took a bite and turned up her nose. "Not enough sugar." She finished it anyway and picked up another.

"Speaking of children, Erma," said Willa-May, after finishing her fourth tart. "I hear you're allowing the Sin-Eater's daughter to visit Evelyn. Why would you want to do that?"

Erma took a sip of lemonade and smiled. "As my late husband used to say, you keep your friends close, but you keep your enemies closer."

"Aren't you afraid for Evelyn?" Tilly asked.

"Of course I am!" Erma had hoped Hattie's visits would have remained a secret, but since it wasn't she couldn't very well lie about it. She continued. "Evelyn was compelled to run off into the swamp once looking for her. I don't want it to happen again. If I don't allow the visits, I might lose my granddaughter to some wild animal." The women nodded their understanding and Erma continued. "You mark my words. That child is up to no good, and I intend on finding out what that is. She's been drawing those pictures again that make things happen. I don't have anything conclusive yet, but when I do everyone will see her for what she is - a creature of evil."

"What's on them?" asked Vera. "Can you get your hands on them?"

"I didn't have time to study them carefully. Evelyn hid them before I had a chance to look at them again."

Willa-May was captivated by Erma's discoveries. She took a bite of a fifth tart. "Why didn't you grab them when you had the chance?"

But it was Sally who answered. "As Mr. Gooch has said a few times, you give someone enough rope and they'll hang themselves. These things have to be handled delicately. If we let her implicate herself, then we won't be accused of any chicanery."

The women talked about the article in the newspaper that predicted a violent storm on Halloween night. Erma told them that she was convinced that it was a lie conjured up by Paloma because Hattie was on the block to be expelled from school, and Jedidiah just carried out her plan after she fell ill.

***

"Yes! Yes! Yes!" shouted Carrie-Ann as she and Evelyn crossed the finish line first in the three- legged race. "We did it!"

Mr. McGuire presented a box each of his most expensive chocolates to the girls as the first place winners (which were purchased by Jonas Burnham for the race).

Carrie-Ann turned to Evelyn. "You want to be my partner in the egg relay?"

"I would, but I have to go - ahm - you know where."

"Have you used the water closet yet?" Carrie-Ann asked.

"They have one?"

"Sure! It's really swell. When you're done, you pull the chain, the water swirls 'round and 'round and then the poop goes down a hole. The water fills the bowl again - clean as a whistle. I hope Papa gets one when he gets back from his honeymoon. He said he'd think about it."

Evelyn headed back to the house and met Mary-Beth Coulter. "You missed the race. Carrie-Ann and I won."

"Papa didn't want me to enter," she replied. "He didn't want to take the chance that I might sprain my ankle before my horse jumping competition next week. But he said I could do the egg relay."

"Are you excited about the competition?"

Mary-Beth smiled and sighed at the same time. "Nervous! I just hope I get an honorable mention. Papa will be so proud of me. He's been telling everyone. Everybody I've met has wished me good luck."

Evelyn was dying to tell her that Hattie predicted she was going to win first place, but she held her tongue. She didn't want to jinx her, so she just wished her good luck also and headed for the main house.

As she walked along, she kept looking for her teacher, but didn't spot her. She entered the house and asked directions to the water closet. The servant led her there, told her it was occupied at the moment and gave her instructions on how to use it while she waited. A few minutes later, the door opened and Evelyn saw her teacher standing before her.

"Hello, Evelyn," She bent down and whispered in her ear, "You might want to wait a moment before you go in." She giggled slightly. "I opened the window."

This was her chance! She finally had her alone. "Miss Pickletta - I mean Mrs. Burnham…"

"Doesn't that sound so nice," said her teacher dreamily. "I love hearing it - Mrs. Burnham. Mrs. Pearl-Lee Burnham." She shook herself from her reverie. "I'm sorry, you wanted to say something?"

"Can I talk to you for a minute before somebody grabs you again? I've wanted to talk to you all day."

Pearl-Lee laughed. "I think I can spare a few moments for one of my brightest students. I think the air has cleared in there by now." She nodded to the servant standing by to demonstrate the workings of the water closet, and said she would give the instruction. The two entered the room and closed the door. "What is it you wanted to talk about?"

Evelyn said a quick mental prayer again asking God to forgive her in advance for the fib she was about to tell. She crossed her fingers behind her back. "I was talking to Carrie-Ann. She's really - really going to miss both of you when you go on your honeymoon. You know her Papa always takes her everywhere…"

"You don't have to say anymore," Pearl-Lee interrupted. "Carrie-Ann already told us about the picture Hattie drew and the little cemetery those two miscreants, Robbie and Billy, talked her into making." She shook her head. "Honestly, the things those two boys get into."

Evelyn sighed in relief. She didn't have to lie. "I'm worried about her. There's a storm coming."

Pearl-Lee put an arm around her. "You are a sweet child, Evelyn. I wish more girls were like you. Mr. Burnham and I have already discussed taking Carrie-Ann with us. We don't know if there is truly a storm coming or not, but neither of us want to take that chance. We haven't told her yet, but she's coming with us. Carrie-Ann has never seen the ocean, so we've decided to make it our first family event." She held her finger to her lips. "But don't say anything. We want to keep it a surprise. She's staying with the Hamilton's tonight and then we're going to pick her up in the morning before we leave for the coast."

Evelyn gave her a hug. "You don't know how glad I am to hear that." She looked at her teacher, smiled and pointed to the contraption against the wall. "Now, how do you use that thing?"

***

Evelyn was finally able to relax and enjoy the rest of the wedding celebration now that she knew Carrie-Ann would be safe. She played games with the other children and even followed Robbie and Billy to the cow pasture with several others. The boys told the group they had something really fun to show them called cow tipping. Evelyn and the others watched as the two snuck upon a cow that stood asleep in the field. They pushed the cow on its side, and the startled animal fell over, hitting the ground with a thump. Most everyone laughed. Evelyn couldn't help snickering herself but told them she thought it was stupid, as well as a mean thing to do to a dumb animal.

A while later, all the children under the age of fourteen who had parents that were staying for the ball, were taken up to the playrooms of the mansion. When the sun had gone down, Evelyn and the others were escorted to the courtyard for the dazzling display of fireworks.

Carrie-Ann stood next to Evelyn. "This has been the best day ever! I now have a Papa and a Mama. We are going to be sooo happy together."

Evelyn smiled and could confidently say, "I know you will."

***

Monday came and Evelyn waited for Hattie at the edge of the field that she usually crossed to come to school. She was anxious to tell her of the news about Carrie-Ann. When Evelyn saw her, she ran to greet her. She wanted to be sure that the gravestone would be gone, and she'd done the right thing. The two girls sat down, and Evelyn pulled out a piece of paper. Hattie started to draw. The picture had changed - but not completely. It was more confusing. Hattie had drawn Carrie-Ann lying in bed, with her parents sitting at her bedside - the gravestone was the headboard of the bed!

Chapter 30

Monday Evening - Five Days till Halloween

Hattie sat down at the dinner table with her family. They joined hands as Jedidiah said the grace. "Dear Lord, we thank you for the food upon this table and our well-being. We pray for the life of our beloved Paloma that you give her back to us, and if not that she will sit beside you at your table. We also ask you for your help in healing the child of Jessica Trainor, that she and her husband will be able to love and care for that small gift you gave them - Amen."

Abigail passed Jedidiah a bowl of beans. "Ya' going again tonight?"

"I couldn't say no," Jedidiah replied. "The child has Cholera. He needs all the prayers he can get. She sent a telegraph to her husband in Texas. He could be here by now."

Abigail sighed and shook her head. "Poor woman."

Hattie took a piece of fried rabbit from the plate. "Daddy, I didn't think you were going to do that anymore for town folk."

Jedidiah thought for a moment. "There's a line in a poem that was written a long time ago by a man named Alexander Pope that says, *'To err is human, to forgive divine.'*"

"What does that mean?" Hattie asked.

"It means everyone makes mistakes. Doesn't matter if they're large or small. The way I figure it, Jesus is divine and He forgave those who killed him. That was a big mistake. My feelings were just hurt. Though I'm nowhere near divine, I just needed time to think about the right thing to do. Does that make sense?"

Hattie nodded her head and changed the subject. "Did ya' finish your new leg?"

Jedidiah grinned and lifted his pant leg. "How does it look?"

"Like a wooden leg." The three of them laughed and continued eating dinner.

***

When dinner was over, Jedidiah got dressed and left. Abigail and Hattie were getting ready to feed Paloma her broth when they heard a knock at the door. "Who in the world?" Abigail was surprised. They never had visitors who actually came knocking. She peeked out the window. "Well, bust my britches!"

"Who is it, Mama?"

"It's Uncle Ennis and Aunt Josie!" Abigail opened the door. "What in tarnation are you two doin' here?"

"Now is that anyway ta' greet kin what has come ta' visit?" asked Ennis. "Are ya' gonna have us in or stand there gawkin' at us with yer eyeballs a poppin' out?"

Abigail invited them in. Josie handed her a clay pot. "We hear'd Paloma Day were feelin' poorly. I brought ya' some of my famous chicken soup. Maybe it might help her git well."

"Thank ya', Aunt Josie. That's awful kind of ya'." She put the pot on the counter. Her aunt's cooking was nothing to write home about - except for that one recipe. No one in Shadrack could make chicken soup that could hold a candle to it. The only question was - why? Her uncle has only been there twice. The first time was when he forced Jedidiah to marry her years ago, and the second was to convince her to help him catch gators several months ago. Her aunt had never been there at all.

Abigail asked them to have a seat in the good chairs by the fireplace, and she pulled up one from the kitchen table for herself. After her aunt and uncle finished the uncustomary compliments to Hattie's looks and noting how much she'd "growed," Abigail sent her daughter in the other room to start giving Paloma the broth.

Abigail was tempted to say something sarcastic, but she held her tongue and smiled. "I'm a pleasured for yer company. Can I fix ya' some coffee? It's still warm."

"Thank ya' kindly…" Josie started to accept, but at a nod from Ennis, she added, "But we won't be stayin' long."

Ennis cleared his throat. "We come 'bout two matters. First, we hear'd a storm was a headin' this way when someone who could read found a newspaper from Black Water. What ever'one wants ta' know, did Paloma say anythin' 'bout it hittin' Shadrack too?"

"Not as I recollect," Abigail replied. "The only place I know is Black

Water. But that don't mean it won't."

"Hmm." Ennis was disappointed, but continued. "Well, the second thing we come 'bout was to see if ya' could put another one of them Gypsy blessin's 'round us again."

"A what?"

"You know - like ya' did when Ennis tried ta' hornswaggle ya' out of yer gator money," Josie said. Ennis poked her in the rib and Josie poked him back.

"Ohhh! That blessing." Abigail tried not to laugh. She remembered that day fondly. But she was curious all the same. "How come?"

"Cause of all the good luck we been havin'," Josie replied. "First, ya' know yer Cousin Jubal's wife has been tryin' for years to give him a son." She held up her fingers. "Five younin' and nary a boy among'em. Well, she was at the house that day, pregnant with baby number six, and don't ya' know she popped out twin boys last week!"

"Congratulations!" said Abigail. "What did he name them?"

"Bucky and Bubba," Josie replied. "They're as cute as a button!"

"Before that," Ennis added. "I met a fella what told me I was bein' cheated on the price I was gettin' for all them gators. When the gator buyer made another contract with me for more hides, I upped my price and told him he could take it or I'd sell'em ta' someone else. The man took the deal. Now with the storm that's supposta be comin', ever' man-jack in Shadrack has been hired to harvest crops 'cause they're afraid of losin' em."

When Ennis hesitated in continuing, Josie nudged him in the ribs. "Go on! Tell her the rest and ask her."

He frowned at his wife. "I was, if'n ya' let me catch a breath." He looked at Abigail. "After the harvestin', ever'body's pullin' up stakes and head'n back ta' Kentucky."

Abigail was surprised. "Really! I thought ya' liked it around here."

"It ain't bad, but we's tired of bein' looked down on by them high'n mighty Black Water folk," said Josie. "A preacher came through Shadrack a couple of months ago. He stayed for a few weeks and held our Sunday-go-ta' meetin' service whilst he was here. He talked ta' us 'bout being educated and learnin' things, especially the things in the Bible. Only a hand full of our people can read'n write. We had a town meetin' and decided ta' send our youn'ins ta' school." Josie frowned. "Their school board said no. They said they don't want no more Shadrack trash associatin' with their children. We decided ta' go back home." Josie lifted her chin proudly. "We got respect there!"

"We got enough money from all them gator hides that we can now git a piece of bottom land ta' have a real nice farm. I got a cousin over in Pine Knot what wrote me awhile back 'bout a piece than can be had for a lick and a promise," added Ennis. Josie nudged him again when he hesitated in asking her the question. He glared at her. "Damn it, woman! If ya' don't quit pokin' me in the ribs, I'm gonna have ta' git a sawbones ta' tape'em up!" He looked back at Abigail. "Do you and Hattie wanna go with us?"

Abigail didn't know what to say. She would love to go back to Kentucky, but there was a lot to consider. "I don't know. I'd have ta' ask Jedidiah…" she looked toward the bedroom. "…and then there's Paloma."

Ennis scratched his chin. "Hmm, I didn't think 'bout ya' wantin' ta' bring them."

Abigail folded her arms. "I ain't leavin' my husband or Granny Paloma."

Ennis shrugged. "I guess if ya' wanna. We might need a good sin-eater at that for the trip back. He does do some damn good prayin'!" Ennis and Josie stood. "Well, ya' got time ta' consider it. So, does ya' think ya' can do it?"

Abigail rolled her eyes. "I just told ya', I gotta talk ta' Jedidiah!"

"I'm talkin' bout the blessin'!" Ennis shook his head. "Can ya' do it?"

Abigail laughed slightly and regained her composure. "I don't know if it will work again, bein' that Paloma is sick'n all. It's been a spell since I said it."

"Well, it can't hurt, can it?" Josie asked. "We just wanna make sure ever'one has a safe trip back."

Abigail smiled and told them to have a seat and fold their hands. In a soft tone, she preceded to say the bedtime prayer she usually said with Hattie, only in the Italian language that Paloma had taught her. When she was done, Ennis and Josie thanked her and left.

Hattie came out of the bedroom. She'd been listening at the door. "Are we gonna move, Mama?"

She heard the concern in her voice and knew immediately what it was - leaving Evelyn. "I don't know, sugar." She smiled and put an arm around her. "It's something we'll have ta' talk about." She looked toward the bedroom. "A lot depends on yer granny."

***

Lieutenant Jack Trainor stopped the carriage in front of the sin-eater's bell and got out, as did Jedidiah. "Can I pick you up tomorrow?"

"That will be fine," Jedidiah replied.

The young man extended his hand. Jedidiah took it. "I don't' believe in this sin-eating thing you do that Jessica and her parents believe in, but your beautiful prayers give my wife hope for our son's sake."

"Your boy is a fighter. Most children would have passed on by now. And," Jedidiah smiled. "It's not the sin-eating that I believe in either. The only thing I consider I do is just give comfort to the living, and ask God for help in healing the body or the aching soul."

The young man nodded his head in agreement. "You do - do that. Whatever happens with the life of my child, I owe you a debt. Maybe someday I can repay what you're doing for us now."

They said their good-byes, and Jedidiah watched as the man drove away. He wished more people in Black Water were like Jessica and Jack Trainor. He turned toward the woods and headed home.

Tuesday - Four Days till Halloween

Hattie sat down on the edge of Evelyn's bed and leaned against the post of the footboard. "I'd hate to move."

"I'd hate to see you move," said Evelyn. "But if you did, you'd probably go someplace where you could have more friends."

"As long as I have you, I don't need nobody else."

Evelyn smiled and sat beside her. "Well, let's don't talk about it. You said that as long as your granny was sick, you weren't going anywhere. Even though I don't wish your granny ill will, Mama told me that people who suffer with brain sicknesses rarely get better. She could live a long time like she is."

"That's what Daddy said." She sighed and changed the subject. "Now, we gotta decide what ta' do with those pictures. Either we give 'em out, or we don't."

Evelyn stood and started to pace. "I thought sure Carrie-Ann was now safe. But now the gravestone is hanging over her head."

Hattie picked up the picture and looked at it. "It's like you saved her from one death just for her to face another one."

Evelyn looked at the picture with her. "The way I see it, death might be hanging over her head, but she still might live. Maybe in this picture she's sick, and it could go either way."

Hattie agreed and told her about the little boy her father was praying for everyday - that his life was hanging in what he called "the balance." Hattie said she was tempted to draw his picture, but was afraid to.

Both girls studied the picture in silence for a moment and then Hattie spoke first. "I don't think we should give 'em out. What if we do and they change what they were going to do. Maybe that change is what causes them to get hurt. They're mostly your friends. It's up to you."

Evelyn sat down at the desk and looked though all the pictures. "So many people might either be hurt or die. I don't know what to do." Evelyn stood with the pictures in hand, walked to the closet and put them in her secret place. "You're granny and my mama are smart. I think we should listen to them. We won't give them out."

There was a knock at Evelyn's door, and then her grandmother entered. "Evelyn, dear, the cook just pulled a pecan pie from the oven. Tell the cook I said it was all right for the two of you to have a small piece before dinner."

Erma didn't have to ask the girls twice. Pecan pie was Evelyn's favorite. Hattie said she only remembered having it once, but she liked it. They left the room and headed down the steps. Erma watched them and smiled. "If you don't give them out - I will!" She'd been listening at the door as the girls talked. She went to Evelyn's closet and opened the secret place. She'd spent hours looking for it while Evelyn was at school. She pulled out the pictures and took them just in case the girls decided to destroy them. Without the pictures as evidence against the witch child, she would never get the girl out of Evelyn's life.

Wednesday - Three Day's till Halloween

Hattie looked out the window as it poured rain. Her parents always kept her home from school on those days because they didn't want her to catch her death of cold. The decision she'd made about the pictures and agreed to by Evelyn weighed heavily on her mind. Did she do the right thing? Her granny told her that with her gift she had a responsibility, but that responsibility extended to knowing when to say something and when not to. Was it a time to tell or be silent?

***

Evelyn sat in the classroom looking out the window. She saw a streak of lightening and heard a loud crack of thunder. She looked around the room. She wished she could have stayed home, but she was the mayor's daughter, and had to set a good example. Her father brought her to school in their enclosed carriage, and she wore her raincoat so her hair and clothing would stay dry.

As she looked around the room, most of the desks were empty. They always were on days like those. She thought about the pictures and how empty the school might be after the storm on Halloween. She was starting to have second thoughts.

Thursday - Two Days till Halloween

The sun was shining that morning and once again all the seats in school were full. Evelyn was anxious to talk to Hattie that morning, but she was later than usual in arriving and barely made it through the door before the final bell was rang.

Evelyn could hardly wait for recess. Time seemed to stand still as their substitute teacher went on and on about some dead poet named Shakespeare. But finally it came and the two girls separated themselves from the others. "They're gone! I tore my closet and my whole room apart looking for the pictures. I thought sure I put them in my secret place. You didn't take them home with you did you?"

"No! I saw you put'em away."

Evelyn groaned angrily and clenched her fists as she paced. "It was Grandmamma! She took them! I know she did."

Hattie thought for a moment. "Well, maybe it's a good thing she did. If she realizes what they are, she can warn the people in them and we won't have to."

"Maybe." Evelyn calmed a bit. "But I don't trust her anymore. Ever since we became friends, she's not been a very nice person."

"Only to me," Hattie reminded her. "Everybody doesn't like somebody. I don't like Robbie Harp or Billy Tate."

"You're right," she sighed. "I don't like them either. But the difference between you and them is, you're nice and their not and my grandmother can't see that."

The two girls talked until the bell signaled that recess was over. Evelyn asked if she would be able to come over after school, but Hattie said she was going frog giggin' with her daddy. Evelyn cringed, and Hattie giggled at the face she made.

When school was out for the day, Evelyn and Hattie said their good-byes and both hoped they would be around to see each other after Saturday night. School was not going to be held on that Friday because the teachers were on the decorating committee, and they needed to get things ready the for party at the town hall.

Friday - One Day till Halloween

McGuire's General Store

Jimmy Johnson was sweeping out the store room when he heard Mr. McGuire call. He put his broom down and went up front. "Yes, sir?"

"I need you to go to the town hall and pick up that box of dynamite to take it to Mr. Baxter's house. Mayor Welch wants it out of there today."

"What if he's not home again? Mrs. Baxter wouldn't take it before."

"Tell her she's just going to have to take it," he replied adamantly. "Her husband purchased it. It's their responsibility."

Jimmy took off his apron and went to the stable to get Mr. McGuire's team of horses and wagon. He went to the storage room of the town hall and saw the boxes of fireworks and next to it the dynamite. He started to pick it up, but a voice from behind startled him.

"Hi, Jimmy Johnson."

He turned around and saw Alice McGuire leaning against the door frame. "Alice! You just about scare me ta' death! What if I'd dropped this box of dynamite?" He shook his head. "What are you doin' here?"

"I heard Daddy tell you to come here." She sashayed up to him and batted her long eyelashes. "You gonna dance with me tomorrow night at the Halloween party?"

"Now, you know before your daddy hired me, he said YOU were off limits."

"That's not fair!" she huffed and sat down on one of the boxes. "Every boy I like, my father says he's not good enough for me. I'm sixteen. If my mama were still alive, she would approve of you. I wish you'd just quit working for daddy and work for someone else."

Jimmy sat next to her. "Listen Alice, I care about you a lot. But working at the store gives me some valuable business experience. I'd like to run a store like his someday. I'm not cut out to be a farmer."

"Can't you work for one of the other businesses?" she pouted.

"None of them were hiring," he sighed. "I just barely got the job with your dad."

"Then you won't dance with me." She looked at him with her big, brown, puppy dog eyes.

Jimmy put his arm around her. "I didn't say that." He smiled and kissed her. When their lips parted, he brushed a strand of hair from her face. "In two years, when I'm eighteen, maybe we'll go away together." He stood and picked up a box. "But in the meantime, I can't afford for your father to fire me."

Alice walked out to the wagon with him. "Can I ride out to the Baxter's with you?"

"What if someone sees us together and tells your father?"

"I can hide in the back of the wagon until we get out of town," she suggested.

He thought about it for a moment. He used to love spending time with Alice when they were in school together. He hated sneaking behind her father's back, but how else could they get to know each other better if they were separated? He smiled, put the box in the back of the wagon and nestled it between the bales of hay to keep it from jarring too much. "Jump in. Cover yourself with that tarp. We'll have to pass your daddy's store to get to the Baxter's."

Alice got in the back and once they were out of town, she climbed up in the seat next to him. It was a twenty-minute ride to the Baxter Farm. When they arrived, Jimmy was relieved to see Mr. Baxter chopping wood by the house. He didn't relish having an argument with his wife about taking her husband's order, and he didn't want to take it back to the store either.

"Howdy, Mr. Baxter," Jimmy said as he pulled up next to him. Alice greeted him as well.

The man wiped the sweat from his brow and smiled at the two. "Jim, Alice," he acknowledged. "Sorry you had to make another trip out here, Jimbo. I'm guessin' you've got my dynamite?"

"It's in the back. Oh, Mr. McGuire said that the Mayor wants you to inform the…."

"…Sheriff before I blast." The man nodded his head. "I know. I've already made arrangements with Sheriff Wright. If you don't mind, just put it in the barn for me. I'll tend to it in a few minutes."

"Sure thing." Jimmy drove the wagon to the barn and put the box just inside the door. He got in the wagon and snapped the reins. "See ya' later, Mr. Baxter!"

"Thanks, boy! And hey!" he shouted to them. "Don't let ol' man McGuire catch you with his daughter!" He laughed and continued chopping wood. When he was finished, he went to the barn to put the explosives up until he used them. He pried open the box and removed the top layer of straw. "What the hell!" He picked up one of the long sticks. "That's not dynamite. It's a roman candle!" He laughed. Normally he'd be angry at having to make a trip into town to exchange a wrong delivery, but he imagined McGuire's daughter had something to do with Jimmy's lack of attention. He figured that since he was taking his family to the Halloween party, he'd just exchange it then.

HALLOWEEN - 12:30 p.m.

Jedidiah wiped a tear from his eye, as he stood next to the crib of Jack and Jessica Trainor's little boy. He'd come every day and prayed with the child's parents for the boy's life. Dr. Jackson had just given them the news. He sighed and looked at the parents. "The fever is broken. I believe he'll be fine."

Jedidiah watched as the two young parents hugged each other joyously. Not wanting to break into the happy moment, he slipped out of the house. He'd come early that day because of the Halloween celebration that night. The bell was only a mile's walk.

Jedidiah barely passed the gates of the property, when Jack Trainor pulled up beside him in the carriage. "I turned around and you were gone."

Jedidiah smiled. "I didn't want to interrupt the moment."

"Hop in. I'll take you back."

He didn't have to be asked twice. They talked as they rode, and Jack laughed when Jedidiah told him the story of the sin-eating he'd done for his wife's dead cat. When they reached the bell, Jedidiah got out of the carriage.

Jack pulled the money clip from his pocket. "I'm told that sin-eater's get paid for what they do."

"Put your money away." Jedidiah waved it off. "I've already been paid - your son will live. That's payment enough."

Jack smiled and put it away. "Then I won't insult you. I owe you a debt. Someday I'll pay it."

"Then do me a favor," he said seriously. "Don't go to the Halloween party in town tonight. Keep an eye out. I think there's a storm coming."

"I'll heed your warning." He snapped the reins and headed for home.

Jedidiah looked up into the sky before he entered the woods. It was one o'clock in the afternoon. There was a slight breeze, but the sky looked clear. Paloma predicted a storm. He didn't see anything that looked like a rain cloud. He wondered if her prediction could have been wrong. He headed for home.

Welch Residence 3:00 p.m.

"Evelyn, sweetie, are you sure you don't want to go?" Emmaline asked. "I think this is going to be the best party your grandmother has ever put together. Your father has even included fireworks."

"No!" Evelyn sat in the window seat of the drawing room and looked out. "There's going to be a storm, and you shouldn't go either."

"There's not a rain cloud in the sky," said her father.

"I'm staying here," she pouted. "I don't want anything to do with Grandmamma's party! Storm or no storm."

Henry folded his arms. "Don't be arrogant, Evelyn. I know you and your grandmother have been at odds lately, but she's still your elder."

"Well, she invaded my privacy and took something that didn't belong to her!"

Emmaline rolled her eyes. They went through that a couple of days ago, but Evelyn wouldn't tell them what her grandmother was supposed to have taken. All she said was, "She knows." When Emmaline confronted Erma about it, she too had been evasive, and asked in a smug manner, "What is it I'm supposed to have taken?" Without Evelyn telling her what it was, they were at a standoff. They ended up sending their daughter to bed that night without supper because of her rudeness.

Emmaline turned to Henry. "Come on, dear. Your mother wants us to help with some of the last minute decorations."

As they headed for the door, Henry turned. "If you change your mind, just have Fredricks bring you."

Evelyn didn't look back. "I won't change my mind." When her parents left, she looked up at the sky. A few clouds had gathered, but it didn't look like any kind of storm was brewing.

The Swamp - 5:00 p.m.

Hattie stood on the porch looking up at the sky. The clouds had increased, and they were moving a little more swiftly, but they didn't look like the normal storm clouds. She was glad they decided not to give out those pictures. What if the storm happened on another night? She would have caused people to worry for nothing.

Abigail joined her daughter on the porch. She had an idea about what Hattie was thinking. "Ya' never know 'bout storms. One minute the sky can be bright and sunny and the next, black as coal. Best ya' quit worrin' 'bout it."

"It's kinda hard not to. Me and Evelyn have been worrin' about it for a while."

"Well, how about we make some popped-corn balls ta' take yer mind off of it? It'll make a nice desert for after supper."

Hattie gave her a smile and went inside.

Welch Residence 6:00 p.m.

There was a knock at the door, and Evelyn opened it with a tray of peanut butter cookies. She saw two boys dressed as pirates.

"Trick or treat, smell my feet, give me somethin' good to eat!" They laughed.

"Robbie and Billy! The two of you are disgusting!" She extended the tray. "Just take a cookie and go away." The boys picked up a couple of cookies each. "Hey! I said one!"

They ignored her and ate one of them. "How come you aren't trick or treating?" Billy asked.

"I've got my reasons," she replied.

"Because she's being stupid," Robbie laughed. "Remember the newspaper? She thinks a big tornado is coming and going to blow us all away!"

"You've got your treats, now go away." She started to close the door, but as an afterthought she turned and said, "If you plan on smoking a cigarette tonight, don't. You might get caught, and I think you'll get in trouble." She closed the door.

"I wonder why she said that?" Billy asked.

Robbie pulled a pouch out of his back pocket. "I was going to show you later. Look what I found. Someone dropped his makin's." He opened the pouch to show Billy. "There's enough tobacco, paper and matches for us to roll a couple of cigarettes."

"When we gonna smoke'em?"

"Later while the party is goin' on. Nobody will pay any attention to us then."

Billy then had a thought. "How did Evelyn know about us smokin'?"

Robbie shrugged. "I don't know. Maybe Hattie drew one of those pictures." They thought about egging Evelyn's house, but they only had a couple of eggs left and decided to save them for someone who didn't have a treat for them.

Town Hall - 8:00 p.m.

The wind had started to pick up but still no rain. No stars were visible and the moon was covered by clouds making it a dark night. The majority of the trick or treating had ended and people started arriving at the town hall for the big party. The inside of the town hall was decorated with orange and black ribbons. There were tombstones hanging on the walls and scarecrows or ghosts in the corners. Tables of sweets for the children or anyone who enjoyed confectionary treats ran along the side of the wall. Erma had also arranged for an orchestra - not just a banjo and fiddle players.

Erma, as well as the other members of the women's committee, Sally Gooch, Willa-May Petty-John, Tilly Tate and Vera Harp greeted the people as they entered and complimented all the guests on their costumes. The committee members themselves dressed as angels. They wore white gowns, halos on their heads and wings on their backs.

Erma was disappointed that some of the people she'd invited decided to stay home. She silently cursed Paloma Day, believing the newspaper article had kept them away. But - as she looked around the room, she did notice that the majority of everyone in the pictures Hattie drew was there.

Now was the time to set her plan in motion. She conversed with the various pirates, ghosts, monsters, queens and kings and then spotted Silvia and Bob Cannapple. She started with a little small talk about the party, the décor and then mentioned their son. "I'm sorry that your son broke his arm."

Bob and Silvia looked at each other. "George's arm is fine." They looked around the room. "There he is."

Erma turned and looked. "Hmm." She pulled out one of the pictures. "Hattie drew a picture of him. His arm is in a sling." She gave it to them.

The boy's mother stared at the picture. "He's never had a broken arm. I wonder why she drew it?"

"I don't know. That girl is a strange one. I think she takes after her grandmother, Paloma Day." Erma smiled. "I wouldn't worry about it though. It's just a picture."

Erma excused herself to seek out another from the pictures. She had similar conversations with many of the guests and made little derogatory remarks about Hattie, leaving them to wonder why the girl would draw pictures that depicted injuries to their family members.

***

Emmaline and Henry were enjoying themselves thoroughly. They couldn't help but think of their daughter, waiting at home for a storm that hadn't come. They saw Sheriff Wright approach.

"I see you made it back in town, Hiram," said Henry as they shook hands. "Catch any fish?"

"A few, but you should have seen the one that got away." He chuckled. The sheriff took a sip of punch and looked around the room. "Your mother out did herself this year. I think this is her best party yet." Then he laughed. "But maybe I shouldn't have come."

"Oh?" Henry questioned. "Why would you say that?"

He pulled out a picture from his back pocket. "Look what your mother gave me. Something the Sin-Eater' daughter drew."

Emmaline and Henry looked at the picture with a board protruding from the sheriff's back. "Mother gave you this?" Henry asked.

The Sheriff laughed. "That kid sure can draw. It's a bit gruesome, but what do you expect. It's Halloween." He spotted Victor Gooch. "Excuse me a moment. I need to talk to the Judge."

Emmaline looked toward her mother-in law. She hadn't noticed it before, but as Erma was talking to Ezra Katts, she was showing him a couple of pictures. "Henry, do you suppose these pictures are what Evelyn was talking about when she said your mother took something?"

Henry glared at his mother. "Most definitely! I think we owe our daughter an apology."

Emmaline looped her arm around Henry's. "We've made our rounds. What do you say we go home? I feel guilty for leaving her alone."

"I'll just talk to Victor, and let him organize the fireworks display and then we'll leave. I'll also see if he'll bring mother home."

***

Robbie and Billy had just been scolded by their mothers. They'd showed their sons a picture of them smoking and warned them if they'd ever caught them, it would mean a trip to the woodshed. The boys stayed in sight of their mothers for a while, until their attentions were diverted to the goings on of the party.

"I told you Hattie drew some sort of picture of us," said Robbie and then he laughed. "Come on. I say we don't make her picture lie."

"Where're we going to do it?" Billy asked.

"The storage room. Nobody will see us in there."

The two boys made sure they left the main room unseen. They sat down on a couple of boxes and made an attempt to roll their first cigarette. They kept dropping tobacco and had trouble rolling the paper.

"My dad makes this look easy," Billy grumbled as he scooped tobacco from the floor.

Robbie kept working with his. "I think I've finally got one!"

"Well, I hope so, we're out of papers. How 'bout sharing yours?"

Robbie pulled out a match and tried striking it. When it wouldn't light, he threw it behind him, and it landed in a small bale of hay. He tried another, and the same thing happened.

"Come on, Robbie! That's the last match," Billy grumbled.

This time when he struck it - it lit. He held the match to the cigarette, inhaled the smoke and started to cough. "Pretty - good," Robbie coughed out and passed it to Billy.

Billy tried it and coughed as well. "Good! It tastes terrible!" He passed it back.

"Well, the grown-ups do it." He took one more draw and heard someone start to open the door. He had to get rid of the evidence quickly, so he threw the cigarette behind him. He hoped it wasn't his mother coming to look for him. Robbie sighed slightly when he saw Judge Gooch and Mayor Welch."

"What are you two doing in here?" Henry asked.

The boys shrugged. "Just sittin'."

Victor took one whiff and knew they'd been smoking. "Get out of here before I tell your mothers what you were doing. There are boxes of fireworks in this room. The two of you could have caught the building on fire."

The boys quickly ran out of the room. Henry pointed to the boxes the boys were sitting on. "There they are."

"Sure you don't want to stay for the big event?" Victor asked.

"I'm sure. I went outside to have our carriage brought around and noticed the wind is starting to pick up a little. You might want to set them off a little earlier."

Victor looked at his watch. "It about nine-thirty." He smiled at Henry. "Be on your porch around ten-thirty, and you can see some of the show from there."

They exited the room and closed the door. The cigarette Robby Harp had thrown behind him was smoldering in bale of hay beside the boxes. The hot ash fell on one of the matches Robbie had trouble igniting - the match caught fire.

Time 9:35 p.m.

"What do you mean you're leaving!" Erma was outraged. "Henry, you're my son, and I forbid it."

"I'm not a child anymore, Mother. We're going to watch the fireworks at home with our daughter."

"Well, she should have come," Erma chided. "The two of you indulge her whims too much. You should have insisted she come."

Emmaline glared at her. "So she could watch you give out the pictures that - you took from her room. Why would you want to give out those horrid pictures? I saw the one you gave the Sheriff, and the Canapple's showed me the drawing you gave them of their son a moment ago."

"You should be glad I did," Erma returned. "This is proof of how wicked the Sin-Eater's daughter is. Who but a wicked person could draw such havoc? Mark my words. She's the product of all those sins carried by her father."

"I don't believe it!" Emmaline exclaimed. She thought of her own father's drawings. "If the girls hid them away, they did it for a reason. You invaded their privacy."

Henry extended his hand. "Give me the rest of them."

"I don't have any more," Erma lied. "I gave them all out." She wasn't about to relinquish the rest of the drawings. They were her evidence.

Henry was angry with her. "Good-night, Mother. Victor will bring you home."

Time: 9:40 p.m.

Henry and Emmaline were about to walk out the door, when they were greeted by Alvin Baxter. "You're just getting here, Alvin?" Henry asked.

"Yeah. My kids were late getting back from trick or treating, and one of the boys got a chocolate handprint on his mother's ghost costume." He laughed. "I told her she would look more unique if the boys put chocolate hand prints all over her costume. But she told me not to be ridiculous, and it took her forever to get a clean sheet adjusted."

"Well, have a good time. The fireworks will be starting shortly," Henry replied.

"Oh, speaking of fireworks, have you seen Jimmy Johnson? He accidently delivered me a box of fireworks instead of my dynamite. I don't want him to get in trouble with ol' man McGuire. He's a good kid with a good head on his shoulders when it isn't turned by Alice," he chuckled. "I don't want the man to fire him for the mistake."

"I saw Jimmy sneak out the back with Alice a few moments ago," said Emmaline. "I think they make a cute couple."

"Alice's old man is an idiot," Alvin replied. "He wants Alice to marry some rich bastard -ahm…." He looked at Emmaline apologetically. "Pardon my language."

Emmaline laughed. "Apology accepted."

"You don't have to bother Jimmy," Henry said. "Your dynamite is in the storage room. McGuire didn't want it in his store so I told him he could keep it here." He turned to Emmaline. "If you'll wait in the carriage for me, dear, I'll be just a moment."

Emmaline grinned. "I know what your moments are. You'll stop and talk to at least five or six people on the way there and five or six on the way back. A moment could be as long as thirty minutes."

"Who me?" Henry said innocently as he walked away with Alvin. He turned and shouted back, "Ten minutes tops!"

Emmaline shook her head. "And men say we women talk too much."

Time: 9:50 p.m.

As Emmaline predicted, Henry and Alvin stopped at least five times to talk to this person or that. What would have taken them about thirty-seconds to walk across the room, ended up being ten minutes. They finally reached the door to the storage room.

"We better hurry," said Henry. "You know how our wives don't like to be kept waiting."

Alvin laughed. "And they talk about us!"

Henry put his hand on the metal doorknob and pulled it away quickly. "DAMN!" he shouted. "It's hot!"

Alvin look at the floor and saw smoke coming out from under the door. "There's a fire in there. SHIT! The dynamite!"

Henry and Alvin turned and shouted. "EVERYONE! RUN! CLEAR THE BUILDING! IT'S GOING TO BLOW!"

Meanwhile - The Swamp

Hattie sat on the floor playing with Esmeralda, their black cat. She looked at her parents. Just like her picture had indicated for Halloween night, her mother was sewing and her father was reading one of her school books. She stood and looked out the window. The wind had started to really pick up. Suddenly, she heard some noises in the distance. "There's a lot of popping and whistling going on."

Jedidiah and Abigail also heard the sound and the three of them went outside. "Probably fireworks," said Jedidiah. But then there came a noise that he was all too familiar with - a sound he remembered from his days in the army. "That was no firecracker!" He started to leave the porch.

"Where ya' goin', Daddy?"

"To town. That was an explosion. There could be people hurt."

Abigail put her hand on his shoulder. "I have a bad feeling about this, Jedidiah. Maybe you should stay here."

He put his hand on hers and smiled. "It's something I have to do. If I turn my back on them, I'd be no better than they are. The two of you stay here. Don't worry. I'll be fine."

They watched as Jedidiah walked down the path Hattie usually took to school. It was a shorter route to the town hall. Suddenly, they heard a shout, "Jedidiah! No!"

"It's Paloma!" Abigail exclaimed. She and Hattie ran into the house and sat down on the bed beside her. She was tossing and turning, but her eyes were still closed. She called his name twice more and then was quiet again.

"Does this mean Granny is going to get better, Mama?" Hattie was hopeful.

Abigail shook her head. "I don't know, sugar." Where Paloma was concerned, anything was possible.

Meanwhile - Welch Residence

Evelyn sat on the front porch swing. The wind blew through her hair. "There *is* going to be a storm," she mumbled. She heard noises coming from the town hall and sighed. "I guess they've started some of the fireworks."

Fredricks, the butler, and Martha, the cook, heard the noises and came out on the porch expecting to see the display. "I love fireworks," said Martha. "Don't you, Miss Evelyn?"

She was about to answer when suddenly, they heard an ear bursting explosion, and even though it was dark outside, they saw a large cloud of black smoke rising from the direction of the town hall. Evelyn's eyes widened. Hattie's pictures came to mind as well as their first thoughts when she drew it. *Someone was going to blow up Black Water!* She didn't say a word to the help but ran off the porch heading for town. All she could think of at that moment was her parents. The butler and the cook followed after her.

Rewind - Back at the Town Hall

"EVERYONE! RUN! CLEAR THE BUILDING! IT'S GOING TO BLOW!" Henry and Alvin had shouted as they urged people to the front door. No one knew what was going on, but they quickly headed for the exit. When they heard the words fire and dynamite together, the people pushed and shoved their way to get out not caring who was hurt in the process. One elderly woman fell and a man stepped on her. He didn't stop to help her up. Some of the people were jumping out the windows of the building. The fireworks started popping and whistling and then the EXPLOSION!

The building blew completely apart. Wood, brick, metal, glass and other debris flew out in all directions. Some of the people were not fortunate enough to get out in time. Sheriff Wright was urging people out and trying to help those who were trampled. The force of the blast blew him ten feet up in the air, and he landed on the ground with a board protruding from his back. The Canapple boy was pushed to the ground, and a man fell on top of him, breaking the boy's arm. The people who'd made it outside fell to the ground and covered their head or sought shelter from the flying debris.

When the dust settled, everything was quiet for a moment. The people who were not dead, unconscious or otherwise injured, lay on the ground stunned, not completely sure how something like this could have happened. Henry slowly sat up and felt a sharp pain in his shoulder. He thought sure it was dislocated. His thoughts went to his wife. He stood and looked around. "Emmaline!" he called and walked among the people sitting or lying on the ground. He finally spotted her lying unconscious and ran to her side. Blood flowed from the side of her head. He took a handkerchief from his pocket to try and stanch the bleeding. She groaned and he thanked God she was still alive.

Other people started to stand and call out the names of their loved ones. Alvin Baxter looked for his wife and children and found they were all safe except for a few scrapes. He had his oldest boy take the family home while he stayed to help.

Ezra Katts looked around and called for his boys. He found his youngest son, Orin. He was leaning up against a wagon wheel holding his head - just as he was in the picture the Sin-Eater's daughter drew. "Oh God!" he cried. "Kyle!" He prayed that his oldest son, his pride and joy, was not like the picture showed. He looked for a pile of bricks and saw a body half covered by them. Ezra started picking up bricks and throwing them right and left, not caring where they landed or who they hit to get his boy out. When he finally freed him, he sat down and cradled Kyle's body in his arms. "Come on, boy, wake up - open your eyes."

Dr. Jackson was making his way from one person to another. He'd left the party early, and when he heard the explosion, he knew there would be people who needed help. He saw Ezra with his son.

"Help him, Doc!" Tears ran down Ezra's cheeks.

The doctor felt for a pulse and listened for a heart-beat with his stethoscope. He looked at Ezra and shook his head. The boy was dead.

Sally Gooch walked from one person to another asking if anyone had seen Victor. She called his name over and over, but he was nowhere to be found. Victor had also been one of those at the back of the pack of people urging them to leave and helping those who'd fallen.

Mr. McGuire looked around for his daughter, Alice. She was sitting on the ground holding Jimmy's head in her lap.

Alice was crying. "He protected me from the blast, Daddy. A brick hit him."

McGuire checked to see if the boy was still breathing. Fortunately, he was. He called to Dr. Jackson.

Robbie and Billy found their mother's. The women cried joyously as they hugged their son, relieved that their little lambs came through unharmed.

Reverend Donner was kneeling beside the body of a five year old little boy he had taken into his home a few months earlier. The child was thought to have been an orphan, but the boy was his from an indiscretion no one in Black Water knew about. He'd supported him over the years, but now his mother was dead from a cancer and named him as guardian.

Erma Welch walked around in a slight daze. She couldn't believe this had happened to her wonderful party. Her face had little nicks and scratches where debris had hit her - her angel wings were broken and her halo was missing. All she could think of were the pictures. It was all in the pictures. She saw Henry sitting on the ground with Emmaline's head in his lap. She knelt down beside him. "See Henry. She did this. That little witch child made all of this happen."

Henry glared at her. "Shut up, Mother! Can't you see Emmaline's hurt!" He then heard a small voice calling and looked up to see Evelyn running down the street calling for them with their butler and cook chasing after her. He called to her, and she turned and ran towards them.

Evelyn wrapped her arms around her father. "Is Mama okay?"

But it was Emmaline who answered. "I'll be fine, sweetie. Mama is just going to have a bad headache for a few days."

"I was so scared! I knew you shouldn't have come. I told you something bad was going to happen," Evelyn cried.

"It was that friend of yours," said Erma. Her tone was hateful. "She made this happen, and she is trying to corrupt you."

Evelyn frowned. "No! I asked her to draw those pictures to warn the people when we realized something was going to happen. We thought it was going to be a storm."

Suddenly, a stranger came galloping into town on his horse shouting at the top of his lungs, "EVERYONE! TAKE COVER! IT'S COMING!"

Chapter 31

Jedidiah made it to the wall and was able to climb it with no problem. He crossed the field and entered the street. He saw the space where the town hall had been and the people milling around helping the injured. He figured they may not want his help, but he decided he would offer it anyway.

***

George Tyler had attended the party briefly to see who was wearing what and write about some of the more unique costumes for his society column. He particularly liked the man who came dressed in a suit of armor. When interviewed, John Wallingford said he was dressed as Sir Galahad, a Knight of King Arthur's round table.

George laughed inwardly upon seeing the ladies from the women's committee dressed in white with halos and angel wings. He thought a more fitting costume would have been red dresses, devil's horns and pitchforks. But to say anything derogatory about these "fine ladies of society," he considered he might be burned in effigy, so he decided he would write something complimentary about them anyway.

After gathering all the material he needed for the next day's issue, he went back to the newspaper to write the article. When he heard the popping and whistling of fireworks, he went outside to enjoy the spectacle, but thought it strange when he saw people running from the building. At first, he thought one of the boys set off a string of firecrackers for a laugh, but then to his utter shock, the town hall exploded. As debris flew everywhere, he ducked back inside his office to escape the matter that started raining down upon him. A few minutes later, he went back outside and saw a cloud of smoke rising from where the town hall used to be. He ran to help the injured - all thoughts of a story erased from his mind.

George was about to fill a bucket with fresh water to wash away the blood from the injured, when he saw someone walking toward them in the distance. He recognized the man's particular stride. It was Jedidiah. He looked around and saw no one was paying him any attention at the moment. This was not the place for the Sin-Eater at this time. He put down his bucket and ran toward him.

Before Jedidiah could greet him properly, George grabbed him around the shoulder and pulled him behind a building.

"What the hell are you doing here, Jedidiah!"

"I heard the explosion. I came to help."

"Your heart is in the right place, but your head isn't. They won't appreciate you being here. If you want to help, wait until they ring the bell. There are many injured and some dead. I've also heard mumblings, but the people shut up when I come near. Something about pictures and evil."

"Pictures - what does that have to do with what happened here?"

George shook his head. "I don't know, but I suggest you go home, and for God's sake, don't let anyone see you!" With that last word, he turned and headed back to help the injured.

Jedidiah stood behind the building and watched for a moment. He shook his head. As many years as he'd lived there, he still didn't understand these people. He turned to walk down the alley and then heard a man shouting as he galloped down the street, "EVERYONE! TAKE COVER! IT'S COMING! A TWISTER IS HEADING THIS WAY."

The last place Jedidiah wanted to be was in the open. The buildings near him had crawlspaces but they were too narrow to shelter him. He had no choice. He had to make it back across the wall.

Most of the time, he didn't think about his lack of a leg, but it was at times like these that he cursed the war that caused him to lose it and the stepfather who'd sold him into it. His run was more like a skip as his good leg did most of the work. He made it to the field, stopped to take a breath and listened. There were no sounds. The crickets and the night birds were silent - and then a faint noise came to his ears. It sounded like a distant train rumbling down the tracks. He picked up his pace crossing the field. The sound kept getting closer and closer. He looked behind him, but even in the darkness of the night, he could make out the swirling winds of a funnel cloud.

Jedidiah's heart pumped violently as he saw the monster land on buildings blowing them apart. It retracted into the sky momentarily and touched down again in the field behind him. He turned his eyes forward and headed for the wall. The swirling winds zigzagged across the field, tearing up a crop of soybeans as it went. He made it to the wall and scaled it just as the twister changed directions again and headed toward him. The sound was now almost deafening. Traveling down the path toward home was an effort in futility, for he felt the pull of the twisting monster drawing him into it.

He knew he had to stop and secure himself, or become one of its victims. He found a vine lying on the ground and picked a large tree with a thick trunk to lash himself to. He sat down, closed his eyes and prayed for the safety of his wife and daughter as well as for himself. It felt as if the tornado was going to suck him right through the trunk of that tree. Leaves, branches and other foliage from the woods smacked him in the face as it was added to the debris the twister collected. Rocks from the wall sailed past him. He didn't dare look for fear of being hit, but he could see in his mind's eye the monster plow through the wall that divided the town from the woods of the swamp.

Though it felt like an eternity to Jedidiah, the tornado was only there for a few minutes and then turned direction again. He didn't move just in case it decided to come back. All was quiet for a few minutes until he heard the sounds of the night echoing though the swamp. He sighed in relief and leaned his head back against the tree to let his nerves calm. He was about to stand, but noticed his wooden leg was missing. The tornado had taken it, and he'd never felt a thing. "Now what!" he said to himself, and as he said it, it started to rain.

Meanwhile - Back in Town

All heads turned when they saw the man on horseback shouting and riding fast toward them. He reined in his horse and was stunned to see the devastation that had happened. He thought that a twister had already come through and now another was on its way.

Henry stood and ran to the man. "A twister! Where is it? How far away?"

"I just barely stayed ahead of it," the man said. "I passed a farm 'bout five miles back and saw it skim the roof off of the house. I saw the flash in town and figured there was some goin' ons here, so I come ta' warn ya'. Ya' better get somewhere safe quick. Ya' don't have long." The man turned his horse, snapped his reins and galloped off.

Henry turned to address those standing around. "Everyone! Help the injured to their feet and get yourselves to safety. Get under a building with a crawlspace. Elvin's stable is the sturdiest building in town. Get under something sturdy and lash yourself down. Just wherever you might think you'll be safe - hurry!"

"What about the dead?" shouted Ezra Katts. He looked at his dead son. "We can't just leave'em here lyin' in the street!"

Henry felt for the man, but there was a choice to make. "Ezra, it's up to you. Stay with the son who is living, or the one gone." He turned to help his family to safety.

The town folk only had minutes to spare. Families left their dead in the street and went for cover when they heard the roar of the twister coming toward them. Most everyone headed for the stable - some for the church - McGuire's store and the hotel had the largest crawlspaces to shelter them.

The tornado rumbled through the town, demolishing three buildings in its path. It engulfed the debris from the town hall, including the dead, before it headed for the soybean field. When the whirling winds could no longer be heard, the people peered out from their hiding places thankful that the whole town wasn't destroyed.

Everyone headed for home. Henry and Emmaline offered her Aunt Sally to come home with them so she wouldn't be alone, but she declined. She said she would be closer to Victor surrounded by his things, but asked Erma if she wouldn't mind staying with her. They had just reached their carriage when it started to rain.

The Swamp

Abigail and Hattie watched out the window as the rain came down in buckets. Though they could hear the wind blowing through the trees, the tornado never entered their little niche in the swamp. Abigail was beginning to worry. Jedidiah had been gone way too long. She didn't relish the thought of leaving Hattie alone, but she had a nagging feeling that something was wrong. She went into her bedroom and got her raincoat, scarf and a hat to help shield her slightly from the elements. She also pulled the shotgun from the mantle that they used for hunting. She turned to Hattie. "I hate leavin' ya', but I need ta' see 'bout yer daddy."

"I'm fine, Mama. I'll take care of Granny." Hattie was also worried about him. She was tempted to draw a picture to see why it was taking him so long to get home, but somehow knowing was more frightening than not knowing.

Abigail kissed her daughter on the forehead and went out into the driving rain. She could feel small pieces of hail sting her face as she traveled the path he'd gone down. The trees that surrounded the path helped block some of the rain, but it was dark and the rain was loud. She called Jedidiah's name several times, but there was no answer. She was about half way to where they usually crossed the wall, when she saw a form moving slowly across the ground in the distance. She readied her gun just in case it was some wild animal. She called out. "Jedidiah! Is that you!" She thought she heard something, but the rain muffled the sound, and she couldn't make it out. She picked up her pace slightly, and as she neared, she heard a faint voice calling her name. It could only be Jedidiah, and she ran to help him. When she reached his side she dropped to the ground and wrapped her arms around him. He was muddy and shivering with cold.

His teeth chattered as he shouted to be heard over the torrential rain. "We live in a wooded swamp, and there wasn't a damn tree limb I could find to use as a crutch!"

"Let's get ya' home."

Abigail helped him to his feet, and between the strength of her slender shoulders and the butt of the shotgun he put under his arm to use as a crutch, they slowly traversed the woods and finally made it to the clearing.

***

Hattie was beginning to worry about both her parents. Her mama had been gone for over an hour. To busy herself, she gathered blankets and towels to put close to the fire so they would warm. She also put pots of water on the stove to heat. She'd remembered her mama doing that several times when they knew her daddy was going to come home soaked to the bone from the rain.

As she watched intently out the window, she finally saw two figures coming toward the house. She opened the door when they were on the porch.

"Hattie, go to the bedroom and get yer daddy some dry clothes," Abigail said as she helped Jedidiah to sit down by the fireplace. She stripped off his wet shirt and put one of the blankets around him that Hattie had thoughtfully put before the fire. When Hattie returned with the clothes, Abigail sent her daughter back into the bedroom so she could strip

Jedidiah the rest of the way.

Jedidiah was bone cold even with the warmth of the blanket. "What a waste," he said, his teeth still chattering as his wife took off his britches and started rubbing him dry with another blanket.

"What is?" she asked.

"We could be in the bedroom instead of Hattie."

She looked up at him and gave him a twisted smile. "Here ya' are, half-drowned, caked with mud and that's all ya' can think of?"

"What can I say? You know where we men keep our brains."

Abigail threw a warm towel over his head. "Well, dry off that empty skull and put them brains back where they belong before ya' catch yer death."

She called Hattie back into the room and had her pour the hot water into a small tub so Jedidiah could put his foot in it, while she went to the bedroom to get out of her own wet clothing. The heat from the water sent welcome waves of warmth through his body. But even though he was feeling warmer, he felt weak and feverish.

When Abigail came back into the room, she sat by the fire. Jedidiah told them that the town hall blew up, but he didn't exactly know why. He also told them about being chased by the tornado, and how it took his leg when he had tied himself to the tree.

Jedidiah looked at Hattie as he remembered something that George Tyler had said. "Did you draw and give out any pictures?"

Hattie's eyes turned to the floor. "Yes, sir. I drew some pictures. Some were bad." She looked into her daddy's eyes. "But me and Evelyn decided not to give them out. She hid them, but when she wanted to look at them again, they were missing. She thinks her grandmother took them."

"Sugar, didn't Granny Paloma tell ya' ta' stay out of it?" Abigail scolded mildly.

"Yes, ma'am. But we only wanted to help people with them. We thought we'd helped Carrie-Ann when she went with her daddy and new mama on their honeymoon. But when I drew another picture, it changed a little, but it still showed she might die. That's when we decided not to give out the pictures. We didn't know if they would help or hurt people." A tear ran down her cheek. "I'm sorry."

Hattie started to cry, and Jedidiah took her into his arms and hugged her. "We're not angry with you. We know your heart was in the right place."

Abigail stroked her hair. "'Course not, sugar. Now dry them tears. It's late. Why don't ya' try and get some sleep."

Hattie kissed both her parents and went off to bed. She said her prayers, thanking God for keeping her daddy safe and said an extra prayer for Evelyn, hoping that she and her parents were safe as well.

Chapter 32

The Hamilton House

It rained for days. Black Water was in dire straits. Though only three buildings were destroyed in town, the surrounding areas were devastated. The rock wall that divided the swamp from the town was over half gone, including the dam over the river that let water flow through but kept the alligators behind it. The farmers who didn't harvest their crops either lost them to the tornado - or the rain. One farmer, who did manage to harvest some of his cotton crop, still lost it when the twister took his barn. Only a few farmers saved their harvests but were hurt in other ways. If the barn wasn't taken - the house was.

The Hamilton's house was one of them. Hattie had drawn the roof being taken off and a man hanging over a tree limb. The majority of the picture came true, except for the man in the tree. Though Richard Hamilton, who was now ninety-two years old, had never seen the picture, he'd read the article in the newspaper. Years ago, when Paloma was a young girl predicting bad weather, he always listened. His was one of the crops saved during the last great weather related disaster that almost put an end to their town.

His grandson, Scott Hamilton, took care of managing the farm since his parents' death years earlier. Scott argued with his grandfather about harvesting early, but the older man told him that he was still the owner of the farm and head of the family. So with great reluctance, the younger Hamilton respected his grandfather's wishes and harvested. Scott also planned on taking his family to the Halloween party in town for an hour or so, but the senior man put his foot down on that as well. Though none were too thrilled about it, they all stayed home.

When it started getting late, the younger man put his children to bed and went out to the porch to convince his grandfather, whom he thought was now entering senility, to do likewise, but he refused. While they argued everything suddenly got quiet - no crickets - no night birds. They saw three deer sprint across the lawn. Their dog's ears perked up, and it started to bark frantically - and then they heard it - the faint sound of a freight train. Scott had managed to gather his family just in time to make it to the storm shelter that was by the barn. The younger Hamilton thanked God that he'd listened to his grandfather. After hearing what happened in town, if he'd gone to the party, not only could they have been hurt there, he and his family could have run right into the tornado on the way home.

The Burnham's

Pearl-Lee and her new family were on their way home from the coast. They were anxious to get back to Black Water and tell what a good time they had. But - on their way home, it started to rain. The shades in the stagecoach barely kept out the rain, and all were soaked to the skin before they reached the next station to change horses and get shelter.

Carrie-Ann was chilled and shivering. They had changes of clothing in their travel trunks, but everything was damp. When the rain let up, and it looked as if the sun might stay out, they started the journey once more. But again they ran into rain about an hour before they hit Black Water. When they finally reached home, Carrie-Ann was sick and feverish - she'd come down with influenza.

Ezra Katts

Ezra Katts sat in his chair looking out at the rain. He put the whisky bottle to his lips and took a drink. He beloved son, Kyle was gone. He couldn't even have a proper funeral for him since the tornado swept away his body. He'd spent the entire next day following the debris trail through the rain to see where the storm might have deposited it, but he found none of the bodies. The trail ended at the swamp, and if the bodies were there, the gators or some other wild animal would have gotten them.

He took another drink. Now there was just Orin - his youngest son who took his beloved wife during his birth. He inwardly blamed the boy for his mother's death. Though he never intended to be cruel to him, he was harder on him than Kyle - the son he loved the most. But now Orin was sick. Though it was raining, the cows still needed to be milked and the horses in the barn fed. He had gone for Doc Jackson and was told the boy had influenza. The doctor said that there was now an epidemic, especially among the children.

Ezra took another pull from the bottle and looked at the pictures Erma Welch had given him. "Something has to be done," he mumbled. He then heard his son call, and got up to tend to him.

McGuire's General Store

Evan McGuire looked out the window of his general store. He hadn't had a customer in three days, and that meant no money coming in. He also wasn't too happy when his daughter, Alice, informed him that she loved Jimmy Johnson, and she planned on marrying him when and if he got better. He would have objected to the marriage, but what could he say now - the boy saved his daughter's life. If he fired the boy, he'd look like an ass to his customers. The explosion and the rain were highly inconvenient. The tornado would bring him income from supplies for rebuilding, but not until the rain stopped.

He shook his head and sat down behind the counter. He'd heard the rumors about the Sin-Eater's daughter causing all this trouble. He believed it. He hated that gimpy Jedidiah anyway, and his kid came from Shadrack trash. Once a month, he was obligated to hand out supplies at no charge to him. That ate into his profits.

Finally, the bell above the door jingled and he stood. "Good-day, Mrs. Welch," he said to Erma as she walked in with the carriage driver holding an umbrella over her.

"There's nothing good about it, Mr. McGuire." Erma turned to the driver. "Wait outside. I'll be a few minutes. I'll call you when I'm ready to leave."

The driver did as she asked to avoid an argument. "Uppity bitch!" he mumbled, pulling the raincoat around him. "To hell with this!" He went next door to the barber shop. After all, Mrs. Welch wasn't his employer. He used to be Judge Gooch's driver. Though he never had much conversation with the man, the judge would have never treated him as Mrs. Welch had just done. He'd decided that as soon as he found another employer, he was quitting. Mrs. Gooch was just as bad as Mrs. Welch.

When the driver left, Erma shook her head. "Honestly, Mr. McGuire, I don't know why the Judge kept that man on. I think he hit every rut in the road purposely."

Mr. McGuire just smiled, nodded and changed the subject. "What can I do for you today?"

"Some headache powders. Burnham's Apothecary is closed. I don't see how he expects to stay in business if he doesn't open."

"His daughter is sick, you know."

"Well, he now has a wife to take care of her." She walked to the window and looked out. "People are dropping like flies. Influenza is running rampant through the town. Mrs. Gooch has taken to her sickbed."

"How is the poor dear woman anyway?" His caring tone was just a front. He could actually care less. Mrs. Gooch was the world's worst about buying something one day only to bring it back the next and exchange it for something else. They'd argue for a while, and he'd end up taking it back just because she was the judge's wife.

"The poor dear is grieving terribly for Victor. She's barely eaten a morsel in days. I've been staying with her."

Mr. McGuire shook his head. "I still don't know how it happened."

Erma was waiting for him to bring up that very subject. "It was that swamp girl, Hattie. You know about the pictures, don't you? The one's she draws to make things happen."

"I've heard, but I've never seen one."

Erma pulled one from her purse. "Look at this one."

She showed him a picture where the town's people were lying on the ground. The storekeeper gasped in astonishment. The scene looked exactly the way it did when it happened. She then showed him the picture of the sheriff.

"Horrible! Absolutely horrible."

"Three disaster all at one time! The explosion, the tornado and now all this sickness. Nothing has ever happened like this until she started coming around."

"Something has to be done," McGuire said. "I think we should call a meeting. The only leadership we have right now is your son, and his wife is injured. With the sheriff and judge gone, all we have left is the sheriff's deputy, Sam Waters, and he's practically useless on major decisions."

Erma smiled. "I think you're right, Mr. McGuire. It's something to think about." After accomplishing her main mission, she paid for the headache powder and looked out the window. She didn't see the driver. "Horrid man," she mumbled. "My hat will be ruined by the rain."

She quickly went outside and got into the carriage. The driver came out of the barbershop and received a severe dressing down for his absence when she needed him.

Mr. McGuire sat back down behind his counter. A meeting," he thought. "Not a bad idea." The thought of tar and feathering Jedidiah and running him out of town came to mind.

Reverend Donner

Reverend Donner sat behind his desk writing his sermon for Sunday. He didn't know what to write until Erma Welch stopped by. He'd been trying to figure out how God could let all these disasters happen in this town. The people were basically good - there were no saloons or brothels and most everyone attended church. The collection plate always brimmed with offerings to the Lord, which he managed. He wondered why there had been no warning signs.

He thought about his child, whom he'd renamed Timothy. Though biologically the child was his, he was going to officially go through the procedures of adoption. He had a whole series of sermons planned on helping the poor and unfortunate with Timothy being the center - but now it wouldn't be.

When Erma showed him the picture Hattie had drawn of the disaster, he recognized himself kneeling over the child. Now he knew. These disasters were not of the Lord - they were of evil. The witch child, Hattie, was the instrument of the devil's handiwork. Her innocent face belonged to that of a trickster. He had to recant what he'd said about the child originally. His child was dead. He didn't care anymore about the Sin-Eater's daughter. The more he thought about it - the more he convinced himself.

The Welch Residence

Emmaline was feeling much better. Doctor Jackson said she had suffered a concussion and to stay off her feet. Henry, on the other hand, started developing a fever. With all that had happened, he thought it important to take care of the town's business, even though it was raining.

Emmaline insisted he go to bed and stay there before he became the next victim of influenza. She tucked him in bed and had the butler stoke up the fire in their room for more warmth. She had wanted to ask Henry if he knew how the disaster happened, but didn't want to discuss it in front of Evelyn, who practically never left her side while she was in bed. But now Evelyn was downstairs having her lunch, so she inquired. Between sneezes, he told her that he and Victor had caught Robbie Harp and Billy Tate in the storage room. Though they didn't actually see the boys in the act of smoking, they believe they'd gotten rid of the evidence before they came through the door. He told her he had no proof, and it was only an assumption since he just smelled the scent of tobacco smoke.

***

Evelyn had quickly finished her lunch and headed upstairs. She was about to go in her parents' room, when she heard them talking about the explosion. She decided not to interrupt and listened. Her curiosity was just as peeked as her mother's. When her father finished talking, she understood the meaning of Hattie's picture of the two boys smoking. They were responsible for the explosion, the death of the sheriff, her Uncle Victor and all the others. They were to blame!

Evelyn went to her room, sat in the window seat and looked out. The rain seemed unending. She hadn't seen Hattie in a week and missed her. School had been canceled because of all the sickness and the rain just kept - raining.

Doctor Jackson

"AhhChoo!" Dr. Lucian Jackson sneezed, as he walked in his house which also served as his office. It was late, and he was dog tired. He'd visited six patients today. All of them had the same thing -Influenza. Somehow he needed to get them all together in one place to treat them instead of traveling from one end of the countryside to the other. He'd spent more time in his buggy than he did in the homes.

As he shut the door, the thunder cracked. "Damn! All this rain." He put down his bag and after changing clothes, he sat in his easy chair. For a few minutes today, it looked as if the rain might ease up, but then a dark cloud covered the one bright spot in the sky, and the rain came down harder. Though he wore a rain coat, his clothing stayed damp.

Just as he was about to fall asleep, there was a knock at the door. "Now what!" He opened the door and saw Joseph Wineman carrying his ten year old son, Luke. The boy's leg was wrapped with a blood soaked rag.

"My boy's hurt real bad, Doc," said the father.

They went into the examining room. "Put him on the table." He started cutting away the make-shift bandage. "What happened?"

"Ya' know we live close to the river. My boy let his dog out ta' do his business. We heard it start barkin' something fierce. Luke tried callin' the dog ta' come in, and when he didn't, he went outside ta' get him. There was a gator on the bank. My boy didn't see it until it was too late. I just barely got ta' Luke before he was dragged to the water."

"Gator! There hasn't been an alligator on this side of the wall in years."

"Wall ain't there no more. Twister got it."

Doc shook his head and went to work on the boy. It took twenty-seven stitches on both sides of his right leg to close up the wounds. He offered Mr. Wineman and his son a room to stay the night and wait until tomorrow to leave, but he said they needed to get home. With gators in their part of the river, he needed to be home with the rest of his family.

When Doc was alone again, he sneezed. He felt chilled. "I can't get sick. Not now!" He knew the symptoms - he was coming down with Influenza himself.

Chapter 33

Finally, after four days, the rain stopped. But it was cold and overcast. As sick as Dr. Jackson was, he'd made arrangements to turn the school into an infirmary. Traveling from house to house as he was doing now wasn't doing his own health any good. He'd also gone to the newspaper office and asked George Tyler if he could print some handbills and distribute them throughout the community informing the residents where to bring their sick. The newspaperman started on the project immediately and soon had posters in every store and printed on the front page of the paper.

The Swamp

Though it was a school day, Abigail kept Hattie at home. Not only did she have to care for Paloma, Jedidiah was now burning up with fever. She needed Hattie to help care for them while she went hunting for food. Since the night Abigail pulled him out of the woods, Jedidiah's health steadily worsened. Hattie applied cool compresses to her daddy's forehead. She worried about him. He'd been sick before, but she never remembered him being this bad.

Surprisingly, she heard a knock at the door. She thought it might be her aunt and uncle again. When she opened it, her eyes widened when she saw Evelyn standing there wearing a white sweater and a pair of overalls. The two girls hugged and were glad to see that the other had survived the storm. "What are ya' doin' here?"

"I snuck out of the house." Hattie invited her in, and they sat down by the fireplace. "I can't stay long. I waited for you to come down the path this morning to go to school. When I didn't see you, I was worried."

Hattie looked toward the bedroom. "My daddy's really sick. Mama's huntin'."

"My papa's sick too. A lot of people are. That's what I came to tell you. There won't be any school for a while. That's where all the sick people are going. Even Dr. Jackson is sick." She hesitated a moment. "So is Carrie-Ann."

Hattie sighed. "I've been worried about those pictures. Maybe we should have given them out."

Evelyn frowned. "They already were. My grandmother did take them, and she passed them out to everyone."

Hattie smiled. "Then that's a good thing…" Her smile disappeared when she saw the look on Evelyn's face. "…isn't it?"

Evelyn shook her head slowly. "I - don't - think - so! There's a lot of whispering going on in town about them. I went with Mama to the general store the other day. They gave me funny looks."

"What kind of looks?"

"You know - the kind when they feel sorry for you for something, and then they shake their heads. Only I don't know what they're shaking their heads about." She shivered. "Made me feel strange."

Evelyn told her what happened in town on Halloween, including that her father thought Robbie and Billy started the fire that caused the explosion. Now Hattie understood what the picture of the boys she drew meant when they were trying to figure out who killed the sheriff.

Evelyn stood. "I better go before I'm missed."

Hattie walked her to the door. "I don't know when I'll get ta' see ya' again."

"I hope your daddy gets better. My grandmother's been staying with my Great Aunt Sally." She looked down. "My uncle was killed in the explosion, and the tornado took away all the dead people. They're having a memorial service at the church tonight."

As Evelyn left the porch and started for the woods, Hattie yelled to her. "Hey Evelyn! What if ya' see a snake?"

"I don't even try to look!" she yelled back. "I just start running and don't stop until I'm out of the woods!" When she got to the edge of the clearing, she took a deep breath, let it out and took off.

Hattie laughed and went back into the house to tend to her father. Jedidiah opened his eyes. He felt cold and hot all at the same time. "I heard voices. Is your mother home?" He shivered and was only partially coherent.

"No, that was Evelyn. She was worried about me."

Jedidiah closed his eyes, and before he went back to sleep, he mumbled to her, "She's a good sister."

"Sister!" she repeated. But then she thought that he probably meant that she was like a good sister. She took the compress from his forehead, moistened it and put it back. He didn't feel as hot as he did before. She hoped that was a good sign.

The Church

Reverend Donner stood at the pulpit and looked at the people who had gathered for the memorial service. There were not very many. Basically just the families and close friends of those who died in the explosion. He was disappointed, but attributed the lack of attendance to the illness that had beset their town. Even the mayor was bedridden, but just as he was about to start, he saw Emmaline and her daughter walk through the door and take a seat next to her aunt and mother-in-law.

He started. "Gone - but not forgotten. We are here today to honor the memories of our dearly departed." He said the names slowly and looked at each family group whom that death affected. "Kyle Katts - our beloved Judge, Victor Gooch - Sheriff Hiram Wright - ninety year old Amberlyn Peabody, whose heart gave out while running from the building... " He wiped a tear from his eye. "And my own five-year-old Timothy Henderson, whom I brought into my home as a poor orphan boy and was about to officially give him my name and call him son." He turned his back a moment, partially for effect and partially for genuine sorrow. He turned around, dried his eyes and continued. "We also pray for Jimmy Johnson whose life still hangs in the balance as well as all those struck down by Influenza."

He looked down at the pictures Erma Welch had left with him and then at the congregation. "I'm sure we all have asked why God let these three tragedies happen; the explosion, the tornado that affected so many in our community and then swept away our dead without proper cleansing of their sins. Now they will suffer to haunt the Earth and be unable to enjoy the riches of heaven. We can't forget those who hang at death's door with illness." He knitted his brow. "There are two forces that control the destiny of our lives - the fearsome power of the Lord our God, and the devil and his minions that were cast out of the heavens." He was silent for a moment, closed his eyes, turned his face upward and raised his fist. "REVELATION! That is what has come to me." He opened his eyes and slowly scanned the room as he usually did when he wanted to get a serious point across. All eyes were fixed on him. He could almost hear their hearts beating in their chest. "Evil has befallen us." Paraphrasing Ephesians 6:12-17 to suit his needs, he said, "The Bible tells us, 'For our struggle is not against flesh and blood, but against the forces of darkness, and of wickedness. We must therefore, take up the full armor of God, so we will be able to resist the evil of this time, and stand firm in our resolve.'" He then held up the pictures Hattie had drawn. "We must gird our loins and put on the breastplate of righteousness and extinguish the evil one." He then called her by name. "Hattie! The Sin-Eater's daughter." He picked up the Bible. "2 Corinthians 11:14-15 says, 'And no marvel; for Satan himself is transformed into an angel of light. Therefore it is no great thing if his ministers also be transformed as the minister of righteousness; whose end shall be according to their works!'"

There was a rumbling in the congregation. Ezra Katts stood and held up the picture of his son. "Look what she did to my Kyle! He was a good boy! He would have become a good man! Now he's dead and won't be able to enjoy heaven's light."

"The sheriff!" said Deputy Sam Waters. Erma Welch had given him a picture.

Sally Gooch stood, though there were no pictures drawn of him. She put a handkerchief to her eye. "My dear Victor." She could say no more. She sat back down, tears rolling down her cheeks as Erma consoled her.

Emmaline and Evelyn were shocked. But it was Evelyn who stood first. "No!" she shouted. "Hattie had nothing to do with it. She's not evil. She's good." She turned her head and looked at the Harps and the Tates who were sitting toward the back. She pointed her finger. "It was Robbie and Billy who set the fire! They caused the explosion because they were smoking when they shouldn't have been." More murmuring could be heard among the people.

Vera Harp stood. She held up a picture. "My son was compelled!"

Robbie knew he was guilty, but he feared punishment. Tears rolled down his eyes and he cried. "Billy and me couldn't help ourselves! We didn't know what we were doing."

Tilly Tate also stood. "Our sons were possessed." She stroked Billy's head gently. "My son is a timid child. He couldn't do something like that purposely." She looked at Evelyn and pointed. "She's been possessed!"

It was Emmaline's turn to stand. "How dare you! How dare you all! These things were ordered by..."

"The devil!" interrupted Ezra Katts. "Let's get 'em. We need to avenge our families and our town. Eye for an eye. The Sin-Eater's daughter and her family are the cause of all this." He turned to one of the men in the congregation. "Able Duffy - get your dogs. We'll hunt them down in that swamp and hang 'em!" The man nodded his head and left the building. "You other men - get your guns and some rope!"

But Sally Gooch stood. "No! You bring them here. I want to see that child of evil get what she deserves for killing my husband!"

"No!" shouted Emmaline. Suddenly, Evelyn broke away and ran for the door.

"Grab her!" shouted Ezra Katts.

Emmaline shouted, "Run! Go tell your father, Evelyn!" She sat down and turned to her mother-in-law. "Please, for God's sake, say something!"

Erma patted her on the hand and smiled. She stood. "Please, don't look upon my granddaughter harshly. Once the Sin-Eater's daughter is out of her life, the influence will be gone. Just as Jesus purged the demons from people possessed by evil, when the witch-child is gone, Evelyn will be fine."

"Amen, Sister Welch," said Reverend Donner.

Emmaline couldn't believe what she'd just heard. She saw a pleased smile come across Erma's face as she sat back down. This was like the Salem Witch hunt of long ago. She couldn't believe this was happening in this day and time. Memories of what her father had told her about their ancestor and how he had a brush with death in Salem all those years ago. Emmaline shouted, "It's not Evelyn who is possessed - you all are!"

She started to leave, but Ezra called for her restraint. "Put her in the backroom of the church until we've gone."

Emmaline turned to Reverend Donner. "Please - this isn't right. Tell them to let me go!"

He looked at her with a stone-faced expression. "It's for your own good. Things will be set to rights soon."

Chapter 34

The Swamp

Tears streaked Evelyn's face as she ran. She heard her mother shout to go tell her father what the men in town were about to do, but there was no time. She had to warn Hattie and her family. They had to leave everything behind and go now. She cut between the buildings, crossed the tornado torn field and entered the woods. Suddenly, she stopped dead in her tracks. A snake was coiled up in her path. Her heart beat frantically. She was torn between her deadly fear of snakes and her deep concern for Hattie. She couldn't go back - she couldn't go forward. The only choice was to go around. But as she started to move, so did the snake. Evelyn screamed and ran deeper into the woods. The snake was following her - of that she was positive. Tree limbs tore at her dress and scratched her arms and face. Something hit her on top of the head, and she stopped, shook her head and vigorously brushed her fingers through her hair thinking some type of bug landed there. Relieved she wasn't assaulted by some eight-legged creature, she looked around - first left and then right. Which way to turn? Panic started to set in. She closed her eyes for a moment. "Calm down, Evelyn. You can do this. You can track like Hattie taught you. Just retrace your steps back to the path."

***

It was a couple of hours before sundown. Abigail sat beside Jedidiah and felt his forehead. She was relieved. His fever had finally broken, and now he was complaining about being hungry. A few moments later, Hattie brought him in a bowl of Aunt Josie's famous chicken soup. Abigail gave him a spoonful.

He swallowed and closed his eyes. "Now I know why your uncle married your aunt. That's the best chicken soup I've ever had."

Abigail laughed slightly. "I don't think it was her cookin' he married her for." She gave him another spoonful. "Chicken soup is about the only thing she makes that's worth eatin'. She may not look it now, but she were a looker in her prime. Now, she's had too many younins and too much Uncle Ennis."

Jedidiah grinned. "What do you mean by too many younin's? I thought you wanted ten or twelve?"

"If I recollect, I said I wanted to keep it *under* ten." Abigail put her arm around Hattie. This 'in is all I want or need."

Hattie smiled and gave her mother a hug. "It would've been nice ta' have a brother or sister though."

Jedidiah and Abigail eyed each other, but said nothing. On this matter, they could read each other's thoughts. Even though they considered Hattie their daughter through and through, occasionally both felt guilty that they couldn't tell her the real truth of her relationship with Evelyn.

Meanwhile- Edge of Town

While Able Duffy went to get his dogs, each man had gone home to gather food, a canteen of water and a bedroll. Since they were getting a late start, they wanted to be prepared in case they had to spend the night in the swamp. The men met at the sin-eaters bell. Joining in on the hunt were Ezra Katts, Evan McGuire, Reverend Donner, Able Duffy and ten other men who, when it came to religion and superstition, were the most fanatical of the members that belonged to the Church of Black Water.

Able Duffy, a potbellied, middle-aged man, held the leads of his two bloodhounds. "Ezra, if the dogs are gonna do their job, they need a scent ta' follow."

Ezra thought for a moment and looked toward the bell. "The bench. No one sits there except Jedidiah."

The dogs picked up the scent and headed down the path.

Welch Residence

About thirty minutes after the men left the church, Emmaline was released. She got in the carriage and headed home as quickly as she could. She entered the house and called Evelyn's name, but there was no answer. She ran upstairs again calling her name as she looked in her bedroom, but it too was empty.

Henry heard the frantic tone in his wife's voice. "Emmaline, what's wrong?" he called from his sick bed.

She entered their bedroom. "Didn't Evelyn come home and tell you?"

He sat up. "I haven't seen her. What happened?"

Emmaline explained what took place in church. "Do you think she's gone into the woods?"

Henry pushed himself up from the bed and pulled on his britches. "I don't think - I know that's where she's gone!" He took one step and felt woozy. Emmaline grabbed him. "I'll be alright. We've got to go after her."

"I'm going with you!" Emmaline insisted.

"You'll have to. I don't know how to get to their cabin. You've been there more than I."

As they were going down the steps, they met Erma about to come up.   "What are you doing out of bed, Henry. Get back there at once. You're still unwell."

"It's a necessity, Mother," Henry said harshly. "Because of your petty hatred, Evelyn is missing."

Erma smiled. "She'll be home before it gets dark. You'll see that what I have done is for her benefit."

Henry closed his eyes and shook his head. "You'd actually have harm done to a child!"

"An evil child!" Erma said hatefully.

"Mother - you're insane!"

"Henry!" she frowned. "That's a horrible thing to say to your own mother. I insist you apologize to me at once."

"If any harm has come to my daughter, I'll never speak to you again!" Henry exclaimed.

"I told you - she'll be back."

"You'd better hope so!" Henry and Emmaline pushed past her.

Meanwhile -Buehl Residence

Jessica and Jack Trainor were in the parlor of her parents' home playing a game of chess as they watched their sleeping little boy rest comfortably. "You're move, Jack."

"Just wait a minute! Don't rush me." He put his hand on his queen and moved it hesitantly.

Jessica laughed and clapped her hands. "I just knew you were going to do that!" She moved her bishop one space. "Checkmate! I win again!"

He pursed his lips and glared at her through laughing eyes. "You cheated! Somehow, I know you cheated!"

"Me! Cheat!" She lifted her chin, turned her head and tried not to smile. "Why Lieutenant Trainor. I am insulted!"

Jack got up, stood behind her chair and wrapped his arms around her. "Okay, I apologize."

She turned her smiling face toward his. "You know what, Jack?"

"What?"

She giggled. "I cheated. I moved your king when you weren't looking."

He grinned. "I know you did. I just wanted to see if you'd come clean about it."

They were about to get into a playful argument when they heard the door open. "Mom and Dad must be home from the church service," said Jessica.

Roland and Olivia Buehl entered the parlor. "Jack! It's just awful. Just awful." Jessica's mother said in worried tones.

"The town has gone completely mad," Roland added.

"What is it?" Jack asked.

"Some of the men are going into the swamp. They're going to capture the Sin-Eater's daughter and hang her for being a witch! No telling what they will do with Jedidiah and his wife."

"No! You've got to be wrong!" Jessica was horrified.

Roland shoved his hands in his pockets. "I wish to God I were. They wanted me to go along. I was afraid to tell them they were wrong and what they were going to do was hideous. They locked up the mayor's wife for doing that very thing. I told them we had a sick grandchild to deal with and left."

Jessica looked up at her husband. "We've got to do something! With the sheriff and Judge Gooch gone, we have no leadership in this town. The other day, Emmaline told me that Henry is sick also. Can you go after them and stop it?"

Jack thought for a moment. "Going after them would do no good. If they're as crazed as your father says they are, they'd turn on me." He hesitated another moment and looked at the chessboard. "We'll have to wait to see if they bring her back. The situation will have to be handled in town."

"Then what can we do?" Jessica asked.

His face was ridged. "Cheat."

Back at the Swamp

Jedidiah sat up. He was still weak and slightly dizzy. He started to reach for his crutches, when Abigail came through the door.

"Jedidiah Lucas - what in tarnation do ya' think yer tryin' ta' do?"

"I think I'm going to get up and go outside."

"And catch yer death again! I don't think so."

"Well, if you don't let me go out, you're going to be cleaning my britches - again!"

Hattie was standing at the door. "Maybe we should get one of them water closets Evelyn told me about."

"A what?" They both asked.

"A water closet. Evelyn says you sit on this white bowl that has water in it and a hole at the bottom. You pull a chain when ya' done yer business - the business and the water swirls around, goes down the hole and fill up again clean as a whistle."

Jedidiah laughed. "Are you sure she wasn't pulling your leg?"

"How can water stay in a bowl with a hole in it?" Abigail laughed as well. "I ain't too bright on some things, but even I know that don't make sense."

Hattie shrugged. "I don't know. That's just what Evelyn said."

Abigail turned to Jedidiah. "Well, I tell ya' what. You ain't goin' outside. I got a white bowl that ain't got a hole in it. You can use that till ya' feel better." She turned to Hattie. "Come on, sugar. Yer daddy has to use the - water closet."

Jedidiah grinned. "Abigail - where's the water?"

She grinned back. "Make it yer'self."

No sooner had Abigail closed the bedroom door, when the front door burst wide open. Both Abigail and Hattie drew a deep breath. Evelyn was standing there. Her fancy yellow dress was practically torn to shreds. Her face was dirty with scratches and dried blood. She was crying.

"Evelyn! What…." Abigail's words were stopped short when the girl ran to her and wrapped her arms around her.

"They're not here yet." She looked up at Abigail. "Please, Mrs. Lucas! You gotta go. You gotta take Hattie and get as far away from here as you can. Right now!"

Abigail gently put her hands on the girl's shoulders and met her eye to eye. "What is it child? What's wrong? Who's comin'?"

"The people," she cried. "They say Hattie is a witch, and she caused everything that happened to the town - the explosion, the tornado, the rain, the sickness, everything! It's my fault. I asked her to draw the pictures. I'm sorry! I only wanted to help."

Abigail held her for a moment. "Hush now, child." When she'd settled, she looked her in the eyes and said calmly, "That's all right. You ain't done nothin' wrong, ya' hear? Do ya' know how far away they are?"

Evelyn choked back her tears and took a deep breath. "I don't know. I saw a snake and got lost in the woods. I don't know how long I was there. I do know they went after Mr. Duffy's dogs. It would've taken him about ten minutes to get to his place on a fast horse."

Jedidiah came out of the bedroom using his crutches. He'd heard everything. "Abigail, get a couple of canteens of water and some food. You and Hattie take the long way to Shadrack through the swamp. You know the way - they don't. It'll be harder to track you."

"You're not coming, Daddy?" Tears started to run down Hattie's face.

"I'd slow you down, sweetie. Don't worry about me. I'll be fine," he smiled. "I'm the Sin-Eater. They wouldn't dare hurt me with all the sins they believe I carry."

"Please, Hattie. You gotta go. You're the one they really want," said Evelyn.

Abigail kissed Evelyn on the forehead. "Thank you, sugar." She brushed a strand of hair from her face. "Get outa that torn dress. Hattie'll give ya' a pair of her overalls."

Evelyn went into the other room and quickly changed. She looked at Paloma. "I wish your granny was better. Maybe she could do something."

Hattie went to Paloma's bed and kissed her. She whispered in her ear. "Please, Granny, wake-up. Daddy needs you."

Suddenly the bedroom door burst open. "Hattie! Go! Out the window," shouted Abigail. "They're here!" She saw her hesitate and this time pointed to the window. "NOW! PLEASE! I'll catch up!"

Hattie did as she was told. Evelyn followed behind her. "Where are you goin'? They won't hurt you."

"Where you go - I go!"

***

Abigail went to the window and watched as the girls disappeared into the woods. While she was gathering food, she'd heard the faint sound of the barking dogs. She'd turned to tell Jedidiah and saw him wobble on his crutches. She'd barely caught him before he fell. Though he was feeling better, he was nowhere near well. She'd managed to get him to the chair. He'd started sweating again. Just that little amount of activity had set him back. Abigail knew if Hattie had heard the fall and seen her father in the condition he was now, she would not have gone.

When Abigail saw Evelyn also go out the window, she didn't call her back. She figured that if these people saw the girl with them, it wouldn't go well for her either. She also knew Hattie would take care of her. Her daughter knew the swamp and the long way to Shadrack. She was confident her daughter could make it. "God protect 'em!" she mumbled and went back into the main room to tend to Jedidiah.

"Go Abigail, the dogs are getting closer," Jedidiah moaned.

"Ya' can't get shed of me that easily, Jedidiah Lucas. The preacher said for better or for worse. I figure this is 'bout as worse as it can get!" She knew if they took him to town, no one would touch him, and he'd need help. She had to stay with him. She just hoped they wouldn't kill them in cold blood.

"What about Hattie?"

"Our daughter ain't helpless. Right now, you are." She looked toward the bedroom. "So is Paloma. They'd probably shoot her as ta' look at her, if they's as crazy as Evelyn says." Abigail stroked the side of his cheek and smiled. "We both learned her good. She knows the swamp as well as town folk knows the town. She can hunt, fish, trap, build a fire and do 'bout anything a full growed man could do."

A moment later, the door was kicked open. Ezra Katts entered with rifle in hand. Abigail stood defiantly and pointed to the door. "Get outa my house!"

Ezra ignored her and turned to one of the men who'd followed him in. "Check the other rooms."

The man looked in Jedidiah and Abigail's room first, and then the other. "Just the old witch, Paloma Day. She's breathin', but she ain't movin'."

"Thought she'd be dead by now," Ezra sneered.

"She could have been, no thanks to all of you," Jedidiah said.

Ezra turned to Jedidiah. "Where's that daughter of sin you spawned."

"Leave her alone. She's done nothing to you or anyone!" shouted Jedidiah.

Ezra pulled out the drawings he had in his pocket. "Nothing! Her pictures killed my son!" He was crazed with anger. He dropped the pictures and raised his gun. "Kill the root that spilled the seed!"

"No!" Abigail shouted as she put her arms around her husband."

But Reverend Donner stepped into the room and pushed the barrel of the rifle down. "This is not the place, Brother Katts." He looked around the room. "This place is permeated with evil. If you kill a Sin-Eater by your own hand, it may not go well for your other son. The sins he carries could form into a monstrous evil spirit that could wreck havoc on our town."

Ezra glared at both of them. "Take'em into town and throw them in the jail."

"I'm not going anywhere," said Jedidiah.

"Your wife's not a sin-eater. You'll go..." He raised his rifle again. "… or she dies."

Abigail looked at Jedidiah and nodded. She helped him stand and adjusted the crutches under his arms.

"What happened to your wooden leg?" asked Evan McGuire as Jedidiah headed toward the door.

"The storm took it."

McGuire laughed. "God's punishment for your wicked ways. That's what you get for robbing me blind every month for all these years with my goods you've been getting."

One of the men turned to Ezra. "What do we do about the old woman?"

"Just leave her. Without them, she'll be dead in a couple a days."

They went outside, and Ezra had half of the men take Jedidiah and Abigail back to town and the other half took the dogs to go look for the child. They took a blanket from Hattie's bed so the dogs could get the scent. After a few minutes of the dogs sniffing the area, they finally picked up the girls' trail.

Paloma's Dream

"Where am I? Where is this place?" Paloma walked in a fog. It wasn't dark - it wasn't light. There was nothing around her. The last thing she remembered was being in the newspaper office. She'd sat down with a headache and closed her eyes while waiting to speak with George Tyler.

The next thing she knew, she was here - wherever that was.

As she walked, the fog started to clear, and she could just make out the trees before her. Soon, the fog completely dissipated, and she found herself in the woods. She smiled. This was her woods. The path soon opened into a clearing, and she saw her cottage. To the left, a man pushed a child on a swing. Their backs were to her, but she knew it wasn't Jedidiah and Hattie. A moment later, the child stopped swinging and both looked in her direction. Paloma took a deep breath. She saw Benjamin. The little boy smiled brightly, jumped up from the swing and ran to her.

"Mommy!" He wrapped his arms around her.

"Alexander?" she said as she stroked his dark brown hair. She'd never seen this boy, but she knew who he was. He was the child she'd miscarried in her youth. She knelt down and hugged him tightly.

"Daddy and me were waiting for you, Mommy." The boy kissed her on the cheek. "You know what today is?"

She looked into his blue eyes. "What is today?"

"My birthday! I'm six years old today. Are you going to bake me a cake?"

"Most definitely." Paloma looked up and saw Benjamin standing next to her. He was young, strong and handsome. He wore no eye patch and his face was unscarred. His blue eyes sparkled like Alexander's. She stood, and he put his arms around her.

"We've missed you," Benjamin said, and then he kissed her.

Paloma knew this was a dream, but it felt so real. Benjamin's kiss and embrace felt exactly as she remembered it. She was about to say something, but he put a finger to her lips. "Shhh. Enjoy the moment," he'd said to her. She felt the boy tug on her dress. She looked down and saw his eyes were covered by his other hand.

"Are ya'll done kissin'?" Alexander asked.

Benjamin laughed and swung the boy up to his shoulders. "We're done. Come on, Alexander. Let's let your mom get started on that cake. You can help me churn some iced-cream."

Paloma watched the two head for the shed. She wondered where they were going to get the cream, and then she heard a cow moo. She looked to the other side of the house and saw it eating out of a trough. That answered her question. She shrugged. "I guess I'll bake a cake."

As soon as she opened the door to the house, she was stunned. All the furnishings and fixtures were different from what she actually had -

yet by the same token, it was always as she'd imagined it could have been. Her hardwood floors shined - a fancy Persian rug was spread before the fireplace - the tables around the room had a glossy sheen and looked like they belonged to a grand estate. There was a pump in the kitchen and an icebox. She looked in the bottom draw of the icebox and saw the huge block of ice. It felt cold to the touch. She shook her head in amazement. "It's ice."

When she went into the bedroom to get her apron, she saw herself in the mirror and gasped. Her hair was long and dark and her face was young and beautiful again. The dress she had on was as fancy as anything she'd seen the younger women in town wear. She spun around and laughed, put on her apron and went to the kitchen to start on her cake.

Paloma had a wonderful day. She and Benjamin celebrated their son's birthday, and he opened presents. His father had given him a knife and her gift had been a new snake skin belt which she knew she'd made for him. His father also surprised him with a puppy. Somehow she also remembered the discussion she'd had with Benjamin about giving him one.

The night was also pleasurable. They sat by the fire and watched Alexander play with his new puppy. When it was time for bed, they listened to his prayers and tucked him in. When they retired for the evening, Paloma felt Benjamin's warm embrace. His touch felt real - the love he'd made to her felt real. She wondered if this were heaven or a dream. If it was a dream, she never wanted to wake.

***

Time passed in Paloma's mind. The days came and went as did the wonderful nights with Benjamin by her side. She watched Alexander grow to become a strong, handsome young man like his father. One day he brought a girl to their home and introduced her as the woman he was going to marry. As more time passed, Alexander and his wife gave her grandchildren, and she and Benjamin played with them. It was a dream life. She and Benjamin grew old together again just as she had always wanted it to be.

One night, Paloma called out in her sleep. She had an awful dream. She saw a young man lashed to a tree during a storm. "Jedidiah!" she called out several times. She woke and saw Benjamin smiling down at her.

"It's almost time, my love." He kissed her on the forehead.

"Time for what?" Paloma didn't understand.

"Time to wake up. They need you."

"But I am awake. It was just a dream." But in her heart, she knew which was the dream and which was the reality. She wrapped her arms around her beloved husband. "I don't want to leave you."

Benjamin kissed her long and tenderly and then looked once more into her eyes. "We'll be together again." He held her in his arms and whispered. "Close our eyes, my sweet Paloma."

***

Henry and Emmaline made their way through the woods. Several times they had to stop when Henry started feeling dizzy. Though he was ill, concern for his daughter spurred him on. It was almost dark before they finally found the clearing and saw Jedidiah's cottage. The door was wide open and they walked in.

"Hello!" Henry called out, but no answer came. "The men have probably already been here."

Emmaline was worried. "Do you think Evelyn is with them? Did she even make it here?"

Henry looked in the bedroom where Paloma was lying quietly. He bent down to see if she was dead or alive. She still lived. He stood when he saw a tattered yellow dress draped neatly over a chair. He called Emmaline into the room. "She was here. At least we know she's with someone."

Emmaline embraced her husband and started crying. "I'm afraid, Henry."

Suddenly they heard Paloma start to moan and mumble in her sleep. Emmaline sat next to her. "Mrs. Day." She touched her gently on the shoulder.

Paloma opened her eyes, and Emmaline slowly came into focus. She looked around and saw Henry standing behind her. "What…" she could barely speak. Her throat felt dry.

"Henry, get her some water," said Emmaline.

There was a pitcher of water on a nightstand with a glass and hollow reed next to it. He poured the water and handed it to Emmaline. She helped Paloma sit up and gave her a sip.

"Are you alright?" Emmaline asked.

"I don't know," she whispered. "I feel stiff, and my bones ache. "She took another sip of water. "What are you two doing here?"

"There are some bad things happening in town," Henry said. "Evelyn came here to warn your family, and we came looking for her. She was here, now no one is. Can you tell us anything?"

Paloma closed her eyes a moment and concentrated. She shook her head. "Nothing is clear." She'd asked them to help her out of bed.

"Should you be getting up?" Emmaline asked concerned.

"Girl, I've been lying in this bed for the past fifty years. I think it's about time I get up."

Henry and Emmaline looked at each other. Her statement didn't make much sense, but they did as she'd asked. The two stood on either side of the old woman. Her legs were as wobbly as a newborn calf. They helped her into the main room, and she sat down in her rocking chair. She looked at Henry. He was sweating profusely. "Maybe you should sit down as well."

He took her advice - the room was starting to spin. Paloma told Emmaline to put some water on the stove to boil and then go to the cupboard and bring her the pouches she found as well as a cup. She took a few pinches from the pouches, put them in a cup and gave it to Emmaline. She told her to pour the boiling water over the herbs, and when the liquid had steeped for a few minutes, to give it to her husband.

Henry took the cup and looked at the dark liquid. "What is it?"

"It'll make you feel better," Paloma replied. When he continued to hesitate, she added, "A little tea, plus a pinch of this, a dash that and a touch of something special. If you want, your wife can add a little sugar like we do for Hattie when she's sick."

Henry stared at it another moment and drank it down. It tasted bitter, but wasn't totally disgusting. "Sugar would have helped it."

Emmaline looked out the window. It was now dark. Clouds shielded the moon and stars. "What do we do now? We'll never find our way in the dark."

"Stay here tonight," Paloma said. "There's nothing you can do till morning. I've extra blankets in the trunk in my room. You can make a pallet on the floor..." she grinned. "...unless you want to sleep in Jedidiah and Abigail's bed."

"Thank you, the floor will be fine," Henry replied. The thought of sleeping in the Sin-Eater's bed made his spine tingle.

Chapter 35

"Come on, Ezra! It's gettin' dark. We gotta make camp," said one of the men.

"He's right," said Able Duffy. "My dogs are hungry. I gotta feed 'em. We can start again first light."

"The kid will probably be hold up somewhere too," said McGuire.

As much as he hated to stop, Ezra knew they had to. The swamp was bad enough in the daytime. At night the place made his skin crawl. There was no telling what they would run into in the dark.

***

Hattie and Evelyn made their way through the woods. They'd stopped for a short time at Hattie's little cabin that she called her special place. They gathered a few things they would need: a mason jar of dried fruit that Hattie kept there to nibble on, her knife, her slingshot and a blanket. When they heard the faint sound of dogs barking, they left.

Evelyn kept her eyes on Hattie. She tried not to show it, but she was a nervous wreck. She couldn't believe that Hattie was so calm and confident even now that it was dark. "Hattie, I don't hear the dogs anymore. Maybe we lost them."

"Most likely they camped for the night. It's getting' dark."

"Maybe we should too?" Evelyn looked around. The trees looked all twisted, and the branches moved in the breeze as if they were going to come down and grab them.

"There's a shelter just up ahead," Hattie pointed. "Me and Daddy use it when we go deer huntin'. There's also a spring not far away where we can get water."

Evelyn was glad to have at least three walls around her when they reached the small shelter. The structure was basically tree branches lashed together with a thatched roof and blankets on each side that Hattie untied and rolled down. Next she watched her build a small fire with nothing but sticks and brush. "Won't they see the fire?"

"Probably not," she replied. "I looked around first to see if I could see theirs."

"How do you know they built one?"

"Take a sniff. What do you smell?"

Evelyn closed her eyes and inhaled. There were several scents she could detect on the breeze. Only one was familiar. "Coffee?"

"That ain't a natural smell in the swamp." She picked up the canteen and started to walk away.

"You're not going to leave me here alone, are you?" Evelyn started to feel a little panicky.

"You'll be fine," Hattie assured her. "The spring is just over there. I'm just a shout away - but don't shout, they might hear you." Before she left she added, "Oh, you need ta' keep that fire goin' - it'll keep the snakes away." She grinned when she saw Evelyn quickly gather dried twigs and throw them into the flames.

Hattie went to the spring and filled her canteen. She spotted a rabbit sitting on a log. She pulled her slingshot and a pebble from her back pocket. "Gotcha!" She thought about cleaning the rabbit there, but didn't want to leave Evelyn alone for too long. She returned to their little camp holding the rabbit up by its ears. "We're in luck, Evelyn. I've got dinner!"

Evelyn was shocked and slightly horrified. "You - killed a bunny?"

Hattie smiled. "Sure did! It's a nice fat one too. It'll make good eatin'. I hate goin' ta' sleep on an empty stomach. Don't you?"

Evelyn heard the enthusiasm in her voice over the kill. If she'd found a chicken or even a deer that wouldn't have bothered her. But a bunny - they were cute and cuddly. She then had to remind herself that Hattie and her family had to survive on whatever meat they could find.

"Anything wrong, Evelyn?" Hattie asked when she didn't answer.

"Oh, no," she replied. "I guess I'm just tired."

"Well, I'm goin' over there ta' clean it. Be back in a few minutes."

When Hattie returned with the skinned rabbit skewered on a long stick, Evelyn could barely look at it. She listened as her friend told her how it would taste a lot better with the spices her mother and grandmother would have put on it. But as the smell of the rabbit roasting over the flames started to get done, her stomach started to rumble reminding her how hungry she was.

Hattie stood and pulled a couple of large leaves from a nearby plant and handed one to Evelyn. "It ain't a fancy plate like yer used to, but it'll do in a pinch." She took her knife and cut a portion for her friend to try.

Evelyn stared at it for a moment. "Ahm - maybe we should say Grace first?" she suggested mostly to delay the inevitable.

"Yer right," Hattie agreed. "I plum forgot." She said the dinner prayer, thanking God for the rabbit he put in her path and then asked Evelyn, "Tell me what you think."

It couldn't be avoided any longer. Evelyn closed her eyes, put the bunny meat in her mouth and started to chew. She just knew she was going to hate it, but as the juicy meat hit her taste buds, they craved more. She was pleasantly surprised. "Tastes like chicken!"

Hattie laughed. She'd been completely aware of Evelyn's disgust about eating this rabbit. "Well, if it'll make ya' feel better, just think of it as a chicken on the spit not a - bunny. So - you want a wing, breast or a drumstick?"

Evelyn felt slightly embarrassed. She realized Hattie's good natured sarcasm for what it was and said sheepishly, "Drumstick please."

As they settled down for the night, Hattie thought of how uncomfortable Evelyn was. Her mother told her to go to Shadrack, but she had to do one thing first - take Evelyn home.

Back in Town

Jubal Hagen, Abigail's cousin, had come into town to pick up a few things for their trip back to Kentucky. He jiggled the knob on McGuire's store, but it was closed. "Dang it! Paw ain't gonna be happy." He shoved his hands in his pockets and walked back to his mule, grumbling about how he'd have to come back tomorrow.

As he mounted, he heard a commotion at the edge of town by the sin-eater's bell and rode that way to satisfy his curiosity. His chin dropped and his eyes bulged when he saw Cousin Abigail and Jedidiah surrounded by angry men with guns heading for the jailhouse. He turned his mule around. "Come on, Berthie, get a move on! Abby's in trouble." He kicked the mule to spur it to a run and headed home.

***

Jack Trainor headed for town just as soon as his father-in-law had explained everything that happened. He thought about putting on his uniform to look more official, but it was Union, and there were many people in the community who were still Confederate minded, though the war had been over for a long time. With the state of mind the people were in now, they may decide to hang him as well.

He decided to wait in the hotel's restaurant for the return of those who went into the swamp, but he saw a sign on the door that read, *Closed due to Influenza.* There was a rocking chair on the front porch so he sat down, propped his foot on the railing and waited. He heard snatches of conversations as people passed him. Fear and anger seemed to permeate the air as they talked about the witch child and how they were going to purge the town of this evil. They even had the audacity to bring God into the picture as if they were doing his will by wanting to hang her.

Jack just shook his head. "This town is pathetic," he mumbled.

"What did you say, young man?" asked an older woman he hadn't seen approach.

"I said this town is panicked," he lied.

"This used to be a great town to live in. But now with two witches and one of them born with all those sins in her! I shiver to think about it. Evil is in the air."

"I couldn't agree more," Jack replied. When the woman passed, he mumbled, "An you're attitude is part of the evil."

The sun started to set. He looked at his pocket watch to check the time. A few minutes later, he heard noises coming for the other end of town. As they got closer, he saw Jedidiah and a young woman, he assumed to be his wife. He stepped onto the street to join the others that surround them and was almost run down by a young man on a mule that galloped past.

He joined the group practically unobserved and listened to some of the people taunt them.

"Where's the witch child?" asked one of the women in the crowd.

"Somewhere in the swamp," replied Sam Waters, the deputy. "Ezra and the others are tracking her down. They'll get her."

"My daughter is a good girl!" Abigail cried. "She ain't a witch. She ain't evil!"

"What else would the mother say!" shouted another in the crowd. "We should hang her too."

Jack saw one women spit on Abigail. He thought it a disgusting display of a town gone insane. A few people shouted that they should hang them now. A few people agreed and someone shouted to get a rope. Jack thought quickly. "Wait till daylight so everyone can see! Besides, evil thrives in the dark!" He rolled his eyes. The latter sounded pretty stupid when he said it, but apparently it worked. Whispers of agreement filtered through the crowd, and they continued on to the jail.

***

Jedidiah fell to the floor when the deputy took away his crutches and pushed him into the cell. He lay there barely coherent. The trek through the woods caused a relapse in his condition.

"Please, let me help him," cried Abigail as she was pushed into a cell next to his. "He's sick. Can't ya' see!"

"He won't be sick for long," said one of the men as the metal bars clanged shut. "We're sending both of you to hell where you belong!"

"And when we catch that creature you gave birth to, she'll join you," added the deputy before he and the others went into the office and shut the outer cell door.

Abigail sat on the cot and cried for a few moments. She couldn't believe this was happening to them. No matter what she'd said on the way there, they wouldn't listen. All her words were twisted and turned to make it fit what they believed.

Jedidiah moaned. Abigail dried her eyes and looked into his cell. She called his name several times, begging him to try and get off the cold floor and onto the cot. The words slowly filtered through his dulled senses, and he pulled himself up to it. Abigail reached through the bars, grabbed his belt and helped him the rest of the way.

"You should have followed Hattie," he mumbled. "Then both of you would be safe."

She reached through the bars and took his hand. "Life without you wouldn't be life." Tears rolled down her cheeks. "If we's destined ta' die tomorrow, we'll be havin' supper with the Lord at his table tomorrow night - together."

Jedidiah kissed her hand, put it next to his heart and closed his eyes.

***

Jack Trainor leaned against the wall in a corner of the sheriff's office, listening to the plans that they were making to rid themselves of the Sin-Eater and his family. The owner of the sawmill said he'd donate the lumber to build a gallows, and four others offered to start building it at first light.

"Who's gonna do the hanging?" asked Sam. The room suddenly went quiet. "Any volunteers?"

"Yer the deputy, that's yer job!" said one of the men.

"Are you crazy! And have their ghosts' haunt me for the rest of my life?" He shook his head. "Not me!"

The men mumbled among themselves for a few minutes. That was the one thing they hadn't thought of. What do they do about their ghosts? Several ideas were tossed about as to who would do the deed. Jack had been formulating a plan. "Draw lots. The one chosen will do the deed and have custody of the ghosts." He found it difficult to keep a straight face when mentioning the ghosts, but managed. All eyes turned to him, but before anyone commented on it, George Tyler entered the Sheriff's Office.

"Like hell you will!" He slammed the door. He'd just caught what Jack had said. "You're condemning a man and his family for what? A few damn pictures!"

"You didn't see the pictures, Tyler," said Sam. "That witch child drew the sheriff exactly how he died."

George folded his arms. "So you're just going to hang them. No trial - no nothing."

"They had their trial in church. We all say they're guilty as sin," said Carlin Baker, the owner of the butcher shop.

"Alright, Baker," George grinned. "I say we hang you."

The man raised his eyebrows. "Me! What the deuce for?"

"For the past two months, you've owed me for three ads you placed in the paper. I haven't seen a penny from you yet. So if you're going to hang a girl for drawing a picture, I say we hang you for thievery."

The butcher stepped up to Tyler and looked him in the eye. "I ain't a thief."

"That's different!" Sam interrupted. "Carlin isn't evil."

"I say he is," George shot back.

Jack listened intently. He had an ally. The newspaperman had just given him another idea. "As much as I hate to admit it - he's right. Even Salem had trials for their witches. After all, this isn't the dark ages. We are civilized, aren't we?"

There was mumbling among the men, and then Sam turned to Jack. "Who the hell are you anyway? I've never seen you before."

"Jack Trainor," he answered.

"Yeah, you married Roland Buehl's daughter, Jessica," said Carlin Baker, and then as an afterthought he added. "I thought your son was sick."

"His fever broke. Heard what was going on and Roland asked me if I could come to town and help." Jack didn't exactly lie - he just didn't say who he was going to help.

"Good man, that Roland," said Sam.

The men talked a while longer and decided they would discuss the matter more tomorrow when Ezra and the others had caught the girl and brought her in. When everyone left the jail, George Tyler caught up to Jack, grabbed him by the arm and jerked him around to face him.

"Are you out of your damn mind! Why are you siding with them? I thought you had better sense, being that you were never an actual member of this community."

Jack grinned. "Have you ever heard the saying - you can draw more flies with honey than vinegar?"

George looked at him from the corner of his eye. "What the hell does that mean?"

"It's called infiltration, Mr. Newspaperman. I have a plan, and I'll need you to help. Come to my in-law's house this evening, but don't let anyone see you." Jack saw the deputy approach. "But right now, Tyler, I apologize for this…." Jack hauled off and punched George in the gut which caused him to drop to his knees.

"What the hell did you hit me for," George choked out.

Jack gave him a wink and then shouted, "What do you mean I have no right to say what goes on in this town? My wife's parents live here so that makes it my business, Mr. Newspaperman."

Sam walked up to Jack. "What's the problem?"

"Do my opinions in this town count around here or not?" Jack grumbled to the deputy.

Sam sneered at George as he stood. "More so than college boy." Sam turned to Jack and smiled. "Come to the meeting tomorrow morning."

The young lieutenant looked at George and rubbed his fist. "Glad to."

George watched the two walk away and shook his head. Either Jack Trainor was just as crazy as the people in this town, or he was a shrewd individual.

The Town - After Midnight

George Tyler had just returned from the Buehl residence. He had come to the conclusion that Jack Trainor wasn't just crazy, he was crazy-shrewd. His idea had merit, but it was very risky. However, he'd do anything in his power to save that little girl if they caught her. Yet saving Jedidiah and Abigail was another issue they hadn't quite figured out.

The newspaperman stabled his horse and walked down the street to his office. He wanted to put some finishing touches on tomorrow's paper. As he walked past the alley by the sheriff's office, he thought he heard a noise. He pulled his gun. Normally he didn't carry a weapon in town, but since his trip took him a little ways out, he'd put it on. Now he was glad he did. He thought it might be one of the town's fanatics attempting to rid themselves of Jedidiah and Abigail by shooting them from the jailhouse window. He saw three figures in the dark stacking crates to reach the cell window.

"Stop where you are!" George said, but before he could say another word, three, two-barreled shotguns were pointed in his direction.

"I'd be puttin' that little peashooter down, Mister. And if'n ya' call out, my boy'll put a hole in ya' as big as that rain barrel yonder," warned Ennis Hagen. "We means ta' get my niece out'a this here jail, an ain't nobody gonna stop us."

George put his pistol away and grinned. "If you wanna get her out, I've gotta better way."

Ennis, his son, Jubal, and Ennis's brother, Hannibal, looked at each other. "You gonna help us?"

"I was trying to think of a way without implicating myself." He motioned them to come closer. "Here's the plan."

***

George quickly opened the door to the sheriff's office. The deputy had just taken the mid-night watch. "Sam!"

The startled deputy stood and pulled his gun. "Damn it, Tyler! I could'a shot ya'!"

"Well, keep it out! I heard noises behind the jail."

Sam came around the desk and followed George outside. As soon as they stepped out, Sam felt a hand go over his mouth and his gun stripped away. The same thing happened to George.

"If'n ya's don't wanna get shot, I'd hold real still," Hannible warned Sam.

Ennis went into the sheriff's office, took the keys from the wall and opened the outer cell door. Abigail sat up. She was shocked to see her uncle. "What in tarnation are ya' doin' here, Uncle Ennis."

"We's come ta' get ya', Abigail." Ennis put the key in the lock and opened the door. She put her arms around him, relieved that he'd come to rescue them.

Normally, Ennis wasn't one to show affection in this manner, but he hugged her back. He cleared his throat. "Come on, now. Get a move on."

"What about Jedidiah?" she asked.

Ennis looked at him. He wasn't moving. "He don't look none to good."

Jedidiah stirred and managed to sit up. "Take her, Ennis. I'd slow you down. I'm too sick to go anywhere." He leaned against the bars and closed his eyes.

"No, Jedidiah! We can't just leave you!" she cried.

"Abigail - please. For our daughter. Go! God willing, she'll make it to Shadrack sometime tomorrow morning."

Abigail reached her hand through the bars and took his hand in hers. She knew he was right. "I love you."

"Come on, girl. We gotta go!" insisted Ennis.

When the two exited the jail, Ennis nodded to Hannibal. His brother hit Sam over the head and watched him drop to the ground. Ennis then turned to George. "Ya' sure ya' want it this way?"

"It's the way it's gotta be, or they'll never believe I wasn't in on the escape. I need the lump to prove it." He closed his eyes tightly. "Make it quick." Jubal hit him over the head and gently lowered his limp body to the ground.

"Let's go," said Ennis.

They made their way down the alley to retrieve their mules. Abigail mounted behind her cousin and looked back. She prayed for Jedidiah's safety.

Chapter 36

The Swamp

The sun had not yet risen. Hattie shook Evelyn awake. She knew her friend had gotten very little sleep. The noises of the night had her sitting up every few minutes until weariness finally overtook her, and she closed her eyes.

"It's not morning yet." Evelyn sat up and rubbed her eyes.

"It's morning enough. They'll be on our trail again in a while. I can smell their coffee brewin'. We gotta go."

Evelyn followed wearily. With every little sound, she would quickly jerk her head in that direction, but she never uttered a word of complaint. Hattie knew it was a right decision to get her home. She twisted and turned through the woods until she was sure Evelyn's sense of direction was confused, and then she set her path toward her friend's home.

The Trackers

The sun was just barely up. Reverend Donner put out their campfire. Able Duffy let his dogs reestablish the scent from Hattie's blanket, and they were on their way. They'd only gone a relatively short distance when they found where their quarry had camped. Ezra bent down and held his hand over the ashes from their fire. "It hasn't been out long." He couldn't believe they'd been that close. He stood and kicked at a partially burnt piece of wood. "If we'd only gone a little further last night, we wouldn't have had to spend the night in this God forsaken swamp!"

"Patience, Brother Katts," said Reverend Donner. "As the Bible says, in Galatians 6:9, *'Let us not become weary in doing good...'"* His eyes narrowed as he looked toward the area that the dogs were sniffing to pick up the scent. He continued reciting the passage in a cold tone. *"'...for at the proper time we will reap a harvest....'"*

Ezra nodded his agreement, and they continued on their way. But the trail they followed didn't seem like it led anywhere.

"Ezra, I thought you said she might head to Shadrack?" asked Able.

"Yeah. That's my guess. What of it?"

"Well, this ain't the way. Either she's lost, or she's doubling back." He knelt down to the ground. "Look. Two sets of tracks. I didn't notice the other set yesterday."

"Two?" asked Evan McGuire.

Reverend Donner thought for a moment. "The Welch girl. The poor child has been bewitched by the Sin-Eater's daughter. Those tracks are probably hers." He folded his hands, closed his eyes and looked toward the sky. "Lord, protect the innocent lamb in the company of the wolf. Do not let her soul be devoured by the evil child she accompanies."

"Amen, Reverend," said one of the other fanatical men accompanying them.

Paloma's Cottage

Henry opened his eyes. The smell of coffee brewing brought him to consciousness. He sat up and stretched his back. The last time he remembered sleeping on the floor was as a child in his best friend's tree house. He saw Emmaline standing by the stove. "Why didn't you wake me?"

"I just woke myself. The coffee smelled wonderful." She yawned. "I didn't sleep well. I can't get Evelyn out of my mind." She poured the coffee in the cups sitting on the counter and took one of them to Henry. "How are you feeling?"

"Actually - somewhat better." He sneezed. "Well, at least my head doesn't ache anymore." He looked around the room. "Where's our host?"

Emmaline walked toward the window. "She's sitting by the fire outside."

Henry joined her. "I never heard her get up."

"She was ill for so long, perhaps she never went to bed. The last I remember, she was sitting in the rocking chair by the fireplace."

Henry finished his coffee. "We better go. I want to get home. Maybe Evelyn's there."

They went outside and approached Paloma. "Thank you for your hospitality," said Henry. But she didn't answer. She stared wide-eyed into the fire. "Mrs. Day…"

Emmaline sat down on the bench beside her and touched her on the shoulder. "Mrs. Day, are you alright?"

The slight touch shook Paloma from her trance-like state. She looked at Emmaline and took her hands. "Go home! Quickly…"

"What's wrong?" Emmaline sensed her urgency.

Paloma shook her head. "I don't know. I just feel something - something isn't right!" She squeezed Emmaline's hands. "Now! Please!"

Henry and Emmaline didn't hesitate. They headed down the path toward home. Paloma watched them enter the woods. She closed her eyes. "God, why am I here? What am I to do? My visions are clouded, and I can't see what's ahead. Please guide my way."

There was a chill in the air. She stood with the help of her walking stick. Her legs still felt slightly wobbly from inactivity. Last night, before they went to sleep, Henry and Emmaline had told her how long she'd been ill and what had transpired in town since then. They also told her that they thought Jedidiah and Abigail might have been taken into town, and they weren't sure about Hattie, but wherever she was, Evelyn might be with her.

As Paloma started toward the house, she heard a screeching noise from above. She looked up and saw a hawk chasing after a small bird. The bird flew amongst the branches of a nearby tree but not before the hawk grazed it with its talons. She saw the bird fall to the ground and approached it. It was still alive, but injured. Paloma picked it up. "You're not too bad. I think I can fix you right up." She took it in the house, tended to its injury and set it on the window sill. It sat there and chirped for a few minutes before it flew away.

She was about to close the window when she heard a distant echo of a rifle followed by a shrill cry. She looked up in the sky and saw the hawk circling. It cried again. She closed the window and started toward her rocking chair, but something inside told her she had something to do. She went to the cupboard, gathered her pouches of herbs and as weak as her legs were, she left the house and went into the woods.

Hattie and Evelyn

Hattie could almost feel Evelyn's fear. She'd just saved her friend from running into a giant spider web when her head was turned. She'd accidently walked into a spider's web herself once and was irked by it. She didn't want to think of what Evelyn's reaction would have been.

They had come to a small stream that was just about ankle deep and Hattie had suggested that they wade through it for a little ways to throw the dogs off their scent. Evelyn hesitated for a moment, but followed her in after hearing the faint sound of baying dogs behind them. After a few hundred feet, the stream started getting deeper, so they got out and continued on their way.

"How much further?"Evelyn asked. To her, it seemed as if they'd been walking for hours.

"Not far."

"I sure don't see how you can keep from getting lost!" Evelyn swatted at a dragon-fly that fluttered around her head.

Hattie laughed. "Have you ever gotten lost in yer backyard?"

"That's silly. Of course not."

"Well, this is my backyard. Me, my mama and my daddy have been all over it."

Evelyn thought about it for a moment. It made sense. She changed the subject and kept asking questions to keep her mind off the strange sounds coming from the swamp. Every time a branch fell or something darted past a tree, all she could think of were snakes. "What are your aunt and uncle like? You don't talk about them much."

"Like any other folks, I guess. We only visit now and again. But I do like my Cousin Caleb. He says when they go back to Kentucky, he's gonna go ta' school like me. I've already learned him his ABCs so he'll have a head start."

As they walked, Evelyn thought her surrounding started to look familiar. There was a large, dead tree lying on the ground to her left. As they traveled a little further, she saw a patch of toad stools to her right. She stopped. "Wait a minute! You're taking me home, aren't you?"

Hattie stopped and gave her a smile. "I appreciate ya' wantin' ta' come with me, but I can tell how the swamp scares ya'. Besides, yer mama and daddy are probably worried sick. I don't want them ta' start hatin' on me like yer grandmother does."

"They wouldn't hate you." Evelyn knew she was right about them worrying. Her desire to be with Hattie equaled her fear of the swamp. She also figured her friend could travel much faster without her. She gave her a hug. "You be careful."

"I will. Can you make it the rest of the way from here?"

"I think so."

They said their good-byes and Hattie headed back the way they had just come. Evelyn started walking the path to home. Suddenly an idea struck her. She rolled her eyes. "Why didn't I think of it before? Mama will take Hattie to Shadrack. I know she will!" She turned in her tracks and followed Hattie's path. She was only a few minutes ahead of her. Evelyn would have shouted, but she was afraid the men that followed would hear. She'd wait to call out when she got closer.

The Trackers

Able Duffy examined the tracks by the water's edge. "The kid is smart. She's taken to the water."

"But which way?" asked Ezra.

"We'll have to split up and look for tracks. The way she's been weaving around this God forsaken swamp, there's no tellin' which way she went or on which side of the stream she came out," Able replied.

Reluctantly the men agreed. Reverend Donner, Evan McGuire and three others went in one direction, while Ezra Katts, Able Duffy and the other two went the opposite. About thirty minutes later, Kevin Jenson, one of the men with Ezra's group shouted, "Over here! I found tracks." He pulled his pistol and was about to fire a shot.

Ezra grabbed his gun hand and stopped him. "What are ya' doin'?"

"I was just gonna signal the others."

"You fire a shot - you warn her too. Best ya' go after them," said Ezra.

"By myself - in this swamp!" Kevin exclaimed. "Nothin' doin'." The man fired the shot anyway. "Knowin' you, you'd take Duffy and the dogs and go off lookin' for her by yourself and leave us." He looked Ezra in the eye. "I wanna get that little witch as much as you do. My daughter might lose sight in one of her eyes because of that explosion." He holstered his gun. "We'll wait."

"He's right, Ezra," said Duffy. "This swamp is no place to be alone."

"Cowards!" Ezra grumbled.

"Damn straight!" Kevin replied. "When it comes to bein' alone in this swamp, I'm as lily-livered as they come!"

Ezra started walking on ahead. Able grabbed his arm. "You're not goin' alone, are ya'?"

He jerked his arm away. "Ya' mind - I got business ta' take care of behind that tree. Unless ya' wanna watch me ta' take a shit right here!"

When Ezra took longer than he should have in returning and didn't answer their calls, they knew he'd taken off after the girl on his own. "Damn idiot!" exclaimed Kevin.

"Can't say as I blame him though," Duffy replied. "Losin' his son like that and not even bein' able to give him a decent funeral, I'd feel the same way."

The three talked about going after him, but decided to wait for the others, which wasn't very long. If Ezra had only waited another ten minutes, they would have all gone together.

Henry and Emmaline

"Are you sure this is the right way?" Henry asked. He looked down at the ground for tracks as he kicked away leaves that had covered their trail. For the most part, the way home had been fairly readable until now.

"Pretty sure," Emmaline replied, as she too kicked away leaves. "I remember that patch of toad stools over there."

Henry walked a little further. "Emmaline - I found tracks!" He bent down and examined them. "I don't know a lot about tracking, but I do recognize small prints when I see them."

Suddenly they heard a shot echoing in the distance. They knew it had to be from the trackers. Emmaline was sure the way home was in one direction, but the small prints headed in the direction that the shot came from. They followed the small foot prints hoping they would lead to Evelyn.

The Girls

Hattie weaved her way through the tangle of the woods. She worried about her parents and wondered if they'd escaped the town's people. As she continued on her way, she stepped on a branch and when it cracked, she heard another noise - the unmistakable sound of a rattlesnake. She stopped instantly, looked around but didn't see it. When the creature quieted, she took a couple of easy steps backward and made a wide path around the area. A moment later, she heard a gunshot ahead of her. She figured the trackers had found her trail out of the stream.

***

Evelyn heard the gunshot. She was getting worried. She thought she would have caught up to Hattie by now. She'd also come upon another problem - two sets of tracks that both looked fresh. But which direction did she go? She called her name in a whispered tone, but there was no answer as she headed down one of the paths. Now she was not only worried about Hattie, she worried about herself. What was she thinking! She was in the swamp - alone! The subtle noises of tree limbs falling, bugs buzzing and then the most horrid sound of all - the rattling of a snake's tail. She froze not knowing where the sound came from. "HATTIE!" she shouted. Tears started to roll down her cheeks until she heard the faint response, "Here, Evelyn!" It had come from the direction of the other trail. She ran toward the voice.

Ezra Katts

As soon as Ezra was out of sight, he left the others. He didn't need Able Duffy's dogs to follow the easy tracks the girls made. The others would just have to catch up. He wasn't going to take the chance on the witch-child getting too far ahead of them. He watched the trail intently, but then heard a voice call the name - Hattie. It had come from a direction different than where the tracks led, and it was fairly close.

Ezra left the trail, pushing away vines and other over-growth until he came to a small clearing. A few yards ahead of him, he caught glimpses of a girl appearing and disappearing between the trees as she ran parallel to his position. "I've got you now," he mumbled. He took a couple of steps with his eyes fixed on her position. He paid no attention to where he was walking and stepped on something that felt like a lump under a pile of leaves. A rattlesnake reared its head. Ezra jumped back, but the creature lunged forward and latched on to the heel of his boot. The shock startled him, and he accidently discharged his rifle.

Two screams could be heard echoing through the swamp. Ezra's, as he yelled while trying to get loose from the snake, and Hattie's, when she saw Evelyn fall to the ground.

Chapter 37

Hattie cried as she ran to Evelyn and knelt beside her. Blood flowed from her shoulder. "Please be alright, Evelyn!" For the moment, she didn't know what to do.

Evelyn opened her eyes and winced in pain as she put her hand to her shoulder. "Go, Hattie. They'll get you."

"No," she whimpered. "I can't leave you like this." Knowing that her friend wasn't dead, she regained the presence of mind to rip the sleeve from her shirt and place it over the hole in Evelyn's shoulder to try and stop the bleeding.

"Get away from her!" Ezra shouted as he pointed his gun at Hattie. He had finally been able to kill the snake that had him. When Hattie didn't move he repeated. "Get away from her or I'll...."

But that was all he managed to say before he felt someone grab his gun and jerk him around. "You shot my daughter!" Henry connected his fist to Ezra's jaw and the man fell.

"It was an accident!" Ezra shouted. "A snake grabbed me and the gun went off." Then he pointed toward Hattie. "It was the witch child. She sent the snake after me!"

Henry ignored him and joined Emmaline by his daughter's side. "Hattie didn't do anything, Papa," Evelyn cried. "She'd led me to the path home."

"Don't talk now, sweetie," Emmaline said. "We're not blaming Hattie." Her voice wavered as she tried to put on a good front. She didn't want to worry her daughter by crying. She'd taken Hattie's place in applying pressure to Evelyn's wound.

Henry knelt down and carefully picked up his injured child. It crushed him when she cried out in pain. He turned to Hattie and spoke in an easy tone. "Can you show us a quick way out of here?"

Hattie wiped her eyes. "This way."

"You're trusting that witch-child!" Ezra grumbled as he wiped a trickle of blood from his lip.

Emmaline picked up Ezra's gun and pointed it at the man. "You say another word, Ezra Katts, or I see you following us, so help me God, I will shoot you dead!"

Ezra watched them leave. He waited until they were out of sight and followed. It wasn't long until he met up with the other men.

"We heard the shot. Did you find her?" asked Evan McGuire.

"Yes, but she temporarily has a rescuer." Ezra told them how Hattie had bewitched a snake to attack him, causing his gun to accidently go off and hit Evelyn. He also told them how the child had manipulated Henry and Emmaline to protect her.

Reverend Donner looked down the path Ezra had indicated. "The devil puts stumbling blocks before those who fight forces of evil!"

"Don't worry, Reverend, we'll get her," said Able Duffy.

***

Hattie led Henry and Emmaline down a path closest to their house. Before Evelyn lost consciousness, she kept asking her parents to please take Hattie to Shadrack and not let them get her.

They finally reached the end of the woods where the rock wall had been demolished by the tornado. "Yer' house is that way," Hattie pointed. She wiped a tear from her eye. "When Evelyn gets better, tell her I'm sorry." She turned back toward the swamp.

"You don't have to go, Hattie. Stay with us. We'll protect you," said Emmaline.

"I've caused enough trouble already. Everything is my fault. She wouldn't have been hurt if it hadn't been for me," she cried and then disappeared into the woods.

***

Emmaline quickly opened the door to their house. "Fredricks!" she shouted as Henry carried in their daughter. "Go for the doctor - quickly!"

The butler was momentarily dumfounded when he saw his employers covered with their daughter's blood, but after being prompted again by Henry, he found his tongue. "I wish to God I could, Sir. Dr. Jackson died this morning of Influenza. They found him slumped over in his carriage when his horse came into town. I'm told there was another alligator attack last night, and he went out to treat the man who was injured."

"What are we going to do now?" Emmaline cried.

Henry shook his head. "I don't know. Right now get some water and bandages." He carried Evelyn up the steps to her room.

Gooch Residence

"Really? They were gone all night?" Sally Gooch sipped her tea and then shook her head as she talked to Erma. "I just can't believe Emmaline's attitude on this matter. She loved her Uncle Victor. You would think that she'd want the person responsible for everything that has happened around here to suffer the consequences."

"My Henry is no better," Erma replied. "I just know they're hiding at a neighbor's house to make me feel some sort of guilt - which I don't! They probably have Evelyn with them." She took a sip from her cup and changed the subject slightly. "I heard they brought in the witch-child's parents yesterday."

Sally cocked her head. "Didn't you hear?"

"No - hear what?"

"There was a daring escape last night. Sam Waters and George Tyler were knocked out. They were found unconscious by the jailhouse steps. Sam has a gash in his head. Since Dr. Jackson was found dead this morning, he had to get Elvin from the stable to stitch him up."

"Did they both get away?" Erma was concerned.

"Just the mother. Jedidiah is on the edge of death himself. I'd say Influenza will get him in a day or two."

"The Lord works in mysterious ways," Erma touted. "It serves him right for fathering a child in the first place. I know Reverend Donner was giving that horrible child the benefit of the doubt, but he now knows the evil those two brought into this world." Erma heard the clock strike. "I'd better go. Perhaps they've come home by now. I'm anxious to hear what excuse they have for not coming home last night."

"Ask Emmaline to come by today. I want her to help me gather some of her Uncle's things. I plan on donating them to the poor," Sally said.

Erma smiled and patted her on the hand. "Even during this time, Sally, your true Christian nature shines through."

The Welch Residence

Erma got into her carriage and headed for home. She smiled when she saw the men building the gallows. She was positive that once Hattie was out of the way, the town and her family would get back to normal.

Once home, her driver let her off at the front door. She was about to take a step upon the porch and saw drops of blood. She closed her eyes and shook her head. "The gardener has cut himself again. Henry is just going to have to speak to him about cleaning up after himself." She opened the door and saw the servants scurrying about. She was appalled when Fredricks completely ignored her and started going up the stairs with linens. "Fredricks! How dare you! Come here at once."

"I've no time, Madam!" He continued on his way.

She heard Henry shout from upstairs. "Fredricks! Where are those linens!"

"Coming, Sir!" he replied.

"Well, their home," Erma huffed. She was about to go up the stairs, when the cook pushed past her with a kettle of steaming water. "Where are your manners?"

The only response she got was an, "Excuse me, ma'am."

"Has everyone gone mad around here?" She marched up the stairs. "I'll get to the bottom of this."

Henry was at the door of Evelyn's room. "Martha! Where's the…" he saw the cook. "Good. Pour it in the basin and get us another kettle."

Erma saw her son's back when she got to the top of the stairs. "Henry! Where have you been?" she scolded. But when he turned around to face her, she saw the front of his white shirt was covered with blood. "Oh my God, son. You're hurt!" She ran to him.

He firmly grabbed her shoulders before she could embrace him. "It's not me that's hurt, Mother. It's Evelyn. She's been shot."

Erma drew a deep breath. "Shot! Who would do such a thing? I've got to see her."

She started to push past him, but he held her firm. "No!" he said adamantly. "I don't want you near her. You're the one who caused her to go into the swamp to warn her friend, and you're the one who has gotten this whole damn town in an uproar. Ezra Katts shot her. He said it was an accident, but I have my doubts about that! If the worst happens to my daughter - I never want to see or speak to you again! So go away, Mother! Go back to Sally's so the two of you can revel over your little witch hunt. It's only a matter of time before she's caught." A tear ran down his cheek. "In trying to kill another man's child! You've practically…" his voice started to crack "…killed mine!" He let go of her, went back into Evelyn's room and closed the door.

"You were a little hard on her, weren't you, Henry?" Emmaline said as she held pressure to her daughter's wound.

"I meant to be. Her prejudice and hatred has spread like a cancer throughout the community. Even if my words had an effect on her, it's too late for the town and God help her, I don't know what I can do for Hattie."

***

Ezra and his men proudly walked into town leading Hattie by a rope tied around her wrists. "We've got her! We've got the witch-child!" he shouted.

The people in town gathered around them. Some asked Hattie why she hurt their families. Some of the women in the crowd prayed loudly for the evil in their midst to be purged and that peace and tranquility would reign once the witch-child was gone.

The trackers had thought they would probably have to storm the Welch residence to take her, but as they followed the trail, they spotted Hattie running through the woods. But capturing her was no easy task. She darted around trees and brushes. She kicked the shins or the private parts of those who managed to get a hand on her. She even picked up a Rat snake and threw it at Reverend Donner. But they'd finally managed to surround her and close in. The preacher then trumpeted that God hath delivered her into their hands.

"What happened to your eye, McGuire?" asked one of the men in the crowd. He was holding a bloodied piece of cloth over it.

"Damn witch hit me with a rock using her slingshot. Damn near took my eye out. Where's Doc? I need a few stitches."

"Best see Elvin 'bout that," replied the man. "Doc's dead. Fever got 'em"

"Where ya' gonna put her, Ezra?" shouted another from the crowd.

He rolled his eyes. "Jail, where do ya' think!"

"Not if ya' expects ta' keep her fer the hangin'," replied the man. "Her kin folk busted her mama out."

Hattie heard what he'd said and wanted to shout for joy, but they told her if she opened her mouth, they'd hang her parents first and make her watch.

"What about Jedidiah?" McGuire asked. "Did he escape too?"

"No, but he'll probably be dead in a day or two. He ain't hardly moved a muscle. He's sick with the fever."

Hattie started to cry and Ezra jerked on the rope. "Shut up, you! No one's gonna be swayed by those fake tears." He turned to the people gathered around. "Any suggestions as to where to keep her?"

A voice came from out of the crowd. "Since the hotel is closed due to the fever, put her in the linen closet. It'll be easily guarded. There's only one door and no windows. Anyone who tries to come for her will have to go through too many guards to get her out."

"Who said that?" Ezra looked around.

The man stepped forward, smiled and extended his hand. "Jack Trainor."

"I don't believe we've met," said Ezra as they clasp hands.

Sam Waters stepped forward and patted Jack on the back. "Jack's a good man. He's Roland Buehl's son- in-law."

"Good to know you, Trainor. Your suggestion is sound." Ezra turned to the others. "Let's get her locked up." They continued toward the hotel.

Jack stood there and watched as the conquering heroes led that little lamb to the hotel to keep for the slaughter. It sickened him. Instead of shaking Ezra Katts hand, he wanted to pull his revolver and put a bullet between his eyes. He rubbed his hand down the side of his britches as if to wipe off the essence of Ezra's touch.

"I hope you know what you're doing," said George Tyler as he approached and watched the mob walk down the street.

"I hope I do too." He started to walk away.

"Where are you going now?"

Jack turned. "The hotel - to join the other lunatics. I need to try and convince them to let Jessica be the child's keeper."

George watched as he ran to catch up to the mob. "Lunatic is right!" He shook his head and went back to his newspaper office.

***

Ezra balked at having a trial. He thought everything had been said and done at the church. He figured they'd just catch 'em, hang 'em and be done with it. But the others told him that if they didn't have some sort of trial, George Tyler could make trouble for them and have outside authorities brought in. That was one thing he didn't want. Their town's affairs were no one else's business. When Ezra suggested that they put a guard on Tyler, Sam Waters told him that it had already been taken care of. Since the escape of Abigail Lucas, they had guards posted at both ends of town. Until after the hanging, no telegrams were being sent and no mail was going out. Incoming stagecoaches and strangers were being diverted saying that their town was quarantined because of the fever. Black Water was basically sealed.

The hotel lobby was filled with people who'd followed their "conquering heroes." They discussed the matter of the trial. Henry Welch may have been the leading town official, but since his daughter was injured, he was out of the picture and more than likely he wouldn't have presided anyway. It was decided that Sam Waters would be the acting judge being that he was the deputy. Practically everyone in the room volunteered for the jury. The town's prosecuting attorney died after being attacked by an alligator while fishing. He was the man Dr. Jackson tried to save before he died. Ezra Katts was elected prosecutor. The other lawyer who practiced in Black Water had been out of town for weeks. Since the only man in town who verbally spoke up for the girl was George Tyler, they volunteered him as defense attorney.

"Who's going to be the hangman?" asked Ezra.

"While you were gone, Ezra, Jack had a suggestion on that," answered Sam. "We can draw lots."

"That's the only fair way, as I see it," Jack added. "All men who enter the courtroom the day of the trial will put their name in a jar at the door. If she's found guilty and sentenced to hang, only one person will suffer the wrath of any ghosts." With that last statement, he had to bite his tongue to keep from laughing. But even though he thought it was ludicrous, no one else did. They accepted his idea.

All the players were in place for that farce of a trial they were going to hold. Jack approached Ezra to volunteer Jessica as matron to the girl, since he seemed to be the ring leader. Ezra hadn't even thought about it. He was just going to throw her in the closet with guards and forget about her until the day of the hanging. But Jack convinced him that, even witches had to piss, shit and take care of any other female thing that a girl of almost twelve might need to have done - done. Ezra reluctantly agreed.

Jack mounted his horse and headed for home. He'd managed to embed himself within the enemy camp and planted his wife right where he needed her. She was the lynch pin. He just hoped he could teach her what she needed to learn before the hanging because if it failed....

***

George Tyler put the last letter in his typesetter and printed a test copy. He looked at his main headline: INNOCENT CHILD TO BE SLAUGHTERED BY CITIZENS OF BLACK WATER. "Who am I kidding!" He wadded up the paper, threw it across the room and then took the letters of his typesetter and dumped them out in the floor. He flopped down in his chair and propped his foot on the desk. "They'll never let me distribute it!" The last newspaper he'd printed with words of the same sort, they'd confiscated and burned. A few of the town's fanatics told him that if he'd printed such slanderous material again, they'd not only burn the papers, they'd burn his newspaper office as well - with him in it. He tried to send a telegram to the U.S. Marshall's office, but was told the line was down. He knew it to be a lie, since the machine had been clicking while he'd talked to the telegrapher. He'd tried leaving town, but was stopped at gunpoint.

The bell above the door jingled, and he looked up. It was one of the fanatical men who'd threatened him before. "I've got a story for you to print, Tyler."

"So you're going to actually let me print one?" he asked sarcastically.

The man grinned. "It's a free country. Freedom of the press and all that - as long as it's the truth."

"As you see it, you mean." He glared at the man. "What's the story?"

The man handed him a list of names. "We've set the day of the trial for tomorrow. The gallows will be finished by then. These are the people presiding."

He looked down the list and saw his name. "Me!" He looked at the man. "I'm her defense attorney."

"You can always turn it down - no one will care. She can defend herself." The man walked to the door and turned. "It's just a formality anyway. The witch-child will hang."

After the man left, George bent down to pick up the typesetting letters from the floor. While he was down there, he prayed. "God, if you're listening, I pray that Jack Trainor's plan works." He stood and looked at the letters he put in the box. "This town has gone to hell!"

***

It was almost dark before Paloma made it to the end of the woods and sat to rest once more. She wasn't surprised to see the demolished rock wall that separated the town from the swamp - she'd envisioned it before. The old Gypsy woman could only take a few steps at a time before stopping to rest. Her legs ached and tingled as if walking on needles and pins. A few times when she rested, she'd closed her eyes and visions had come to her in hazy snatches. She saw Hattie in a black dress with a man she didn't recognize. She saw glimpses of a hangman's noose. But right now, the visions that disturbed her the most were those of Evelyn. Blood was everywhere. She heard echoes of voices in her head that she couldn't understand. But the ever pressing thought in her mind was to go to her. After resting for a few moments, she stood with the help of her walking stick and continued toward the Welch residence.

Welch Residence

"What do you mean they won't let you leave!" Henry shouted at the butler.

"The men at the edge of town told me that no one from your household was allowed to leave town until after the trial. They threatened to shoot me if I tried," Fredricks replied.

"But Evelyn needs a doctor. Emmaline and I don't know what we're doing. Did you tell them that?"

"I told them. I tried everything. I even went to the other end of town. No one there would let me leave either."

Henry turned and slammed his fist against the wall. "Damn all the people in this town! Damn them to hell!"

He'd sent for Elvin, the stable man, but he'd said the only thing he could do was stitch her up, that his hands were too shaky to remove the bullet. He'd said if he tried, he could kill her. The old man had done what he could to stanch some of the bleeding, but it only slowed it down.

Henry was about to go back into Evelyn's room, when he heard raised voices coming from downstairs.

***

Erma had been sitting in the drawing room. The room was dark. No lamps had been lit for her. The servants paid her no mind, but that was understandable since they were helping with her granddaughter. She bent her head and prayed. With the doctor dead, and that old coot, Elvin, not being of any use, she asked God for someone to help.

There was a knock at the door and since the butler and cook were upstairs, Erma resigned herself to answer it. She was shocked to see who it was. She scowled. "I thought you were practically dead! What are you doing here?"

"I've come to help," Paloma replied.

"Help! No one needs your kind of help, Paloma Day. Go on back to your swamp where you belong."

Paloma shook her head and spoke calmly. "Erma Welch, hasn't this unrealistic jealousy of yours gotten just a little out of hand and gone on for too long? I never had any interest in Alvin Welch or any of the young men who tried to court me when I was young. The only time I ever spoke to Alvin was after I married. Benjamin Day was the only man I'd ever had eyes for."

Erma was incensed. "How dare you speak to me like that! Jealousy has nothing to do with it. You're an evil woman, Paloma Day. Go away before I have the authorities..."

"Mother!" Henry shouted, interrupting her next words. He came running down the stairs.

"You didn't hear what she said to me, Henry. I'll not allow this - witch in my home!" Erma bellowed as she pointed at Paloma. "She's caused nothing but problems ever since she came to this town."

"These days, I seriously doubt that!" Henry put his arm around Paloma to help her in. "Can you do anything?"

"That's why I've come. I have some knowledge and some skills. With the Lords help, I'll try my best."

"Evelyn's upstairs. Can you make it?"

Paloma smiled. "I've traveled this far. With your help, I can manage the stairs."

Erma watched her son help her hated enemy. "You're letting the devil's minion see to Evelyn."

Henry turned on the stairs. "No, Mother, an angel. It's the devil's minion who's trying to stop her." He continued on taking most of Paloma's weight on his shoulders.

Emmaline saw Henry leading the old Gypsy woman into the room. She stood and gave her a hug. "She's so weak." She looked back at Evelyn. "She's our only child. We don't want to lose her."

Paloma wanted to say something about that, but now was not the time.

She put a hand to Evelyn's forehead. The child had a fever. She removed the bandage from her shoulder. "I'll have to open up these stitches."

"Elvin brought Dr. Jackson's medical bag and left it here," said Emmaline.

Paloma asked to see the clothing Evelyn was wearing. They had the butler retrieve it from the trash bin, and she examined the hole. "There's a piece of material missing. If it's in the wound, it could cause infection."

Though she was unconscious, Paloma had Henry hold Evelyn steady in case she woke, while Emmaline held a lamp. The old Gypsy's hands were steady as she carefully removed the bullet. She also found the piece of material and cleaned out slivers of tree bark from the wound.

"Do you have any honey?" Paloma asked.

Henry nodded to the butler who was standing by for anything they might need and then asked, "What's that for?"

"It helps in healing."

When the butler returned, she applied the honey and bandaged the wound. When Henry asked about putting stitches back in, she told him that it was best to let the wound heal naturally, and the concern now was tending to the child's fever.

Emmaline told Paloma that she could sleep in the guest room, but the old woman declined and said a rocking chair in Evelyn's room would be satisfactory so she could keep an eye on her during the night.

The rocking chair was ordered as well as a dinner tray for their guest. Emmaline considered Paloma a godsend. Having faith that their daughter was in good hands, she and Henry retired for the evening.

Chapter 38

The School House- Next Morning

Pearl-Lee and Jonas Burnham sat beside their daughter, Carrie-Ann. They watched another body of a dead child being carried out. Jonas shook his head. "Nothing I have in the apothecary seems to be working. I don't know what else to try."

Pearl-Lee put another compress to her step-daughter's forehead. "I'm sorry, Jonas. I've prayed until I don't have any more words I can say."

One of the town's residents entered the building and started passing out papers. Jonas took one, read it and crumpled it slightly. "I wish to God we'd never come back to this town." He passed it to Pearl-Lee.

She read that they were holding the trial of Hattie Lucas that afternoon. She shook her head. "It's a mockery of justice," she whispered. "I wish there was something we could do."

Jonas thought for a moment. "You could testify on her behalf. Everything is based on those damned pictures everyone is talking about. "You showed me the pictures she drew of us before we married. Perhaps they could help."

"If I do, what if there is retaliation against us?"

Jonas brushed the side of his daughter's cheek. "There are enough dead children in this town. If we'd left our daughter here while we were on our honeymoon, she could be dead instead of ill." He looked up at Pearl Lee. "I feel we owe the child something. Go to the trial. I'll stay here."

Coulter Residence

Braden Coulter had returned to Black Water with his daughter anxious to brag about Mary-Beth's first place win in the equestrian event she'd competed in. But his news was squelched by all the tragedy that had taken place in their absence.

His wife, Corinne, didn't attend their daughter's championship. She had argued with Braden that it wasn't a proper thing for a young lady to do. She wasn't impressed by Mary-Beth's win. She scolded that their boastful display of pride was one of the seven deadly sins. She'd wanted to have Mary-Beth get down on her knees and pray that her soul wouldn't go to hell for such prideful thoughts. Braden put his foot down on that. He told his wife that if their daughter prayed for anything, it would be to thank God for the talent he'd bestowed on her in horsemanship.

The breakfast table had been quiet. Braden and Corinne weren't speaking and Mary-Beth was afraid to say anything. There was a knock at the door and her father answered it. A man delivered a paper telling about the trial.

Corinne looked at it. "It's about time they do something about that horrid witch-child."

Braden was stunned. "I can't believe you're in favor of hanging a little girl!"

"She's evil! You weren't in church when Reverend Donner had his revelation."

Mary-Beth also couldn't believe what she'd heard. As far as she was concerned, Hattie was responsible for her having a horse. If she hadn't drawn the picture, her father would never have seen it and made the decision to get one for her. She stood. "No, Mother. Hattie is good! Hattie predicted I'd have a horse. I've got one."

Corinne frowned at her husband. "See, Braden! I told you that horse was a devil's inspiration." She stood. "If you don't get rid of that animal right now - I'll shoot it!"

Braden stood. "You're out of your cotton-pickin' mind, woman! I knew you were a religious fanatic when I married you, but this is insane!"

"NO!" Mary-Beth shouted. She ran out of the house and went to the barn.

Braden threw his napkin down on the table, glared at his wife and ran after his daughter.

"Please, Daddy, don't let Mother shoot Sampson!" she cried as she wrapped her arms around her horse's neck.

Braden stroked her hair and then took her in his arms. "Don't you worry about that." He dried her tears. "You get on Sampson, and ride to Mayor Welch's house. Right now, he's the only one in this town I trust. Stay there until I come for you."

"What about Hattie? Is there anything we can do for her?"

"Probably not a thing, honey. But I'll say something at the trial before we leave."

"Leave? Where are we going?"

"I was talking to some men at the championship. I heard that Lexington, Kentucky is prime horse country."

"What about Mother?"

He smiled at her. "Do you really want her to come?"

Mary-Beth thought for a moment. Her mother rarely showed her any type of affection. Mostly she just pointed out all of her faults, and she spent the majority of her time on her knees praying for things she didn't understand were sins. Once when she heard her parents arguing, she'd heard her mother say that *she* was the product of her father's lust. She returned her father's smile and simply said, "No." Mary-Beth mounted her horse and rode off.

The Hagen's

Abigail paced the porch at her uncle's home. Hattie should have been there by now. She knew her daughter would have had to spend one night in the swamp, but not two. Her uncle sent Jubal to town to see if they'd captured her.

Her Aunt Josie joined her on the porch. "Don't worry, Abigail, it won't do ya' any good."

"I wish Jubal would hurry up and come back. If she's not there, I'm gonna look for her."

No sooner had she spoken the words than Jubal came riding up on his mule. He dismounted. Ennis joined them.

"Well, boy!" Ennis asked.

"Town's sewn up tighter than a man in a bundlin'bag," Jubal replied. "They saw me comin', and before I got a word out, the men at the edge of town started shootin' at me."

"So ya' didn't get ta' see if she's there or not?" Abigail asked.

"Didn't say that," Jubal grinned. "I tied up Berthie at the edge of another part of the swamp and worked my way around. You should see the wall. It's tore up to hell and back. Ya' know that the dam over the river…"

"Jubal!!!" Ennis rolled his eyes. "Git to the point, boy! Do they got her or ain't they?"

"They got her."

Abigail turned to her uncle. "We gotta go get her, Uncle Ennis."

"Ain't no way possible," Jubal replied. "They's all got them repeatin' rifles. All we got is shotguns. They'd cut us down like hogs in a slaughterhouse. She ain't in the jail. I checked there too. Couldn't find out where she was. But I did find this here paper." He took it out of his back pocket. "Don't rightly know what it says."

Abigail wished she'd paid more attention to what Hattie was learning in school. She could read a few words, but not all of them. "They's puttin' her on trial today." She looked up at her uncle. "Maybe we can get her then?"

Ennis scratched his head. "I weren't gonna say nothin', lest we know'd she'd been caught. But there's a couple a men in town already workin' on a plan ta' get her. The man what help us git you out didn't say what it were, but if we go bustin' in, we could spoil the whole shebang and get us all killed ta' boot."

Josie put her arm around Abigail. "Best thing ta' do is pray and wait." She smiled and added. "Maybe that Gypsy blessin' ya' put around us will give ya' luck where Hattie is concerned."

Abigail couldn't help but smile thinking about the bedtime prayer she'd said in Italian that they thought a Gypsy blessing. "Hopefully so, Aunt Josie."

Buehl Residence

Jack put his hands on Jessica's shoulder. "You know what to do? Do you think you need to practice one more time?"

"I've practiced so many times I can do it in my sleep, but I'll do it again if you want me to?" she replied.

"How's the child?" asked Olivia Buehl.

"I brought her breakfast this morning. She's scared, poor thing. I wanted to tell her what was going to happen, but the guards were with me the whole time. I didn't have a chance." She turned to Jack. "How am I going to do it if they don't leave me alone with her?"

Jack thought for a moment. He shook his head. "I don't know. I've got to be at the trial." He turned to Roland. "Maybe you can call the guards away on some pretext."

"I could, but what?" Roland replied.

Olivia's eyes brightened. "I know! Wait right here!" She ran upstairs and about fifteen minutes later, she returned with one of Jessica's childhood dresses. "I couldn't bear to part with this one. It was my first attempt at making you a dress instead of buying a ready-made one or hiring it done." She smiled. "I didn't do a bad job on it."

"Mom, I don't think they would let me put a pretty pink dress on a girl they plan to hang," said Jessica.

Olivia shrugged. "So, we rip off the frills and fluff, tear out the crinoline and die it black. You've got to admit, black is appropriate for a supposed witch. They'd have to leave you alone with her to get her dressed."

Jack nodded his head. "I think it could work!" He put his arm around Olivia and kissed her on the forehead. "I believe I'm just about the only man in the world that loves his mother-in-law."

"Flatterer!" Olivia laughed, gave him a peck on the cheek and turned to her daughter. "Come on, dear, we don't have much time to get it fixed, dyed and dried."

The Hotel

The Trainor's pulled up in front of the hotel. "I hope this works," Jack whispered and then gave Jessica a kiss for good luck.

Jessica got out of the carriage and picked up a box. She put her hand on the door knob, took a deep breath and entered the hotel with a big smile for the guard. "Hello, Barney."

The big man looked at her skeptically. "You were here just a couple of hours ago. What are you doing back here again?"

"Why, to get her ready for the hanging, of course, silly" she replied with a flip of her hand.

"What's ta' gettin' ready," he shrugged. "We just put a rope around her neck and drop the trap."

"When I got home, I was thinking about the way she looks. Have you had a real good look at her?"

"She looks like a kid. How's she sposta' look?"

"Exactly my point. She looks like any other kid with those innocent looking braids and overalls. Why, if she shed a tear looking like she does now, she'd break someone's heart. The next thing you know, they'd be letting the girl go free."

The man laughed. "I seriously doubt that. She's killed too many people with them drawin's of hers." He looked at the box. "So what have you got there?"

Jessica opened it. "Just a plain ol' black dress and a black ribbon for her hair. I figured I'd brush out those braids and tie her hair back. She'd look more fitting for the trial and the hanging."

The man took the dress and examined it. "I don't see what difference it makes." He hesitated a moment. "But we do have a few bleedin' hearts around here who wouldn't know evil if they looked it in the eye."

"You are surely right about that, Barney," Jessica agreed, knowing that he was one of them.

"Well, I guess it's alright." He opened the door and let her in.

Jessica turned and looked at him. "Well, you're not going to stand there and watch! It's indecent. Go on now." She waved him off. "I'll be out in about fifteen minutes. If I need you, I'll give a shout."

"Oh! All right!" He shut the door.

Hattie was sitting on the floor and looked up at the woman who'd brought her breakfast this morning. She'd eaten a few bites, but was just not hungry. "Am I goin' to the trial now?"

"In a little bit," Jessica whispered. "Stand up, sugar. I've got a lot of talking to do and you've got a lot of listening. Now, take off your clothes and be quick."

As Hattie started to disrobe, her eyes widened when the woman started to take off her dress. But, even stranger than that was what she was wearing underneath it. "What is…"

"Don't talk, just listen," Jessica interrupted in a whisper. "I'm a friend of your daddy's. You've got to be brave and do what I tell you. If I don't do this right, you can still be hurt. This is what's going to happen…."

***

The guard outside looked at his watch. Jessica had been in there a long time. He knocked on the door. "You about done in there? It's almost time."

Jessica opened the door. "I was just about to call you." She looked at Hattie. "What do you think?"

The guard looked at the girl and curled the corner of his upper lip. "I guess it does make her look older. Not so much like a kid." He shut the door and locked it back.

"My thoughts exactly. More witch-like dressed in black like that." Jessica walked toward the door. "I'll see you at the trial, Barney. I want to get a front row seat."

"Good luck with that! It'll probably be standing room only."

The Jail

Sam Waters looked at himself in the mirror after putting on Judge Gooch's official black robe. He thought he looked rather smart as he grabbed the lapels. He opened the door separating the office from the jail cells and looked at Jedidiah lying on the cot. "You still alive, Sin-Eater?"

"What do you want?" Jedidiah mumbled.

"Just thought I'd let you know we're gonna be hangin' that thing you brought into the world."

Jedidiah managed to lift his head. "I hope all of you rot in hell!"

"I think you've got that backward. We're purging our town of the wickedness. It'll be you and her that burn in the pit."

Jack Trainor walked into the Sheriff's Office and saw Sam in the back. "It's almost time. They need you at the courthouse."

"My replacement isn't here yet."

"I'll stay for a few minutes. You go ahead."

Sam Waters left and Jack went into the back room. "How are you feeling, Jedidiah?"

"You son-of-a-bitch! I thought you were my friend. I hear you're involved in this...nightmare."

"I am," he whispered. "But not in the way you think. Have faith and trust me. I can't tell you any more than that."

Jedidiah laid back down. In his weakened condition, he couldn't hold himself up any longer. "Do me a favor. I have to see Henry Welch now. It's imperative."

"I don't know if he'll come. His daughter was gravely injured. But I'll try." He heard someone come in. "Believe me, Mr. Sin-Eater, you'll get what you deserve." He turned his head and saw Evan McGuire at the door.

"What are you doing here, Jack?"

"I was walking by. Sam had to take a shit before the trial. I told him I'd watch the prisoner until you got here." He walked from the back and shut the door.

"I guess he's nervous," said McGuire.

"Maybe, but I tell you what, I'd be more nervous if I was selected as the hangman."

"Damn straight about that."

Jack walked out the door. He had about thirty-minutes to spare before he had to be at the courtroom. He got in his carriage and headed toward the Welch residence. He figured he would at least deliver Jedidiah's message.

Welch Residence

Paloma changed the bandage on Evelyn's wound. The child still felt feverish, but she seemed to be resting comfortably. She sat back down in the rocking chair and closed her eyes. For the first time in a long while, her dreams finally had clarity. They were no longer shrouded in a haze, and she knew what she had to do. A short time later, Emmaline entered the room.

"How's she doing?" She went to her daughter's side.

"The bleeding is starting to lessen. She mainly needs rest and quiet." Paloma stood. "May I use your kitchen?"

"Of course. Is there something Martha can fix you?"

"No, this is something I need to prepare myself." She stood and walked toward the door. "Oh, and you're about to have a couple of visitors."

Emmaline looked at her curiously. "How do you know that?"

Paloma smiled. "I just know."

***

Fredrick's opened the door. "May I help you?"

"I need to see Mayor Welch."

"He's unavailable at the moment, Sir. You'll have to call again at a later time."

The butler was about to shut the door, but Jack put his hand on it. "It's important." He pushed past the butler.

"Really, Sir! This is highly irregular!"

***

Henry was in his study. His head ached with all that was on his mind - his daughter - his mother - the whole town - Hattie. He wondered what his father would have done in this situation if he were still alive. He heard raised voices in the foyer and went to see what it was about.

"What's going on?" He saw a man with the butler. "Who are you?"

"Jack Trainor. I don't have much time. I have a message for you."

"What is it? I've got a very sick daughter. Any business you have with me will have to wait until a better time."

"Just one thing. Jedidiah Lucas wants to see you. He says it's imperative."

Henry looked at him from the corner of his eye. "What have you to do with Jedidiah?"

"I'm just a messenger. But the way he said it, it sounded like you owe him. Now, I've got to go."

Henry walked to the door and watched his visitor run to his carriage and snap the reins to spur the horse to a gallop.

Emmaline walked into the foyer after hearing voices. "Who was that, dear?"

"A man named Jack Trainor."

"Jessica Buehl's husband? What did he want?"

"He said Jedidiah wanted to see me."

"Are you going?"

Henry thought about what the man had said. He nodded. "I'll go later. I suppose I do owe him since I'm one of the people responsible for him become the town's Sin-Eater if only to say how sorry I am for what's happening."

Emmaline agreed. She started to walk toward the stairs and thought of something. "Hmm. Paloma said we'd have a visitor."

"We generally do at one time or another," Henry replied. "Don't be reading anything into it. We've got enough problems with talk of witchcraft around this town."

Emmaline laughed quietly as she continued on her way and remembered something else. "Oh, Paloma wants to see you in the kitchen."

"What for?"

"She didn't say."

Henry went into the kitchen. "You wanted to see me?"

Paloma handed him a Mason jar. "Give this to Jedidiah when you see him."

For a moment, he wondered how she knew he'd planned on visiting their Sin-Eater, but he just shook his head and figured she'd overheard the conversation. Henry looked at the contents of the jar. It was full of that dark liquid she'd given him at her cottage. "I can't leave right now. My daughter…"

"...needs you," she finished. "I know. If Jedidiah wants to see you, trust me - you'll want to hear what he has to say. I'll tell Emmaline you'll be back in a while."

Henry thought Jedidiah's request and the old Gypsy woman's insistence very mysterious. He didn't want to leave, but Paloma had done him a good turn in helping them with Evelyn. If she hadn't come, they'd probably have lost their daughter by now. If she wanted him to go now, he couldn't refuse her.

He went out the back door toward the stable and saw Mary-Beth Coulter riding up. She practically jumped off her horse before it stopped. "I'm sorry, Mary-Beth, Evelyn can't have visitors. She's very sick."

"Please, Mr. Welch. My daddy sent me here. He says you're the only one he can trust. My mother wants to kill my horse. She says it's a devil's gift." She patted her horse on the neck. "Sampson is a good horse. Can we stay here until Daddy comes for us?" She smiled. "We're going to Kentucky."

Henry could definitely relate to the girl's mother problems, since he had issues with his own. He gave her a smile. "I'll help you put Sampson in the stable, and if you go on in the house, I think Martha just pulled a cherry pie out of the oven. Tell her I said you can have a piece. But be quiet. Evelyn needs her rest."

"Thank you, Mr. Welch."

Henry watched as the girl ran into the house. He felt sorry for Mary-Beth. In listening to some of the things Emmaline had told him about the fanaticism of the girl's mother, he was surprised Braden hadn't taken his daughter and left her years ago. After the stableman saddled his horse, he mounted and rode off.

***

Emmaline had just come out of Evelyn's room after being informed of Mary-Beth's arrival and was going to see to her comfort. She saw Erma walking down the hall dressed in her best.

"You're not going to that hideous trial, are you?" Emmaline asked.

"I intend on seeing justice done! I'm going in support of your Aunt Sally in your place. I completely understand why you can't go."

Emmaline rolled her eyes. "Justice! I don't even what to discuss it. All I can say is I'm ashamed of both of you. May God have mercy on all of your souls!" She passed Erma and continued down the steps.

Erma closed her eyes and shook her head. "She just refuses to see the truth." She continued on down the stairs and went outside to wait on the porch for her carriage. She saw Paloma come from around the back of the house. "I hope you're going for good."

"It's a good possibility."

"Good riddens! Soon, that witch's apprentice of yours will get what she deserves."

"Of mine?" Paloma cocked her and grinned. "I believe you spoke to Emmaline about seeing the truth. A revelation is forth-coming." With that said, she continued on her way.

Erma frowned. She wondered how the old witch knew what she'd said. No one was around them when she'd said it. She saw the carriage come to the front and got in. She sat back in the seat and watched as they passed her hated enemy. She wondered. "What revelation?"

The Courthouse

The courtroom started to fill. Jack Trainor stood by the door and had each man who entered to write his name on a piece of paper and put it in a jar. Braden Coulter walked in and was given a piece of paper. "Sure, I'll put my name down," he said in a sarcastic tone. "But if it's drawn, we'll be standing on that gallows until hell freezes over. I'll not pull the lever."

"You on her side after what she done, Coulter?" asked one of the men waiting behind him.

Braden turned around. "I'm not up on the Bible, but I think somewhere it says, *'Vengeance is mine saith the Lord.'* I say it's His call - not ours!" He turned to Jack. "I'm a witness for the defense. I don't count."

"Go on in," Jack replied.

The man behind Braden shook his head. "Damn bleedin' heart. If Reverend Donner says the witch-child is evil - she's evil. He's closer to the Lord than that damned idiot banker!" He looked at Jack. "Give me one of them papers! I'll even put my name in twice!"

"Once is enough," Jack replied.

The man put his name in the jar and found a place to stand. Jack thought it a pity. Only one man and one woman appeared for the defense - Braden Coulter, the town banker and Pearl-Lee Burnham, the school teacher.

The seats filled quickly. Soon there was standing room only. Jack saw

Jessica come in. She gave him a nod which meant Hattie understood what was going to happen. He just hoped it wouldn't fail. If it did, the girl would die. He closed his eyes and said a silent prayer.

The Jail

Henry rode down the street. It was empty. The gallows erected before the courthouse stood as monument to the madness that had consumed his town. He shook his head. His town - he was ashamed to call it that. He decided he was leaving it when Evelyn recovered, and he had faith she would. Not by black magic or witchcraft as his mother tried to convince him, but from God's Grace.

Henry went inside the Sheriff's Office and found no one was guarding it. The keys were left hanging on the wall, and he opened the outer door to the cells. Jedidiah looked half-dead. He entered his cell and hesitated a moment before touching him. "What the hell," he mumbled. He jostled him. "Jedidiah - wake up." The man opened his eyes slightly. "You wanted to see me." When Jedidiah closed his eyes again, Henry pulled him upright to lean against the bars and slapped his cheek slightly to bring him around.

Jedidiah opened his eyes and tried to focus. "Henry Welch?"

"Yeah." He pulled the Mason jar from his coat pocket. "Drink this."

Jedidiah drank it down. No one had given him anything to drink since he'd been there. Though the familiar tasting liquid was bitter, it did quench his thirst. "Needs sugar." He looked at Henry. "Tastes like something Paloma would give me."

Henry smiled. "She did. She's at my house now."

Jedidiah shook his head slightly to clear it. "Did I hear you right?"

"She's awake. She walked out of the swamp and came to my house."

Jedidiah closed his eyes a moment. "Thank God for that at least."

"You wanted to see me?" Henry repeated.

"I've got a confession to make," he mumbled. "There's something you've got to know." Jedidiah was about to tell him, when they heard the door to the Sheriff's Office open. A man entered.

"What are you doing in his cell, Mayor? You're not supposed to be here," the guard warned.

"Give me a minute," Henry demanded. He looked back at Jedidiah. "What is it?"

"I rescued something that belonged to you," Jedidiah continued, but he was starting to get woozy.

"Mayor!" insisted the guard.

"Shut up!" Henry said to the man and looked back at Jedidiah. "Tell me. What did you rescue?" Jedidiah started to slide down the bars toward the cot. Henry grabbed him by the collar.

The guard pulled his gun. "Mayor! I'm not telling you again!"

Jedidiah motioned for him to lean closer and whispered, "I kept the secret!"

"Jedidiah!" Henry shook him and called his name again. But it was no use. He was still alive, but unconscious. When the guard cocked his gun and he stood. "I'm going!"

Henry walked out of the office and mounted his horse to head home. He couldn't fathom what the hell Jedidiah meant. He passed the courthouse once more and saw his mother's carriage there. He shook his head. "She still came!" As he rode, he continued to wonder. *What secret? What did I throw away that Jedidiah could have possibly rescued?* Nothing came to mind. He racked his brain over the puzzle. Except for recently, the only time he'd ever seen the Sin-Eater was at funerals. Jedidiah had only been to his house twice that he remembered. His father's funeral and… "Oh, God! It couldn't be!" He wheeled his horse around and galloped toward the cemetery.

The Courtroom

Hattie stood tall with her head up and shoulders back as she was brought into the courtroom. Her hands were bound in front of her. The crowd barked insults and called her names. She did her best not to cry and be brave as Jessica had said, but tears rolled down her face anyway. She sat down beside George Tyler. The man told her he was going to defend her, but she'd only spoke with him for about two or three minutes and that was five minutes ago.

"Are you okay," he whispered.

Hattie just nodded. She dared not say a word. She thought of how Evelyn had been scared in the swamp. It was her turn - she was scared in this room. To her, these people seemed more dangerous and fearsome than any creature that lived in the swamp.

Sam Waters came out of the back room and sat at the bench. He banged the gavel. "Court is now in session!" He looked at the prosecutor. "Alright, Ezra. You're first."

Ezra stood and grabbed the lapels of his coat. "Gentlemen of the jury, I will prove that the defendant…" he pointed to Hattie, "…is guilty of witchcraft that caused the deaths and sickness of everyone in town because of her drawings."

Sam banged his gavel again. "Alright, Tyler. What do you say?"

"Hattie pleads innocent. Her drawings were just that - drawings. She meant to help people with them. Not hurt. They were warnings that no one listened to," George said.

The crowd mumbled and shook their heads. Sam called order again and told Ezra to call his witnesses. He called everyone up to the stand who had a drawing that was given to them by Erma Welch. Each of them blamed Hattie for what happened.

When George tried to counter their arguments, he was accused of being out of order or over ruled by Sam. It didn't take long for him to realize that nothing he said would make any difference. They'd already made up their minds.

When the prosecution rested, it was George's turn. He called Braden Coulter to the stand and he held up a picture. "Hattie drew a picture of my daughter riding a horse. That was something Mary-Beth had been asking me to get her for a long time. I always said no. I love my daughter, but she had no talent at anything. She can't even boil water without melting the pot on the stove!" The crowd laughed, the court was called to order and Braden continued. "But horses - there's where her talent lies. She won a first place at an equestrian event." He held up the picture again. "If I hadn't seen this picture, she wouldn't have the horse or the blue ribbon. How is this evil?"

The crowd was quiet for a moment, until Corinne Coulter stood from among the crowd. "A devil's gift! A bribe! Remember what Reverend Donner said? Darkness often disguises itself as light!"

"I object!" George shouted.

Sam banged his gavel. "You're out of order, Tyler! Call your next witness."

George threw his hands up in the air. He called Pearl-Lee Burnham to the stand.

"I also have pictures. She drew me in a wedding dress. No one expected me to ever be married. Not even me. But I'm married. I've got a wonderful family."

Ezra stood to cross examine. "Carrie-Ann is sick, isn't she?"

"Yes, but she got sick before we came home. We got caught in the rain."

"Isn't it true that the witch-child drew your daughter's name on a headstone?"

"Carrie-Ann drew her own name on a headstone." She pointed to Robbie Harp and Billy Tate who had previously testified. "Those two convinced my daughter that it was good luck to do that. That is what Hattie drew, Carrie-Ann's fake cemetery. Evelyn Welch helped her take it down."

Vera Harp stood. "I object! My boy didn't mean any harm."

Sam banged his gavel and said calmly, "Settle down now, Vera. Let Ezra - I mean the prosecution to do his job."

"Thank you, Your Honor." Ezra laughed. "Boys will be boys. They are always full of jokes." The crowd laughed as well.

"I object, Sam!" George shouted as he stood. "The prosecution is twisting the testimony of my witness as well as taking testimony from someone not sworn in."

Sam banged his gavel. "It's Your Honor, not Sam. Show a little respect for these proceeding. Over-ruled! If you do that one more time, I'll fine you fifty dollars for contempt of court and give you ten days in jail!"

George turned his back and rolled his eyes. *This is idiocy!* he thought. Sam looked at Pearl-Lee, and said in a sensitive tone. "You're excused, Mrs. Burnham. Go back to your daughter." He glared at George. "You got any more witnesses, Tyler?"

There was nothing else he could say. If he put Hattie on the stand, Ezra would just torture the poor child and twist her words as they were doing his. There was nothing anyone would listen to. "Defense rests."

Sam grinned at him. "Smart man." He turned to the jury. "You wanna go in the back room and deliberate?"

The foreman of the jury stood and looked at the other eleven men who were nodding their heads. "We're in agreement, Sam. Hang the witch!"

The crowd was in an uproar of agreement. "Hang the witch now!" they demanded almost in one voice. Sam banged his gavel several times before the crowd settled. "We'll do it in a minute. We've gotta draw the name of the hangman first." He looked around the room for Jack Trainor and saw him in the back. "You got the jar?"

"Right here, Sam." He brought it forward.

A hush came over the room. Everyone wanted Hattie to hang, but they were also afraid to do it themselves.

"Who wants to draw the name?" Sam asked and looked around the room.

The room was still for a moment and then Sally Gooch stood. "I'll do it. For my beloved Victor." Jack brought her the jar. She pulled out a name and read it aloud. "Jack Trainor!"

Jessica immediately started crying loudly. She stood and ran to her husband. "No, Jack! Not you!"

He held her close so the crowd couldn't see her face. She was laughing in his jacket. "There, there, we knew it could happen." His tone was consoling and loud enough for those around to hear. He then whispered in her ear, "If you don't quit laughing, they'll know something is up!" He kissed her on the forehead and motioned for her father to come and escort her from the building as planned.

Jack, stone-faced, stood before Sam. "Now?"

Sam nodded and Jack took the rope that was tied around Hattie's wrists and led her down the aisle between the people who still called her names and taunted her. They went outside with the people following behind. They filled the street before the gallows as Jack led Hattie up the steps. Reverend Donner followed next and prayed for the healing of the town as well as condemning Hattie's soul to the pits of hell.

Jack put the rope around her neck, adjusted it and put a black bag over her head. "Be brave," he whispered as he put his hand on the lever to spring the trap door.

The Cemetery

Henry dismounted at the cemetery and jerked on the gates, but they were locked. Behind him he heard the voices of the people shouting as they came out of the courtroom. He climbed the fence and ran passed mausoleum after mausoleum until he reached the one belonging to his family. He opened the door and entered. There it was - the unmarked vault. He hesitated, wanting to pray, but didn't know what to pray for. After prying off the stone plate, he carefully took out the small box that was supposed to contain the body of Evelyn's twin sister and gingerly set it on the stone table in the center of the room. He removed the lid to the coffin.

The Gallows

As Jack put his hand on the lever, the winds started to pick up. The crowd was silent. Suddenly, a cry deep and eerie came from behind them. It was a continuous, gut-wrenching howl that sent chills down everyone's spines - and it came from the cemetery!

When Jack said, "And may God have mercy on your souls," he pulled the lever and the trap door opened.

The crowd remained quiet as they saw the little girl fall. They heard her scream briefly until her body dangled at the end of the rope - lifeless. But there was still the wailing that echoed from the cemetery. Jack closed his eyes a moment and shook his head. He came to the edge of the railing and scanned the crowd with his eyes. He thought whoever it was crying in the cemetery couldn't have timed it any better. "Isn't anyone going to cheer? The evil is dead! All your troubles are over. You've successfully killed the child." He hesitated. "Why are you all so quiet? Everyone cheers at a hanging!"

One by one, the people turned away - the crying still ringing in their ears. It was as if the dead were raising their objections to what had just happened. Ezra looked up at Jack. "Take her down."

George Tyler stepped forward. He glared at Ezra. "I hope you can sleep at night after what you've done. I'm taking the body to her mother in Shadrack. Have you got any objections?"

Ezra shook his head without saying a word. He started to go back into the courthouse until someone ran up to him and said his son, Orin, had taken a turn for the worse. He ran to the schoolhouse.

George walked to the gallows. Sam was standing by the steps. "You want me to help you?" he asked sheepishly.

George gritted through his teeth, "I don't want you to touch her!" He walked underneath the gallows and called up to Jack to lower her down. There was a wagon ready with a coffin that he laid her. After putting on the lid, George climbed up and drove away.

Jack walked down the steps of the gallows. The wind had really started to pick up. There was a crack of thunder and lightning struck the platform starting a fire. The people screamed and ran toward the nearest building. Jack looked up to heaven and winked. "Nice touch!" He went to the stable to get his horse and it started to rain. He looked back up to the sky and laughed. "I could have done without the rain though!"

Chapter 39

The Cemetery

Henry couldn't cry anymore as he sat on the cold, stone floor of the mausoleum and looked toward town. That beautiful little child who'd lived in the swamp had been his daughter all along. The one he'd kept secret from Emmaline and Evelyn.

Thunder cracked and he saw a bolt of lightning streak across the sky. It would rain soon - he could smell it in the air. "I'm too late." As he closed his eyes to picture Hattie's face, he could see the subtle resemblance to Evelyn and now understood why the two were so close - they were drawn together. He stood, walked out of the mausoleum and vomited. All he wanted to do was go home. He suffered the pain of losing the same child all over again - only this time it was worse. Hattie was dead, and he did nothing to stop it. "I may as well have pulled the lever myself. I killed my own child!"

The Welch Residence

Emmaline looked out the window in Evelyn's room. She shook her head. "Raining again!"

"Mama?"

Emmaline turned her head quickly at hearing that small voice. She ran to her daughter's bed side. "I'm here, sweetie." She gently stroked her cheek.

"Where's Hattie? Did you take her home?" Evelyn said faintly. Her eyes were still closed.

"Shhh, you go back to sleep so you can get better."

Evelyn quieted and Emmaline said a small prayer of thanks. Just those few little words were a good sign that her daughter would recover. But she also felt an overwhelming sadness wash over her. She would have to tell her daughter that Hattie wasn't safe. That was going to be heart-wrenching.

Emmaline went downstairs to share the good news with Paloma and the staff that Evelyn had spoken. As she headed for the kitchen, she saw the front door open.

"Henry!" She ran toward him and wrapped her arms around him. It didn't matter that he was soaking wet. "She spoke! Our daughter spoke!"

At hearing those words, he broke down and cried as he hugged her. He couldn't speak. Emmaline felt that these were not tears of joy. She pulled slightly away from his embrace and looked into his sad eyes.

"She's dead. They…" he then corrected himself. "…we hung a child."

Emmaline closed her eyes and put a hand to her heart. Her happy feeling was just shattered by the news of this tragedy. She ached for her husband's sadness - she ached for Evelyn when she would find out - she ached for Abigail, Jedidiah and Paloma - and then there was something she felt deep inside. She ached for herself and cried.

They held each other for a few minutes, and then Henry said he was going upstairs to change and sit with Evelyn for a while. Emmaline went into the kitchen to inform Paloma, but when she got there, Martha handed her a note and told her she'd left. She opened and read it.

Thank you for your hospitality. Apply honey with every bandage change. Martha has plenty of tea I brewed, just add a little sugar and give it to Evelyn when she wakes - and you and Henry don't worry. Life has a way of surprising you. ~Paloma

Emmaline read the last lines again. "Hmm. I wonder what she meant by that?" A moment later, there was a knock on the back door. Martha opened it, and Braden Coulter walked in.

"Good afternoon, Mr. Coulter," Emmaline said.

"I wish I could say it was." He shook his head. "Ghastly day. Just ghastly."

"Henry just came home and told me. I'm just sick about it. Right now he's upstairs sitting with Evelyn."

"How is she? I heard what happened."

"I think with time her body will mend, but her spirit, when she hears about…"

"…I know," Braden interrupted. "I've got to tell Mary-Beth. Where is she?"

It was Martha who answered. "In the stable with her horse, Sir. That's where she was just before it started to rain."

He chuckled slightly. "That figures. She'd sleep in the stable if I'd let her."

Braden asked Emmaline if she and Henry would mind if he and his daughter spent the night. He told her that they'd be leaving first thing in the morning for a new town - rain or shine. He said he'd talk to them later about his plans in detail. When Emmaline said he was more than welcome to stay, he excused himself and went to the stable to join his daughter.

The Schoolhouse

Pearl-Lee had gone back to the schoolhouse after the trial. She couldn't bear to watch the hanging. Jonas put his arms around her as she cried. "It was horrible! There was no justice. It was just pure insanity. "

"When Carrie-Ann is better…" He closed his eyes to say a silent prayer and looked back toward his wife. "…we're leaving this damn town. I still have my uncle's house in California. I'm thinking about moving there. I want to get as far away from here as possible!"

Pearl-Lee dried her eyes and put her hand to the child's forehead. "She's still burning up."

They heard a woman cry from another part of the room. Her child had just died. Jonas shook his head as they watched the parents leave and their child's body being removed from the room. "I don't know what else to do."

Shortly afterward, they heard the door to the schoolhouse open and a low murmuring of whispers circulate the room.

Pearl-Lee drew a breath in surprise. "It's Paloma Day!"

Paloma scanned the room and spotted who she was looking for. She approached the Burnham's. "I have something that might make her feel better." She handed Pearl-Lee a Mason jar. "Just add a little sugar if you wish."

Pearl-Lee gave it to Jonas, and he looked at the dark liquid. "What is it?"

Paloma smiled. "A little tea, plus a pinch of this, a dash that and a touch of something special."

"I'm surprised you'd want to help any of us after…" Jonas couldn't bring himself to say it.

"Life has its twists, turns, and surprises. I had a dream. Sometimes things are darker than they appear."

"You speak in a riddle," Pearl-Lee said.

"Life is a riddle," she shrugged.

Jonas looked toward the others in the room. "What about them? This is only one small jar? If this helps…"

"That's why I came to you. You're the apothecary. They'd accept what you gave them. They wouldn't accept it from me."

Jonas smiled. "How did you know I would?"

Paloma grinned. "I had a dream." She handed him a pouch stuffed with herbs. "This is my mixture. Get the largest pot you can find and brew it as you would tea. There should be enough for all in this room."

Paloma turned to leave and Pearl-Lee stood, extending her hand. "I want to thank you. Can we take you anywhere? It looks like rain."

"Thank you, no. I won't be going far."

"Will you stay here in Black Water now?"

"I think I've been here long enough. There are other places to go." She walked to the door, turned and gave them a wink. "Perhaps California. Someplace close to the ocean." She left the building.

Jonas's eyes widened. He whispered to Pearl-Lee, "My uncle's house is near to the ocean!" He shook his head and considered it just a coincidence. He looked at the dark liquid again and poured some in a cup.

Ezra had seen Paloma talking to the Burnham's and walked up to them. "You're not gonna give that stuff to your daughter, are you? It's probably poisoned."

Jonas handed the cup to Pearl-Lee and stood. He balled his fist and struck Ezra across the jaw, knocking him to the floor. "The only thing poisoned around here is your mind!" He looked around the room. All eyes were upon him. "And that goes for the rest of you!" He held up the pouch. "I don't know if what Paloma has given me will work or not. But I'm going to give it to my daughter. Nothing I have in my shop is working. At this point, I'll try anything! If any of you are of the same mind as I am, we'll brew this!"

Maurice Shaw, the owner of the hotel, looked down at his sick family - his grandchild, his son and his son's wife. He remembered how Paloma's fortune telling at the hotel brought him a tidy profit. He stood. "I, for one, trust Paloma Day! We can use the stove at the restaurant. If anyone here wants some of it, bring a Mason jar and everyone will get a share."

Jonas handed Maurice the pouch, and he ran from the building. One by one, a parent left his or her child to go to the general store for a jar. Ezra got up off the floor and started to walk back to his son, but changed his mind and followed after the others.

The Welch Residence

Erma had gone home with Sally when it started to rain. She had taken an open carriage to the trial, and if she'd gone home, she would have been soaked to the skin, not to mention that the new hat she'd just bought would have been ruined. She was also glad she'd gone home with her friend. Sally was in a state of fear after the scene at the hanging with that eerie cry and lightning striking the gallows as it did. She had told Erma that she had an unexplainable sense that they had done the wrong thing. Erma told her that the noise was probably being made by one of those who opposed what had happened to scare them and the lightning strike was just an untimely coincidence.

The rain stopped just before dark. It was after eight o'clock when Erma arrived home. Everything was quiet. She figured the help had retired to their quarters, and Henry and Emmaline were upstairs with Evelyn. She didn't want to go to bed quite yet, so she fixed some tea and went to the drawing room to unwind. When she opened the door, she saw the silhouette of her son sitting in the window seat.

"What are you doing sitting in the dark, Henry?"

"Waiting for you," he said evenly.

"Well, it's nice to think that you actually worried about me for a change." Her tone was sarcastic.

Henry didn't respond. He just continued to look out the window.

Erma walked to her table to light a lamp. "How's Evelyn?"

"Sleeping peacefully - thanks to Paloma Day."

"The less said about that woman the better! But I'm relieved about my granddaughter." She settled in her chair and sighed. "What a day! You should have been there. George Tyler didn't have a case. Ezra Katts prosecuted quite well, considering his inexperience."

Henry looked at his mother with a blank expression. "Did he now. So everything went exactly how you wanted it to go!"

"Yes it did, and don't be flip with me, Henry," she scolded and then added, "Except for the hanging." She shivered. "There was this eerie sound coming from the cemetery and just after the hanging, lightening struck the gallows and it caught on fire. It practically scared the life out of me at first."

Henry had wondered who had set it on fire. Now he knew.

Erma continued. "I talked to several people afterward. They're beginning to wonder if we'd done the right thing." She took a sip of tea.

"Maybe that was God's way of telling all of you..." He corrected himself, "...all of us something."

"Don't be ridiculous! Lightning strikes happen all the time. A nail probably attracted it."

"And I'm sure you'll set everyone straight!"

This time Erma ignored his sarcastic tone. "Things will get better soon, you'll see." She smiled. "Evelyn will no longer be under the influence of the horrible witch child. She'll go back to associating with proper friends. Not a swamp urchin."

Henry stood, folded his arms and faced his mother. "You're so proud of yourself, aren't you?"

"Mind that tone, Henry. I'm still your mother."

"I tell you what, Mother..." He went to the drawing room doors and closed them. "...I'll let you have the honor of telling Evelyn how you enjoyed her...twin sister's hanging!"

She frowned. "That wasn't the least bit funny."

Henry closed his eyes as he leaned against the doors. The memory of that empty little coffin pained him. A lump developed in his throat and when he regained his voice to speak, he stood before his mother. "You wanna know who it was crying in the cemetery? It was me!"

She looked at him from the corner of her eye. "Why would you do that?"

He turned his back and walked toward the mantle by the fireplace. "I visited her grave after talking to Jedidiah. I opened the coffin."

Erma stood, dropping her tea cup. "You defiled her grave!"

He faced her. "There was nothing to defile! The coffin was empty."

"What!" Erma put a hand to her chest.

"Jedidiah told me, before he went unconscious, that he rescued something that belonged to me. He said he kept the secret. The secret he kept was my daughter - Hattie was my child!"

"It's a lie!" Erma shook her head. "He must have done something with the remains to trick you. I know he's lying. I know!"

"Jedidiah is half-dead, Mother! He's racked with fever. He wouldn't lie about something like that."

"He's going to hell anyway, so what difference does a lie make!"

"You know what, Mother! After today, I've lost complete faith in what we've been taught about the Sin-Eater. Have you ever really - and I mean really listened to the way he prays? How can a man say such beautiful prayers with such feeling and go to hell!"

"Then why didn't he give her back?" Erma chided.

"He didn't have a chance to say, but I can guess. We all thought the child dead, including Dr. Jackson. The people who knew about her were sworn to secrecy." He folded his arms. "What would those people think if they thought a dead child was brought back to life, especially if Paloma Day was involved? Look what you…" he corrected himself again, "…what we did to Hattie for just drawing some damn pictures." Henry paced for a moment before facing her again. "And then there's Emmaline. We lied to her, Mother, and I'm sick about it! I've been sick about it for years." He walked to the drawing room doors. Before he exited, he added, "So congratulations, Mother, you were the lynch pin in killing your own grandchild. I hope you're proud of yourself."

Erma's knees went weak and she sank into her chair. She sat quietly for a moment. "It's a lie. It's got to be a lie." A solitary tear trickled down her cheek, before she buried her face in her hands and wept.

Chapter 40

Earlier – After the hanging

Though it poured rain, it didn't take long for Jack to catch up to George in the wagon. The newspaperman stopped, and Jack tied his horse to the back and climbed up next to him.

"No one's following. I think it's safe to let her out," Jack said.

George laughed. "She doesn't want out."

"The hell you say? Why not?"

"To use her words, and I quote, 'My mama and daddy didn't raise no fool. It's rainin' out there, and I ain't gettin' wet and you are!' unquote."

"She's got a point," Jack chuckled. "If there was room - I'd join her!" The two continued on their way to Shadrack.

***

Two men stood under a tree by the rickety Shadrack sign to at least partly shelter themselves from the rain. "Paw! How much longer we a gonna sit out here in the rain waitin'?" Jubal asked. "I could be home a snugglin' with my wife."

"Quit yer belly-achin', boy, and git yer head outa yer britches," said Ennis. "All I knows is sometime ta'day. That's what that newspaper fella said. He don't know where we live so I told him we'd meet him at the sign."

"Well, what if the plan didn't work?" Jubal shielded his eyes from the rain and looked off into the distance.

Ennis shrugged. "Eye fer an eye, boy. We'll shoot'em dead!"

"Well, look yonder," he pointed. "I sees a wagon comin', but I only sees two men. I don't see Hattie."

Ennis and Jubal mounted their mules and rode out to meet Jack and George. When they saw the coffin in the back of the wagon and no Hattie, they raised their shotguns.

"Where's the girl?" Ennis asked. "I thought ya' said ya' had a plan?

"She in the coffin, Mr. Hagen," George replied. "She…"

"The two of you got five seconds ta' say, yer prayers, before we blow yer heads off!"

"Hold on, there!" Jack exclaimed. "She's not dead. She's just in there."

"The hell you say?" Ennis dismounted and lifted the lid.

Hattie smile. "Howdy, Uncle Ennis."

"Girl! What the hell ya' in there fer when ya' ain't dead?"

"Keepin' dry."

"Git on outa there! Yer mama'd have an apoplexy if she sees ya' come home in a pine box." Ennis mounted his mule and extended his hand to help her get on behind him. "Yer just like yer mama was when she was a youn'in. Ain't got the sense God gave a goose!" He turned to the men in the wagon. "Ya'll come on with us. I'd kinda like ta' hear what that plan was."

***

Abigail looked out the window. She'd been praying that Hattie would be alright. Suddenly, Caleb came busting through the door. "Cousin Abby! She's comin! She ain't hanged!"

Abigail followed Caleb out into the rain and met her uncle on the path to the house. When Hattie spotted her mother, she jumped from the back of her uncle's mule and ran to her waiting arms. Abigail smothered her with kisses and held her tightly as they both cried.

"Glad ya' didn't get hanged, Hattie," said Caleb.

Hattie wiped away her happy tears. "I did get hanged."

Caleb was confused. "Then how come ya' ain't dead?"

"We'll talk about that in the house," Abigail replied. "Before we all catch our death."

They went into the house and sat by the fire. "Now," said Ennis. "How did ya' keep Hattie from gettin' her neck stretched?"

"I told ya' already, I did get hanged," Hattie giggled. "Had a rope around my neck and Mr. Jack did the hangin'."

"Tain't possible," Jubal replied. "I ain't ever hear'd nobody livin' after they'd been hung."

"It is - if the hangman knows how to fool a crowd," Jack replied.

"Mr. Jack's wife put this contraption around me," Hattie answered. "Under this dress, I'm harness up like a team of mules. I got harnesses between my legs, wrapped around my chest and more harnesses around my back and shoulders."

"I hooked the contraption, as she called it, to the noose," replied Jack. "The rope that went around her neck was a fake. It just looked like the real thing. The actual noose tightened up around the harness when the trap dropped."

"Ya' ain't hurt none?" Abigail asked her daughter.

"Jarred my teeth a bit when I dropped, and I might have a couple of bruises here 'n there. But other than that, I ain't hurt none." She started to fidget. "But I'll be glad ta' get this contraption off."

Abigail stood. "Come on, sugar. We'll do that right now." She took Hattie into another room and the others continued the conversation.

"So how did ya' finagle yer way ta' becomin' the hangman?" Ennis asked.

"We drew lots at my suggestion. They all wanted the deed done, but no one wanted to do it. When no one was looking, I switched jars with one that had my name on all the papers."

When Abigail returned, she asked the men about Jedidiah. They told her that when they got back to town, they would see what they could do. Jack told them about lightning striking the gallows and the cries from the cemetery. He said that the people might just let him go after that.

It was almost dark when the rain stopped. Before they left, Jack warned them not to let Hattie be seen by anyone in Black Water, or everything they did might become undone. Ennis said they wouldn't have to worry about it much. None of the town folk came to Shadrack, and besides, they would be leaving for Kentucky in a couple of days when everyone was ready.

The Sheriff's Office

Just before sunrise, Sam Waters walked down the street to the office. He tossed and turned all night. The trial and the hanging kept replaying over and over in his dream, and when he saw the gallows struck by lightning, he woke with a cold sweat dotting his forehead.

When he unlocked the door to the office and lit the lamp by his desk, he turned around and saw Paloma Day sitting in a chair. "How did you get in here?"

"The door was unlocked and I walked in," she replied.

"But I just..." He didn't complete the sentence and just shook his head. Where Paloma Day was concerned, anything was possible. He frowned. "What happened yesterday - happened. That's it - it's over and done. So what do you want?"

"I'm just waiting."

"For who?"

"Someone," she grinned.

The door opened and Sam turned around. His eyes widened when he saw Jack Trainor standing there with a colt revolver pointed at him. "What's the meaning of this, Jack?"

"I'm relieving you of your prisoner."

Paloma smiled. "I guess he's the one I'm waiting for."

Jack didn't have a clue who she was or what she meant. He looked back at Sam. "Unlock his cell - now." When Sam hesitated in doing what he'd asked Jack added, "I didn't have any qualms about hanging that little girl, so I definitely don't have any problems putting a bullet through you."

Sam got his keys and headed for the back room. "As far as I know, he might be dead by now."

"He's not," Paloma replied.

Jack followed the deputy into the back. When he unlocked Jedidiah's cell, Jack hit Sam on the back of the head with the butt of his gun and knocked him out. He shook Jedidiah to try and wake him. He opened his eyes slightly, but closed them again. "I guess it's the hard way!" Jack picked him up and threw him over his shoulder. "Damn! He's heavier than he looks!"

When he left the back room, the strange old woman was gone, but when he went outside, he saw her sitting in the wagon he'd had around the side of the building. After putting Jedidiah in the back, he climbed up in the wagon and smiled at the old woman. "I take it you know him?"

"I'm Paloma."

Jack nodded. "I should have guessed. I thought you were gravely ill?"

"No, just asleep." She recalled the dream life she'd had with her beloved Benjamin. "A very wonderful sleep. Shall we go?"

Jack snapped the reins and headed for Shadrack.

***

Abigail and Hattie were both shocked and excited to see Paloma with Jack. They were also relieved that Jedidiah was still alive. Jack took him into the house and went back to his wagon.

"Sayin' thank you' just don't seem enough fer what ya done," Abigail said to Jack. She put her arm around Hattie. "Ya' gave me back my daughter and my husband."

"On the contrary," he said humbly. "I told Jedidiah that I was in his debt. Though I don't believe in the concept of sin-eating, I do believe in the power of prayers. I believe that it was Jedidiah's heart-felt words that not only helped my little boy get well, but they also gave my wife and her parents hope. That was worth a lot to me."

"When Jedidiah is better, maybe you and yer Misses could stop by and visit before we leave in a couple a days. I'm sure he'll wanna see ya'."

"I would, but after what I did to Black Water's deputy this morning, my wife and I think it best to make ourselves scarce. We're heading back to Texas as soon as I get home. Jessica's parents plan on making arrangement to sell their house and in a couple of weeks they're joining us." Jack looked at Hattie and chuckled slightly. "You try and stay out trouble, young lady." She told him she would, and he snapped his reins and drove off.

Abigail and Hattie joined Paloma in the house. She was tending to Jedidiah.

"He should be up and around in two or three days," Paloma said before they asked. "All he needs is a little love and care." She then turned to Hattie and smiled. "I also have some news for you."

"About Evelyn?" Hattie guessed. "Can you tell if she will be alright?"

"I saw to it personally. She's a very sick girl, but I believe she'll be fine."

Hattie sighed in relief. "I wish I could tell her that I'm okay."

Abigail gave her a hug. "Not right now, sugar. Maybe when we get ta' where we're goin' you can send her a letter. We don't want any of them crazy town's people comin' after ya' agin."

***

For three days, Jedidiah was in and out of consciousness. When his fever finally broke, he woke to see Abigail by his side. "I'm sorry, Abigail. Our daughter..." He closed his eyes. "...I couldn't..."

"Shhh." She put a finger to his lips. "Hattie is fine. She's alive n' sassy as ever! Your friend, Jack, saved her. He wrote down where he lives. Said if'n we're ever down by way of Texas, ta' drop on by."

He sighed in relief. "Thank God!"

"I have - over and over. When yer better, I'll tell ya' bout it. If'n Hattie don't tell ya' first." Abigail laughed. "She's become right popular mungst ever'body since the hangin'. She tells the story over and over. Got a lot more friends too."

As Jedidiah became more coherent, he felt the sensation of movement and noticed he was in a covered wagon. "Where are we?"

"On our way to Kentucky with my kinfolk. The whole community left yesterday."

He pushed himself up to a sitting position and shook his head. He still felt a little dizzy. "Where is Hattie?"

"Walkin' long side with Paloma. About took my breath away when I saw Mr. Jack bring you and her in the wagon."

Jedidiah told her that he thought he remembered being told Paloma was finally well, but everything was hazy. Abigail turned to call Hattie to the wagon, but he put a hand on her shoulder. "Wait a minute. Before you do, I need to tell you something." He hesitated a moment. "I think I told Henry Welch the truth about Hattie. I'm not sure. I thought I was going to die, and I know I said something, but I don't remember exactly what." He closed his eyes. "It's all a fog. Part of me wanted to tell him the truth so maybe he might do something. Another part wanted to punish him for not doing anything to prevent it."

Abigail nodded her understand. "It don't matter none. Ever'one in Black Water thinks she's dead, 'cept fer a few what helped."

Jedidiah took Abigail's hands in his and looked lovingly into her eyes. "I think we should tell Hattie the truth. She should know about Evelyn."

Abigail was silent for a moment. "Can I think on it a spell?"

"Take all the time you need. This is something we have to decide together."

Suddenly Hattie popped into the wagon. When she saw her father sitting up, she wrapped her arms around his neck and hugged him for a long while. Her eyes sparkled as she looked in his. "I'm makin' somethin' for ya', Daddy." She opened a chest and pulled out a piece of wood. "I ain't done with it yet, but what'da ya' think?"

Jedidiah nodded his head and smiled. "I think it looks like a wooden leg."

Hattie laughed. "An almost finished wooden leg!"

Jedidiah listened as Hattie told him all about her trial and the hanging. The way she told it, and how she embellished each person's part in the ordeal with hand gestures, facial expressions and the highs and lows in the tone of her voice, it was almost as if it were a story one might tell at a campfire.

When Hattie finished, she remembered what she had come in to tell them. The news had been passed back from wagon to wagon that they were going to stop at the next town which was about three miles ahead.

When they arrived, Abigail and Paloma took Hattie with them to the town's general store to pick up things they needed. Before they'd left Black Water, Paloma had Abigail go back to their cabin to retrieve a hidden money pouch that contained fifty dollars in coins. Paloma told her it was some of the money she'd saved from her fortune telling days at the hotel years ago.

As they walked along the street, Hattie stopped momentarily and looked at one of the buildings. Above it read - Post Office.

"Come on, sugar!" Abigail called when she'd noticed her lagging behind.

"Comin' Mama!"

Chapter 41

The Schoolhouse

A week had passed since Paloma had left her mixture of herbs for the people at the Black Water schoolhouse to give to their sick. Gradually, fevers started going down. Pearl-Lee and Jonas were overjoyed when Carrie-Ann finally woke and said she was hungry. They decided the best place for her was home. He picked his daughter up and carried her outside. The sky was still overcast, and it rained on and off for days. It was as if a permanent, dark cloud had settled over Black Water.

They passed Ezra Katts who was sitting on the schoolhouse steps. Jonas and Pearl-Lee looked at each other and shook their heads. His son, Orin, had died. They thought it poetic justice. Ezra was instrumental in killing the child, Hattie, now both of his sons were dead. Jonas told his wife, that if the man had been caring for his son instead of out in the swamp on that witch hunt, the boy would probably be walking out the door now. The attention Ezra gave to the boy was too little - too late. Not even Paloma's miracle mixture, as the people called it, fazed him.

The Burnham's got in their carriage and made sure Carrie-Ann was wrapped up in a blanket to keep warm. They saw the mayor on their way home, and Jonas reined in his horses to inquire about Evelyn's health. Henry told them that she was now up and about on a limited basis, but even though her physical health was coming along, her emotional state was a different story. The news of Hattie's death seriously affected her.

"Maybe you should consider moving," Jonas said. "Being here would just remind her of what happened. We'll be moving just as soon as she's well enough to travel." Jonas smiled at his daughter.

"We're going to California to live by the ocean," Carrie-Ann said. "When Evelyn feels better, maybe you can move there and live by us."

Henry chuckled slightly. "It is definitely something to think about."

When Henry asked Jonas about his house and business, he said as far as he was concerned they could sit there and rot. With that said, Henry looked around to make sure no one was in earshot of what he was going to say.   "I've been thinking about moving since – that day. Now it's more than just a possibility. Braden Coulter hasn't just gone out of town on business as everyone thinks. He's left permanently. With him gone, there's no bank." He held up an envelope. "I just received a letter from him. He'll be back in a week to settle up all accounts. But keep it confidential. I don't want another panic to start."

"I won't say anything. I don't do much banking here anyway."

Jonas told Henry that they would stop by to say their farewells before they left town. They bid one another good-day, and Henry continued on his way to the stable. Elvin was sitting on the bench outside, chawing on a plug of tobacco and whittling on a piece of wood. "You want to hook up my rig for me, Elvin?"

The old man spit. "Can't say as I want to…" His toothless grin stretched across his face. "But that don't mean I won't." He got up and went into the stable. "Did ya' talk ta' Deputy Sam yet?"

"Not today. How's his head?"

"Dumb as ever! He's still rantin' 'bout gitten a posse together and goin' after that Jack Trainor fella what hit him over the head and let Jedidiah go free."

"I told him it wasn't going to happen the other day. With no witness, it would just be Sam's word against Trainor's anyway. Besides, I was going to have the Sin-Eater released anyway."

Elvin spit and shook his head. "Bad feelin's goin' 'round these days. I hear tell ever'body's havin' bad dreams."

Henry smiled. "How do you sleep?"

"Me?" he pointed to himself. "Like a babe. I stayed outta that damned mess. If'n I'd been a younger man…" he shook his head and walked away.

When the old stableman finished hooking up his rig, Henry headed for home. But first he stopped by the general store to pick up a licorice whip for Evelyn, hoping it would cheer her up. Evan McGuire was leaning on the counter looking through a catalog. "What are you so engrossed in, McGuire?"

"Looking at wedding dresses," he grumbled. "My daughter is bound and determined to marry Jimmy Johnson. I may as well get used to the idea and give them my blessing. If not, she said she was going to follow him to New Orleans whether I consented or not."

"I don't know why you object to him, McGuire. He's a good, hard working boy who's looking to better himself."

"The boy may be looking, but I'd rather my daughter marry someone who's already found better! You'll know what I'm talking about when your daughter is of that age."

Henry didn't bother to respond. The only thing Evan McGuire concerned himself about was a man's net worth, not his worth as a man. He bought the candy and left.

***

Evelyn sat outside on her swing rocking back and forth and staring off in the direction of the swamp. Her shoulder still hurt and her arm was in a sling. She looked around the yard where she and Hattie used to sit and make clover necklaces for their mothers and then at the tree where Hattie first taught her to climb.

"There you are, sweetie." Evelyn turned her head at hearing her father's voice.

Henry bent down beside her. "You're not overdoing it, are you?"

"I'm just sitting here." She looked up in the sky. "It might rain again."

Henry looked up as well. "I think you're right." He smiled at her. "I saw Carrie-Ann today. She's much better."

Evelyn sighed in relief. "I was worried about her." She thought about the picture Hattie had drawn with the gravestone hanging over Carrie-Ann's bed. She knew if Hattie was still alive, she would be relieved too.

"I've got a couple of things for you." Henry handed her the licorice.

"Thank you, Papa."

"And this." He put a hand in his pocket and pulled out a letter.

"For me? Who'd be writing to me?"

"There's no return address, so I don't know. The postmark says Jackson, Mississippi. Do you know anyone there?"

Evelyn shook her head. She felt a drop of rain and followed her father inside.

Erma was in the kitchen. She smiled at her granddaughter. "Martha baked some fresh cookies. Would you like some?"

Evelyn walked passed her as if she wasn't there. She turned to father. "I'm going to my room to read my mystery letter."

Erma shook her head. "I don't know how to get through to her. I've tried to apologize several times. She won't look at me or speak to me."

"I warned you a long time ago, Mother. You wouldn't listen." He walked out of the room. Even though Henry told his mother that she would have to break the news about Hattie's death to Evelyn, he didn't. It was his responsibility. Though he didn't place blame or indicate her grandmother in anyway, Evelyn still did.

***

Evelyn went to her room and sat on the window seat. It was pouring rain - again! She sighed and then turned her attention to the letter. "I wonder who it's from." She opened the envelope. Her mystery letter was still a mystery. There was nothing on the paper but a few straight lines. Depending on which way the paper was turned, it could either have been an "I" or an "H" or just two lines with another between the two. She laughed slightly. "What a curious thing to send." She shrugged her shoulders and threw the paper away.

As the days passed, the rain continued. It would ease up a bit and then start again. Another week went by and Evelyn received another letter. This one was postmarked from Tuscaloosa, Alabama. She opened it and found a paper with three lines again, only this time they formed a different shape. It was either an "A" or a "V" with a line through it. This time she kept the paper. Someone she knew was playing a game with her. It was a curious puzzle, and she was anxious to receive the next piece.

Evelyn wasn't disappointed. In the weeks to come, she received two more letters containing the strange lines that could have been either "H's" or "I's." The third and fourth letters were postmarked from Tullahoma and Springfield in Tennessee.

Henry and Emmaline were relieved to finally see their daughter excited about something. Every day she wanted to go to the post office to see if she received another letter. They too were curious as to who was sending these mysterious letters with no return addresses. They'd asked her what was in them, but she would just smile and say, "Letters."

***

Well over a month had passed, and it continued to rain in Black Water. When it wasn't raining, the sky remained overcast. Henry left his office for the day. He'd said farewell to another resident. Between all the rain and the river flooding the area, farmers were leaving. Several businesses had also closed due to lack of customers. With the bank gone and business sorely lacking, Maurice Shaw closed the hotel and moved to New Orleans to be near his son and his family. They had moved to get away from the gloomy weather. Maurice had said they didn't want to take the chance that their child would get sick again. George Tyler packed up his typesetting equipment and said he was heading for Texas. He said he'd received a letter from Jack Trainor stating that their town could use a good newspaperman. Reverend Donner hadn't been seen since the hanging. As far as Henry knew, he said nothing to no one. When he didn't show up for Sunday service, someone checked his residence and though all his furniture was still there, all his personal belongings were gone. Elvin had said that he'd come into the stable and asked for his buggy to be harnessed and he hadn't seen him since.

Henry walked to the post office. "Good afternoon, Mrs. Potts."

"Hello, Mayor," said the elderly woman.

"Where's Mr. Potts today?"

She shook her head. "Suffering terribly from the gout today, Lord love'em."

"Well, give him my best." He changed the subject. "Any posts for me today?"

She looked in his slot and pulled out several letters. "None for you, Mayor, but Evelyn is very popular today. She has several." She looked at the postmarks. "There's one from California, and three from Kentucky."

"Thank you, Mrs. Potts." He turned to leave.

"Oh, Mayor."

Henry turned. He saw an uncomfortable look on the woman's face. "Yes, ma'am?"

"I just wanted to tell you that…" she hesitated a moment. "You'll have to get someone else to take care of the mail. Mr. Potts and I plan on moving in a couple of weeks."

Henry smiled. "I wondered when that was coming. Pretty soon, the only inhabitants in Black Water will be the ghosts."

"Well, they can have it." She shivered. "This used to be a pleasant town. Now those who haven't left already are moody and irritable. Some say they're being haunted by ghosts of the dead."

"There's a lot of that going around," Henry replied and then added, "You're not being haunted are you?"

"Gracious no!" she laughed. "The only thing that keeps me awake at night is Mr. Potts' snoring." She told Henry that she and her husband were getting along in years and wanted to move to Alexandria where they both had family.

After bidding Mrs. Potts a good journey, Henry went home and found Emmaline in the drawing room with her Aunt Sally and his mother. Evelyn was sitting in the window seat ignoring them. "Is this the meeting of the minds?" he asked.

Emmaline stood and greeted him with a kiss. Evelyn ran to him and promptly asked if she'd received any mail. He handed her the letters, and she went back to the window seat.

"We were discussing the town's situation. We need to find a way to revitalize it," said Erma. "Your father would roll over in his grave if he saw what was happening."

"I'm afraid it would be a lost cause," Henry replied. "Black Water is like a sinking ship. The bank is gone, the hotel, farmers are being flooded out, now, in a couple of weeks, the postmaster."

"As much as I hate to admit it," said Sally. "I think I have to agree with Henry. I received another letter from my daughter the other day. Barbara wants me to come live with them. I've been seriously thinking about it."

"Oh no," Erma sighed. "Not you too?"

"With Victor gone, my house seems so empty. Being near Barbara would fill the emptiness."

"Mother, the only reason we haven't left yet is because I'm the captain of the sinking ship. It's only a matter of time before we leave as well."

"Henry and I have been discussing where we might go," said Emmaline.

Erma frowned at her son. "Well, were you going to include me in on your decisions?"

"There's no need to get testy, Mother. We are just talking about places."

As her family talked, Evelyn opened her letters. The one from California was from Carrie-Ann. She'd written about how much she loved her new house and their town by the ocean and hoped she'd write soon. Evelyn was glad that she was happy. The next letter was from Mary-Beth Coulter. She wrote that her father had bought into a horse farm near Lexington, and she'd never been so happy in her life. She said her mother had written her father a letter asking him for a divorce. When Evelyn read why, she started laughing hysterically.

"What's so amusing, Evelyn?" her mother asked.

"I got a letter from Mary-Beth. Her mother wants a divorce and you'll never guess why?" She continued to laugh.

"Well, are you going to tell us or leave us in suspense," Henry replied, getting caught up in her laughter.

"Mary-Beth's mother wants a divorce so she can marry…" she hesitated a moment to build the anticipation.

"Don't leave us wondering, dear, who?" asked her Aunt Sally.

"Reverend Donner!" Evelyn got the shocked response she was looking for. She saw eyes widen and chins drop. "According to Mary-Beth, her mother had wanted a divorce for a long time but was afraid she'd be stuck having to raise Mary-Beth. She said when they left for Lexington, her mother left town with Reverend Donner. She says they're with a traveling revival show somewhere in Alabama the last they heard."

The adults continued to discuss what they had just heard, while Evelyn opened the second letter from Kentucky. It was from her mystery writer. Only this time there wasn't an "H" or an "I" it was an "E." She opened the last letter and read:

Dear Evelyn,

You don't know how much I wanted to officially send you a real letter, but my mama said I couldn't until we got to where we were going. Most of my kinfolk have gone on to a place called Pine Knot. My daddy decided he wanted to stay in the place where we'd made camp. That's why you are getting this letter so soon after I sent the last. The town is called Bowling Green, here in Kentucky. All of us like it here.

I know how you love puzzles and trying to figure out things, so that's why I sent you all those other letters. I'm not signing my name to this here letter, so you can guess. But I do want to tell you, when you figure out the letters, I'm not a ghost, and have I got a story to tell you!

Very Truly yours,
P.S. When you figure it out, please don't tell anyone!

Evelyn's heart pounded in her chest. She jumped up from the window seat and ran out of the room without so much as an, "I beg your pardon."

"What do you suppose has gotten into her?" Emmaline asked.

Erma sipped her tea. "Really! Henry, you and Emmaline need to do something about her manners."

"Mother!" Henry frowned. "Don't start."

Erma held up her hand. "My last word on the subject!"

Evelyn went to her room and pulled out all the letters from her desk draw. She had twisted those H's or I's many times and couldn't figure it out. Now she knew why. One of the H was actually two "t's" connected together. She laid all the papers side by side and drew and "H" to replace the very first one she'd thrown away. It read: H −A − tt − I − E.

She gathered all the letters to her chest, spun around and laughed and cried at the same time. She left her room, ran down the steps and entered the drawing room. "I know where we can move to!" she said with an over abundance of enthusiasm. "It's where I really, really want to go! I don't want to live anywhere else but there!" She jumped up and down. "Please! Please! Please! We can move tomorrow or the next day or any day, but please!"

Henry and Emmaline hadn't seen their daughter that excited over anything since before that terrible day. Henry laughed. "Where is it you propose we go? You didn't say."

"BOWLING GREEN..." She threw all her papers up in the air. "KENTUCKY!"

***

As the weeks passed, more and more people left Black Water. When Evan McGuire, the owner of the general store finally announced that he was pulling up stakes, the town officially died. Sally Gooch had moved to Baton Rouge to be with her daughter.

Evelyn kept pushing for them to move to Kentucky, but she refused to say why. Erma insisted they move to Baton Rouge, since Henry had a few connections there and they would also be reunited with Emmaline's Aunt Sally and her cousin, Barbara. Emmaline said she'd go wherever Henry thought best. Henry didn't care much one way or another just as long as it was away from there. But now he was caught between the desires of his daughter and the logic of his mother. He'd about made up his mind to disappoint Evelyn and make their home in Baton Rouge, until he picked up the final mail delivery for Black Water from the stagecoach. The driver informed him that was his last run to their town and any residents left would have to make arrangements for their posts to be picked up in one of the other towns.

Henry went into the Post Office. It was left up to him to sort the mail and put it in the slots for the people who were still there. He saw a letter to Evelyn postmarked from Bowling Green, Kentucky. He stared at the envelope. Normally, he wouldn't invade his daughter's privacy, but his curiosity was too overwhelming. He opened it. There was a picture of two boys included, dangling from a tree limb with an alligator beneath it. He laughed. The two looked a lot like Robbie Harp and Billy Tate. As he started to read the letter, his heart pounded in his chest. Now he understood Evelyn's urgency to move to Kentucky. Tears of joy rolled from his eyes. He laughed and cried at the same time as Hattie wrote a very detail letter as to how Jack and Jessica Trainor as well as George Tyler had tricked the whole town with her "faked" hanging. Henry felt as if an enormous weight had been lifted off his chest. His daughter was alive!

***

Henry entered the house. "Emmaline! Evelyn! Mother!"

Everyone ran into the foyer from different parts of the house. "What on Earth are you shouting for?" his mother asked.

"I've decided. We're moving to Bowling Green!" Erma was about to object until Henry raised his hand and added, "Mother, you can come with us if you wish or I'll settle you in Baton Rouge close to Sally. It's your choice. I've made up my mind. End of discussion."

Evelyn wrapped her arms around him in a great hug. She considered it the happiest day of her life. When she told her father she was going upstairs to start packing, he called her back and handed her the letter. Evelyn looked at him curiously when she saw it had been opened, but when he gave her a wink and a smile, she was glad he'd opened it. Soon she would be reunited with Hattie once more.

Epilogue

Three weeks later, the Welch family packed up everything they attached either a personal or sentimental value to. Henry told them they were going to start their life over in a new place, with new furniture and fixtures and leave the old things with their memories to the ghosts of the past. Erma decided to accompany her son and his family, using the excuse that perhaps she could bring a little culture to the citizens of Bowling Green. In truth, she just didn't want to be left alone.

Except for a few scavengers who planned on stripping the town of everything thing they could load up on a wagon and sell that residents left behind, the Welch family were among the last to leave Black Water. The only other couples who hadn't left were the Harps and the Tates who were still crating things to take to their new homes. They were heading a little further south to Thibodaux, Louisiana, where Ralph Harp and Gordon Tate had acquired jobs through a friend who lived there.

Before Henry headed to the railroad station, he stopped at the Harp's residence to see how they were getting along. Ralph said that he and Gordon would be leaving within the next couple of days, if they could round up their missing boys to help with the packing. Evelyn remembered the picture Hattie had sent and wondered. She told Mr. Harp to check by the river and look in one of the trees with an alligator under it, and he might find them there. Ralph laughed and told her that Robbie would give any gator indigestion and spit him back out. With that said, Henry snapped his reins and they were on their way to the train station.

***

"Great idea, Robbie!" Billy exclaimed as he held onto the branch of a tree for dear life. "Look what you've got us into now!"

Robbie looked down at the alligator beneath the tree. "Well, you're the one who said it would be funny to put a baby alligator in your sister's trunk!"

"Since when do you ever listen to me!"

The branch they were on started to crack and the boys screamed as they dangled from the branch.

***

The sounds of the day filled the cool air of Black Water swamp. Bullfrogs croaked their love songs to any female that would listen. The hissing of a snake echoed in the breeze as it was about to acquire a meal. Leaves rustled on the trees, and dead branches fell to the ground. The cacophony of sounds blended together as a soothing noise. But in Black Water Township everything stopped. The quiet was deafening.

Other Books by Michele L. Hinton

High Seas: The Cabin Boy
High Seas: A Matter of Blood

Tales with a Twist & Tales Totally Twisted

Children's Books

Princess Courtney and the Magic Suit

Children's Book By Betty J. Rees
(Michele's Mother)

Beauregard Blue